The Belches
Book
By
Andrea Frazer

The Belchester Chronicles Books 1 - 3

Other books by Andrea Frazer

1

<u>Contents</u>

STRANGEWAYS TO OLDHAM

(The Most Efficient Route to Eternity)

The Belchester Chronicles - Book 1
A Lady Amanda Golightly Murder Mystery
By
ANDREA FRAZER

DRAMATIS PERSONAE

Anstruther, Dr – elderly GP

Beauchamp – butler and general factotum at Belchester Towers

Campbell, Dr Andrew – new, young GP

Cholmondley-Crichton-Crump, Hugo – a permanent house guest at Belchester Towers

Edwards, Malcolm – head of a private nursing service

Foster, Derek – a care worker

Golightly, Lady Amanda – owner of Belchester Towers

Matron – head of the Birdlings Serenade Nursing Home, whose name is known to no one

Myers, Richard – an elderly local resident

Pagnell, Reginald – a resident of the Birdlings Serenade Nursing Home

Plunkett, Nurse Sarah – an employee at the Birdlings Serenade Nursing Home

Tweedie, Enid – cleaner, friend, and co-conspirator of Lady Amanda

Updyke, Dr Cedric – an orthopaedic consultant at Belchester City Hospital

Williams, Young Mr – an elderly partner of Freeman Hardy, Williams and Williams

Police Personnel

Inspector Moody

PC Adrian Glenister

A NOTE ON PRONUNCIATION

Beauchamp's name is usually pronounced Beecham in England, but Lady Amanda insists on the French pronunciation, Bo-sham.

Hugo's surnames are pronounced Chumley-Cryten-Crump.

PROLOGUE

Belchester was a small cathedral city, about fifteen miles from the south coast; the largest dwelling in its environs Belchester Towers. Belchester Towers had been built in the early nineteenth century by one Godfrey Golightly, nouveau riche, and out to display his newly found wealth.

That the man had no taste or breeding mattered not a jot to him, and he celebrated his recently acquired title with a heap of a red-brick building, ugly, four-square, with a huge crenellated tower at each corner and a faux moat surrounding the whole – a raspberry to all the other fine houses that had a wealth of history behind them.

Godfrey Golightly would build his own dynasty, and his house would mature into its surroundings over time, of this he had had no doubt.

In the last almost two hundred years, the fortunes of the Golightly family had fluctuated, down to the present day, and last member of the direct line of descent, Lady Amanda, who was now of a certain age – i.e. wouldn't tell anyone that she had recently become the recipient of a state pension. She lived there with only the company of a general factotum called Beauchamp, and an army of casual cleaners and gardeners, whom the aforementioned Beauchamp summoned at intervals, as and when they were needed, to turn the dwelling back into a decent place in which to live.

Lady Amanda's parents had been killed in an accident on the London to Brighton Rally some years before, after driving straight into a tree. They had been drunk to the wide due to frequent nips from their hip-flasks of cocktails, and Lady Amanda considered that there could not have been a better way for them to go.

The car behind had said they were laughing their heads off at the time of the accident, after 'Daddy', as she always thought of her father, had lost control of the steering. It was considered not to be speed that had been the main cause of their death, because the old car didn't have it in her to go very fast, more the sheer bad luck that they had both broken their necks and fractured their skulls when they had been thrown from the body of the vehicle, face first, into said venerable and unmovable tree.

Lady Amanda was an aficionado of cocktails; in fact, she had been since she was a teenager, having been brought up with them, one could say, and she hoped that she had a suitably bizarre and fun ending – if death can ever be fun! – to her own life, when the time eventually arrived.

A formidable character, she conducted her life openly and honestly, and would have no truck with slyness, prevarication, untruths, or any hole-in-the-corner, or cloak-and-dagger behaviour. She was hardest of all on bad manners, and would not tolerate them from anyone, no matter what their station in life. Being a blunt woman, however, Lady Amanda called a spade 'a bloody shovel' if she didn't call it 'trumps', although she very rarely used coarse language and frowned upon it in others.

Physically, she bore no relationship to the figure that most imagined, having only heard her name. She was not tall and willowy, a waif – a go-lightly, in fact, whom a gust of wind would bowl over. Instead, she was short and squat – what she liked to refer to as portly, where others said she was just fat – with piercing green eyes, and blond curls.

Her hair was her only vanity, but more of that later …

Chapter One

'Beauchamp!'

The name was shouted in a glass-shattering screech, which echoed round the vast entrance hall of Belchester Towers. 'Beauchamp! Where the dickens are you! Come here, at once! Beauchamp!'

Thus, she summoned the one and only other occupier of her vast house. She was standing now, in the entrance hall, holding a piece of paper in her hands; holding it at arm's length and squinting furiously at it.

'How may I be of assistance, my lady?' Beauchamp had appeared at her side as if by magic, his footsteps silent as always on the stone-flagged floor. Lady Amanda didn't know how he did it, but he had often caused her to jump nearly out of her skin, with this inexplicable trick of his, to move around like a shade, with no intimation at all that he was near her. He was just, suddenly, there.

'What, in heaven's name, is this?' she demanded, thrusting the piece of paper in his face, without preamble.

Beauchamp took the proffered document, and scrutinised it in detail. 'It would appear to be a fine for speeding, my lady,' he informed his enraged mistress.

'Just what I thought, but how the devil can it be? I haven't had the Rolls out for ages. The thing's covered in dust and cobwebs, out there in the stables.' She followed this with a noise that it is only possible to write thus: 'Hrmph!'

'It does not concern the Rolls, my lady – it is, in fact, a notice for speeding on your tricycle.'

'My tricycle? Absolute rot! How could I possibly have been speeding on my trike? Don't know what the world's coming to, when a respectable woman can't even ride her own trike without breaking the law. It's a load of absolute rot, Beauchamp, and I shall phone the Chief Constable about it. His father used to be a good friend of Daddy's, you know.'

'I fear that would do little good, my lady. It states here that you were travelling along the entrance road to the hospital, where the speed limit is only five miles an hour, and you nearly 'had' the senior orthopaedic consultant with your conveyance.'

Ignoring him completely, she continued, 'I mean, what sort of damage can one do, with a tricycle?'

Beauchamp eyed Lady Amanda's generous figure up and down, considered the weight of the ancient machine she had been propelling, and decided not to voice his conclusion, which was 'a considerable amount'. 'And the gentleman mentioned, my lady?' he prompted her to further explanation.

'He got out of the way in time, didn't he? I didn't exactly hit him!'

'No, but he only escaped being hit by your trike, by jumping off the entrance way into a rose bush, thus sustaining considerable damage to the material of his shirt and trousers, and a number of small scratches and abrasions.'

'Piffle!' retorted Lady Amanda, her face bearing a mutinous expression with which Beauchamp was only too familiar.

'The accompanying letter says that you didn't even stop to see how the poor man was.'

'I was late for visiting. Old Enid Tweedie, you know. How ridiculous, having to have her tonsils out at her age. Absolutely shaming, if you ask me. It's the sort of thing that children have done, then get a week of ice-cream and jelly until the pain goes away. Had it done myself, as a matter of fact, when I was about seven. And then, a couple of weeks later, she had to go back in to have her gall bladder removed. There'll be nothing left of her, if she keeps having bits taken out at this rate.'

'It also says here, that you are lucky not to be charged with what is referred to in common parlance as "hit-and-run".'

'With a tricycle?' she shrilled, her voice rising with indignation. 'I shall dispute it, of course!'

'There were witnesses, my lady. I think they've got you by the proverbial "short and curlies",' Beauchamp informed her calmly. He was used to her moods by now, and didn't let it disturb him, even when she threw a firstclass tantrum.

'Don't be coarse, Beauchamp!'
'Sorry, my lady.'

'So, what do I have to do now?' she asked him, her colour subsiding a little, as she realised she could probably leave this to Beauchamp to deal with, as he did with most things that arose in the household which required thought.

'I suggest that you just pay your fine like a model citizen, my lady, and bear in mind the speed limit in future. Mrs Tweedie wouldn't have been the worse for you arriving just a minute or two later, and you wouldn't have found yourself in this situation if you had observed the roadside speed limit signs.'

'Very well, Beauchamp. Get on with it.'
'There's just one more thing, my lady,' he asked.
'And what's that?'

'My name is pronounced Beecham, not that French variation you have used for some years now.'

'I'm sorry, Beauchamp, but your name is an ancient one that came over with the Conquest, and I cannot find it in myself to use its Anglicisation. Take it or leave it! You should be proud to bear such an ancient name!'

It was a long-running battle between them, and Beauchamp gave in with a good grace, the way he always did, but one day – one day, he might just persuade her. And pigs would fly across a blue moon, when that happened, was his last thought on the matter.

'I'm going out this afternoon, on the trike, but I shall take what you've said into consideration. Enid Tweedie informed me, as best as she could, of course, with her throat being so sore, that old Reggie Pagnell has gone into a nursing home.'

'Poor old thing! I haven't seen him in absolutely yonks! I expect he was before your time, but he and Daddy used to be business partners when I was a wee one.'

The thought of Lady Amanda ever being a 'wee one' made Beauchamp wince, but he managed to make it a mental wince that didn't appear on his features, lest his employer decided to take offence.

'Anyway, I thought I'd tricycle over there this afternoon, and see how he is; cheer him up; you know, that sort of thing?'

Beauchamp knew that some people were only too delighted to have the pleasure of Lady Amanda's company, and would gladly have run up a flag if they knew she were coming to visit. Others were not quite so fond of her, and were more likely to run up a side street at the rumour of a visit from her, but he maintained a respectful silence, knowing which side his bank account was buttered.

'Perhaps you would be good enough to get the old steed out for me, Beauchamp. Just leave it round the front, as usual, and check the horn, to make sure its bulb hasn't dozed.' Attached to the handlebars of the tricycle that used to be her mother's was a small version of an old-fashioned car horn, brass with a rubber bulb, and she was always worried that the rubber might have deteriorated to the point where she couldn't use it any more.

In fact, she had used it, she remembered, when that chappie at the hospital had got in her way, and it had been in fine fettle then. Remembering this, she went to prepare for her visit with a smile on her face, hoping it would be a long time yet before she had to resort to one of those horrible little bell thingummyjigs.

Belchester was less than a mile away, now, as the little city's suburbs crept ever-increasingly outwards, towards Belchester Towers, and it was a relatively short ride for Lady Amanda to the Birdlings Serenade Nursing Home, (Nursing & Convalescence Our Speciality. Enquire about respite care), next to St Anselm's Church, and on the city's old northern border, just south of the cathedral.

She had never visited the place before, but surveyed in dismay its surroundings. To the west of the nursing home lay St Anselm's, and its beckoning graveyard. To its north was the city hospital, and, to the east, a doctor's and a dentist's surgery. The poor residents were surrounded on all sides by decay, illness and death, and it must be very depressing for them, she thought, as she propelled her tricycle, at a snail's pace, given what had occurred previously, up its drive to the main entrance.

The reception area that greeted her reminded her of how lucky she was not to be reduced by health and finances to live in a place like this. Despite the scents of polish and disinfectant, there lingered the odour of boiling greens and, underneath everything, a decided tang of urine, which made her wrinkle her nose in distaste. To think of poor Reggie Pagnell, ending up here.

At the desk, she announced in a booming voice that she had come to visit an old family friend, but when she announced that friend's name, the receptionist turned a little pale, and asked her if she'd wait, so that she could check with Matron, whether that would be all right or not.

'Stuff and nonsense!' declared Lady Amanda, watching the woman walk off down a corridor to her right, and then, consulting a handy list of residents, which had been pinned to the wall to the side of the desk, she spotted her target's room number, and toddled off down the left-hand corridor, in search of her father's old partner. Her eyesight was still good enough to read things at a distance, and she had learned all she needed to know. What did the woman want to involve Matron for?

Room number five was only a few steps away, and she gave a brisk knock on the door, and entered it hurriedly before that interfering receptionist woman came back with some excuse or other about why she couldn't pop in on poor old Reggie. Closing the door carefully behind her, she turned, ready to greet a familiar face, and was staggered to note that he wasn't tucked up in bed, as she had expected, but rather was laid out; the whole length of him, including his face, covered with a white sheet.

Startled into silence, she approached the shrouded figure almost on tiptoes, noticing as she did so that his bedside table bore two cocktail glasses, both of them empty. That was odd! She wouldn't have expected cocktails to have been served in a place like this. Almost instinctively, she bent her nose to the nearest glass, and gave a very unladylike sniff, then moved on to the other glass.

The first had smelled the same as the second, and she knew she recognised it, but could not put a name to it, off the top of her head. Her long experience of imbibing cocktails meant that she had an encyclopaedic knowledge of just about every cocktail that existed, and she knew she had come across this one before. Without even thinking about it, she placed one of the glasses in her capacious handbag, noticing, at the same time, that some liquid had recently been spilt on the carpet, in front of the cabinet.

Without a trace of embarrassment, she got down on all fours, and leant her nose towards the still-damp stain. Another gargantuan sniff confirmed what she had suspected she would find. This, too, was a recognisable cocktail, but there was something else there in the background, which she had detected in the glasses too.

Her thought were interrupted, however, as, at that moment, the door sprang open, and a whippet of a woman with an angry face confronted her. 'Who are you? And what the devil are you doing in here?' she barked, furiously.

Still on all fours, her forearms flattened before her as she bent forward, her nose almost touching the carpet, she thought furiously. 'I'm praying to Mecca, for the soul of the departed,' Lady Amanda improvised, in double-quick time. 'And, if it comes to that, who the devil are you?'

'I think you'll find that east is in the opposite direction, madam. I am Matron of this home, and you had no right to enter this room. The patients' privacy is secondary only to their welfare,' Matron yapped, looking at Mr Pagnell's strange visitor.

'In that case, why is poor old Reggie dead?' she asked, piercing the woman with a gimlet eye.

'He passed away not half an hour ago, and the doctor hasn't arrived yet to issue the certificate, although what business it is of yours, I haven't a clue. Who the devil are you, madam?'

'I,' began Lady Amanda, rising ponderously from the floor, and pulling herself up to her full height of five feet four, with the aid of the bed frame, 'am Lady Amanda Golightly of Belchester Towers.' That usually did it. The woman would be quelled now.

But she wasn't. 'I don't care if you're the Duchess of Cornwall. You can't just come waltzing into the private room of one of my residents without a by-your-leave. Now, I insist that you vacate this room this instant. You had no right to be here in the first place.'

'I didn't realise this was a prison,' Lady Amanda threw back at her. 'I thought this was a home, and one can have visitors at one's home, can't one?'

'Not without my say so,' spat Matron, sure that she had made her point this time.

As if to indicate the end of round one, a male voice called plaintively from a few doors down the corridor, 'Nurse! Nurse! I haven't had my tablets yet!'

The timbre of the voice registered in Lady Amanda's subconscious first, speeding through the twists and turns of Memory Lane at the speed of light, back on down it to her youth, and before she even realised what had just transferred itself to her conscious mind, yelled, 'Chummy!' and did an abrupt about-turn, to leave the room, and march purposefully towards the place whence the voice had sounded.

Through the doorway of a room on the other side of the corridor, the owner of the voice looked her up and down, and enquired, 'Manda?' unbelievingly.

'Chummy!' she hooted again, approaching the figure in a wing chair beside the window. 'Well, bless my soul, if it isn't old triple-barrelled Hugo! What the blue blazes are you doing in a place like this?'

'So it is you after all! I heard you bellowing at that old witch of a matron, and I thought, "good for you". It certainly sounded like you, but I couldn't believe it could possibly *be* you, not after all this time.'

'But what are you doing here?' asked Lady Amanda, hardly able to believe her eyes, that the elderly man she was looking at was the friend she hadn't seen for decades.

'It's the arthritis that got me, Manda. I had to have someone in to look after me a few times a week, and then it got even worse, until I just couldn't cope on my own anymore, so I put myself in here. God's waiting room, we all call it. And that matron! What a gorgon! The old besom calls me Mr Cholmondley-Crichton-Crump! I've tried explaining to her that it's pronounced Chummley-Crighton, but she won't listen to me – thinks I'm in my dotage, just because I have difficulty in moving around.'

'Oh, how ghastly for you, you poor old thing! What an ignorant woman, and such bad manners to keep on doing it, after she's been corrected. I have the same trouble with my Beauchamp – you must remember him from the old days. He insists that his name is Beecham, and won't listen to a word I say on the subject. Well, I'm not standing for you being subject to that sort of thing! I'm getting you out of here. You simply can't stay. And whatever's happened to the house? Lovely old place!'

'I've got it on the market. Can't afford to stay here for long, at the prices they charge. I'm not made of savings, you know.'

'Just precisely what is the fee, per month, Hugo?' asked his visitor, with genuine interest.

At this question, he gestured her towards him, so that he could whisper in her ear.

'*Combien*, Hugo? How much?' she shouted, scandalised at the figure he had named. 'That does it, Chummy! You're moving into The Towers today. I can't think of you incarcerated in here for another day.'

'But how are you going to get me out,' asked Hugo, rather pathetically.

'I'm going to see that dried-up old hag, and get her to prepare your paperwork for you to leave, then I'm going back to The Towers to fetch the Rolls, before driving back here and moving you out, bag and baggage.'

'But how am I going to manage?' queried Hugo. 'You know, the nursing and helping side of it?'

'You'll have me and you'll have Beauchamp. If you're not paying out a fortune every month to stay in this urine drenched prison, you can afford to have someone in, like you used to, for whenever it's necessary. I know The Towers isn't the most luxurious of homes, but it's got to be better than this.'

'A bed of nails in a pig sty would be better than this, Manda. Do you really think you could swing it with old Mato?'

'Course I can. I'm still the gal I used to be, and I was a match for anyone in my youth.'

Lady Amanda Golightly treated everyone in life equally, no matter what their station, and had not yet met her Waterloo. That woman – that Matron person – had three strikes, then she was out. Those were the rules. She had had her first one, when she had been so rude to Lady Amanda, on finding her in Reggie Pagnell's room. Strike one! She had, even after repeated requests, refused to acknowledge the proper pronunciation of Hugo's rather protracted surname. Strike two! This would be her last chance.

With the light of battle in her eyes, that Hugo remembered of old, she marched out of his room, calling, 'Matron! Matron! I need to speak to you. *Now*, you wretched woman!'

For the next ten minutes, Hugo Cholmondley-Crichton-Crump was aware of raised voices, coming down the corridor to his room from the reception desk, and sat, quivering, wondering what was going on; what was being said about him, and where he'd be sleeping tonight. If it was to be here again, he knew he was probably in for a very rough time. Matron didn't like her word being questioned, let alone completely trampled over, and he knew his Manda of old.

When the disagreement, argument, fight – whatever it had been – had ended, Hugo heard brisk footsteps approaching his door from the corridor, and cowered down in his chair. Ooh-er, he was probably for it, now!

Lady Amanda erupted into his room, her appearance as sudden as that of a pantomime demon that had just shot up through a trapdoor in the floor. 'Did you know Reggie Pagnell was in here?' she asked, quite inconsequentially in Hugo's opinion, and when he answered in the affirmative, she nodded her head in approval, then told him, 'Right, that's all settled then.'

'What's all settled, Manda? I can't keep up with you.'

'You never could, Chummy, and I'm afraid you never will. That's it! I've sprung you! You're free to go! I've phoned Beauchamp on my mobile, and he says he'll fix the old trailer on to the Rolls, and come down to fetch us. You're coming to live with me, in Belchester Towers, and I won't hear a word to the contrary. Now, let's get your stuff packed.'

'Thank God!' said Hugo, on a loud sighing exhalation of breath.

'Thank *me*, if you please,' replied Lady Amanda, already pulling a suitcase from the top of the wardrobe. 'I shall also be telephoning round the local estate agents with reference to your house. I don't see why you should have to sell it, when it can bring you a perfectly good income. We'll get them to assess it for rent, and you can let it out – let it work for you, with a little something to make you more comfortable. Of course, if, when the property market rises again, you want to go for the lump sum, that's completely your affair. But nobody but a fool sells at the moment, Hugo, dear. Prices are so low. And now you won't have to line the pockets of the shysters who run this place anymore.'

'I simply don't know how you do it. You're like a whirlwind, still. I would've considered that, after all these years, you might have slowed down a bit, but you've still got all the get up and go you had when you were a gal.'

'I have Hugo; it just takes me longer to recover from one of my tornados, now.'

Chapter Two

After settling Hugo into a suitable room on the ground floor, Lady Amanda and he took afternoon tea in the drawing room, as she explained Beauchamp's current job description to him.

'Bertie Wooster had Jeeves, Lord Peter Wimsey had Bunter; I have Beauchamp, who does his level best to live up to the impeccable record of his fictional counterparts. He's a sort of old family retainer-of-all-work. He seems to be good at absolutely everything, except the appreciation and pronunciation of his own name. I believe you met him first when he was Daddy's butler?'

At that moment, Beauchamp appeared in the doorway, silently as usual, to enquire about supper. 'What have you planned for us this evening? I know it's short notice, to feed another mouth, but we'll have to manage,' she enquired. 'You remember old Hugo, don't you?'

'Of course, my lady. Good evening, Mr Hugo. Nice to see you at Belchester Towers again, after all these years.' He turned to Lady Amanda. 'I had planned Dover sole, new potatoes, and a green salad,' Beauchamp intoned. He did a lot of intoning, when they had guests, she'd noticed.

'Stuff and nonsense!' she replied. 'Deal with the fish the best you can to feed three. Chuck it in some batter, chip the potatoes, and we can have it all fried, with some baked beans. My secret supply is in the camphor-wood coffer in my bedroom, Beauchamp.'

'I know, my lady. Thank you, my lady. Will there be anything else with that?'

'Yes. A pot of really strong Assam, a plate of white sliced bread, suitably buttered, and lashings of tomato ketchup, thank you, Beauchamp. And we'll have a nice kipper for breakfast. Fried, mind – none of that grilled nonsense! You may go.'

'Thank you, my lady.' Beauchamp melted back through the doorway, and it closed without a sound.

'He's a bit unnerving, isn't he, Manda?' commented Hugo, having noticed the noiseless arrival and departure. 'I'd forgotten all about that trick of his, moving around without a sound.'

'Oh, Beauchamp's all right. Started here as a boot boy, donkey's years ago, and worked his way up, until he was the only one left. Serves him right! Haha! Good old stick, though, Beauchamp. Would trust him with my life,' she finished, full of the man's praises, even though the two of them often fell out.

'Loyalty! That's what it all comes down to in the end: loyalty, Hugo. And talking of loyalty, tell me about Reggie Pagnell. Did you see much of him in Stalag Birdlings – the place even has a sickening name!'

'Not really, Manda. He was in quite a bad way. Marbles gone, you know. I tried popping into his room, when I realised he was in there too, but he didn't have a clue who I was, so I stopped going. Too depressing, making me think that I was headed there too.'

'Tommyrot, Chummy! You'll still be compos mentis when we're all gaga! Now, back to Reggie – did he have any visitors?'

'Only the one, that I'm aware of. Came once a month, for the last three months. In fact, yesterday was his third visit. Sorry if I sound a bit like an old biddy peeking round the net curtains, but there's bally little else to do in a place like that, but keep an ear and an eye out for what's going on around one.'

'Don't apologise. If I'd been stuck in there, I'd probably have committed murder by now, and be locked up in Broadmoor, if it still exists. So who was this infrequent but regular visitor of his?'

'One of the nurses said it was his nephew,' replied Hugo, unsuspectingly.

'His *nephew*?' boomed Lady Amanda. 'But he was an only child and he never married. How the hell can a nephew visit him, when he hasn't – sorry, hadn't – any brothers or sisters, or in-laws?'

'I don't know, Manda. I'm only repeating what I was told. Don't shoot the messenger. It was your father who was in partnership with him, back in those antediluvian days. I was still a bit of a stripling, back then.'

'Sorry, Hugo. I just don't understand it. Any other information?'

'Yes. Apparently, this 'nephew' always brought along a hip flask filled with Reggie's favourite cocktail, and they shared it during his visit.'

'Yes!' Lady Amanda was back in booming mode.
'Careful, Manda. You nearly made me spill my tea.'

'Again, sorry, but you've just jogged my memory. So much has happened this afternoon that I just forgot all about it. Look here,' she commanded, scuffling in her capacious handbag and pulling out a cocktail glass, a fine old linen handkerchief a barrier against her leaving any fingerprints on its surface.

'I say, old girl! You haven't taken to drinking during the day have you?' enquired Hugo, aware of her love for cocktails when he had last known her.

'Of course not. I actually went into Reggie's room. That's why I was at that ghastly place. Enid Tweedie told me he was in there, when I went to see her in hospital ... But that's a completely different story.

'I went there with the specific goal of visiting him, just for old time's sake, you know. But when I got there, that person on reception told me she'd have to ask Matron first. Well, you know me! I wasn't going to wait to be given permission to visit an old family friend, so I checked his room number with the list pinned on the wall, and toddled down to see him, *sans* permit.'

'But he was dead, Manda.'

'I know that now!' she exclaimed in exasperation. 'But I didn't know it then – just shot into his room before anyone saw me, and there he was, covered from top to toe in a white sheet. It gave me quite a turn, I can tell you.'

'So the cocktail glass is from his room?'

'Bingo, Chummy! There were two glasses on the bedside table, and they looked rather out of place in a joint like that, so I sniffed 'em.'

'Ah, the old Golightly nose! Can identify a cocktail at a hundred paces.'

'That's right! And I got it straight away. The cocktail was a 'Strangeways to Oldham': one measure of dark rum, one measure of gin, half a measure of Rose's Lime Cordial, two measures of mandarin juice, one measure of passion fruit juice and two measures of lemonade,' she informed him crisply.

'But there had been something else in those glasses, too – something nasty. And some of the liquid had been spilled on the carpet, so I got down on all fours like a dog, and sniffed that too.'

'Oh, you didn't, Manda. You're quite shameless, you know.'

'And that's how Matron caught me – on all fours, sniffing the carpet.'

'Whatever did you tell her?' asked Hugo, amused at the turn of this tale.

'I told her I was praying for Reggie's immortal soul, nicked an empty glass, and swiftly made my retreat, because I'd heard your voice. Your room seemed as good a place as any to hide, and I didn't fancy being chased by that old harridan, down the drive, with my proof in my handbag. If I'd hesitated, she might have asked why I had my nose to the carpet, and I'd have had to be very rude to her, and told her I was trying to trace the smell of wee that pervades the home.'

'Proof of what?' asked Hugo, referring back to something Amanda had said, almost in passing.

'Why, proof that Reggie Pagnell was murdered, of course. Don't be so dense, Hugo! She even asked me, when I was arranging your escape, if I'd noticed how many glasses there were on his bedside cabinet, so I told her, of course, that I'd only seen one. Let her look amongst her own staff for the phantom cocktail glass snaffler!'

'That's taking two and two and making five, isn't it?'

'Rot! Reggie's gaga. He gets three visits from a nephew who can't exist. The "nephew" always brings a cocktail for them to share. Reggie dies suddenly, after the third of these visits. I turn up, and smell something suspicious in the glasses. Ergo, he was murdered, but by whom, and why?'

'But both the glasses had something nasty in them, you said.'

'Hence the stain on the floor. He had to pour out two drinks, just like he'd done before, and then, when Reggie had drunk his, he must have poured the other back into this hip flask. Have you ever tried pouring anything into a hip flask without a small funnel? It's impossible not to spill something. Hence the spill on the floor. Hence, murder. QED, Hugo.'

Lady Amanda sat with her arms folded, eyeing her old friend with a mutinous glare. 'Well, Hugo?'

'Actually, I think you might be right, after all you've told me. But what are you going to do about it, eh?'

'You mean, "what are *we* going to do about it", Hugo. Well, firstly, I'm going to ring for Beauchamp, and tell him to put this glass somewhere very safe ... I suppose, actually in my safe would be the best bet.'

'I wondered why you'd been holding it in your hankie like that. And secondly?'

'That's the bit I don't know yet. I think we'll have to sleep on it, but it'll probably involve going to the police station and seeing if I can get anyone to believe my story.'

'And now I believe it is a couple of minutes past the Cocktail Hour, so what can I get you?'

'I haven't the faintest idea. I don't know much about cocktails. You choose!'

'Then we'll have what I consider to be the cocktail of the day. *Beauchamp*! A couple of Strangeways to Oldhams, if you please.'

And thus, Lady Amanda Golightly stumbled into her first ever experience of murder: innocent, guileless, but with the inherited cunning that had kept her family in Belchester Towers for a great many generations.

And she had used the 'm' word: murder. Lady Amanda didn't believe in beating about the bush, as has been mentioned before, and she wasn't going to tolerate murder amongst her friends and acquaintances. That was absolutely beyond the pale!

Although she had been aware of its presence in the trailer at the rear of the Rolls the day before, Lady Amanda was shocked and dismayed, the next morning, to see Hugo shuffling along the corridor propelling a Zimmer frame in front of him, on the way to breakfast.

'I say, old crock. I didn't know you were as bad as that!' she declared, as he finally reached the breakfast room door.

"Fraid so, old stick. Doctor says there's nothing to be done about it, though,' he replied ruefully.

'Who's your doctor?' she asked, abruptly.

'Old Anstruther,' he replied, concentrating on getting his frame over a crack in the flagstones.

'Anstruther? Why, he must have been Methuselah's doctor! Have you had a second opinion? Been to the hospital for X-rays? Had blood tests?'

'He says there's no point, Manda.'

'No point? The silly old coot. He was practically in his dotage when I was a gal. I'll give my own doctor a ring – sharp young chap, he is – and get you signed on to his books. If there's anything that can be done, he'll not only know about it, but put it into practice. We can't have you trailing round the house like a tortoise, with that thing as your foregoing shell.'

'If you say so, but I can't see him coming up with anything new.'

'Anaesthetics are probably new to that old windbag you've been going to. I'll phone after breakfast and make an appointment for you. In the meantime, we've got to get you mobile, and out in the fresh air for some exercise, to strengthen up those old muscles of yours.'

'I know what we'll do,' decided his hostess, as they entered the breakfast room and took their places at the table. 'Did you see my old black trike yesterday?'

'Of course I did. It went in the trailer with my walking frame, when you collected me from the home,' replied Hugo, with some dignity. He was neither blind, nor unobservant.

'Well, that was Mummy's everyday conveyance. For high days and holidays, she had a red one – not quite so heavy, or difficult to steer, and it's in the stables. Also, Daddy used to have a bicycle with a little motor-thingy. If I can get Beauchamp to transfer the motor-thingy from the bicycle to Mummy's red trike – he'll work something out to take into account the extra wheel – we can go out for picnics, even if we never get out of the grounds.'

'That sounds jolly pleasant, Manda,' he replied, his good humour restored, at the thought of outings and outside – two things he'd been severely deprived of, of late.

Beauchamp laid out a dish of fried kippers on the table, and as Hugo was starting to enquire about what they would do with regard to their suspicions of murder, Lady Amanda upbraided him with, 'You know one never discusses business at table, Hugo. We'll talk about it after we've eaten. While we're at breakfast, tell me about your extraordinarily long surname, and how it grew that big. I never have known the full story.'

'Oh, that's an easy one,' he began, interspersing the tale with breaks, while he forked mouthfuls of kipper from his plate, and chewed them appreciatively. 'Two strong women were all it took. Grandpa Cholmondley-Crichton-Crump married a Miss Crichton and, anxious that her name should not be discarded so lightly, she insisted on adding it to his, making it double-barrelled.

'My father, in his choice of bride, married an equally strong woman, but with the unfortunate surname of Crump. Well, she prevailed, probably egged on by, and in the same fashion as, her mother-in-law, and the name became triple-barrelled, as you now know it.'

'But you never married, Hugo?'

'Didn't dare to, in case I chose a similarly strongminded bride. Might have ended up with a moniker so long, I'd never be able to fill in a form for the rest of my life. It's bad enough as it is, without making it even longer. Pen keeps running out of ink, don't yer know.'

'Don't be flippant, Chummy. Is that the real reason you never married?'

'Of course it's not. Just never met the right gal, I suppose.'

'Never mind. We can keep each other company now, can't we?'

'I was going to ask you about that,' Hugo replied. 'Didn't know if it was quite decent, the two of us living under the same roof, and all that. It's all been a bit sudden. I'll understand completely, if you think you acted rather rashly, yesterday.'

'Don't be absurd!' she spluttered, her mouth full of tea. 'I'm glad of the company, to be quite honest, and we have known each other for a very long time.'

'But with an exceedingly long gap in between.'

'Certainly! But we're still the same people, aren't we? I know I haven't changed my nature very much, and from what I've seen, neither have you. Now look here, Hugo: we can be lonely separately, or we can choose to be in company together. Which is the most attractive option to you? I know which I'd choose, and I have. When one is older, sometimes the luxury of one's pride and independence is something one shouldn't even attempt to pay for. Do you want to go back to that dreadful home?'

'No,' agreed Hugo, and addressed himself to a clean plate, for toast and marmalade. 'Do you remember how I used to carry you around on my shoulders, when you were still quite a tot?'

'Of course I do,' she replied. 'I sometimes wonder if it was that lofty view that made me a bit haughty at times. One never knows, does one?'

A little later, as Beauchamp cleared away the breakfast things, Lady Amanda decided to make some telephone calls, and, spotting Hugo over by the window, she called over to him, 'Do you think you could get me my little address book? It's on the whatnot.'

Looking round quizzically, Hugo enquired mildly, 'What whatnot?'

'The window whatnot.'
'What's on the window whatnot?'

'I'll get it myself. If we go on like this, we're going to slide into the "Who's on next?" sketch that Abbot and Costello did.'

'What?' asked Hugo.

'Never mind! I just want to make a few calls, then ring for an appointment for you with my doctor, and check out a couple of estate agents about getting tenants for your house. And you can ring up the one who's trying to sell it, and tell him to take it off the market. Then, we've got to work out what to do about the "you-know-what".'

'What "you-know-what"? Is the "you-know-what" on the window whatnot, or what?' Hugo replied, nearly restarting the surreal conversation that Lady Amanda had just forcibly ended, before it got out of control, and drove her mad.

Chapter Three

After a very intense hour on the phone, Lady Amanda was as good as her word earlier, and instructed Beauchamp on the alterations she required, with the motor from the bicycle being suitably adapted and transferred to Mummy's best red trike, then mounted her own machine, having decided that she owed it to the police, to give them a crack at solving this case of murder she and Hugo had uncovered.

She arrived in South Street in Belchester, where the police station was situated, just beyond The Goat and Compasses public house. Leaving her tricycle firmly chained up, she went through the police station doors and presented herself at the desk, where a fresh-faced uniformed officer sat, reading the sports pages of a daily paper that she would never allow to darken the letter box of her own home.

'Can I help you, madam?' he asked, pushing the newspaper aside and looking up, his facial expression freezing a little, as he noticed that she was neither young, nor pretty.

'I sincerely hope so, young man,' she replied, thinking that he looked no older than a schoolboy. Wherever were the police recruiting from nowadays? It'd be from the nursery next. 'I wish to report a murder,' she stated baldly, and watched his face change from slight disappointment, to 'we've got a right one, here'.

'How can I help you with this "murder", madam?' he asked politely, the word murder obviously carrying inverted commas, and with a sarcastic gleam in his eye. 'I'd like to speak to the officer in charge, if you don't mind. Murder is a serious matter, and should be treated as such, don't you think?'

'Of course, madam. I'll ring upstairs for the inspector, if you'll be so good as to wait here.'

Lady Amanda took a seat on a hard wooden bench on the wall opposite the desk, but her hearing was still acute, and she heard the young man's end of the conversation without any difficulty. 'Got a right one down here. Some batty old biddy wanting to report a murder. Wants to see someone in charge. Do you think you could have a word with her?'

The answer must have been in the affirmative, for he proceeded to conduct her up a flight of stairs and into a small, unaired office that smelled of sweat and 'fags smoked out of the window'.

In five minutes, she found herself back outside once more, feeling both silly, and furious at the same time; silly, because the inspector – too young for his rank, in her opinion – had treated her as if she were senile, and furious, because she had let him get away with it, which wasn't like her at all. She hadn't had much to do with the police, in her time, however, and it could have been that which threw her so far out of her normal commanding and forthright character.

More likely, however, it was the insolent and superior attitude of the inspector, who had asked her if she thought she was some sort of 'Miss Marple' character, and enquiring if she watched a lot of detective programmes on what he had referred to as 'the telly'. She had retorted with as much dignity as she could muster, by informing him that: A) Miss Marple was a fictional character, B) Miss Marple was portrayed as a very elderly lady, and C), Miss Marple managed to traverse the decades without ageing a day, and that, as she was none of these three things, she certainly did not see herself in such a role; and she marched out of the police station in high dudgeon.

So, that was that! The police were going to take no notice of her whatsoever. Granted, she hadn't brought the cocktail glass with her, but they'd probably just have taken it, washed it up, and put it away behind the police social club bar.

So, she'd hang on to it. And she and Hugo would find out who killed poor old Reggie Pagnell themselves.

She rode back to Belchester Towers via the back routes, taking her time, to allow her temper to subside, and to try to come to terms with the fact that the police thought her a silly old fool. As she entered the grounds, she looked across to the building where she had spent her entire life (when not at boarding school).

There it stood, its red brick dulled by age now, though it was less than two hundred years old, with its silly moat empty, overgrown by weeds. There it stood, with its daft towers, and all its unrealistic fairy-tale architecture, and she loved it. Tears came to her eyes as she thought of all the happy times she had spent there throughout her life, accompanied by tears of self-pity, at how she had been treated at the police station.

Well, she had Hugo for company now, and they'd show that snotty inspector how to track down a murderer, and then who would be laughing? Eh?

When she had parked her trike, she went into the morning room and encountered Hugo taking a leisurely look at the newspaper. Looking up, he was immediately aware that Manda was not herself – something had happened that had 'got to her'. 'What's up, old thing?' he asked, in a gentle voice.

'Oh, nothing, Chummy. I've just discovered that when one is old, nobody notices one, or listens to one any more. The elderly become invisible, and I feel that, today, I have joined their silent and unnoticed ranks.'

'Rot, Manda! You? Old? Utter and complete tommyrot!'

'Very gallant of you, Hugo, but I have to face the fact that I'm just a meddling old woman in most people's eyes.'

'What's happened to make you feel like that?' asked Hugo, with concern. This wasn't the Manda that he remembered and ... was – well – very fond of, at least.

'I went to the police station to report Reggie Pagnell's murder, and was treated as a silly old trout with an overactive imagination,' she informed him, looking thoroughly crestfallen.

'How dare they! We must speak to the Chief Constable, now. That really takes the biscuit!' Hugo retorted, now full of indignation.

'Times have moved on, since we were in our prime, Hugo. The Chief Constable's a young man in his midforties, I believe, and although Daddy knew his father, I predict that if we put our little problem before him, he'd just think it was dementia setting in, as so many people now presume, about anything esoteric, said by someone over pensionable age.'

'Then we'll just have to investigate it ourselves. Can't have a murderer wandering about out there, scot free and undetected.'

'I hoped you'd say that, Hugo. That's what I'd more or less decided myself, on the way home. I just didn't know if you'd go along with it or not. I'll start with the nursing home: see what details I can get about this "nephew", and about when and where the funeral's to be held.'

'That's more like my Manda of old. Up and at 'em! Don't let 'em grind you down! When are you thinking of going?'

'After luncheon,' she replied, tugging on a chintz bellpull to summon Beauchamp, and announce that they were ready for their meal.

Unnervingly, Beauchamp slipped through the door the moment she grabbed the bell-pull, and she gave a little shriek, at this immediate attendance upon her wishes. 'I wish you wouldn't do that, Beauchamp. At least give a little cough, to warn me you're just about to appear, like a pantomime villain, as usual.'

'Sorry, my lady. And it's Beecham,' the man declared, his dignity not ruffled one jot.

'Tell me, did you study French at school, *Beauchamp*?' she asked, emphasising the pronunciation of his surname.

'No, my lady. I studied woodwork. But it's still Beecham.' And with that, he disappeared out of the room, to bring the food to table in the breakfast room, where it was cosier to eat, at this time of day, than in the vast panelled dining room.

Over their meal, the proposed investigation banned until after they had finished eating, the conversation was of a nostalgic nature – not unexpectedly, given the circumstances that had suddenly thrown them together again, after such a long time.

'Nice name that – Amanda,' Hugo mumbled through a mouthful of food. 'Lady Amanda, now that's just the same as the woman in those Campion books by whatshername – Margery Allingham. That's the chap. Lady Amanda Fitton, wasn't it? Did you ever read those books, Manda?' he asked.

'Actually, Mummy named me after her. The writer only had the copyright on the books, you know, not the characters' names as well. But Mummy loved all those old murder mysteries, and I read them when I was growing up. Used to imagine it was me, marrying silly young Albert. And here I am, never managed to find Mr Right, or even Mr Wright – that's with a 'W', Hugo, as one can't hear spelling. Joke!'

'Jolly good! Play on words. I seem to remember you were rather good at those, when we were younger, but that one definitely needs to be written down to appreciate it.'

After a few seconds of silence, Hugo declared, 'Damn shame, you being orphaned like that!'

'Damned lucky escape, if you ask me!'

'Whatever do you mean, Manda? That sounds rather cruel, and that's unlike you.'

'It's just sheer logic, old bean. The only people who never have to face up to the loss of their parents, are those who die young, and I never had any intentions of doing that.'

'Ah, see what you mean. True enough! You always were a sensible old thing.'

'And not so much of the "old". I've had a bellyful of that today already, and you're a good few years my senior, if my memory really isn't failing.'

'Touché!'

'Oh, by the way, Beauchamp has transferred that motor thingy from Daddy's bicycle to mother's best tricycle, so we can get out and about.'

'Bravo, Beauchamp!' Hugo replied, waving his fork about, in his excitement. 'We could be like those Hell's Angels chappies, what?'

'More like Hell's Wrinklies! And mind your fork! You nearly chucked your food on the floor, waving it about like that.'

'Sorry, Manda.'

After coffee and a suitable period for digestion, Lady Amanda mounted her three-wheeled steed and set off to see what she could learn from the rest home where she had discovered Hugo incarcerated, the day before.

She had a legitimate family reason for knowing when, and where, Reggie's funeral would take place, and the same thing applied to getting in touch with his so-called nephew, to pass on her condolences. She'd present a humbler version of herself today, and explain away her behaviour of the day before as shock, pure and simple.

If anyone made a fuss about her 'kidnapping' of Hugo, she would say that had also been due to the shock of Reggie's demise, and stumbling upon her old friend, after so long a time. She could certainly tell them that he was happy and settled, and that they needn't bother themselves about his welfare any more. He would be more than adequately cared for at Belchester Towers. Maybe the address would impress them. Maybe her own name would, too, for she didn't remember formally introducing herself on her last visit, and thought that remedying that might improve their treatment of her no end.

She duly parked her trike and chained it to a sturdy chain-link fence and then entered, her hopes of success high. The woman on duty at reception was the same one as the day before and, on seeing Lady Amanda approach her for the second time in two days, cringed, and put her hand under the desk, presumably to ring a panic bell.

'Good afternoon, young lady,' cooed Lady Amanda, holding out her hand in greeting. 'I'd like to apologise for my rather excitable behaviour yesterday, and introduce myself properly. I am Lady Amanda Golightly of Belchester Towers.'

That seemed to have done the trick, and by the time that Matron arrived at the double, prepared for anything, after the panic bell having been used, she surveyed the figure of Lady Amanda, and inhaled hugely, to give her a piece of her mind.

It was only the immediate intervention of the receptionist that deflated her bubble. 'This is Lady Amanda Golightly of Belchester Towers,' the woman informed the purple-faced tyrant, 'and she's come to apologise for yesterday. Shock, you know, at finding one old friend dead, and another resident here.'

That was Matron efficiently torpedoed, and the sour faced woman had to force a smile on to her disapproving countenance. 'So pleased to be introduced to you at last, my lady,' she dripped, shaking hands with a hand like a wet fish. 'What can we do for you today? Let you remove another resident or two? Why not the whole lot, then you can have a very jolly time at The Towers.

Hmph! The woman wasn't quite dead in the water yet, thought Lady Amanda. She'd have to continue with the charm offensive.

'Apart from apologise, all I wanted was to get details of poor old Reggie Pagnell's funeral, and maybe his nephew's address, so that I could convey my condolences on the loss of his uncle.' She sounded almost like Mary Poppins, so anxious was she to get her hands on the information she needed to start the investigation.

But Matron wasn't giving in that easily. It took more than Lady Amanda on her best behaviour to make her crumble and fly the white flag. 'I'm afraid we're not permitted to give out personal information about our "guests",' she intoned, a wolf-like smile shaping her lips. 'However ...' Here, she held up a hand, to stem the flow that was preparing itself to fall from Lady Amanda's sneering mouth.

'However,' she repeated, 'we can provide you with the name of Mr Pagnell's solicitor, who will provide you with any information he deems necessary, in the circumstances.'

'Thank you so much.' Lady Amanda was back in purring mode. The solicitor's address would probably net her more than she was ever likely to get from this old harridan, and if she needed any inside knowledge about Reggie's residence here, Enid Tweedie could prove to be just the right cat's paw to get her insider information.

If Lady Amanda footed the bill, she was sure Enid would not be averse to a few days – a week at the most – convalescing here, and being her 'agent' on the inside. It would also give her another excuse to be here on the premises, as she still might need to return.

Clutching the piece of paper with the name 'Freeman, Hardy, Williams and Williams' and an address in East Street in her hand, she walked thoughtfully out to her trike, placed the piece of paper carefully in her handbag, put it in the front basket of the vehicle, and made her way back to Belchester Towers, determined to make a proper appointment to visit Reggie's solicitor. She'd almost suspected the name of the law firm to be fictitious, when she had first learnt it. 'Sounds just like a shoe shop we used to have in the town,' she'd muttered under her breath, when she'd read it, but it obviously wasn't.

But she must make a good fist of this next part of the exercise. It wouldn't do to 'blow it', as she had done at the nursing home. Advance warning of who she was might make all the difference to how they treated her at the law firm, and she didn't want just to blunder in and make the wrong impression. She'd already done that at the police station, and look where that had got her – playing at sleuth, actually!

She'd have to get her violin out when she got home. Oh, and have a rummage around for Daddy's old deerstalker. (Lady Amanda had undertaken tuition, in her schooldays, in playing the violin, flute and piano, and had, of course, excelled at all three!)

Back at Belchester Towers, she dug her violin out of the lumber room, where it had slumbered for many a year, and shoved some old sheet music on to the lectern in the library, to have a good old play. She was only halfway through the 'March' from *Scipio* (for the third time) when Hugo shuffled through the door, propelling his walking frame before him.

'What's that dreadful racket? Thought someone was torturing a cat in here, so I came to investigate,' he asked, closing the door behind him, lest Beauchamp should become aware of the fearful row, and poke his nose in.

'Bit out of practice,' Lady Amanda excused herself. 'Couldn't find you when I got home, so I thought I'd look out the jolly old fiddle – Sherlock Holmes, and all that. See if it put me in the right frame of mind for this sleuthing we've decided to take on.'

'I was having a little nap,' explained Hugo, looking slightly embarrassed. 'Food makes me feel rather like a snake after a large feed. I just want to curl up somewhere and snooze.'

'No need to make excuses to me, Hugo. We are the age that we are, and we must just live with that. The alternative's unthinkable. And we must, therefore, ensure that we don't indulge in too large a feast before we have to go out investigating. Wouldn't want to be caught asleep on the job, would we?'

'I should hope not. What's the next move then?' asked Hugo eagerly.

'I've made an appointment with Reggie's solicitor for tomorrow morning. I couldn't get a thing out of that mato at the nursing home, except for the name of his legal representative, so I thought I'd go and beard him in his den, so to speak.'

'Jolly good idea. You will be gentle with him though, won't you, Manda?'

'Gentle? I'll charm his socks off. You might not know it, but I can be darned persuasive, when I want to be.'

'I don't doubt that for one moment. So, what happens now, or is that it, for today?' enquired Hugo, wondering if he might not be able to slip off to continue his forty winks.

'We're going outside so that you can test-drive your new mode of transport. I told you Beauchamp had finished the job. Now we need to see how you get on with the thing.'

'What, right now?' asked the elderly Hugo, disappointed that yet more action was called for.

'Yes. Right now! You know there's no such thing as a dull moment with me, old stick,' she declared.

'No such thing as a peaceful one either, if I remember correctly,' mumbled Hugo, but he did it very quietly, not wanting to hurt her feelings, after she'd been so kind as to take him under her wing like this, and rescue him from that living grave he had been existing in before.

His spirits raised considerably, though, when she announced that it was much later than she had thought, and that it was, once more, cocktail time, and that they must hurry inside, so as not to miss a moment of it. She had earlier instructed Beauchamp, to set out two of the 'cocktails of the moment' in the drawing room, and they should be waiting for them now, icy cold and deliciously relaxing.

Chapter Four

The next morning, after breakfast, Lady Amanda requested that Beauchamp give the Rolls a bit more of a buff-up than it had needed to collect Hugo, and meet her outside the front entrance (a proper road-crossing having been provided, many years ago, over the old moat) at ten-thirty sharp. 'Oh, and wear your chauffeur's livery,' she commanded him.

'One wants to make a good impression,' she informed her ever-patient employee, 'and you always looked so amusing in that cap.' This addition rather spoiled what had sounded very much like a compliment, but Beauchamp took it all in his stride, as he did Lady Amanda's many strange ways and eccentricities, and was ready and waiting in the car, at two minutes before the half hour.

Lady Amanda emerged as the stable clock was chiming, dressed very smartly in a silk summer suit and her best hat. (Blimey! thought Beauchamp. She *is* going to town.) Entering the car and settling herself comfortably, she blew through the speaking tube to get his attention. 'Yes, my lady?' he replied, sliding open the window between the back and the front of the car.

'Oh, do use the tube, Beauchamp. It's so much more fun if you use the tube,' she implored him.

'Yes, my lady. If you say so, my lady, but I can't understand a word you're saying when we use the tube. You'll just have to tell me through this here window, and then pretend that we did it down the tube,' he advised.

'Very well, but you're a spoilsport and a party-pooper, Beauchamp!' she retorted.

'That's Beecham, my lady!' he replied, but he said it down the tube, so that she wouldn't be able to decipher what he'd said.

'Take me to East Street. I have an appointment at Freeman, Hardy, Williams and Williams at eleven o'clock, and I don't want to be late.'

Half an hour may seem a long time, for a journey of a little more than a mile and a half, but in the ancient Rolls Royce, it would take them all of that time to achieve their goal, and both of them understood that. The ancient vehicle shuddered to a start, and Lady Amanda set off on the next stage of her adventure.

The receptionist at the legal firm informed her that her appointment was with *young* Mr Williams, so she was therefore very surprised when an ancient man with two walking sticks and only a few wisps of white hair, beckoned her into an office opposite the reception desk.

'Do take a seat, Mrs ah – Mrs um ...' he quavered, creaking slowly down into the seat behind the desk; a large padded leather seat that dwarfed him, and made him look like an elderly child.

'Lady Amanda Golightly,' his client trilled, on her very best behaviour.

'Speak up, Mrs – Mrs?' young Mr Williams spake.

'Lady Amanda Golightly,' she almost shouted, and that seemed to do the trick, for he nodded his head very slowly, and muttered, 'Belchester Towers! Well, well, well!'

'That's right, Mr Williams, and I'm here to see you about the death of a very old family friend who has just passed away. Mr Reginald Pagnell.' She hated euphemisms, but she could hardly have told him that Reggie had been murdered. She was on her best behaviour, and must not stray from the path.

She was glad she was not consulting the old boy on anything confidential, for she knew that, at this volume, everything she said would be clearly audible in the reception area, and probably in the adjacent rooms as well.

'Mr Pagnell? Pagnell?' There was a pause, as the little gnome of a man gathered his woolly thoughts together. 'Ah, yes, Pagnell! What can I do for you in respect of the late Mr Pagnell, dear lady?'

'I'm trying to find his "nephew"', she could not help herself uttering this last word in a voice clearly indicating disbelief in the existence of such a person. 'Apparently he had got into the habit of visiting his uncle once a month, at the nursing home, where he was residing. I should like to speak to him about his uncle, whom I had not seen for a number of years, just for old times' sake.'

'A nephew? Nephew? Can't recall any nephew, dear lady. I shall just call for a little assistance, and maybe Carole in reception can have a look in the records.' Thus saying, he picked up the internal telephone, of which he had no real need, considering the volume to which his own voice had risen, so that he could hear himself speak, and asked if the receptionist could have a quick scan of their records, in search of a nephew for Mr Reginald Pagnell (deceased).

The answer came almost immediately, that they had no record of any living relatives for their late client, the last one being a cousin who had died some five years ago.

Having received this unhelpful information, Lady Amanda tried another tack. 'Would it be possible to know the terms of Mr Pagnell's will?' she asked, in as charming a voice as she could muster, given the decibels at which this request had to be made.

'Hoping to be remembered, are we?' shouted the old man, with a wheezy chuckle.

'No, no, nothing like that, I assure you, Mr Williams. I'd just like to know, for the sake of personal interest,' she cooed, like a pigeon using a megaphone.

'Can't just give out confidential information like that, dear lady. I'm sure you understand,' Mr Williams countered.

'But the will will be read soon, and then it will be published, and in the public domain,' she pleaded.

'Have to wait a bit then, won't you,' the old solicitor informed her, a wicked twinkle in his eye, at having thus thwarted her.

Gathering her considerable resolve together, Lady Amanda made one last thrust. 'Can you give me the details of the funeral, then – time, place?' She almost, but not quite, begged him.

At the mention of the word 'funeral', the old man drifted off in to a brown study, and began muttering: quite loudly as it happens, but because of his deafness, clearly audible to Lady Amanda.

'Queer thing, that, about the funeral. Mr Pagnell left clear instructions that he was to be interred in the family plot, in the churchyard of St Michael-in-the-Fields. Sole beneficiary, after a number of small bequests, or rather his representative, has been pestering to have the old boy cremated. Don't fancy that, myself. Want my skull and cross-bones all together, when the Last Trump sounds.'

Now, looking up at his client once more, he continued, as if he had intended her to hear what he had been saying to himself all along, 'Absolutely impossible in the light of my late client's wishes. Cremation, my gouty old foot! He shall be interred where he requested to be interred.

'That was his last wish, and it is my job to make sure that that is how things happen. St Michael-in-the-Fields, next Wednesday at ten-thirty, then afterwards, at the deceased's old address, High Hedges, The Butts, Belchester. I think that is all the information I can give you, but it has been arranged that the will-reading take place after the wake. Perhaps you might find yourself there at the appropriate time, young lady. I shall certainly not object to your presence,' young Mr Williams concluded, constructing on his crumpled old face what Lady Amanda correctly construed to be a conspiratorial smile.

'Is there any information you can give me as to the identity of the sole beneficiary?' she asked, hopefully.

'Sorry, young lady, but you will just have to be patient, and all will be revealed.'

She blushed with pleasure to have been addressed as 'young lady', not just once, but twice, and made her farewells suitably appreciatively, if a little on the *fortissimo* side.

As she re-entered the Rolls, she mused on what she had learnt. Next Wednesday; and it was Friday today, so she and Hugo had five days to determine whether they were capable of discovering the identity of the young man who had visited the nursing home, with such deadly refreshment about his person.

On arrival back at Belchester Towers, she shared what little she had learnt with Hugo.

'Well, that seems to be that then, old thing,' he commented when she had made her little speech. 'Nothing we can do now, but wait.'

'Rot, Hugo! There's plenty to be done.'
'Well, I can't see it.'

'No, but, luckily, I can. And don't you find it very suspicious that that "nephew" of Reggie's – because that's who this mysterious representative of his beneficiary is – has kept banging on about cremating his "uncle", when it was strictly against Reggie's dying wish? I do, and it sounds like he's trying to prevent the opportunity for an exhumation, should anyone suspect him of poisoning his "uncle".

'So, the first thing I'm going to do is phone the hospital and find out when Enid Tweedie is going to be discharged. Then I'm going to visit that ghastly nursing home again, and book her in for a week's convalescence.'

'I say, that's a bit mean, isn't it?'

'Not at all,' retorted Lady Amanda. 'She'll be an undercover agent, for us.'

'Oh, I see what you mean,' said Hugo, nodding his head of thick, wavy white hair.

'And anyway, I'll be paying, so she can hardly complain, can she?'

This was a rhetorical question, and was recognised as such by Hugo, so he just kept his mouth shut, and waited to hear what other plans she had made. 'On my third visit to the nursing home,' she commenced, spearing him with a gimlet-eyed glance, 'I shall ask to see the rooms they use for short-term convalescent patients.

'It said on their sign outside that they also offer convalescent and respite care, and I shall be perfectly within my rights, as I intend to send some business their way, much as I abhor the idea, but Tweedie's a tough cookie. She has to be, as when she's fit, and up and about, she comes in here once a week to 'do the rough', and she's got a real horror of a mother living with her, too. She'll cope. She'll be glad of the break.

'What I can't ferret out on my visit, I can leave it to her to do, chatting to the staff, and drawing them out. She can pretend to have been old Reggie's cleaner at some time, and improvise some reminiscences, to allay any fears her prey may have.'

'Top hole, Manda!' cheered Hugo, amazed at the tenacity and inventiveness of his old friend. 'Then what?'

'If we still haven't got our bird, going to the funeral and the wake should give us more idea of the identity of this mystery beneficiary, and we just take it from there. I refuse to go back to the police again, until I have the murdering beggar bang to rights, and can have him charged for the dog he is. That'll show that uppity, disrespectful inspector a thing or two!'

'Don't turn this into a personal crusade, Manda,' Hugo implored her, knowing what she could be like.

'It IS personal. Daddy and Reggie were partners, back when they were young. Reggie dissolved the partnership and moved away to do something else, but he obviously returned to the town of his birth, when he retired. I remember him from when I was a tot, and I'm not going to let a personable man like that get himself murdered, and no one be any the wiser.

'Whoever shortened his life by even a day is going to pay for that theft of time, and do some time of his own. Hmph!' she concluded, a determined expression on her face. 'Let's see, today's Friday, so tomorrow's Saturday. I'll go to the nursing home tomorrow, when they should be swamped with visitors who usually work during the week, so they'll be busy, and not so "on their guard".

'But, now, to more practical matters. There is a very elderly lift in this building, which was put in for Grandmama, who needed to use a wheelchair. I'll get Beauchamp to oil the thing up, and get it into working order. That way, you'll be able to explore a bit more of the house, if you get bored.

'I've also noticed that you have some trouble with your walker thingy, getting up and down the steps in the corridors, where the floor levels change. No, Hugo! Let me finish! We used to have dachshunds, and when there was a litter, the pups' legs were so short that they couldn't get round the place very easily, so we put ramps at all the steps.

'BEAUCHAMP!' Here, she broke off to give an earsplitting yell, and Hugo winced at the assault upon his ears. 'I'll get Beauchamp to get them out of the attics and put them in place again. That will make life much easier for you, getting around.

'And, by the way, you have an appointment with my GP tonight, at five-thirty, to see about those worn-out old pins of yours. I shall, of course, accompany you, and Beauchamp can take us there in the Rolls. Argh!' she suddenly screamed, for Beauchamp had just appeared at her shoulder. She hadn't even noticed him entering the room.

'Dammit, Beauchamp, I'm sure you're not human. There's something of the supernatural about you that just can't be explained.'

'That's Beecham, my lady,' intoned Beauchamp, in a bored monotone.

While Beauchamp went about his business as instructed by his employer, Lady Amanda escorted Hugo outside, to have his first lesson in riding a motorised tricycle. He was rather averse to the idea, himself, but she insisted, and even fetched his walking frame for him.

'You just wait outside, and I'll ride them both round to the front. Then I'll show you how to control the motorised one – once I've worked it out for myself – and you can have a go, yourself' she informed him.

'I'd rather not, Manda. The whole idea terrifies me.'

'Stuff and nonsense! It's no different to driving round in one of those motorised shopping thingies that so many old people seem to have. It's just cheaper, that's all – recycling, in its best form. Recycling! Haha! Good one, don't you think? Maybe I should have said "re-tricycling"?' She went off into peals of delighted laughter, at her own accidental joke.

Recognising a lost cause when he saw one, Hugo gave in, with as good a grace as he could muster, considering how apprehensive he felt.

Lady Amanda disappeared off to the stables and, in due course, appeared again, pedalling the black tricycle that she used almost on a daily basis. She then trotted off once more, there was a muted roar, as of a motor being overrevved, and, amid a cloud of black smoke, an apparition appeared, rounding the corner of the house, emitting loud hooting noises of despair, and Lady Amanda shot past him, managing to stop, just short of the moat.

As the smoke began to clear, Hugo could make out her figure more clearly, pushing the ancient velocipede towards him, the engine not engaged. 'Bit trickier than I thought,' she puffed, as she drew up alongside him. 'I'll have to get Beauchamp to work out how best to handle it, and then we'll try again. No point in going off at half cock, is there, Hugo, old bean?'

'Absolutely none, Manda,' agreed Hugo, with great relief. He would be spared the indignity of making a fool of himself, for today at least, and would do his best to discourage her from trying again in the near future.

'Best go in and have a little lie-down, I think. Then we can think of afternoon tea, and getting ready to drag you off to the quack's – get something positive done to make you a bit more mobile.

'His name's Dr Andrew: Campbell Andrew, and he's a very helpful and obliging young chap, so listen to what he says, and no arguments. Agreed, Hugo?'

'No, ma'am,' replied Hugo a trifle testily. He knew perfectly well how to behave towards doctors: he'd seen enough of old Anstruther in the last couple of years to last him a lifetime, and he'd never uttered a discourteous word to the old man, no matter how cross or disappointed he was at his diagnoses.

They were sitting in the surgery's waiting room, keeping an eye on the red light above the door of the doctor's consulting room. The receptionist had informed them that they were after the old lady with the shopping trolley, and she was in there at the moment. They would not see her leave, as a door from the consulting room let patients debouch into another corridor, but once the red light turned green, they could go in.

With a buzz, the red light abruptly changed its colour, and they were off, Lady Amanda knocking on the door, Hugo following slowly behind with his walking frame. He had a feeling he would not have much contribution to make in the ensuing consultation, and he just wanted to get it over and done with.

Dr Andrew turned out to be a man in his early forties, still with a full head of hair, and a kindly face, and after greeting them both, he bade them take a seat. Having waited for Hugo to get comfortable, Lady Amanda rather thoughtlessly, in Hugo's opinion, opened the proceedings, and immediately ordered him to stand up and walk about, so that the doctor could see how bad his problem was.

'Come along, Hugo! Right turn, and walk! Left turn, and walk! Sit! Rise! Atten-shun! Stand at *ease!*' she barked, like an RSM.

'I think that's enough for now. He's not on parade, or at Crufts,' said Dr Andrew, and thoughtfully came round to the other side of the desk to feel over Hugo's worn-out joints, not making him climb up on to the couch usually used for such examinations.

'Had any X-rays done by your last GP?' he asked, and was flabbergasted when Hugo replied in the negative.

'Who was your last GP?' he then asked.

'Dr Anstruther,' replied Hugo, feeling slightly flustered at what he felt was a defection.

'Ah!' Doctor Andrew needed to say no more, and Lady Amanda just snorted.

'I'll just ring the hospital now, and make you an appointment to see a specialist – get you in to see him as soon as possible. Can't have you tottering around like that, if there's something simple that will remedy it,' Dr Andrew explained, as he waited for his call to be answered.

'Ah, hello there. Dr Andrew from the Summerfield Road practice. Could I have a quick word with Dr Updyke, please? It is rather urgent.' As he waited for his call to be put through, he smiled reassuringly across his desk. 'Cedric and I go back a long way,' he informed them – a clue that he might be able to massage the length of the queue to see this particular specialist, through a bit of 'knowing the right person'.

The call was obviously picked up at the other end, for he bent his attention to the receiver again, and began, 'Hello, Cedric. Got a rather interesting case of advanced arthritis here – hips and knees. Not had any prior treatment at all, not even X-rayed as yet. Dr Anstruther. Nuff said. I wondered if you could fit him in at all, urgently.' He paused, then continued, 'A Mr Hugo Cholmondley-Crichton-Crump – an old friend of Lady Amanda Golightly,' he added, for the sake of Lady Amanda's pride.

There was an irate squawking noise from the other end of the telephone, which took Dr Andrew a couple of minutes to quell. 'How terribly unfortunate, but I'd rather you didn't let that colour your judgement, of course. This is really of the utmost urgency, in my opinion.' He was silent for another minute and a half, then made his goodbyes, and ended the call.

'Monday at nine thirty a.m., Mr Cholmondley-Crichton-Crump. Dr Cedric Updyke, at the main hospital.' He then turned his attention to Lady Amanda, and speared her with his eye. 'Who's been a naughty girl then?' he asked, fighting a grin.

'What have I done now?' Lady Amanda asked in puzzlement, unable to understand why attention should suddenly have turned to her, when the phone call had been about Hugo.

'I hear you've been riding that trike of yours at high speed, without due care and attention, and have been involved in a hit-and-run, the scene of which you left, without reporting the matter,' he explained.

Lady Amanda blushed, as she remembered the man who had had to dive for safety, as her trike had careered down the hospital drive. 'I say, it wasn't *him*, was it?' she asked, now thoroughly embarrassed.

'It was! And I understand that you've been fined for speeding,' Dr Andrew added, no longer able to suppress his amusement.

'Stuff and nonsense,' she blustered. 'He shouldn't have got in my way.'

'Well, you're lucky, in a way, that he did. The thought of you taking another crack at him got him thoroughly rattled, and that's why Mr Cholmondley-Crichton-Crumpmond's appointment is so soon. He assumes that you will arrive in a more orthodox vehicle, given your friend's condition, and he said that if he could get it over with as soon as possible, it would save him getting paranoid every time he has to walk down or cross the entrance road.'

'Oh, we will, we will,' Lady Amanda assured him. 'We'll get Beauchamp to bring us in the Rolls,' she said, with relief.

'Good! And I'm sure we can improve the quality of your life, with all the modern techniques we have these days,' he assured Hugo. 'Soon have you up and about, and getting about, with a lot more ease. I can't promise you that you'll ever get back on a tennis court, for we can do nothing about reaction time, but I'm sure we can get you walking with minimum discomfort, and maybe indulging in a bit of dancing – just for exercise, and to strengthen the muscles,' he reassured a rather alarmed Hugo. He'd never liked tennis, but wasn't completely averse to a slow waltz or two.

'Thank you very much indeed, Doctor. It's very good of you to take the time like this,' he spluttered, unable to believe that his pain and struggle for mobility might soon be things of the past.

'No trouble, Mr – uh, may I call you Hugo? Just to save time, you understand. Your surnames are a bit of a mouthful, I'm afraid.'

'No problem, Doctor. And thank you, once more, from the bottom of my heart.'

'I think you ought to thank Lady Amanda as well. If she hadn't nearly run over Dr Updyke, and frightened the life out of him, he'd never have agreed to see you so promptly.'

'Marvellous!' exclaimed Hugo, accepting the walking frame offered to him by Lady Amanda, and they exited the consulting room, well-satisfied with the visit.

Back at The Towers once more, and seated in the drawing room, Lady Amanda hardly had time to consult her watch, before Beauchamp entered, silently as ever, bearing a silver salver which held two cocktail glasses, filled to the brim. 'Your drinks, my lady,' he intoned, and put them down on a small side table.

'Strangeways to Oldham,' he informed them, before slipping away as noiselessly as a cat.

Chapter Five

The next morning, armed with the knowledge that Enid Tweedie would be discharged on Monday afternoon, Lady Amanda set out early – a passenger once more, in the Rolls – to visit the Birdlings Serenade prison camp, to make enquiries about that lady's convalescence.

Monday was scheduled to be a very busy day, what with Hugo's visit to the orthopaedic consultant, and Enid needing to be transferred from hospital to care home, and then they had the funeral on Wednesday. Life suddenly seemed a lot busier than it used to, she was happy to note, for it was now much more interesting as well.

On arrival at the home, the receptionist recognised her, this time without feeling the need to press the panic button. Lady Amanda's civilised persona, on her last visit, to make enquiries about one of their late clients, had reassured her that she wasn't an escaped lunatic, but a member of the aristocracy, and she greeted the stout figure with a smile.

'Lady Amanda Golightly,' Lady Amanda introduced herself, in case the woman's memory wasn't up to it. 'I understand that you provide convalescent care, as well as full-time,' she stated, hoping for confirmation that this service was still available.

'Of course, your ladyship,' replied the woman, with the slight bob of a curtsey, which she could do nothing to avoid. Her legs just responded to the title automatically. 'We always keep a couple of rooms free for people who wish to convalesce with us, or for relatives of the sick and bed-ridden to take a break, by taking advantage of our respite care.'

Lady Amanda nodded happily at being thus informed. 'I have a friend, you see,' she said, 'who is being discharged from hospital on Monday, and I wondered if it was possible for her to spend a week here, to get her strength back up?'

'Absolutely no problem, your ladyship,' the woman informed her, and did another little bob, feeling surprised at herself, for reacting thus. 'I can get someone to show you the rooms we use, so that you can choose which one your friend might prefer, and then, if you could return here, we can sort out the paperwork.'

'Splendid!' declared Lady Amanda, her face breaking out into a beaming smile. Everything was going like clockwork, so far.

A nursing auxiliary was summoned, and led her off down the corridor, opposite to the one where Hugo's and Reggie's room had been situated. At the end of it were two rooms, both with views of the grounds, and in reasonably cheery decorative order.

'I'll just leave you alone here for a while, so that you can make up your mind,' chirped the auxiliary. 'Can you find your own way back to reception?'

'Of course I can, my dear,' cooed Lady Amanda, then muttered, 'Do you think I'm in my dotage yet?' under her breath, as the girl left the room.

It didn't really matter to her, which of the rooms was allotted to Enid, but she supposed the one second from the end would put her slightly nearer any action, and Enid wouldn't mind the faint tang of urine. She looked after her ancient mother who lived with her, and Enid's home always had just a slight whiff of pee. Thus engaged in thought, she heard footsteps coming slowly down the corridor, then another set, moving considerably faster, and a call of, 'Nurse! Nurse Plunkett! Stop this instant!'

The action was about to take place, whatever it was, right outside the room in which she was standing, so Lady Amanda made herself as still as possible, hardly daring to breathe, in case the two women outside became aware of her presence, and moved their 'business' elsewhere.

'I've just had a complaint from Mr Perkins on Poppy Wing, that, not only did his false teeth taste of soap when you returned them to him, but that they weren't even his own teeth. You'd given him back the wrong set.'

'I can't see how that happened,' replied the meek voice of someone trying to stand their own ground.

'What have you got in that bucket, Nurse Plunkett?' asked the first voice, mean, grating, and easily identifiable as Matron's.

'False teeth,' replied the meek voice, even quieter, knowing that the battle was lost, and Matron was about to scrag her, metaphorically speaking.

'How many times have I told you that you can't just lump all the teeth together in a bucket of soapy water, then run them over with a scrubbing brush?'

'Sorry, Matron. I forgot!'

'Forgot? Stuff and nonsense,' Matron admonished her. 'I know you're only an agency nurse here, but we do have standards and procedures, and they do not include cleaning the patients' false teeth in the manual equivalent of a dishwasher.'

'No, Matron! It won't happen again, Matron.'

'You can bet your shirt on that, Nurse Plunkett, for if I catch you doing this again, I shall send you back to Edwards's Nursing Services with a flea in your ear and a reference that will ring in your mind for ever. Do I make myself clear?'

'Yes, Matron!'

'Then get off to the sluice room, and clean those teeth properly, and get them back to the right patients, if it takes you all day to do it. And start with Mr Perkins. He's got a bag of toffees that he needs them for, although I don't know why; they always gum him up, then he has to ask for

help, to get the bottom set unstuck from the top.'

'Yes, Matron!'

Two sets of footsteps disappeared down the corridor in the direction of reception, and Lady Amanda was left alone with her thoughts, again. 'Must remember to tell Enid to clean her own teeth, when she's here. Disgusting! Absolutely disgusting!'

She dawdled back to the reception desk, having noted the number of the room, and proceeded to deal with the form-filling that was necessary to admit Enid Tweedie for a week, then left, to return to Belchester Towers, with a rather amusing tale to relate to Hugo. She must remember to ask him if he had ever had his teeth taken away to be cleaned, while he was staying there.

That evening, at six o'clock sharp, cocktails were served once more, and Hugo decided that this was a part of Manda's life that he could easily get used to. It was not only very civilised, but helped to relax his muscles, where they had been tensed against the pain in his legs. That she had kept up such a daily habit while living on her own amazed him, but he was glad of it.

Sunday was spent teaching Hugo the mysteries of operating the elderly lift that Beauchamp had got back into working order, and although it groaned and creaked alarmingly in its ascents and descents, he had assured them that it was perfectly sound, and safe to use.

Lady Amanda showed Hugo how to open the cage-like doors, and entered with him, to instruct him in the use of the contraption should he wish to visit the first floor. Unfortunately, the lift did not travel up to the second floor, or to the attics, so maybe he'd have to wait until after his raft of mobility-improving operations before being ambitious enough to tackle exploring at those levels.

There was barely room for two people in the little cage, let alone two stout people, and to begin with they were jammed in back to back, and had to indulge in a perfect fandango of wriggling, to end up both facing front, and in a position to exit the lift, when it reached its destination.

She indicated to Hugo the button that would close the metal doors, then the button which would open them again. Finally, she pointed out the button which would cause the lift to ascend to the first floor. Pressing the 'doors open' button, she instructed Hugo to take them upstairs, as a test of how well he had absorbed her simple instructions.

'I can't, Manda,' he pleaded helplessly. 'The doors are still open.'

'You dolt, Hugo! That's part of using the thing. Close the doors, take us upstairs, then open the doors to let us out. Nothing could be simpler!'

For a few minutes, the lift doors slowly ground closed, then open again: closed, then open again. 'May I suggest that somewhere in the procedure, you actually use the ascend button, Hugo, old bean,' advised Lady Amanda, not cross, but merely amused by his ineptitude.

'I'm terribly sorry, old stick, but I can't seem to remember which button takes us up. Can you just go through the procedure again for me, then I'm sure I shall be able to do it without fault.'

It took a good half hour, but by the end of that time, Hugo was as proficient at ascending and descending in the lift as if he had been operating it all his life. 'I say, old girl, this is jolly rot isn't it, being able to go upstairs without all that darned climbing?' he exclaimed.

'Save your poor old legs no end, won't it?' she offered, in agreement.

Lady Amanda also took him round the various ramps that Beauchamp had restored to their previous positions, and she ascertained that none of them was too steep or too narrow for Hugo to negotiate with his walking frame.

Apart from that, they did little more than take a slow – very slow – toddle in the grounds, and play a few hands of piquet. Monday was to be an unusually busy day, and they both wanted to conserve their strength, for the stamina they would need to find, to get through both Hugo's appointment with the consultant, collecting Enid Tweedie from the hospital ward, and seeing her safely installed in her temporary lodgings.

Lady Amanda had got Beauchamp to drop into the hospital grounds, on their way back from the nursing home, so that she could inform Edith of her upcoming role of 'undercover spy', and why this was necessary; so the stage was set. They had only to wait for curtain-up, the following morning.

Hugo had been offered another lesson in riding the trike, even though he had not yet had the displeasure of actually trying to ride it himself, but had politely refused, and received another stay of execution by the ringing of the telephone.

There was nothing to do now, but wait.

Chapter Six

Monday morning dawned bright and sunny, and they reached the hospital's main entrance with fifteen minutes to spare – just as well, considering how long it would take to get Hugo down the various corridors, and up in the lifts to reach the necessary waiting area. On their way, however, a kindly nurse had seen their difficulty, and promptly fetched them a wheelchair to hasten their progress.

Although Hugo had protested about being pushed around in a bath-chair, like an elderly Edwardian gentleman, the nurse's pretty smile had persuaded him, and she had then volunteered to wheel Hugo to his destination, to Lady Amanda's obvious relief. He was no lightweight, and she was no stripling, and the whole journey through the maze of corridors was leaving her exhausted and disorientated, so that she actually had no idea whether they had been travelling in the correct direction or not.

With the nurse's help, they reached their destination with five minutes to spare, going through the double doors to the waiting area, only for the most ghastly sight to greet their eyes.

Chairs arranged down two sides of the wall contained waiting patients, but all appeared to be liberally doused in blood, and it looked like a massacre had just taken place. Lady Amanda emitted a foghorn-like scream, and Hugo expressed his horror and distress by uttering, 'Oh dear!' and shaking his head from side to side in disbelief.

A distressed nurse, only now noticed by them, was looking horror-stricken, and paging someone on the inhouse telephone, to come to her assistance. In the middle of the floor lay a blood bag – obviously headed somewhere for transfusion – that she must have dropped, loosening its seal. As she explained to them briefly, it had then squirted out its contents in all directions, with the vigour of a deflating balloon, and liberally sprayed all those waiting to see Dr Updyke.

At the sound of the fuss, the great man himself appeared in the doorway of his consulting room, looked around in amazement at the devastation, and the apparently mutilated patients, caught sight of Lady Amanda, and pointed an accusing finger at her.

'You again!' he boomed. 'This is all your doing, isn't it? Call the police, someone! There's a homicidal maniac on the loose. She's had one go at me already, and now she's starting in on my patients.'

Lady Amanda had gazed upon his features with horror, too. That was the bounder who had nearly had her off her trike, if her memory served her correctly. Dr Andrew had told her so, but she'd forgotten all about that. Crumbs! 'Hugo,' she hissed, as quietly as possible. 'That's the cad who wandered in front of my tricycle, and ended up in the shrubbery.'

Hugo had the grace to blush, at this disturbing admission, and hoped this would not be held against him during his consultation. He idly wondered if he ought, or even if he dared, perhaps, to try to get Manda to remain in the waiting area, but he knew this was a non-starter, as soon as the thought entered his head. Manda did as she pleased and, at the moment, she was looking after him, and looking after him meant going in to the doctor's office with him. No go!

It took longer than it should have done to calm down the consultant and explain the situation to him, because he was so wary of Lady Amanda but, finally, all was peaceful again, and it turned out to be Hugo's turn to be seen, which was quite all right with Lady Amanda. That little pantomime had filled in the time they would otherwise have wasted waiting in silence, and been jolly entertaining to boot.

When they were seated in the consulting room, Lady Amanda apologised very prettily for the unfortunate circumstances that had prevailed at their previous meeting, and Dr Updyke thawed a few degrees, from permafrost, to just well-chilled.

She was delighted to note that, when he addressed Hugo, he pronounced his name completely accurately, and she smiled at the consultant, to mark her approval. She had related the trike incident to Hugo on the day he had moved into Belchester Towers, with the post scriptum of her fine for speeding, and he had laughed like a drain, and exclaimed, 'Good old Manda!'

Lady Amanda's smile slightly unnerved Dr Updyke, but he pulled up the e-mail on his computer from Dr Andrew, and began to question him about his current treatment.

'I'm afraid I don't really have any,' apologised Hugo, looking slightly embarrassed at his dearth of pills and potions, as if it were, somehow, his fault. 'My last doctor just told me to take paracetamol, and accept it as part and parcel of old age,' he informed the consultant.

'Outrageous!' Updyke exploded. 'Who exactly was this previous doctor of yours?'

'Dr Anstruther,' Hugo stated, and both he and Lady Amanda watched as the medical man turned scarlet with wrath.

'Silly old fool should either have retired, or been struck off the Medical Register years ago. The real toll of the harm he's done will never be uncovered, but his treatment of you is typical of the man. He's too old to care, too old to understand modern treatments, and only carries on for the money. Disgraceful!'

The doctor had now thawed completely, and examined Hugo with the tenderness of a mother examining her child. 'Right, Mr Cholmondley-Crichton-Crump, I'm going to send you off for some X-rays now, and for blood tests. I want to see you again in a week. The receptionist in the waiting area will make a follow-up appointment for you.

'In the meantime, I'm going to give you a prescription which you can have filled at the hospital pharmacy, for some jolly strong painkillers and some anti-inflammatory pills. They should ease things for you, and we can follow on from there. I have a fair idea of what the X-rays will show, and I have to warn you that it could be a double hip-replacement and a double knee-replacement for you.

'If this proves so, it will take some time – maybe a year or two – to get everything done, but I can assure you that it will give you a completely new lease of life. If you have any questions, make a note of them, and bring them along to your next appointment, which I sincerely hope,' here, Dr Updyke paused to give a little chuckle, 'will not commence with a bloodbath. Haha!'

He shook hands as they left, in quite a good humour, and it was only as they made to exit his consulting room, that his expression turned to a slight frown of puzzlement. That woman had seemed perfectly OK today, but what was she? Some kind of Jekyll and Hyde personality? When she had come roaring at him on that tricycle of hers, she had looked just like a Valkyrie in full flight. Today she had been as polite as was to be expected, given who she was, and her station in life. He just hoped that he never had the misfortune to encounter the Valkyrie side of her personality again.

The wheelchair had been left in the waiting area, and was still there when they came out. The receptionist, having noticed how slowly Hugo walked into the consulting room, had kindly summoned a porter to push him to wherever he was fated to go next.

Clutching his fistful of forms and the prescription, Hugo lowered himself gratefully into the seat, and made his trips to the

X-ray department, to have his blood taken, and to the hospital pharmacy, with un-hoped for swiftness, and they found themselves back at Belchester Towers in time for lunch, a goal believed unattainable by Lady Amanda, when they had set out on their trip, earlier.

A short nap after lunch to eliminate the rigours of the morning, saw them awake and alert again, at three o'clock, and preparing to go to collect Enid from her hospital discharge, and settle her in at the home.

When they located Enid's bed in Robin Ward, she was already dressed, and sitting on a bedside chair, her bag packed and waiting beside her, her discharge papers clutched in her right hand.

'The doctor came round early,' she excused herself for being ready to leave before time. 'I've been sitting here for almost an hour.'

'Do you good to be out of bed,' commented Lady Amanda, gruffly and unsympathetically. 'By the way, I don't think you've met my long-lost friend Hugo,' she stated, having noticed Enid staring at Hugo in an interrogatory way. She rarely saw Lady Amanda in company with a gentleman friend, and she was naturally curious.

'May I introduce you to Hugo Cholmondley-Crichton-Crump?' Enid was fascinated to meet someone with such an exotic-sounding name, and even more so, when Lady Amanda wrote it down for her to see.

'So it's pronounced as you said it, but it's spelled like this?' she asked incredulously.

'That's right, Enid.'

'I've never met anyone before who had a name that sounded differently to what it looked like on paper,' she added, in wonder.

'Well, you have now, so come on, let's get weaving. Now, you know that you're our eyes and ears in that home, don't you? Good! We need to find out who was impersonating Reggie's nephew, what he looked like, and – if you're really good at this – where he might have come across Reggie, to pull a fast one on him and the staff there, like that. Got it? Good!'

The hospital provided a nurse to wheel Enid to the main hospital doors in a chair, and she then transferred into the Rolls, evidently enjoying herself immensely, and acting like Lady Bountiful, as she climbed into the vintage vehicle.

Their destination was only a couple of hundred yards away, but that didn't stop Enid savouring every second of it. Being in a Rolls-Royce wasn't an everyday occurrence for her, and she noticed how people stopped and stared at it, as it passed. Lucky, lucky, Lady Amanda! And she just took this sort of thing for granted!

At The Birdlings, she was clearly delighted with her room, and the thought that she could just take it easy for a week, and be waited on, hand foot and finger – something she had not appreciated in the hospital, due to the way she had felt after her operation, and the fact that the hospital kitchens seemed to have a contract with the operating theatre staff, regarding the provision of meat. There had been far too much offal on the menu for her liking, anything including meat had been unidentifiable, and had left her feeling very suspicious of the source of their butchery requisitions.

After having been shown the room, and its meagre facilities, Lady Amanda turned on Enid and said, 'I suggest that you try speaking to Nurse Plunkett. She doesn't seem very happy here, and has been sent by an agency. I think she'd be willing to give you any of the dirt she knows about on this place, just for the sheer pleasure of it.'

'I'll do my best,' responded Enid Tweedie, looking slightly worried, now she was actually installed here and on the job, so to speak.

'You will do better than that, Enid. You will make me proud of you!' was Lady Amanda's uncompromising reply, and was not so much a prediction, as an order. 'We'll visit every day – don't want to trust important information in a case of murder to the phone lines. Don't know who might be listening in,' she added, somewhat melodramatically, in Hugo's opinion. This wasn't Sexton Blake: this was real life, and real life was safer than fiction, or so he thought, then.

When they finally returned to Belchester Towers, it was too late for afternoon tea, so Lady Amanda requested that dinner be brought forward a little, to compensate, and Hugo announced that he needed another little lie-down, as it was some time since he had been so active.

'Really, Hugo! You spent most of the time we were at the hospital being pushed around in that wheelchair. How can you possibly be tired again?' Lady Amanda asked, casting a sceptical eye over him, and realising that he really did look worn out. 'Never mind! Can't be helped! Off you toddle, and don't worry about me. I'll find something to occupy my time,' at which point the old pullstyle front door bell rang, and she exclaimed in triumph, 'Here we go. I said something would turn up.'

The something that turned up was a representative from the Social Services department, with a wheelchair for Hugo to use, until such time as he was more mobile. 'Dr Andrew phoned and ordered it,' the gentleman at the door explained. 'If you'd just like to sign here – and here – and here? Thank you very much, madam.'

'That's 'my lady' to you,' she informed him haughtily, and took charge of Hugo's new chariot. 'Hey, Chummy, just before you toddle off to bed, look what Dr Andrew's sent round for you. Fantastic, eh?'

'If you like that sort of thing,' replied Hugo, turning his back and shuffling off in the direction of his bedroom, which was where he liked it – on the ground floor, where he felt safest.

Abandoning the new carriage, which Beauchamp could take care of, as far as finding somewhere to stash it was concerned, Lady Amanda arranged her face in a determined expression, removed an old crash helmet of Mummy's from a cupboard, and stumped purposefully off, out of the house, and towards the stables.

She was determined to get the hand of the motorised trike while Hugo was napping. She'd had Beauchamp try it out himself, leaving any alterations or improvements to its running in his capable hands, and was now ready to get 'back on the horse' so to speak. It may have beaten her once, but it wouldn't be given another chance. She would master it, or die in the attempt.

When Hugo entered the drawing room after his nap, still a little bleary-eyed, he found Lady Amanda sitting on a sofa, her hair wildly out of place, oil smudges on her face and hands, and a triumphant expression on her face.

'Been taming the wild beast,' she said, by way of explanation, and when Hugo's face broke into a study of incomprehension, explained in more detail:

'That motorised tricycle that Beauchamp fixed up for you. I've had him do a few alterations, and I've just about mastered driving the thing. It's nowhere near as excitable as it was last time we had it out, and I think it's time you learned to ride it.

'Oh, not now, you silly,' she added, watching fear creep across his features. 'Maybe tomorrow, before we go to visit Enid for her fist debrief of the case. We won't go until after lunch – give her time to settle in, so there'll be plenty of time in the morning. The funeral's not till Wednesday, so we've got time on our hands, and nothing planned to fill it. Are you up for it, old chap?'

'Only if you ride it first, so that I can see it's not wild and dangerous, as it was when you tried it out before.'

'Of course I'll demonstrate,' she assured him, pleased to be able to demonstrate how proficient she had become at controlling the bloody-minded contraption in so short a time. 'I'll give you a performance, explain everything, then you can have a go – and if you wear Daddy's old crash helmet, we should be prepared, in the event of a mishap.'

Hugo didn't like the sound of this last bit, but he was game to try it out, and nodded in agreement before his hostess went on, not waiting for a spoken answer from him.

'Six o'clock, and time for a bit of a belter, I think, don't you, Hugo?' This was another rhetorical question, and Hugo wisely recognised it and remained silent. He'd have to get used to those rhetorical doo-dahs again. 'Where's that Beau ... Oh, there you are! I didn't hear you come in. *Quelle surprise*! Now, pass the tray to Hugo first as he's a guest, then I'll have mine. Thank you very much, Beauchamp.'

As the manservant left the room, he was heard to mutter, 'And my name's pronounced Beecham!'

Chapter Seven

Hugo was delighted, on waking on Tuesday morning, to find that the weather had taken a turn for the worse, and rain was falling relentlessly from a leaden sky. 'Hoorah!' he thought. Now he wouldn't have to have a go on that three-wheeled machine from hell. Manda would have to let him off, because of the weather. There was nothing even *she* could do about that.

Lady Amanda did try to persuade Hugo that they could manage perfectly well if she attached an umbrella to the back of the thing, but Hugo was having none of it. 'The wind's getting up,' he pointed out to her, 'and if the brolly gets caught by a gust, I'm going to look like ET, flying on that thing, or Mary Poppins in the Tour de France, heaven forbid.'

'You win, Chummy. We'll have to postpone it till after the funeral now,' she conceded with bad grace, 'But there's nothing stopping us having a few games of cards, and then we can have a quiet read until lunchtime.'

This suited Hugo's ambitions perfectly, and they played a few rounds of gin rummy, before putting away the playing cards. Hugo then settled down with his newspaper, while Lady Amanda sat at a small table, her hands occasionally darting forward to write something on a piece of paper resting on the table in front of her.

Hugo was quite happily absorbed in his reading, but was disturbed, every minute or so, by a cry of 'Aha', or 'Of course, how stupid of me'.

'What on earth are you up to, old girl?' he asked a trifle querulously.

'Crossword, old stick,' she replied, without looking up. 'But you haven't got a paper?' he observed, logically.

'People put them through the door for me. Cut from their newspapers. They know how addicted I am, and this way I get crosswords from a good cross-section of the papers. Good, eh? Did you know that the French word for a paperclip is "trombone"? Super clue!'

'Perhaps you could moderate your ejaculations, Manda, old girl,' he suggested. 'Keep losing my thread, with you yelling all over the place.'

'Sorry, I'll try to keep it down, but it's just so exciting when I solve a particularly tricky cryptic clue. I'll try just to wave my fist in the air, in future, so as not to disturb your reading.'

Which she did, but Hugo could see it out of the corner of his eye, and found it just as distracting as her yells of triumph had been. Finally, he gave up, placed the open newspaper over his face, and dozed off to sleep. If he was sleeping, at least her raised fists of triumph couldn't disturb his dreams.

After a very satisfying half-hour's nap, Hugo woke up refreshed, and asked, apropos of nothing in particular, 'So you never married either, old girl?'

Lady Amanda looked up from her crossword, and prepared her answer. 'No, Hugo. Of course, I danced with all and sundry during my coming-out year, but, after one disastrous incident, I only ever took one walk in the garden, during a ball.'

'What happened to put you off, old thing?' Hugo was interested now.

'Some boy or other – I can't remember who he was, now – took me outside for a walk by moonlight, and the bounder grabbed me round the waist and kissed me full on the mouth, and actually stuck his tongue down my throat. I was so disgusted I threw up in a rose bush, so I never went for a "walk" again. Gardens contain too many dangerous things, like shrubberies and summer-houses. I really can't be doing with anything wet and sticky, unless it's called "pudding".

'What about you, Hugo? I never fell for that old rot about not taking the chance on having your name lengthened again. That sort of tosh simply won't wash with me. That was a load of old cow poo; a load of doggydoodles. Out with it! What was the real reason?'

'Same sort of thing, really. I was taken outside by a girl, and she kissed me, and put my hand ... somewhere about her person, and I nearly passed out. I'm with you on that one.

'We danced together at a ball once, didn't we?'

'I do believe we did. And at one time, I had a tiny crush on you, Hugo – when you used to visit, in the school holidays. '

'Never!'

'I did. And then I took that ill-fated "walk" in the garden, and I decided I was finished with the opposite sex. Everything's so untidy and undignified in human relationships, and I didn't want to have any part in that sort of thing.'

'Good for you, Manda. I felt absolutely the same about it. Changing the subject somewhat – we've got so much to catch up on, haven't we? Did you have a good time at school? I didn't. I was always being bullied for being, what they call nowadays, a bit of a wimp.'

'Oh, I had a shocking time. I was sent somewhere up north, to be educated along with the lumpen daughters of the aristocratic sod – and right sods they were too – please excuse my language.'

'Don't mention it,' remarked Hugo politely.

'Horrible little beasts they were. Always going on about their ponies, and the gymkhanas they'd ridden in. And when they found out where I came from, they gave me no peace. Separated Belchester into "Belch" and "ester", and from then on, I was known as Windy Esther. Sadistic little sods they were. Children can be so cruel! It was such a relief to come home for the holidays, to some civilised company.'

'I notice you don't use much of the house, nowadays, do you, Manda?'

'Most of it's locked up; the furniture all dust-sheeted. Why?'

'Well, I wonder you don't open it to the public. It'd give you a real purpose in life, and it would bring in a few extra shekels.'

'I've thought about it from time to time, but it all seems a bit too much like hard work.'

'Well, there are two of us, now. Maybe it's something we can organise together.'

'Not until you've had all your treatment and are a bit more mobile, Hugo. If we tried it now, I'd be the one doing all the running around, and you'd be almost chairbound.'

'True, but it's something to consider for the future, what?'

'Maybe!'

After luncheon, they donned their wet weather gear, to venture out to visit Enid Tweedie, to see if she'd managed to gather any useful information with reference to identifying old Reggie's mystery visitor. Rain still fell from the sky in torrents, and Lady Amanda rather hoped that it would clear up before the morrow, for there was nothing more likely to induce a deep depression, than standing by a muddy graveside in the rain, forced to contemplate one's own mortality.

The home smelt of boiled Brussels sprouts today, or at least, that's what Lady Amanda hoped it was! They found Enid sitting in an armchair by the window of her room, engrossed in a ladies magazine of the trashier type, and she put it down reluctantly, at their arrival.

First things first: 'How are you, Enid? Good, good! And who's looking after your mother while you're in here? Come to mention it, who looks after her during your frequent stays in hospital?'

'She goes to my sister down near the college,' Enid replied, and then to avoid further questioning about her domestic arrangements, added, 'And Mrs Next-Door feeds the cat.'

'So your house is empty, then?'
'That's right.'

'Better give me the keys, so I can check you haven't been burgled. We wouldn't want you coming out of here and finding your house ransacked, now would we?'

'Good idea, Lady Amanda. They're in my handbag. I'll just get them for you.'

While she scrabbled around in her handbag looking for her keys, Lady Amanda whispered to Hugo, 'If I can get into her house, at least I can give it a good airing – throw all the windows and doors open, when the weather's a bit better. What with her old mother and the cat, the house simply reeks of 'wee wee' and old pussy.'

Transferring the unexpectedly large bunch of keys into her own handbag, Lady Amanda enquired, 'Have you had a chance to talk to that Nurse Plunkett yet?'

'What a very nice young lady she is!' stated Enid, with a happy smile. 'Always has time to stop and chat; not like some of the others, who are always rushing off to do something or other.'

'What have you learned?'

'That she works for Edwards's Nursing Services, and she's pretty fed-up with being placed here on her own. Quite often the nurses are on temporary contract in couples or threesomes, when it's for a hospital, but Matron here wouldn't hear of having to pay for a second nurse, so she only took the one.'

'That's all very nice to know, but we're trying to place that chap who posed as Reggie's nephew, not extract her woes and troubles from her.'

'I do realise that, and I was just setting the scene, before I got to the interesting bit,' Enid replied, a trifle sniffily. 'She did say that she'd spotted one of the other agency workers here, when she came to look round the place and be interviewed, but he hadn't seen her. She assumed he was visiting someone, as he was carrying a bunch of flowers.'

'Aha!' exclaimed Lady Amanda. 'Does she know his name?'

'She can't remember, for the moment, but said if I was really interested, she'd phone one of her colleagues, and find out for me. It seems he was employed six months or so ago, to nurse an elderly gentleman in his home, but that contract ended, and he's had to move on since then.'

'Aha!' Lady Amanda exclaimed again. 'That's the bunny! I'm sure about it now.'

'How can you be?' asked Hugo, doubtfully. 'You've only got one tiny bit of information.'

'By using the old noggin, Hugo. This chap nurses Reggie, gets him to change his will, then Reggie has to move here. Our chappie then starts to call in on him, to make sure he hasn't been lucid enough to change his will again, and then, for some currently unknown reason, bumps him off. There!'

'There's a lot of conjecture in there, Manda. Mind out! You might get your fingers burnt, if you try accusing an innocent man of murder.'

'Piffle!' she replied. 'I know I'm right! I can feel it in my water.'

'There's a visitor's loo just across the corridor,' they were informed by Enid, 'should you feel the need.'

After their now habitual cocktails, and dinner, Lady Amanda started to look shifty, and began fidgeting in an altogether embarrassed way that Hugo did not at all understand. 'Whatever's got into you, old thing?' he asked, concerned. 'You look as if all the hounds of hell are after you.'

'I have to do something tonight – with Beauchamp,' she explained, looking terribly uncomfortable.

There was a pause, and then Hugo exclaimed, 'Oh, not that, surely? And with Beauchamp? But you said earlier ...' His voice trailed off.

Pulling herself into a very upright position, and assuming a haughty expression, Lady Amanda replied, 'Hugo, wash your mouth out with soap and water. I can read your mind, and it's positively pornographic. It's nothing like that, I can assure you.'

With a jaundiced eye, Hugo retorted, 'Well, what is it then, if it's "nothing like that"?'

Walking towards him and leaning over – a movement which both startled and alarmed him, she pointed at her head and said, 'Being a man, you probably haven't noticed anything amiss, but my hair is turning from blonde to grey, from the roots out.' Here, she lowered her voice to a whisper, 'I have my roots dyed once a month. Can't afford the hairdresser, so Beauchamp does it for me. Much cheaper that way, and it stops all the nosy parkers talking about how my hair isn't its natural colour. *Comprende, senor?*'

'Oh, got you, old girl!' exclaimed Hugo in complete understanding. 'So there is a chink in your armour after all, then?'

'Not so much a chink, as the merest speck of vanity. Now, I'm off upstairs to the bathroom with Beauchamp, and I'll probably not come down again, so sleep well, old stick.'

'Same to you, Manda.'

'And remember – not a word to a soul about this, Hugo. I'm relying on your discretion.'

'I'm loyal to the end, old friend,' he said, saluting her as she left the room.

Lady Amanda left the room and stumped off upstairs to meet her fate. Stopping in her bedroom, she stripped to the waist, and hurriedly wrapped her upper half in large, camouflaging towels, held together with old-fashioned wooden clothes pegs, before presenting herself in the bathroom.

The bathroom itself was so old-fashioned that it had become, now, high fashion again, with its cast iron roll-top bath with lion's feet and 'telephone' hand-shower attachment. The ceramic sink was oblong, with cut corners, and still had the original taps, and the lavatory was the high cistern flush-type, decorated with blue leaves and flowers, and a bumble bee in the pan for the gentlemen to aim at.

In fact, a photograph of it would not have looked out of place in any home-design magazine. Lady Amanda, of course, realised this, and had stopped moaning about renewing the old suite a couple of years ago, when she realised just how trendy her bathroom was.

Beauchamp had everything laid out, and she took her seat in the chair he had provided, with her usual trepidation. Although Beauchamp had been providing this service for several years now, she still felt (and indeed was) naked under the towels, in the presence of a man, and she was very unnerved, every time her roots had to be coloured.

Beauchamp was the soul of discretion, of course – she had no worries on that front. It was just the sensation of nakedness, which she knew was stupid. She was naked under her clothes in his presence every day, and just considered herself decently attired – but this – this just felt different, and made her very uneasy, as if the towels were transparent, or even invisible, leaving her top half exposed for him to ogle.

'Silly old trout!' she muttered to herself, and gave Beauchamp permission to go ahead and apply the stinking stuff to her roots with the harsh-bristled root-brush. Later, when it was dry and combed again, all these negative feelings would be as if they had never existed, but, for an hour or so, every month, she felt like a threatened virgin, and there was no 'again' about it.

While she was 'cooking', Beauchamp kindly fetched her reading glasses and her bedtime book from her room, and left her alone for half an hour, until she was nicely done to a turn, when he would return, and rinse and condition her curly locks, all blonde again, and without a tell-tale trace of grey.

While she was thus on her own, Lady Amanda had what until recently she had taken so much for granted – some time on her own. Although it was lovely to have Hugo staying with her at The Towers, she had lived alone since Mummy and Daddy died – Beauchamp didn't count. He had always been there. But now she was beginning to realise how difficult it was to adapt to having someone else about the place.

Of course, it wasn't Hugo's fault, and she couldn't let him go back to that ghastly home, but it was going to take some time to establish a routine that satisfied them both, with time together, and time in solitude. She knew Hugo had also lived alone before, and he must be feeling very much as she was, but she was sure they could work something out between them.

Chapter Eight

At breakfast the next morning, served half an hour earlier than usual, so that they should have sufficient time to make themselves ready for Reggie's funeral, they discussed what they wanted to achieve that morning.

'Being at the funeral will give us a good chance to have a real eyeful of whoever attends, then, I understand, it's back to Reggie's house for the wake. Young Mr Williams has sort of given me permission to stay on for the reading of the will, and I want to know to whom the dosh has been left.'

'Where did Reggie live?' asked Hugo.

'Apparently he lived in that really old house called High Hedges – the only property that fronts on to The Butts. I've passed it many a time on my peregrinations on the trike, but never realised it was Reggie's place. If I had, I'd have called in to say hello, and now it's too late.' Lady Amanda drew a handkerchief from her pocket and mopped at the corners of her eyes.

'There, there, Manda. Never mind. You might not have got to meet up with him again, for all your efforts visiting the nursing home, but at least you sussed out that he'd been murdered, and are going to avenge his death now, by hunting down and bringing to justice the cad who knocked him off,' replied Hugo in soothing tones, but somewhat pompously.

'*We* are going to bring that bounder to justice, Hugo – *us* – both of us.'

'Fair enough, but I don't see what a useless old buffer like me can do to help apprehend a dangerous criminal.' 'Just do as I tell you and you won't go far wrong,' Lady Amanda instructed him.

'Don't I always!' replied Hugo, helping himself to another slice of toast and the thick-cut marmalade.

'If I take my mobile phone with me,' she informed her companion, 'I might be able to get a photo of that *faux* nephew, and then we can show it to Nurse Plunkett, for identification purposes, and then ... Well, we can get the case wrapped up fairly rapidly, and present it all to that illmannered Inspector Moody – I rang up to check who was on duty when I called in – and show him who are the better detectives.'

'It's all a bit Enid Blyton, isn't it, Manda?' Hugo ventured.

'Tosh! Easy as one, two, three. We'll show that uncivilised buffoon at the police station who knows their onions and who doesn't.'

'Well, just be careful. If that chap's killed once, he may not hesitate to do it again,' Hugo warned, suddenly fearful for her safety – suddenly fearful for his own safety, too, when push came to shove. He'd momentarily forgotten that they were working together.

In the car, on the way to St Michael-in-the-Fields, Lady Amanda informed Hugo that his house was on the rental market. 'But you don't even know where I live!' he exclaimed in amazement. 'I never said anything, when you were referring to the old place, and how lovely it had been.

Didn't like to. Shatter your illusions, and all that.' 'Well, I have a little confession to make,' she told him.

'What have you done now?' he asked, in a resigned tone of voice.

'Oh, nothing much. I'd already worked out that you'd moved on. I lifted your house keys from your jacket pocket one day when you were having a little nap. It's very naughty of you to have an address label on them. It's just asking to be robbed.'

'I hadn't thought of that,' replied Hugo. 'It was so that they could be returned to me, if I ever lost them.'

'You were more likely to be cleaned out, or murdered in your bed – or both!' chided Lady Amanda, amazed at the naïveté of her old friend.

'Holy Moses! So you could've saved my life!'

'Better than that,' she said. 'I phoned round a selection of local estate agents, and got Beauchamp to sort out access – I'm afraid he had to have a few copies of the keys made, but we'll get them all back before anyone moves in. Anyway, they've all valued it for rental, and I've chosen the one who has come up with the most believable figure, and the lowest rate of commission, and I've asked him to advertise it.'

'But ...'

'But me no buts, Hugo. You don't have to do anything. If there's anything you'd like to remove from the property, Beauchamp and I can sort that out. The same with any special pieces of furniture that you'd like put into storage – loads of room at Belchester Towers – and the agent does all the financial checks, collects the rent, and just pays it into your account. All you have to do is sit back and accrue the profits.'

'But what if something needs doing?'

'The agent organises all that, and takes it out of the rent money,' she explained, feeling that she had adequately clarified the process to him by now.

'I say! You have been a busy little bee, haven't you, Manda?'

'I do my level best. I used to hang around the estate manager's office, when we had more land, and tenants, so I had a fair idea of how things worked.'

There were only a handful of people in the church for the funeral. Young Mr Williams was there as Reggie's legal representative here on this earth, there were a couple of people from the nursing home that Lady Amanda recognised, and a couple who introduced themselves as Reggie's former neighbours. The only other person in attendance was a man who appeared to be in his mid-

thirties, who sat in the front row, his face shaded by the hat he had not had the respect and courtesy to remove, inside the church.

It was black! The hat was black! 'There you go, Hugo,' whispered Lady Amanda. 'It's always the man in the black hat who's the baddie.'

'Don't be silly, Manda. That's only in old films and westerns. He's at a funeral. Of course his hat is black.'

'I bet that's the fake nephew!' she hissed back, right into his ear, which tickled a lot, and he had to push her away, while he gave it a good old rub with the palm of his hand, to stop it itching so.

'Shut up and behave yourself!' was his last word on the matter, and they both bent their heads to examine the flimsy piece of paper which contained the order of service. Hugo had barely had sufficient time to take in the details, when she hissed at him again. 'That Moody man should be here, not us!'

'Who the hell is "that moody man"?' asked Hugo, a little tetchily.

'That policeman – Inspector Moody. If only he'd listened to me instead of humiliating me, he could be sitting in the church now, about to pounce on the villain.'

In uncharacteristically demotic mode, Hugo hissed back, 'Can it, sweetheart! It's all about to go off!'

The service itself was short and swift, and started with a couple of verses of 'For Those in Peril on the Sea'. 'Reggie wasn't a sailor, was he?' whispered Hugo, behind his hand.

'Not to my knowledge. I know he was passed unfit for service during the war, and I never heard of him having a boat of any kind.'

The eulogy was short and evidently delivered by a clergyman who had never met the dear departed. Both Lady Amanda and Hugo were surprised that the man they had dubbed the *faux* nephew hadn't risen to speak, but, on more considered thought, realised he probably knew very little about Reggie, being a fake.

Two verses of 'The Day Thou Gavest Lord is Over' finished the swiftest funeral that either one of them had ever been to, and the undertaker's men came in, to ferry the coffin to the graveside.

They made a very sad and sorry bunch – the few of them that there were – standing in the pouring rain and getting soaked to the skin – as the coffin was lowered into the ground, and the clergyman began to say the words of the service of committal. When the time came for someone to throw in a handful of earth, they all looked round at each other, Lady Amanda finally removing her gloves and picking up a handful of almost liquid mud, before pouring it into the grave, to dribble across the coffin, like the trail of a brown snail.

The man in the black hat blushed with embarrassment, and reluctantly copied her action, as did Hugo, as a mark of respect for the departed. The vicar made the sign of the cross, and they all looked around to see who would be the first to leave.

As it happened, it was the man who had sat at the front and claimed to be related to Reggie who scuttled off first, but that was no problem, as there was to be a wake – a very small one, by the looks of it – afterwards, and all Lady Amanda and Hugo had to do was to get Beauchamp to follow the car of Reggie's ex-neighbours, to their unknown destination.

'Actually, I think it would be better to follow young Mr Williams. The neighbours might not be going back to wherever it is – it could be the young man's house. I hope it is, because then we will at least know where he lives. But, if we follow young Mr Williams, we know he'll be going back afterwards, because he's arranged to read the will, after the – the – whatever it turns out to be.

'I don't expect a champagne reception, but a cup of tea and a slice of cake, or a ham sandwich would go down well. It's getting on for lunchtime, or will be by the time we've all gathered there, and I shall, no doubt, be ravenous.'

'Typical Manda!' commented Hugo. 'You always did put your stomach first!'

'Anyway, I've got a thirst on, after all that singing!'

'Pathetic, wasn't it?' Hugo asked, looking round at her for a response.

'It certainly was: a sad and pathetic end to a man's life, and if there's nothing more we can do about it, we'll at least expose the person who caused him to be planted in the ground today.'

'Oh, damn and blast it!' exclaimed Lady Amanda, as the car in front of them turned into the drive of Reggie's old house in The Butts. 'How are we ever going to find out where this cove lives, if he holds the wake at Reggie's old house?'

'Haven't the faintest idea, old thing, but I'm sure you'll think of something,' replied Hugo with confidence.

'Oh, I will, I will. And if I can't get the information today, there are more ways than one to skin a cat.'

'You think this chap's got a cat, do you?' asked Hugo, not really paying attention any more.

'You're dothering, Hugo. It's just a figure of speech, as you jolly well know.'

Young Mr Williams did the honours at the front door, welcoming them all back to Reggie's old home, which seemed very odd, considering there was a 'relative' in attendance. Where had that fellow got to, wondered Lady Amanda? He ought, at least, to act the part, by welcoming the funeral guests. But he was nowhere to be seen, nor did he appear as they sipped glasses of warm, cheap punch, and nibbled on curling ham and cheese sandwiches.

It wasn't until Reggie's next-door neighbours left, that he reappeared, but he moved to the far side of the room, and seemed to take an inordinate interest in a bookcase full of dusty leather-bound volumes, that probably had not been taken out of the shelves in years – nay, decades.

'What's he up to?' asked Hugo, *sotto voce*.

'Avoiding speaking to anyone, if you ask me. He's pulling that old trick of trying to hide in plain view, like that purloined letter, or whatever it was, that Sherlock Holmes had to sort out.'

'He can't hide forever.'

'Probably waiting for us to go. What he doesn't know is that I arranged with young Mr Williams for us to stay on and hear the will being read. That should spike his guns good and proper! Watch this!'

And with this last imperative hissed at Hugo, she approached the rear view of the man who wasn't who he said he was. 'You're dear old Reggie's nephew, aren't you?' she asked, in the sort of piercing voice that simply cannot be ignored, and he had to turn towards his interrogator, no doubt flabbergasted at being addressed as such.

His first reaction was one of alarm, and he simply blurted out, 'Who told you that?' Lady Amanda was on dangerous ground here, but it had not occurred to her that her manner of address might make him suspicious of her motives for being here.

'Can't remember. I just remember hearing that you were,' she assured him. 'Had a great old time in the navy, didn't he, your uncle, during the war?'

'Really enjoyed himself,' came the answer, with great assurance, an utter and complete lie. He was handling himself well under fire.

'Well, nice to meet you,' she said, 'Although, I suppose our paths will never cross again after today,' she finished, turning away, and thinking, until we bring you to justice, that is.

Her hearing was still sharp, though, and, as she left his side, she heard him mutter, 'I damned well hope they don't!'

Young Mr Williams had overheard this exchange, and frowned in puzzlement. He'd have to try to remember to have a word with young Lady Amanda sometime. The poor girl seemed to have got her wires crossed somehow.

As the few remaining guests trickled away, young Mr Williams began to shuffle through the papers in his briefcase, and when there were only 'the suspect', Lady Amanda and Hugo left, he cleared his throat and begged for them to be seated. 'I have here the last will and testament made by Mr Reginald Chamberlain Pagnell, and I propose to read it to you now.'

'Why are those two still here?' asked the suspected murderer.

'Because we're old family friends!' boomed Lady Amanda, in her best Lady Bracknell voice. That quelled him, and the reading of the will proceeded.

After a number of small bequests, it was announced that the residual legatee was a Mr Richard Churchill Myers, of number six Wilmington Crescent, Belchester, another old friend, apparently.

Lady Amanda fixed her beadily accusing eye at the young man sitting with them, and enquired if this were he, to which he replied, smugly, in the negative, and stood, preparatory to leaving.

'Is that *really* not you?' she enquired again of the young man.

''Fraid not!' he admitted, and gave her a cheesy grin of triumph. How had he managed to outwit them? Lady Amanda was simply furious.

'Dammit!' she muttered, rather strongly for her, and nudged Hugo to get him moving. 'I've left Beauchamp outside with the Rolls. Told him to use my mobile to try to get a picture of the cove leaving. We'll just have to follow him now, if we want to find out where he lives.'

'But there was nothing left to him in the will. We've hit a dead end,' protested Hugo. 'If he wasn't left a bean, why would he want to kill old Reggie like that? It doesn't make sense, Manda.'

'It does!' she insisted. 'It's just a complicated puzzle, for which we don't have all the pieces yet. I *know* that young man did for Reggie, and I have the evidence locked securely in my safe to prove it. We'll just have to find out who he really is.'

'Perhaps he was Reggie's home nurse,' suggested Hugo, rather swamped with things medical at the moment and not enjoying it one jot.

''Brilliant!' quoth Lady Amanda, and rushed to catch young Mr Williams before he left. She managed to grab him by the sleeve of his jacket as he was heading out of the room, and asked, in as casual a fashion at she could muster at short notice, and with such excitement flooding her mind, 'Who is that young man who stayed on for the reading of the will? I don't think I've been introduced.'

'That was young Mr Foster – Derek Foster,' he answered, unsuspectingly.

'And how did he know Reggie?' she asked, her face a mask of innocence.

'I believe he used to provide nursing care for Mr Pagnell, before the departed had to be admitted to a home for full-time care. His mind was wandering so much he needed constant supervision, lest he wander away and get lost, I believe.'

'That's very interesting, Mr Williams. Thank you so much for your time and trouble. Do you happen to know where Mr Foster lives?' This would really be a coup for them, if she could get his address.

'I'm afraid I haven't the faintest idea, my dear young lady. He answered an advertisement I placed in the local paper, asking him to contact us. This, he did, and our only other contact has been by telephone.'

'Cow poo!' declared Lady Amanda, as they got back into the Rolls. 'I thought we had it all neatly stitched up there, and now we've lost him. Waiting to talk to that old twit has cost us time we couldn't afford. If I'd thought about it harder, it would probably have been better to follow him to find out his address, then we could have delivered him to Inspector Moody as a nicely wrapped-up parcel, specifically addressed to the Department of Public Prosecutions.'

'But he didn't get the money or the house,' protested Hugo anew.

'No, but he was Reggie's home nurse. There's more of a tangled plot here, than I thought. Did you manage to get a photograph, Beauchamp?'

'I shot off a couple, and one of them's not too bad. He moved in the other one, and he's just a blur.'

'Good-oh!' chortled Lady Amanda. 'A very successful surveillance job, Beauchamp!'

'Beecham,' muttered their chauffeur, but under his breath.

'So, what do we do next, Manda?' asked Hugo, all ears, now that the game was still afoot.

'We show the photograph on my phone to Nurse Plunkett, to see if she can positively identify him, and we proceed from there. It's time we visited Enid again, anyway. I promised we'd visit her every day, and I've not been too good at keeping my promise.'

Chapter Nine

The weather cleared up after luncheon, and a watery sun shone in a pale blue sky. This was grist to Lady Amanda's mill, and she insisted that Hugo have another go at learning to ride the motorised trike. His protest were squashed as easily as swatting a fly, and at two thirty he found himself being escorted outside, wearing an oldfashioned crash helmet, and a pair of gauntlets – 'Lest you fall off and scrape your hands,' Lady Amanda had reassured him.

Except that all this protective gear just made him even more apprehensive about the venture, but he knew there was no escape. Once Manda had you in her clutches, there was no way out. A man resigned to his fate, he allowed himself to be led over to 'that contraption of Satan himself', as he mentally referred to it; but never out loud, for fear that Manda should hear him, and brand him a coward.

'Get on it, then you can just try pedalling, without turning the motor on, just to get the feel of the steering; that sort of thing,' she commanded him. And he did push like the very devil on the pedals, but they moved so very slowly, that Lady Amanda eventually took hold of the back of the saddle, and started to push him, to get him going.

'Don't do that, Manda! It's too fast!'

'Stuff and nonsense! Here, let me push you a little faster – feet on pedals, old boy,' she puffed, heaving him along with all her strength, her hands now firmly on his back.

'Argh!' screamed Hugo, as his feet met the pedals, and found the turning movement irresistible, and were compelled to join in. 'Manda!' he wailed, 'You forgot to tell me where the brakes are.' And thus, hooting and yelling, he propelled himself, slowly but assuredly, into the trunk of a venerable oak tree.

Luckily, he had been travelling at a very low speed, and neither he nor the tricycle came to any harm. 'Now, Hugo,' ordered Lady Amanda bossily, 'here are the brakes, just under your hands on the handlebar.' She pointed at each brake handle. 'Have you never ridden a bicycle before? It's just the same as that.'

'A skill, I'm ashamed to say, I never mastered,' admitted the hapless jockey.

'You just squeeze them gently, and you'll come to a stop. When the motor's going, you just turn this little knob, then activate the brakes.'

'I don't think I want to try it with the motor today, Manda. It's frightening enough without it.'

'Humbug! But, as you wish. But we'll have another go with me pushing, just so that you can try out the brakes. Here we go!' and she fastened her hands firmly against his back, and began to propel the tricycle forward with everincreasing speed.

'Argh!' yelled Hugo again. 'It's much too fast, Manda. Slow down!' the latter being a hopeless request. Lady Amanda had no more intention of slowing down than she had of flying to the moon without the aid of a rocket.

'And away!' she cried, removing her hands and stopping, as she saw Hugo's unwilling feet relentlessly drawn to the pedals again. 'And steer round the tree, not into it, this time.' She called this last instruction after his figure, retreating down the drive at a sedate three miles an hour.

Hugo, however, did not find it sedate, and considered the idea of propelling himself, at all like this, a truly frightening experience, at his age. As a wooden bench hove into view, not far ahead of him on his current trajectory, he could hear Amanda calling to him to operate the brakes, and he clutched desperately at the two little levers below the handgrips of the handlebars.

The trike stopped, as suddenly as if it had run into a brick wall, and Hugo found himself unexpectedly flung across the handlebars, where Lady Amanda found him draped, when she caught up with him, shortly afterwards. 'What happened this time?' she asked, amazed that anyone could make such a muddle of riding a tricycle. Did he never have one as a child? she wondered.

'I pulled on the brakes, like you said, and the thing felt like the Titanic when it ran into the iceberg. It just stopped, only I didn't. Give me a hand, old thing, will you? I'm rather stuck, and need a bit of help.'

Lady Amanda obliged, and sat him gently on the bench he had nearly tried to reduce to matchwood. Having moved the tricycle to one side, she sat down beside him, and announced, 'We'll have another lesson tomorrow. I really think you're getting the hang of it now, Hugo. But before we finish for the day, let me give you one more demonstration.

'I want you to observe very closely exactly what I do, and how I do it,' she cajoled him, as she mounted the conveyance that had caused Hugo so much distress.

'Like this,' she called, looking over her shoulder at him, as she tricycled off. It was unfortunate that she was not paying sufficient attention to the direction in which she was headed. As Hugo observed as closely as he could, he suddenly observed that she had disappeared, as if swallowed by the ground itself.

'Manda, where are you?' he called, rising to his feet and beginning to totter towards the spot that she had simply ceased to occupy. 'What's happened to you? Are you all right?'

A series of strangled cries, still out of his sight, arose from a little way ahead, then Lady's Amanda's head seemed to appear from out of the ground. Hugo stopped his snail-like progress, shocked rigid by the appearance of her head, and called, 'Have you gone down a hole or something?'

'No, Hugo,' replied the erstwhile tricycling teacher, daintily spitting out the flower-head of a daisy. 'I just completely forgot about the ha-ha! Haha!'

After the application of a little iodine, and the partaking in of afternoon tea, they climbed into the Rolls to visit Enid Tweedie, to instigate her second debrief of the investigation.

They found her in a day room, socialising with other patients, and generally having a right good old time. As they entered the room, she noticed them and waved, announcing to the room at large, 'Look! Here are my friends Lady Amanda Golightly and Hugo Cholmondley-Crichton-Crump. Aren't I lucky to have such attentive friends, coming here to visit me?'

They ushered her out of the room as discreetly as possible, which meant, in Lady Amanda's case, ordering her to get on to her feet and get straight back to her quarters, so that they could have a little private chat together.

Back in her own room, Enid plonked herself into the only armchair, proprietorially, leaving her two visitors either to stand, or perch on the bed. Given their ages, they chose the latter option, and Lady Amanda began her interrogation.

'Have you found out anything more about that chap that murdered Reggie? Has Nurse Plunkett spilled any more beans?'

'She spilled a bedpan yesterday. In the corridor,' Enid informed them with glee. 'Matron gave her absolute hell for it, and she's threatened to ask for a transfer to another location. She said she could be treated like dirt at home by her family, and didn't see why she had to come here six days a week for an extra portion, considering what little she gets paid.'

'You're treating this like a visit to a holiday camp, my girl, and that won't do at all.'

'Oh, but I love it here. I'm having a very good time. I'm feeling so much better, and I'm having a really good rest. Thank you so much for arranging it for me, Lady Amanda.'

'Giving you a whale of a time wasn't the reason I booked this little visit, originally, was it, Enid? I want you here to gather information, so that we can bring a killer to justice. You're just not taking it seriously,' Lady Amanda chided her, and when you were chided by Lady Amanda, you knew about it, all right.

'But I am, my lady. Honestly! It's just that nobody else seems to have seen your chap. The time you came in visiting, when he'd not long left, is a very quiet time. It's when all the patients take an afternoon nap, so there was hardly anyone around.'

'Cunning swine! Did Nurse Plunkett know his name? We think we have it from our own investigations, but I'd like confirmation.'

'She thought he was known as 'Del', but that's all she could tell me.'

'Is she on duty this afternoon?' Lady Amanda wanted to know.

'I think so. I'll give a little buzz, and see if I can get her to come down here, so that you can ask her what you want to know yourself.'

Nurse Plunkett was available, but Matron was not happy about letting her 'socialise' with the patients. When, however, she found that this had been a special request from Lady Amanda Golightly, she capitulated. There was no way she'd win a fight with that formidable woman, and her title was the deciding factor.

'How nice to meet you, my dear,' cooed Lady Amanda, a dove of peace, for the moment. 'I wonder if there's anything more you can tell us about that chap you said they call Del?'

'I'm awfully sorry,' the little nurse replied, 'but I don't really know him. He just works for the same nursing agency that I do.'

'And which agency is that?' the cooing had become a positive purr of persuasion.

'Edwards's Nursing Agency. It's run by Malcolm Edwards,' she informed them, then Lady Amanda remembered her mobile phone, and took it out of her handbag, selected the good photograph taken by

Beauchamp after the funeral, and showed it to her, saying,

'Is this the man called Del?'

'That's him. I recognised him straight off, but I really don't know anything more about him,' she replied.

'Well, thank you very much for what you have told us. You may go now.'

Nurse Plunkett seemed nonplussed by this abrupt dismissal, which was something she had not been subject to since she was at infants' school, but left the room nonetheless, feeling that to disobey might bring down, if not quite the wrath of God, then at least the wrath of Lady Amanda, and she didn't think there'd be much to choose between them. She'd heard tales of this woman's first visit to the home, and if she'd intimidated Matron, and 'sprung' one of the patients, then she was a force to be reckoned with, and not to be crossed.

Chapter Ten

The next morning, Thursday, Hugo took breakfast in bed, leaving Lady Amanda free to carry out a little errand she had been meaning to do since Hugo had moved in. She set off into what promised for now to be a fine day, on her trusty trike, for the centre of Belchester.

Travelling through the city centre on her trike was a completely different experience to going through it in the Rolls. One saw so much more, and Belchester was really a very pretty little place, if one raised one's eyes above shop frontage level. Above the sea of plate glass windows with their gaudy displays of wares, one became aware of the history of the place, and the time it had taken to grow to this wonderful mixture of styles and ages.

The latest additions to the terraces of shops had been Victorian, as the city had luckily avoided any bomb damage during the war, and these facades were typical of their era, many of them gothic revival in style. Other buildings had graceful Georgian frontages, unfussy and clean-lined. Moving back through time, one eventually encountered Tudor buildings, with their exposed beams and mullioned windows with leaded lights, above groundfloor level.

Although Lady Amanda's family had caused Belchester Towers to be built nearly two centuries ago, true Belchester families still considered the Golightlys to be incomers – Johnny-come-latelys; mere upstarts – so deeply buried were the roots of these ancient families in this very old city, which still boasted substantial and respectable remains of its venerable Roman walls.

The cathedral itself had been built to serve a living community that already possessed a considerable history, and not just to venerate and pray for the souls of the dead.

Some of the history of this long-established city could be easily read, if one only aimed one's gaze upwards, and Lady Amanda never tired of examining this mixture of architectural styles. This was not her business today, though, and she headed her tricycle for the post office: the goal of her errand.

Her business done, she headed back to Belchester Towers, encountering Hugo just exiting his bedroom, as she appeared in the entrance hall. 'Morning, Hugo,' she called cheerily. 'A bit cream-crackered after yesterday, were we?' she enquired solicitously.

''Fraid so, Manda. I'm not getting any younger, you know.'

'None of us is, Hugo. I've been into town, and I've got something here for you, that I know you need,' she replied.

'Ooh, what is it?' asked Hugo, eager to see if she had bought him a little present.

'It's a post office form to have your mail redirected to this address,' she answered, disappointing him. 'We've been collecting your post from the nursing home every time we visit Enid, but she'll be out soon, and then it'll be a real drag, so I got this form for you to fill in. If you can get it done before this afternoon, Beauchamp can drop it in for you, and Bob's your uncle.'

Hugo heaved a great sigh of despair. 'Whatever's the matter with you?' Lady Amanda enquired, surprised at his reaction. She thought he'd be pleased to get his mail organised.

'I bet it's got "full name" on it somewhere, hasn't it?'

'Of course it has, Hugo. If they didn't know that, how would they know which mail was yours for redirection?' 'I thought so.' Hugo sounded really down in the dumps.

'Whatever is your problem,' she asked, puzzled.

'Hugo Cedric Ethelred Raleigh Tennyson St John Cholmondley-Crichton-Crumpmondley-Crichton-Crumpmondley-Crichton-Crump,' he replied, looking downcast.

'Oh crumbs! Great-grandmother's father?' she enquired, thinking how Enid Tweedie would lap up the information that Hugo had yet another name that wasn't pronounced as it was written.

Hugo knew, without asking, that she was referring to 'St John'. 'Yes,' he intoned dolefully. Back then, ladies hadn't thought of tacking their maiden name on to the end of their husband's surname, so I got lumbered with it, as a memento of times long ago. There's been a St John in the family since Great-grandmama's day, but I shan't be carrying on the tradition, thankfully,' he explained, with a rueful smile.

'See what you mean, Hugo. Well, if you like, I'll fill it in for you, and you'll just have to sign it. What d'ya say, *compadre*?'

'I say – thank you very much. That's most civil of you, Manda. You can imagine how I've dreaded filling in forms, all my life.'

'I can, but I had no idea you were quite so encumbered! You poor sausage!' she replied, taking his arm and leading him into the drawing room.

'I never knew you'd been living only about ten miles out of the city,' commented Lady Amanda, as they sat in the morning room sipping their morning coffee. 'The last I heard, you were living in Town.'

'I came back here when I retired, then I had to go into that horrible home, courtesy of the advice of old Dr Anstruther,' he explained.

'So what happened to the family home then? It was huge, as I remember, with quite sizeable grounds.'

'Papa had to sell it after the war. That's when we moved to where I ended up. I closed the house when they died, and returned to it, as I just mentioned, when I became eligible for my pension.'

'And you never looked me up?' asked Lady Amanda.

'I thought the Golightlys would be long gone. Thought the house would probably be offices, or some sort of ghastly institution by now, and I already had problems *getting around*, and checking that out was one of the things I,' here, Hugo paused for effect, 'never *got around* to! Haha! Mild joke there, you know.'

'Very witty, old bean. You seem a lot more cheerful than when you first moved in,' commented Lady Amanda.

'I'm getting used to having company now. I must say, it was a bit of a shock to the system at first, if you don't mind me mentioning it, Manda.'

'Not at all, Hugo; and I must admit that I felt exactly the same, but it's amazing how adaptable we humans are, and how quickly we get used to new circumstances, isn't it?

'By the way, apropos your current house, I've had a few calls from estate agents who have clients who would like to view your house.'

'So long as they keep them securely locked away when they're not in use, I have no objections whatsoever. I'm quite looking forward to an increase in income, and I doubt I'll return there – oh! Was that out of order, Manda?

Maybe you don't want me hanging round here long-term.'

'Of course it wasn't "out of order", as you phrase it, Hugo. I didn't expect you to go back to independent living. We seem to be jogging along all right together, and I'm sure we'll get into a way of living that allows us to have company when we want it, and a little solitude, when we feel in need of some.'

'You are a kind girl. Always were.'

'The estate agents were surprised to get the chance of letting a house the size of yours. I thought your parents were downsizing!'

'Well, you know how Mama and Papa liked to entertain, and they thought that, although they might have lost their grand house and all its fine grounds, at least they could afford to buy somewhere where they could still entertain – weekend parties; that sort of thing – and have their friends and family to stay.'

'How very sensible of them not to buy some ghastly little bungalow on the coast and moulder away there, for the rest of their lives.'

'They had a great time for their remaining years,' Hugo informed her. 'And it was so much cheaper to run and maintain a house of that size, that they found they could entertain frequently, and, for a couple of those years, they even spent the winter in the Caribbean.'

'And now you shan't moulder away either, in some seedy little nursing home. We're going to get your knees and hips sorted out, then we're going to have some fun!' predicted Lady Amanda.

'But aren't the coffers a bit depleted?'

'Well, I act as if they are, to all and sundry. I'm doing a very good job of publicly displaying the 'mean gene' I inherited from Mummy, for I don't want people making approaches for loans or donations to whatever scrape they've got into, or for their pet charities, but no, the coffers are in very good order, but I fully intend to see that they are severely depleted, by the time I pop my clogs.'

'How did your parents manage after the war? I mean, the county was in a terrible state, and so many of the people like us just went under.'

'If you promise to keep it under your hat, Hugo, I'll tell you. But there's not another living soul knows this. Except, probably, Beauchamp. He is all-knowing and allpowerful, in his way.'

'Cross my heart and hope to die,' said Hugo, in an excited voice, and miming the actions as he spoke.

Lady Amanda lowered her voice, and whispered at him, 'Daddy was big in the black market during the war; and, in fact until the end of rationing in the fifties. When that died out, he became an arms dealer – very hush-hush, don't yer know. But not a word of this to a living soul – not even Beauchamp, even though he knew all along what was going on. Thing is, it's just not talked about. Bad form and all that, as well as it being rather illegal, and liable to be frowned upon, even in these more liberal-minded times.'

'Good Lord! I had no idea!' Hugo was suitably shocked, right down to his pale-blue silk socks.

'Oh, don't look like that! I never had anything to do with it. I wasn't even born when all this underhand business was going on, and anyway, it all ceased when Daddy and Mummy died, but the coffers were overflowing by then, so I've just lived off what they made, ever since.'

'But how did you feel about living off money that was earned on the black market and by the sale of weapons?' Hugo asked, still suffering from the trauma of what he'd just learnt.

'I just considered that money was money. I could either own up, and hand it all over to the government, or I could spend the rest of my days in comfort, wanting for nothing, but acting much more impoverished than I am.'

'You always had the larder well-stocked, whenever we came over, and your parents never seemed to stint themselves with anything. Couldn't understand it at the time, but you never seemed to do without, like a lot of others we knew did.'

'Never had to. Daddy still got deliveries from Harrods and Fortnum & Mason's; he just arranged the delivery of their wares differently. He used to get them to deliver to a meeting place about thirty miles away, in a plain van. The deliveries were always after dark, and Daddy just drove off, collected the goods, and drove home in the Rolls. He'd just bought the car then, and was inordinately proud of it. He also left the cellars well stocked with fine wines, in the same way. Was that so wrong of us, Hugo?'

Hugo thought for several minutes, then looked up and exclaimed, 'You did exactly right! I know the black market was wrong, but, with a choice between deprivation, and an uninterrupted lifestyle, I know what I'd have chosen. Let's have some fun! I'm up for that! Is that why you didn't get requisitioned during the war?'

'Absolutely not! That was because Mummy ran a "knocking shop" for the American soldiers nearby, and that was considered to be her contribution to war work.'

Hugo actually blushed at being told this. 'Manda! How could she?'

'Oh, quite easily, as it turned out. She used the room next to yours as an office, and just approached it as she would any other business venture. Even had an extension for the telephone installed, so that she could take bookings, for the higher ranks.

'It was good money; it kept the servicemen from pestering local girls who wanted to be left alone, and it gave those who didn't the chance to earn a little extra money in very hard times. It was all, of course, kept as hush-hush as possible, the main drive never being used by either client or employees.

'There were several unofficial entrances to the grounds, and if anyone commented on the number of guests we seemed to have, we passed it off as enthusiastic entertaining. We explained the lack of vehicles by citing the shortage of petrol and coupons, and said our friends

were very imaginative in their means of transport.'

'So your father was a black marketeer and a gunrunner, and your mother was a brothel-keeper?' Hugo asked, hardly able to believe what he was being told.

'That about sums it up!' said Lady Amanda, in a very matter-of-fact voice.

'You make it all sound so reasonable, Manda.' Hugo spoke in a horrified voice.

'Well, it was! It was business at its most basic level, and everyone was a winner. You can't be squeamish, when you're faced with either bankruptcy, or a little dodgy business. It was dog-eat-dog back in those days, as you well remember. We all have choices to make in life, and our way to make in the world, and, I must say, I've certainly enjoyed the benefits of my parents' ill-gotten gains, as are you, now.

'May even sell the whole bang-shoot one day, and buy a luxury villa in the Caribbean. I'd take you and Beauchamp, of course, if you wanted to come, and I'd employ some staff, so that Beauchamp can have some sort of retirement, too. I don't think I would survive very well in a dingy little flat somewhere. I'm quite at ease with myself. Does this make any difference to the way you feel about me and this place, Hugo?'

Hugo sat wreathed in silence for another few minutes, and then looked up at her again. 'Not a jot, old girl!' and he smiled. 'One can't change the past. All one can do is make the best of the present, and hope that the future is a little further away than tomorrow, and that it treats us kindly. Oh, and by the way, I'd love to come with you; warm my old bones in some Caribbean sunshine, for the rest of their days, which I hope will be many.'

'That's that, then! And remember, not a word to a living soul!'

'Be like Dad. Keep Mum!' Hugo quoted, from a wartime poster. 'Loose lips sink ships!'

They planned to go to visit Enid Tweedie again after afternoon tea, and, as usual, retired after luncheon, for their usual post-prandial naps. Hugo was first up and about again, today, and as Lady Amanda descended the stairs from her bedroom, she heard Hugo in the drawing room, singing to himself:

'Whistle while you work,
'Hitler is a berk,
'He is barmy,
'So's his army,
'Whistle while you work.'

He had a pleasant baritone voice, but seemed deeply embarrassed when she walked in on him. 'Sorry about that,' he apologised. 'Just a bit of nostalgia, after our little talk about the war, earlier, but I'm really not sure about the third line. I'm sure I haven't got the words quite right.'

'You could hardly be expected to, after all this time. After all, the war is a long time ago, and you were only ta child yourself back then - and I wasn't even a twinkle in my father's eye,' Lady Amanda commented.

'Sometimes those days seem more clear, and nearer, than yesterday. The older I get, the more I forget silly things, like what I had for lunch, or whether I've done something or not, and even where I'm going, and what I was going to fetch, when I get there.

'Memories from my childhood and youth, however, are as bright and colourful as ever. As if I could just reach out my hand and touch them.'

'It comes to us all, Hugo. It's a symptom of getting old, but the alternative's unthinkable.'

'What's that, then?'

'Dying young! Best to just trot along as we are, and get the most out of every day. Live every day as if it were your last, Hugo, because, one day, you'll be right!' she advised him, with unchallengeable common sense and logic. '*Carpe Diem*, Hugo! *Carpe Diem*! I say! Do you fancy another lesson on the old trike, before we have tea?'

'I'm not seizing anything that hard!' Hugo stated, showing a little spirit, at last.

As Lady Amanda went into the hall to collect the light jacket she would wear that afternoon, for their visit to Enid Tweedie, she found Hugo at the foot of the stairs, tapping the barometer. Again!

'Hugo!' she expostulated, 'you're always tapping at that thing. What's the fascination?'

'I've missed having my own, what with being in that place, and everything.'

'But do you have to do it, what seems like every hour, on the hour?' she chided.

'Is it really that often? I had no idea. Short-term memory and all that.'

'If you carry on like that, you'll have to do what Enid did a couple of years ago.'

'What's that?' asked Hugo, turning round in interest.

'Go into hospital and have your 'aneroids' out. That's what!' she told him, and had to stifle a snort of laughter.

Enid was still in her element, being waited on, and generally feeling like a minor member of the royal family. She had also been busy in her role as undercover agent, and had managed to get a surname out of one of the permanent members of staff who was familiar with many of the agency nurses locally.

Using the ruse that the son of a friend used to work here on a temporary basis, she made enquiries about a young man called Derek, having surmised that this was the name from which Del was derived.

Lady Amanda had already confided in her that they already had the name of one Derek Foster, but hinted that she (Lady Amanda) needed to be doubly sure, before she did anything. To have nabbed the wrong man would be unthinkably embarrassing. And on Enid's first enquiry, she had hit the jackpot.

Derek Foster, as he *was* called, had been employed there as an agency worker for only a week or so, a couple of years ago, but one particular nurse felt it her duty to recall not only past members of staff, but the names of anyone visiting the home. Recalling Derek was no problem for her, although she had not actually seen him when he had visited Reggie Pagnell.

'Must have managed to slip in when she wasn't rota-ed for duty,' guessed Lady Amanda, sitting on Enid's bed and munching distractedly on her grapes. 'Don't know how he'd found out, but he must have been very careful about when he came here.'

'The staff has quite a high turnover here,' added Enid. 'The nurse I spoke to said that there was no one here who had worked for the place for longer than eighteen months or so, except her, so he'd have no worries about being accosted by Matron, for she wouldn't know him from Adam.'

'Except for the obvious one, that she's a right old dragon.' This was Lady Amanda again, now sucking noisily on a boiled sweet, purloined from a bowl on the bedside table. 'As long as he was sure your nurse with the photographic memory was out of the way, he had a clear field in which to commit his dastardly deed,' she concluded, in a slightly muffled voice, as the sweet had decided to try to escape from her mouth, and nearly ended up on the bedspread. They could be like that, at times, boiled sweets!

'Well, at least we have a confirmed name to work with now, Manda. That's something, isn't it?' Hugo said hopefully.

'It's not the same as having an address, though, is it?' she retorted. 'How the hell do we find him with just his name? He could live anywhere. There's nothing to say that he has to live in Belchester, is there? I knew we should have followed him after the reading of the will, and not stayed behind to try to pump that old bag of wind Williams.'

There was a silence that stretched out into the eternity of three minutes, then Lady Amanda spoke again. 'I suppose there's no harm in me actually visiting the offices of Edwards's Nursing Services, posing as a client with a relative in need of care, and enquiring after a Derek Foster, whom a friend has recommended to me, as excellent?'

'That's sounds like a good ruse, Manda. You might be able to get his address from there. Who is supposed to be the patient?' asked Hugo.

'Why, you, of course, you silly sausage! Who else around here is as doddery as you are?' she asked, and received a furious scowl and a childish pout in reply.

'Will you go in disguise, Lady Amanda?' asked Enid, memories of post-war spy films flooding her memory.

'Of course not, you dolt! That sort of thing only goes undiscovered in fiction. If I put on a wig and lashings of make-up, anyone would spot at once that I was up to something dodgy. This isn't some caper film! This is real life, Enid. This chap is dangerous, and I don't want to be his next victim.'

'Who says there's going to be a next victim?' asked Hugo, now looking decidedly nervous.

'There always is, isn't there!' declared Lady Amanda. 'The first murder is the hardest, then it just gets easier and easier to kill. It's like a compulsion. Who knows how many victims there will be if we don't stop him.'

'I wish you'd stop talking about it, Manda. You're making me very anxious. He's already seen us once, at Reggie's funeral, and then we turned up at the reading of the will. If he sees us again, he's going to work out that we're on to him, somehow. I don't want him setting his mind to wiping us out, because we've worked out what he's done.'

'Never fear, Hugo! We shall come out of this unscathed, and he will be headed behind bars.'

'Thank you very much, Enid Blyton,' remarked Enid, gleefully getting her own back for what Lady Amanda had said to her just a short while ago, and Hugo offered his two-penn'orth as well.

'Eat your heart out, Agatha Christie. Now, can we get back to Belchester Towers, where I feel rather safer than out and about visiting?' he asked, acidly.

Lady Amanda's retort was curt and to the point. 'Sure can, you yellow-bellied jackal!'

That had been the nearest the two of them had come to a disagreement, and the journey home was unusually silent, both of them too embarrassed to refer to the incident. Although it had been very short, it was the sharpest exchange between them but, on entering Belchester Towers, Lady Amanda's *joie de vivre* was instantly restored, when she checked the time, and found that it was not quite five o'clock.

'There's still time to make an appointment with that chap Edwards, before the office closes,' she declared, heading for the telephone directory, with hasty steps. 'I might even be lucky enough to get an appointment tomorrow.'

Wasting not a second, she looked up the number in the Yellow Pages, and immediately dialled, without giving herself too much time to think of a story. It would be better if it was spontaneous. If she invented and rehearsed something beforehand, it would end up too complicated and convoluted, and she would forget what she had already said, and trip herself up, contradicting things she had already stated. It was much better off the cuff, then Hugo could remember for her, as he'd be listening to her end of the conversation.

Hugo eavesdropped out of necessity, as the call was answered at the other end. 'Good afternoon,' began Lady Amanda. 'I have a relative living with me who suffers mobility problems, and could do with someone visiting, maybe twice a day ... Sorry, I can't discuss this on the telephone. He might overhear.'

He was overhearing perfectly well, thank you, and had been surprised to be referred to, firstly, as a relative, and secondly, as having mobility problems. He might be a bit slow getting around, but he was doing just fine, now he had Lady Amanda and Beauchamp to help him. He was just a bit slow: that was all.

'I wonder if I could make an appointment to come to your offices to discuss my requirements.' Lady Amanda asked, puzzled as to why Hugo seemed to be scowling at her. 'No, I don't need someone to come in as a matter of urgency; that's quite all right.' She paused, listening to the voice at the other end of the line.

'Tomorrow morning at ten-thirty? Yes, that would be very convenient. My name is Lady Amanda Golightly, and I look forward to meeting you on the morrow, to discuss my little problem,' she concluded, putting down the telephone receiver. 'Well, how was that?' she asked Hugo.

'Speaking as your "little problem" he replied, somewhat tartly,

'I don't think you should have given him your real name.'

'Horse poo, Hugo! What harm can that possibly do?'

'When you've made your enquiries about this chap Foster, it might get back to him that someone has been asking about him, and you've just given him your real name on a plate. Round here, it won't take much effort to find out that you live at Belchester Towers, with only an elderly manservant and your 'little problem' for company. Then, where will we be?'

'Don't be so melodramatic! I'm sure he's not going to come tearing round here with a gun or a machete, or even a lethal cocktail. We'll just tell the police all we've found out, hand over the "evidence" – the cocktail glass – and they'll lock him up.'

'Sez who?' asked Hugo, sarcastically. 'That inspector took no notice of you whatsoever before. Who says he's not going to do the same thing, next time you go to speak to him?'

'He won't be able to deny the evidence, when I go to see him again. He'll be compelled to take action,' she replied, somewhat huffily, as the memory of how she had been dismissed out of hand by Inspector Moody, on her previous visit, stirred in the back of her mind.

'Come along! The weather's fine and it's quite a while till cocktails. Let's go and get you on that trike again. It's about time you had another lesson,' she suggested, getting her revenge on Hugo, for his lack of faith in her powers of both detection, and persuasion.

Hugo fared a little better this time, managing both the art of pedalling, and that of using the brakes. He was tired after half an hour, but in that time, he had demonstrated that he was perfectly capable of controlling the tricycle, at very low speeds.

The next, obvious, stage, was to get him controlling the steering and brakes, with the motor running, as Lady Amanda suggested, as they walked slowly back indoors for their nightly cocktail.

'Dear Lord, Manda, give me a break! I've only just got the hang of riding the thing under my own steam. Let me get used to that, before you put a rocket in my saddlebag.'

'It's invigorating, to learn something new,' she retorted, contrarily.

'That's as may be, but not quite so invigorating, if one dies in the attempt. Let me take it at my own pace. I will manage it, but slowly-slowly. I'm not going to let you bully me on this one. You've already had me scare myself half to death on that thing, and it's just going to have to be left up to me, when I'm ready.'

'Fair enough, Hugo,' she agreed, rather meekly for her, but she was just pleased to have, sort of, got her own back on him with the trike lesson, for doubting her detection abilities. She knew she had acted pettily, and was feeling just a teensy bit ashamed of herself.

'Cocktail time, Hugo! Then din-dins! My favourite part of the day,' she said, encouragingly, and led the way into the drawing room for their daily libation.

Chapter Eleven

'Of course you can't come with me, Hugo. Don't be silly! There's no point in me explaining all about my ailing relative with mobility problems, if you're sitting beside me in his office, looking as right as ninepence, is there?'

'I don't know why he has to know I'm the supposed sick relative,' Hugo countered, sulkily.

'Because we might have to carry this charade to the point where someone visits you here, to assess your daily nursing requirements, that's why,' she explained, as if to a child.

'Oh, I see,' he replied, then added. 'I don't think I'd like someone poking and prying around my habits and abilities, let alone my body, to assess me for anything.'

'It probably won't come to that, but we must be prepared to go to any lengths necessary, to catch this chap,' she assured him. 'Just leave this one to me, and I'll do my level best to find out where he lives, from this Edwards person, this morning. If I can wheedle and smarm, and use a bit of charm, I might just come home with the goods, and we can go to visit Inspector Snooty, and give him one in the eye.'

'Might I not come in the car?' asked Hugo wistfully. 'If anything goes amiss, it might be good to have your coconspirator around, for safety's sake?'

'I shall have Beauchamp with me, waiting in the car,' she explained airily. 'You'd better stay here out of the way, in case we need you to be the patient. If you're at all bored, you can write a narrative of our adventure so far – be a Watson to my Holmes. Dr Watson always wrote the stories, didn't he?'

'Holmes and Watson weren't real people, Manda! You really must stop living in the land of fiction,' he replied, getting another one in, on behalf of poor old Enid, yesterday, with her Hollywood-inspired spy fantasies.

'Anyway, I fancied us more as Tommy and Tuppence Beresford.'

'That couple of wet fish? Oh, Hugo, *do* set your sights higher. They were the most ghastly couple of drips who ever disgraced crime fiction!' Lady Amanda made it abundantly clear that she was not a fan.

As the front door slammed, however, Hugo reconsidered the idea of writing a Watson-esque journal, and saw that it was good. If anything happened to them, at least there would be written evidence of what they had become involved in. He also rather fancied the idea of being Watson, faithfully recording the adventures he became caught up in with his friend, Holmes.

Taking himself off to the library, he hunted out paper and writing implements, and sat down at the desk, to await inspiration for his title. After a couple of minutes chewing the end of his pen, he gave a small cry of, "Aha!' and wrote *The Adventure of the Terminal Cocktail*, and underlined it. It might not be the best of titles, but it would do for now.

Taking up his fountain pen again, he began to write: *I find it recorded in my notebook that it was a sunny but not particularly warm day, when this matter raised its ugly head.*

At its launch I was, myself, incarcerated in a nursing home, being cared for after my old war wound had flared up again. Each day being like any other, I whiled away my time solving crossword puzzles, and wandering up and down the veranda with the aid of my trusty walking cane, smoking my faithful old pipe.

On the day in question, I had just finished reading the morning paper, when a familiar old voice called out my name, and who should enter my room, but my faithful friend from childhood, Lady Amanda Golightly.

At this juncture, I had better introduce myself to the reader of my modest efforts at writing, and state that I am Hugo Cholmondley-Crichton-Crump, and have been acquainted with the Golightly family, almost since my birth. A long gap in this friendship had occurred, due to circumstances beyond the control of either party, and quite unexpectedly, I found myself re-united with the family's youngest member, Lady Amanda, still delightful, despite the passage of time.

I greeted her warmly, and rose from my prone position to shake her by the hand. Our previous relations had been warm, but formal.

Before I could utter a word of welcome, however, she raised a finger to her Cupid's bow lips, and bade me be silent, before informing me that, in a room, down the corridor, a ghastly crime had been committed. A man had been cruelly murdered.

At this point, he put down his pen, searched without success for blotting paper, and blew softly across his writing to dry the ink, before he concealed it somewhere where Lady Amanda would never find it. He'd always fancied himself a writer, but had never had the time to put pen to paper. Maybe he'd give it a try, now that he was retired, and had sufficient leisure time to do as he pleased, but he wouldn't say anything to Manda. She'd rag him terribly, and he'd die of embarrassment.

Meanwhile, Lady Amanda had a thoughtful journey to Edwards's Nursing Services, going over her cover story, so that she would be word-perfect when she got there. She had decided that, if asked what relation to her Hugo was, she'd claim him to be an older cousin, fallen upon hard times, and unable to live independently any more. She only hoped that nerves would not get the better of her and make her mind go blank – a not very

'Lady Amanda-ish' thing to happen, but then this was a first, for her.

The offices of Edwards's Nursing Services were in Snuff Street, very handy for the Birdlings Serenade prison camp, Dr Andrew's surgery and the hospital. The building that housed them was a Georgian one, its front still in original state, only a discreet brass plaque by the door identifying this as a commercial property, and not a private dwelling house.

Mounting the three steps that led up to the front door, she stepped inside to find herself confronted with a reception area with huge desk, at which sat a very efficient-looking and forbidding secretary-cum-receptionist.

'May I help you, madam?' this individual enquired, giving Lady Amanda a sharp look under her severely plucked brows.

'I have an appointment to see Mr Edwards,' Lady Amanda replied, with a confidence she no longer felt. 'It's about my cousin.' She knew she was rattled, because this was unnecessary information, and proved that she was heading towards a tendency to babble. It was an outright lie, Hugo being a relative, she decided. Just as she abhorred bad manners, thus did she feel about telling lies, too.

'Name, please?' enquired the efficient female, still giving her the once-over.

'Lady Amanda Golightly,' came the reply, and suddenly the other woman thawed, and positively purred a welcome.

So, her name still carried some weight around here. Her title was doing its job again, as it had on numerous other occasions. Lady Amanda's nerves fled whence they had come, and she began to feel her normal confident self again.

'I'll just buzz through to Mr Edwards and let him know you've arrived,' the receptionist informed her, pressing a button on an intercom service, and announcing to Mr Edwards the arrival of his client.

A voice squawked, 'Send her in, please,' its normal tones distorted by the intercom to an electronic, machinelike voice.

Malcolm Edwards's office proved to be large and luxuriously appointed. There must be a good whack to be made out of providing nursing care, Lady Amanda thought, as she lowered herself into a large comfortable armchair, across the desk from the proprietor.

'Good morning, your ladyship. How may I be of service to you?' asked Mr Edwards, and Lady Amanda immediately identified a slimy tone in his voice, indicating that he was well-versed in creeping and crawling around prospective clients, to hook them into his bank balance.

'Good morning, Mr Edwards,' she replied, then waited for him to make the next move.

'Do call me Malcolm,' he requested, and then continued, 'I believe you have a poorly relative who may be in need of the services which my humble agency is more than happy to provide,' he stated.

Yes, he was definitely an experienced crawler and shoe-licker. No need to get any coarser about the matter! 'It's my cousin,' she stated. 'He's got to an age where he's not very mobile and, although I have taken him under my wing and into my own home, I find that I am rather averse to carrying out some of the tasks with which he needs help.'

'Which are?' Golly, he was going straight for the jugular. She'd have to keep her wits about her, if she didn't want to end up employing a nurse, and not getting the opportunity to ask about Derek Foster.

'Before we go into the details, I want to state categorically that my cousin, the help needed being of the intimate sort, will only consider the services of a male nurse.'

'That's perfectly understandable, my lady.' He was in a bit of a bate himself, considering the way he attempted various ways of addressing her, evidently hoping to be directed to the correct form.

'A friend of mine has recommended a young man in your employ, whom they described as efficient, courteous and well-mannered, and I wondered if I might be able to avail myself of his services.' This was it! Make or break! She'd only get one shot at it here.

'And who might that be?' asked Mr Edwards, leaning confidentially over the desk towards her.

'I believe his name is Derek Foster,' she declared, her cards now on the table.

Mr Edwards leaned back in his chair, and adopted a rueful expression. 'I'm so sorry, Lady Golightly, but Mr Foster has just left our employ, and I am, therefore, no longer able to offer his services to you.'

Oh, goat berries! Piggy poo! thought Lady Amanda, who had just had her guns well and truly spiked. What now? she wondered. She'd have to try thinking outside the box. 'I really feel very strongly, after such a glowing recommendation from my friend, that I'd like to contact Mr Foster at home, to see if he is willing to consider coming to care for my cousin. Or perhaps he's gone to another agency?' Let's see how he liked them potatoes.

He didn't! 'I have been led to believe that Mr Foster has come into a large sum of money, and has taken advantage of this, by retiring from work altogether, and I'm afraid I cannot give out the private address of any employee, whether present or past. I do apologise for not being able to help you, but my hands are tied by the Data Protection Act. However, given the large number of nurses on my register, I'm sure we can satisfy your needs, or those of your cousin, with another male nurse. Just tell me what sort of care he is likely to need, and I'm sure I can recommend another of our staff.'

Cow poo! He had her there, and he knew it. She could tell by his face that he'd seen through her ruse, and was waiting, a slightly amused expression on his face, to see what she would do next.

'In the event of Mr Foster not being available, I feel I shall have to discuss the situation with my cousin, in light of this new information. I shall not, therefore, be able to make any decision on his behalf today. I shall go home and discuss the matter with him, and make a further appointment to speak to you, when he has made up his mind.'

She left the building with a sigh of exasperation. What a waste of time that had turned out to be. Not only would he not tell her where the rascal lived, but it would seem that he didn't work for anyone now. How had he come into money, though? she wondered. He had been left nothing in Reggie's will.

Surely he wasn't going around bumping off old people willy-nilly, after having persuaded them to change their wills in his favour. If this was so, then it hadn't happened with Reggie. Maybe Reggie had had lucid moments when he realised Foster was trying to trick him into leaving him all his money, and Foster had had to get rid of him, before he blew the gaff on his little scam – or huge scam, for all she knew. What next? she considered. She'd have to have a little think in the Rolls, on the way home.

When she returned to Belchester Towers, Hugo was still busy scribbling away in the library, enjoying himself tremendously. 'What are you up to, old bean?' she asked him, throwing her considerable bulk into a sturdy (thank goodness!) sofa.

'Writing up our adventure so far,' replied Hugo, looking up from his labours.

'I was only joking when I suggested that, you know,' she explained.

'Maybe you were, but it's jolly good fun. Ought to make a cracking yarn, once it's finished, provided, that is, that it ever does get finished, and it has a happy ending. I've really enjoyed myself while you've been gone. What about you? Any joy?'

'None whatsoever,' she told him. 'It would appear that our Mr Foster has had a large inheritance, and is no longer in paid employment. That Edwards chappie sussed out that I was fishing, and he played me like an expert. Zilch! Nowt! Nada! Although I did think on the way home, that we might just check Directory Enquiries. He must have a telephone and we've got his name. There is just a chance that they'll be able to find his telephone number for us if he lives in this area.'

'Good idea, old stick! Shall we do it now?' Hugo was getting just a little bit excited, at the thought of actually finding out where their prey's den was, so that they could beard him in it.

Lady Amanda dialled the required digits, gave the voice on the other end of the phone Derek Foster's name, then said that she didn't know his address, but it was definitely in the same telephone area as was her number.

After a short pause, there was a distant squawk from the other end of the line, and Lady Amanda's face fell so fast, it almost made a whooshing noise as it hurtled downwards. 'Thank you so much,' she intoned, in a disgusted voice, and ended the call.

'Any luck?' asked Hugo, already knowing the answer, before she told him.

'Lucked out again! He's ex-directory,' she said, with a sigh.

'Well, then we did learn something,' Hugo pointed out.

'What?' she asked. 'How? We know nothing more than we did before.'

'Yes we do, Manda. If she was looking for him, and discovered he was ex-directory, then that means he definitely lives in this area, you silly sausage.'

'So it does, Hugo! So it does! How blind I am. Why didn't I see that? But then, where does that leave us? We know he lives in this area, we know he's on the telephone, but we don't know whereabouts in this area that telephone is, and without an address, we're still stuffed, whichever way you look at it.' During this speech, her voice had gone from triumphant back to crestfallen again.

'We could always have another shot at young Mr Williams,' suggested Hugo mildly, but without hope in his voice.

'You're right again!' Lady Amanda was back in best crowing form. 'He's a very old man, and quite liable to let something slip, if he's approached in the right way. I'll ring up this afternoon, and make an appointment to see him. I can use the same excuse of wanting to try to persuade him out of early retirement for just one last case.'

'And then we could be back in business again, eh, Sherlock?' Hugo was also back on top form, at the thought that they might be able to move their investigations on again. 'Go, Manda, go! We'll nail the blackguard yet!'

After luncheon, Lady Amanda duly put a call through to Freeman, Hardy, Williams and Williams, Hugo sitting with bated breath, waiting to see if young Mr Williams would be forthcoming with the information they needed. Something, however, was not as expected, as Lady Amanda suddenly crashed down the phone and turned to look at him with an expression of absolute astonishment and horror,

'What is it, Manda? Have they been terribly rude to you?' he asked with concern.

'It's young Mr Williams!' she declared, then grabbed her handbag and made for the main hall.

'What about young Mr Williams?' called Hugo, shuffling after her, keen to be part of the action, whatever that action was.

Lady Amanda suddenly stopped, and informed him, 'He's *dead*, Hugo, and I'm going down to their offices this very minute to find out what happened. I smell a rat here, and I won't rest till I've found out where it nests!'

'Can I come?' pleaded Hugo, like a small child wanting to accompany a parent shopping.

'If you can get yourself ready and into the Rolls in two minutes flat, you're more than welcome. If my persuasive powers for information gathering prove insufficient, yours might be just the job.'

The receptionist at the legal firm's offices was crying when they arrived, but as discreetly as possible, keeping her handkerchief balled into one of her fists, when not mopping hurriedly at her eyes. The blinds on the windows facing the street were all at half-mast, as if in respect for the departed, a fitting gesture for such a long-established firm.

Hugo at once proved his worth, by approaching the receptionist, leaning down as far as he was able, mobility permitting, and put a kindly, avuncular arm around her shoulder. 'There, there, my dear,' he crooned in quiet, soothing tones. 'What ever happened to the poor gentleman?'

Having bottled up the information all morning, the secretary grabbed the opportunity to spill the beans, as a drowning man does a straw, and the dam burst open. 'They said he must have gone down to the orchard at the bottom of his garden yesterday – afternoon or evening; they're not sure which yet. He liked to sit up there in the peace and quiet, just listening to the birds, and having a drink.

'We know he sometimes took down a small jug of Pimm's and lemonade, so that he didn't have to go back to the house to refresh his glass. He really loved it down there: said it made him forget about being old, and just put him in tune with nature. It made him happy, completely cut off from work, and not so much concerned about his own aches and pains.

'Anyway, his cleaner came in this morning, as usual, and found his bed not slept in. The first thing she did was to search the house, to see if he'd had a fall, and couldn't get up again, but there was absolutely no sign of him, so she phoned here, to see if he'd come into work, maybe having spent the night with a colleague, but, of course, he hadn't.

'Mr Freeman suggested she go out to check the garden, thinking maybe he'd collapsed or fallen out there, and might be stranded with a broken ankle or something similar, so she hung up and went to have a thorough search. She called back again after about twenty minutes, to tell us that she had found him in his usual chair in the orchard, a jug beside his chair, a glass fallen from his fingers, and that he was stone dead!'

'My dear girl,' comforted Hugo. 'What a terrible shock for you. No wonder you're upset.' As he spoke, he was aware of Lady Amanda making hideous faces at him from behind the receptionist's desk, mouthing a word. And the word was simply: 'how'?

'Has anyone any idea why he passed away so suddenly? Or had he been ill for some time, and maybe it wasn't so unexpected?' he asked, worming his way effortlessly into her confidence.

'Young Mr Williams was never ill,' she informed them. 'He was as fit as a flea, and we quite confidently expected him to live long enough to receive a letter from Her Majesty. That was why it was so shocking.' Her valiant effort to unburden herself of this information suddenly faltered, and she raised her handkerchief to her eyes again, as a flood of fresh tears overwhelmed her.

'And there's going to be an inquest and everything, because he hadn't seen a doctor for so long. Oh, the shame, and they won't even let the poor old man rest in peace. They're going to cut him about, and do all sorts of undignified things to him which he would have hated, were he alive. It seems so obscene, to subject him to that, even after death.'

'There, there, don't fret. Young Mr Williams is at peace now, and nobody can insult his dignity. He's beyond earthly interference, and with his God.' Hugo did feel a bit two-faced about this, as he had ceased to believe in the Superior Being many years ago, but it seemed to have had a soothing effect on the woman.

'You're right, of course!' she said, blowing her noise loudly, in a most unladylike and indiscreet way. 'I know what you say is true. It's just the shock, you know? It's left me feeling thoroughly rattled, and now I'm neglecting my duties to the firm. What can I help you with? You must have come in here for a reason.'

It was Lady Amanda's turn, now, to be inventive. Smiling as sweetly as she could manage, she plonked herself in front of the desk, and said, 'It's nothing that can't wait, my dear girl. We'll take ourselves off, in the light of the loss you have all suffered, and come back another time, when circumstances aren't quite so trying. Don't give it another thought.'

Once more outside and out of hearing, she took Hugo's arm, and declared, 'Well, I'll be! What a couple of AmDram sleuths we're turning out to be, eh? Perfect team, and all that! You did a marvellous job of getting her to spill the beans. I'd just have sailed in there and demanded to know what was going on, and got the old bum's rush, but you charmed it out of her, and at the same time, made her feel better.'

'You had your part to play, too,' Hugo replied. 'If it hadn't been for your get-up-and-go, we'd never have gone there in the first place. You didn't waste a minute, after you were told on the phone that there had been a death. You just got on with tracking the matter down to its hub.'

'Thank you, so much, Hugo. Ah, there's Beauchamp, with the Rolls. He has been lucky with the parking today.'

'It hasn't got us any further, though, with finding out where Foster lives, has it?' Hugo asked, suddenly downcast again, as he remembered the real reason they had contacted the legal firm. 'And with the old man gone, it looks like a dead-end for us, don't you think?'

'Not necessarily,' replied Lady Amanda, then made a noise that sounded very like 'ping'.

'Whatever's up with you, Manda? Do you need basting, or something?' This was Hugo's attempt to alleviate the mood of gloom that had settled over him.

'What a pair of dolts we've been!' she suddenly exclaimed, her face breaking out into a broad grin. 'Register of Electors,' she declared. 'We must go to the library at once! That's where we'll learn what we need to know.'

'Can't we leave that till tomorrow?' begged Hugo, whose limited store of energy had just registered empty.

'All right! But, first thing, mind you. Sparrow fart! Stupid o'clock! We want to be there as the library opens, and not nearly lunchtime. Agreed?'

'Agreed!' concurred Hugo, with a sigh of relief.

Chapter Twelve

At breakfast the next morning, Lady Amanda stated, 'I bet there was something in that jug of Pimm's, or in his glass.'

'You think it's the same chappie, killing again?' enquired Hugo.

'I do,' she assured him. 'I'll bet they discover enough poison in his system to have killed a herd of elephants. Our young Mr Williams may have spotted something odd, put two and two together, and unknowingly signed his own death warrant.'

'How?' asked Hugo briefly, his mouth still half-full of scrambled egg.

'He knew, as we do, that that young chap was somehow mixed up in Reggie's affairs. We also know that this Del was left hardly anything in the will, but still attended both the funeral, and the wake, with the reading of the will. I wonder how he explained his presence to young Mr Williams. Why should someone, who hadn't nursed the deceased for some time, be interested in attending his funeral, especially as there was nothing in it for him?'

She paused for a few seconds. 'What if he got wind that Foster had been posing as Reggie's nephew, at the home? I mean, it's quite likely, isn't it, if young Mr Williams went to take possession of Reggie's bits and pieces, him having no living relatives, that someone might have said something to him about how nice it was, that Reggie's nephew got in touch with him again, just a few months before he died?

'In fact, I remember hailing him as Reggie's nephew, at Reggie's house. I wonder if young Mr Williams overheard, and became suspicious about Foster? Lord! Then, it could've been me who got him killed. What a ghastly thought! But I do think this was done by the same hand. The modus operandi is the same.'

'You've got a point there, Manda.'

'And if Mr Williams mentioned something, or questioned Foster about it, he would definitely have put himself in danger, wouldn't he?'

'By George! I think she's got it!' exclaimed Hugo, unconsciously echoing words from *Pygmalion*. 'We've got to bring this bounder to justice!'

'Quite right! He's killed twice now, and he won't hesitate to kill again.'

'I rather think you ought to go and speak to that policeman again, Manda. This is getting very dangerous.' Hugo's concern for her safety shone out through his eyes, and behind that was discernible a deep concern for his own safety, as well.

'Tommyrot!' she exploded, showering the table with toast crumbs. 'What, go to that man and be humiliated again? Be treated as a batty old lady who has delusions? I won't, I say! We'll wrap this up ourselves, and then hand it to him on a plate, and watch his embarrassment, as he realises that I was right all along; that's what we'll do.'

'Well, we'd better go carefully. I'm quite happy with my cashmere overcoat, and don't want to be measured for a wooden one, anytime soon. We'll need to tread very carefully. I know the word 'carefully' is probably not in your vocabulary, Manda, so I suggest you go and look it up in a dictionary, after breakfast.'

'Cow poo, Hugo! Doggy doodles! He who dares, wins!' she retorted emphatically.

'As long as it's not "he who dares, dies"!' was Hugo's somewhat waspish reply.

Finding an address at the library for Derek Foster took quite some time, but nowhere as near as long as it could have taken, had they not had a stroke of luck. Lady Amanda had decided that, if they looked at the Belchester map, they could look at the relative positions of the nursing home, Edwards's Nursing Services, and the address of the residual legatee of Reggie's will. As she pointed out to Hugo, he wouldn't want to be too far away from either place, if all this was pre-meditated.

Unfortunately, although Lady Amanda had made a note of the name and address of the main beneficiary of the will, she had carelessly written it down on an old envelope she had found lurking in her handbag, and she had cleared out said handbag, only the night before, as it was getting rather full with things like apple-corers, screwdrivers, tape measures, corkscrews and the like. The envelope would now be residing in the waste paper basket in the drawing room.

'Thank goodness Beauchamp won't empty it, this being his nominal day off, when he does nothing that isn't absolutely necessary,' she said. 'Let's note down the street names that are possible, taking into account the other locations, and see if we're fortunate enough to come up with anything.'

They sat themselves at one of the library tables, and began their search; the next two hours being filled with such comments as: 'I didn't know he was still around' 'I thought he'd moved away' and 'I could have sworn she was dead'. It may have been tedious, but, in some ways, it was a little like a walk down memory lane.

'I say, guess who's moved into that big house near the cathedral', 'I never thought his son would leave home'. They carried on in this manner until the librarian himself came over, and asked them, please, to observe the rule of silence, and they hunted on with only the odd squeak of recognition, as they came across familiar names from times gone by.

It was half-past lunchtime, when Hugo made a *sotto voce* exclamation of triumph. 'Got the wretch!' he whispered across the table to Lady Amanda. 'I'll just make a note of the address, then we can get out of here, and go and get something to eat. I'm starving!'

An extremely loud and long drawn out 'Shhhhhh!' carried across from the desk to their table, the sibilance alerting other users of the reference area, that someone was in trouble, so, putting away their notepads and pens, they gathered themselves together and made as dignified an exit as they could manage, under the stern and disapproving eye of the librarian, who was thoroughly fed up with them.

They were worse than the children that came in, in his opinion, and he was glad to see them leave, at last. His haven of tranquillity had been invaded, for over three hours now, by those two inconsiderate bodies, and he hoped they didn't intend returning in the near future.

Once outside, Lady Amanda did her level best to jump up and down with glee, but with only a modicum of success, given her age and weight, and Hugo, who understood how victorious she felt, simply nodded his head vigorously, in agreement with the sentiment.

Before she could speak, however, he pre-interrupted her. 'No, Manda! Not today! We have to plan this carefully. Our lives could be at stake.'

'Well, at least we can discuss it when we get home,' she replied, her bottom lip stuck out in disappointment.

'We can discuss it as much as you like, but we mustn't rush into anything perilous. As there's probably not a lot of it left for me, I find myself very fond of life. I'd hate to do anything that would hasten its end, and I'm sure you feel the same way.'

'Spoil sport!' she retorted, sticking out her tongue at him in frustration and defiance.

'We'll tackle this with the greatest of caution, or not at all!' declared Hugo, standing his ground, and feeling the very first traces of the development of a backbone. 'Now, let's find the Rolls and get back for lunch. My stomach thinks my throat's cut!'

Given that all three of them had arrived home well past the usual hour for luncheon, and that it was, technically, Beauchamp's day off (he had already driven them to the library and back) the manservant did a pretty slick job of serving them a simple lunch, with the minimum of fuss or delay.

'Now you see why, if I do decide to sell the lot, and beetle off to the Caribbean, I'd take Beauchamp with me. Apart from the fact that he's worked here all his working life, I'm so used to him now, that I feel I really couldn't manage without him.' Lady Amanda was purposefully avoiding the subject of what their next actions should be, with regard to hunting down this double murderer.

However, it wasn't so easy to pull the wool over Hugo's eyes as she thought, and he pierced her with a steely gaze, and said, in as commanding a voice as he could summon, 'I know what you're up to, and it won't work!'

'I'm not up to anything, Hugo. Whatever do you mean?' she asked, innocently, but not fooling her old friend for a minute.

'I know you, of old,' he stated. 'And I'm going to keep an eagle eye on you, for the rest of the day. If I catch you sneaking off anywhere on your own, you'll have me to answer to. You're not young and fit any more, you're old and vulnerable, and you'd better wise up to that fact, now. I don't want you taking any unnecessary risks. After all, if anything happened to you, where should I live?'

This last, apparently selfish question, he had asked with the idea of goading her out of her habitual recklessness, and bringing her back down to earth, by making her think of someone else's welfare, for a change, and not just the opportunity (and risk) of covering herself with glory. It was all very well, her wanting to show up that inspector, but not at the expense of her own life. That would be a hollow victory, indeed.

She sighed. 'You're a fussy old woman, Hugo, but you do have a point. I promise to do nothing without consulting you first. OK?'

'Show me your hands, Manda,' he ordered, scrutinising them minutely, when she held them out for his inspection. As she looked at him quizzically, he added, 'Just checking, to see that your fingers weren't crossed!'

At that point, Hugo toddled slowly off to 'wash his hands'. Giving him sufficient time to reach his destination, Lady Amanda uncrossed her toes (sneaky old baggage that she was) and made her way to the wastepaper basket, where she retrieved the discarded envelope with the name written on it, scanned it briefly, and slipped it back into her handbag, where she could access it easily.

After their meal, Lady Amanda settled innocently in the drawing room with the local paper, which was never delivered to Belchester Towers until the day after it was published. As was her habit, after scanning the front page, she turned straight to the announcements to see who had been hatched, matched, or despatched. Her eyes devoured the columns eagerly, until she came to one entry, which made her shout out in surprise.

'Whatever is it, old girl?' asked Hugo, who was wandering through his copy of the *Daily Telegraph* without much interest. 'Been bitten by something?'

'It's in the *Deaths* column!' she nearly shouted. 'We've got the rotter!'

'What's in the *Deaths* column?' asked Hugo, wondering whose passing could have elicited such excitement from her.

'*Richard Churchill Myers of six Wilmington Crescent, Belchester, died peacefully in his sleep* – let me see, ah! – *Thursday night, at home, after a long illness. Will be missed by his loving nephew, Derek Foster.* That was the day after the will reading! The evil little beast!'

'Whatever are you on about, Manda? At least he was someone's nephew.' Hugo still hadn't quite caught up with events.

'Myers!' she declared. That was the name of the chap who inherited the bulk of Reggie's estate. It says in here that he's just died, and his nephew's only *our* chappie, who seems to like eliminating anyone who gets in his way, concerning his acquisition of money.'

'And you think he murdered his real uncle, too?'

'Of course he did! It's as plain as the nose on your face. First he bumps off Reggie, so that his estate goes to this Myers chap, Foster's uncle, then he does away with this uncle, who's probably not got any other relatives, if his nephew posted the death notice. And, in between, poor young Mr Williams gets wiped out. He probably only got a whiff of what was going on, and tackled him, in all innocence, about it.'

'Well, I never,' exclaimed Hugo. 'We've got him! Can't we just hand him over to the police now?'

'Over my dead body!' said Lady Amanda.

'That's rather what I'm worried about,' parried Hugo. 'Just report him, and leave it at that.'

'But there's not enough evidence. I can see exactly what happened, now. I reckon he was nursing old Reggie at home, until he went a bit gaga. I surmise that Reggie and that Myers chap must once have been good friends, and we know Reggie had no relatives to leave anything to, so he must have made his will in this old friend's favour.'

'This is all surmise, you know. You may be completely wrong,' Hugo said, hoping to temper her enthusiasm with a little common sense.

'Rot, Hugo! You know I'm right!' She rolled right over him like a verbal steamroller, and continued, 'If this blighter nursed Reggie, he'd probably have found out that he was leaving a bundle to his uncle, who was probably already ill – it says here: after a long illness.

'Well, what if his uncle took a turn for the worse, and he thought Reggie would probably outlive him. He'd need to do something about that, wouldn't he? And what better action to take, for his own evil purposes, than to remove Reggie from the equation? The money would then go to his uncle without question, uncle dies, and Bob's your uncle – sorry about that! – and Foster would cop for the lot.

'The only fly in the ointment was young Mr Williams, who smelled a rat, so he had to be removed as well. For all we know, Foster might have hurried his uncle into the next world as well, getting impatient to be a relatively rich man, leading a life of leisure.'

'Why don't you just tell all this to that Inspector Moody, Manda, and let him do the sniffing around?' asked Hugo, demonstrating that he, at least, had some common sense left.

'Because nobody but us, and presumably young Mr Williams, suspected anything in the first place. It was only because I found that cocktail glass in Reggie's room, and smelled the spilt stuff on the floor, that I thought there was something fishy about his death. As far as the law's concerned, Reggie died a natural, peaceful death; young Mr Williams just slipped away due to his age; and the Myers chap, having been ill for a long time, won't even have a post mortem.

There'll be no trouble with the death certificate, because he'd had a long illness: probably cancer – it usually is, these days. So they'll just cremate him, probably; the same with young Mr Williams, and nobody will ever be any the wiser, if we don't do something about it. You remember what Williams said about Foster – that he wanted Reggie cremated, and not buried, but – thank God – he was buried, so we could still force an exhumation.'

'Aren't you running just a bit ahead of yourself there, Manda?' asked Hugo.

'I don't think so, Hugo. Somebody's got to sort out this mess, and it might as well be us. Nobody else is interested, and until we can provide adequate evidence that crimes
have been committed, nobody will listen to us.'

Hugo managed to keep Lady Amanda in check by suggesting that she give him another lesson in taming the trike, and this distracted her for a while, but during afternoon tea, she was back at the 'trouser leg' of the murders again, like a Jack Russell with a rat.

'You never actually gave me the address, did you, Hugo, old boy?' she pumped him, like a car nearly out of petrol and desperate for fuel.

'What address is that, then, Manda?' he replied, playing the innocent.

'You know darned well what address I'm talking about. Don't be obtuse,' she retorted, a growl creeping into her voice.

'The address of my house for the estate agents?' he asked, without hope, but more as a distraction and timewaster.

'The address of that Derek Foster that you found this morning.' Anger was making her sound like a furious cat, disturbed at its food.

'Can't seem to remember where I wrote it down,' Hugo parried, knowing he wouldn't win, but hoping he might distract her sufficiently so that she was put in a foul enough temper to forget what her original purpose had been.

'You wrote it in the little section at the back of your diary, where you always make notes. You haven't forgotten at all. You're just doing this to rile me.'

'It's working then!' Hugo commented, noticing the rise in the pitch of her voice as he continued to prevaricate.

'Hugo!' she shouted. 'Give me that blasted address!'

'All right! Keep your hair on.' Reaching into his trouser pocket, he produced his diary, flicked to the back pages, where he made a note of anything he particularly wanted to remember, and read: 'Eleven, Mogs End, Belchester. That's to the south of the city, isn't it?'

'Yes. It runs off Lumpen Lane, cutting through to Raga-Bone Road. It's only a sort of alley, really, and the houses are just a few tumbledown old cottages; should have been condemned and demolished years ago, in my opinion, but then who am I to contradict the nosy-parker preservation societies that seem to proliferate today?' 'Satisfied now?' he asked, putting away his diary.

'Absolutely! We'll go tonight!'

'What do you mean, we'll go tonight? Go where? Why? This all sounds a bit iffy to me.'

'We'll go and scout out the house – make sure he lives there – that sort of thing. It's only a little tidying up. We need to be absolutely sure of our facts, before we can take this investigation any further,' she explained, in the most rational of voices, as if it were perfectly normal to go skulking about at night, trying to see into people's homes, before getting them arrested for what was now triple murder.

'Manda! You can't be serious! What if he catches us – you? I'm certainly not going peering through folks' windows, spying on them in their own homes.'

'I shall pretend to be an old lady who has come over queer, and would like a glass of water – something of that order should do it,' she informed him, without a hint of embarrassment.

'But he'll recognise you!' Hugo warned. 'What do you do, then, when he confronts you with being at Reggie's funeral, the wake, and the reading of the will?'

'I shall go in disguise,' she retorted, giving him a scornful look, as if this were so obvious that he should have thought of it himself. She seemed completely to have forgotten how she had poured contumely on this idea, when Enid had suggested it.

'You can't!' expostulated Hugo, in as masterful a voice as he could manage.

'I can, Hugo. And what's more, I will. There are no street lights down that alley, and it should be easy enough to sneak into the garden and look through a lighted window – much easier after dark than in broad daylight.' Lady Amanda had made up her mind, and nothing in the world would make her change it.

'Well, how are you going to get there?' Hugo asked. 'Surely not on that tricycle of yours? There's no way you could make an effective escape on that. He'd catch you in no time.'

'I shall get Beauchamp to take us – us, you notice, in case I need your help – in the Rolls, and park it in Lumpen Lane. There's a tiny piece of waste ground at the junction with Mogs End where Beauchamp can park, and

extinguish the car lights. No one will notice it there.'

'I don't see what sort of help you think I could be to you. I'm hardly up for a sprint escape, or for wrestling with villains.'

'You could call the police if anything happened to me; if I didn't come back, or something.'

'Oh, great! So I have to sit inside a pitch-black car, waiting for something dreadful to befall you, before I'm of any use. Beauchamp would be a lot handier than me.'

'Fact is, Hugo, I want you to be there. This is our adventure, and I don't want you to miss out on any of the fun,' she explained.

'Fun?' Hugo was astonished by this view of what they were proposing to do. 'I'm going to speak to Beauchamp,' he threatened. 'I shall forbid him to drive you anywhere tonight after dark.'

'Surely you don't want to force me to carry out this necessary surveillance with the tricycle as my only conveyance and means of escape, do you?'

'Manda, that's not fair. Of course I don't. If you must carry out this hare-brained scheme, then of course I'll accompany you, even though the thought of it worries me to death.'

'Good man, Hugo! That's the spirit!' She was always magnanimous in victory. Getting her own way bucked her up no end.

Chapter Thirteen

It wasn't dark enough for them to leave until half past nine, and it took a further twenty minutes to get Hugo out of the house and into the car. First he had had to go to the lavatory, then he had decided that he really ought to take a light jacket against the cool of the evening, then he claimed to have left his glasses in his bedroom.

When he stated that he had to go to the lavatory again, as anxiety always affected his bladder, Lady Amanda decided that this was the last straw, and rushed him from the cloakroom, through the front entrance, and into the car. She would brook no more shilly-shallying and timewasting, and put her foot down with a firm hand [!]

The drive through Belchester at this time of night was very pleasant. Not being a great centre for night clubs and partying, the few public houses the city did possess were usually frequented by older residents who wanted only a quiet drink. Those who wanted a more riotous time left the city for other destinations with more glittering establishments on offer.

The little city was almost deserted and, with its street lights in the style of Victorian gas lights, charmed anew, with this slip back in time, and its unpopulated streets. Beauchamp turned right, out of North Street in to West Street, then took the first turning left, into a road called simply and accurately West-to-South, then first right into Lumpen Lane, which was shaped like the letter 'U'.

At the bottom of its curve was a right-hand turn into Mogs End, and, opposite this junction, a small piece of ground, unused since a venerable cottage had been demolished due to its unsafe structure; a victim of neglect and lack of care.

Beauchamp drew the car to a halt on this tiny piece of waste ground, handed a torch back to Lady Amanda, then extinguished the car's lights. 'Take care of yourself, my lady,' he mumbled, as he handed it over, and Hugo leaned across to Lady Amanda and whispered, 'Keep your eyes peeled, old girl, and never underestimate the power of a scream.

'If we hear anything of you, Beauchamp can rush to your aid, and I can get in the front and lean on the horn, until everybody living hereabouts comes outside, to see what all the noise is about.'

'Hugo?' she hissed back.
'Yes?'
'Why are we whispering?'

'I haven't the faintest idea, Manda. It just seems appropriate, somehow.'

Lady Amanda slipped from the car, with absolutely none of the grace and elegance of a cat, and immediately caught her toe on a half brick, causing her to exclaim, audibly, in surprise and pain, an action that drew an even louder 'shh' in stereo from the Rolls.

'I'm OK,' she hissed back. 'I'll just put my torch on for a minute, until my eyes get more used to the low light.' There may not have been any street lighting in Mogs End, but it was a clear night, and the sky provided sufficient illumination for her, after just a few steps.

Trying to act as normally as possible, she extinguished her torch and put it in her pocket before starting to saunter down Mogs End, keeping as keen an eye out as she could, in the low visibility, for the house numbers. She was not sure which end the numbering began, nor which side had the odd numbers, and which evens.

She was on the right-hand side of the street, as one approached it from this end, and the second house had, fortunately for her, a large number '4' on its gate, so at least she had the information required, to locate number eleven. The numbers obviously started at this end, and the odd numbered cottages were on the other side of the road.

Looking around her with a nonchalance she did not feel, she crossed the road and began to stroll slowly past the cottages with the odd numbers, counting as she went. 'I must have passed one and three, so, five next, seven – no lights on in there at all, they must be out – nine, television blaring, and *there* – number eleven.'

She whispered to herself to boost her confidence, because, at this very moment, she felt uncharacteristically frightened. Anything could happen to her, going into enemy territory like this. She'd brushed and sprayed her hair flat, worn her tattiest old gardening clothes, and smeared on some very bright make-up, before leaving home, but she suddenly felt naked – exposed as she never had been before, and as if she had a name card round her neck, confirming her identity to all and sundry.

At the garden gate, she paused, and looked over it to see how it opened, undid the bolt with the greatest of care, and then froze on the spot. What if he had a dog? It would come rushing at her a soon as she set foot on the property, barking its head off. What if it was a large dog? A vicious dog?

Scolding herself for such cowardice, she grabbed the gate and began to open it very slowly, stopping after only about six inches, because it was badly in need of oiling, and screeched like the very devil itself. A light came on in the front room of the house, and she ducked down into a crouching position as quickly as she could manage, behind the hedge that fronted the property.

It was quite a height, and very unkempt, and made a good shield for someone of her bulk.

The front door was opened, and a voice called, 'Is there anyone there?' It was Foster's voice, all right. She was definitely at the right place, but this was no consolation, now that he had become aware of her presence. Or had he? He might just put it down to not having shut the gate properly.

She was right. A few footsteps sounded on the very short garden path, and the gate was kicked shut. This was a blessing, as Foster never got as far as actually taking a look out into the street. She'd just have to get in some other way.

When the front door had slammed shut, she crawled along the very narrow pavement, eventually finding a place where there had been a gap in the hedge, and it would be possible for her to swarm her way through, even though the hedge was in the process of managing this breach in its defences. So much for being discreet, she thought. If any of the neighbours were to come out of their houses, she would look like an old soak, crawling home after a binge!

It was no easy job, penetrating that hedge, even though it grew much more sparsely at her point of entry. Twigs and branches caught at her hair and her clothing, and nettles stung at her ankles as she scrambled her way through. One wayward frond of foliage found its way up her skirt in the most undignified way, and assaulted her most viciously, in a place for which she could not possibly seek sympathy. But she was determined to get to the other side, finally reaching it on all fours, and having to put her hand back through it for her hat, which had been whipped off, and deposited back on the narrow paving, on the other side.

Gathering her dignity as best she could, she stayed in her prone position, and approached the side of the house, still on all fours. The light at the front of the house had been switched off again, but there was a light to the righthand side, which she considered might possibly be the kitchen, as the starlight revealed pipes exiting the wall, and disappearing into what she supposed was a drain.

On reaching the window from which the light illuminated an oblong of the garden, she slowly slid into an upright position – it had to be slow. Fast, she couldn't do, at her age – and pressed herself against the wall of the property. Maybe, if she was very careful, she could sneak a peek into the interior.

She had no idea what she expected to achieve by this action, she suddenly realised, and all the adrenalin, which had buoyed her up thus far, suddenly evaporated, leaving her feeling old and foolish. What had she hoped to achieve by this nocturnal reconnaissance visit? Well, it was no good making a bolt for it now. She'd just have to achieve what she had set out to achieve, and get a look into this chappie's house.

The feeling of foolishness continued to nag at her. Had she really expected to find him brewing some sort of devilish potion in his kitchen, intent on claiming the lives of more victims? What was she playing at, and at her age, too? She ought to be ashamed of herself, but that would have needed a grown-up attitude, and she never intended to grow up properly.

Dismissing such negativity from her mind, she remembered that the Golightlys weren't quitters, and she steeled herself to lean round, as rapidly as she could, and sneak a peek into that kitchen. She bunched her muscles, drew in a large breath, which she held, with the suspense of the moment, and bobbed her face rapidly across the window pane, and back again.

There had been nobody in the room. It was empty. Thus emboldened, she took a more leisurely look at the interior of the room, looking for goodness knows what, but alert to any alien item, out of place in such an environment.

As she committed the contents of the room to memory, she became aware of a low, menacing growling, which seemed to be coming from just behind her slightly crouched figure. The hairs on the back of her neck began to rise, and she turned, very slowly, to see just what was to her rear.

As she began to move, the growling turned to a deep baying bark, and a voice ordered her to stay where she was. Completing her one-hundred-and-eighty degree turn, she found herself almost nose to nose with a dog she immediately identified as a Great Dane, its collar held in a firm grip by its owner, Derek Foster.

'Don't move or cry out,' he commanded. 'I've phoned the police and they're on their way. I suggest you just stay where you are until they arrive, unless you'd like to take on Marmaduke here.'

'I'll stay,' she whispered, and gradually straightened up, until she was in a more comfortable position. The dog growled again, and gave two mighty 'wuffs'.

'I also suggest you keep quiet. Marmaduke doesn't take kindly to strangers.' After a few seconds of silence, he asked, 'Aren't you that woman who came to my father's friend's funeral? You can talk now I've spoken in an ordinary social voice. He won't make a move if I act in a civilised fashion towards you.'

'I was there, yes.'
'Why?' he enquired, still speaking softly.

'Because Reggie was an old friend, and an ex-business partner of my father's. I was just paying my respects.' 'Is that all?' He sure was nosy, she thought.

'Of course!'

'Then why did you stay on after the wake, for the reading of the will? Hoped he'd left you something, was it?'

'Something like that,' Lady Amanda agreed, not sure where this conversation was leading, but not enjoying it one little bit.

At that moment, what she considered to be their sinister little exchange of un-pleasantries was interrupted by the wail of a siren, and a police car drew up in the road outside the cottage, its lights providing a bright show of red and blue, but that was not all. A Rolls-Royce approached from the other direction, and also parked, nose to nose with that belonging to the forces of law and order.

'Thank God!' Lady Amanda muttered, her voice drowned by the still unquenched wails of the siren. 'Beauchamp has ridden to my rescue!' and her whole body relaxed, shortening her height by a good two inches, and decreasing the pressure in her bladder, which had grown considerably, during her little conversation with Foster and his hell-hound.

At the gate, Beauchamp was standing aside courteously, to allow a uniformed policeman and one in plainclothes to precede him, and all three figures approached the tableau presented by an elderly lady slumped against the side wall of the cottage, and a man, responsibly restraining a large and angry dog.

'Shall we go inside?' enquired the policeman not in uniform, and Lady Amanda's spirits slumped to new depths. It was that Inspector Moody, who already suspected her of being batty. How was she going to talk herself out of this situation, without confirming his original suspicion?

Once inside the cottage, Beauchamp took over with his usual aplomb, and confirmed, without a shadow of a doubt, that Lady Amanda had bats in the belfry. 'I am Lady Amanda's family retainer,' he explained. 'She often goes wandering,' he continued, in a perfectly reasonable tone. 'It runs in the family. There's many a time, in the past, when I've had to locate her late mother, out for one of her little jaunts, looking through other people's windows, to see how the other half lives.

'She's not dangerous: just wants to watch other people getting on with their lives, in homes so different from her own. If I could only persuade her to get a television set, it would probably solve the problem instantly with, perhaps, an addiction to *Coronation Street*, or one of the other soap operas, that I believe are on offer, these days.

'But she is adamant that she won't have such a thing as a television in the house, and this is the result. Please accept my sincere and humble apologies, and be assured that I will keep a closer eye on her in the future, if she's in one of her exploring moods.'

Moody looked at the dignified figure of the manservant thoughtfully, considering whether he was telling the truth, or just trying to talk his employer out of an awkward situation. After a short silence, he gave Beauchamp the benefit of the doubt, having been subjected to Lady Amanda's visit to the police station, and her ramblings about there having been a murder committed at a local nursing home.

'I sympathise with your predicament,' he intoned, addressing Beauchamp for the first time. 'Do you have transport to get the old lady home safe and sound?'

'I do, indeed, Inspector. The family Rolls-Royce is parked outside, awaiting us for the journey home, if you will be so generous as to permit us to leave.'

Moody thought about it, but had one or two more questions. 'And you'll definitely keep a sharper eye on her in future?'

'Certainly, Inspector,' replied Beauchamp with dignity.

'And do you know how she got here tonight?'

'I strongly suspect it was by tricycle,' he answered, making the inspector gape with surprise. 'No doubt on the route home, I shall find it abandoned somewhere, and simply come back to collect it with the trailer, when I have got my charge settled for the night.'

It all seemed perfectly reasonable to Inspector Moody, who had been convinced, since his first encounter with Lady Amanda, that she was as daft as a brush. Being *Lady* Amanda, probably just meant that the family could afford to pay for a 'minder' for her, rather than put her in a home for old crazies, which is where he, personally, considered she should be.

'I shall release her into your care, then. But I shall be keeping an eye out for her in future. We can't have batty old biddies going around giving people terrible shocks, like that which she inflicted on Mr Foster this evening.'

'You have my guarantee, Inspector,' said Beauchamp, pulling himself up to his full dignified height, and glaring at Lady Amanda, with the command to stay absolutely silent, in his eyes. She was getting agitated, and if she spoke now, it would ruin everything.

'In that case, you may take her away. Trespass is a civil offence, and I understand that no damage has been done. Do you want to press charges for anything, Mr Foster?' he asked.

'No. I just want her to leave me alone,' replied the householder.

'That's good enough for me,' stated the inspector. 'You are to stay away from this gentleman's house – in fact from any house, the windows of which you might want to peer through, indiscriminately. Do you understand me?' he asked, piercing Lady Amanda with his steely gaze.

She made as if to speak, but Beauchamp reached out a foot at the speed of lightning, and trod on her toes. 'Ahhh!' she cried and, getting the message that had been so painfully delivered to her, added, 'I understand.'

'Good!' replied Inspector Moody, not having noticed Beauchamp's swift and effective action. 'I do not expect to run into you again in similar circumstances. Do I make myself perfectly clear to you?'

'Yes, Inspector.'

'You may take her home, now, Mr Beauchamp. And you'd better make sure she stays there, and doesn't go off on one of her little "peeping-tom jaunts" again, or she'll be for it.' Turning to the uniformed officer who had driven him there, he instructed him, 'I want you to keep an eye out for this old lady. She can be a real nuisance. Got that, Constable Glenister?'

'Got it, sir,' replied the navy-blue clad figure, trying his hardest to suppress a smile at the situation. 'If I see her, I'll run her in, and deliver her straight to you, Inspector.'

'Good man!' Turning now to Lady Amanda and Beauchamp, he advised them to be on their way, and to keep under his radar, in the future.

Lady Amanda was speechless with rage, as they walked over to the Rolls, and then speechless with fury when she found Hugo lying across the backseat of the vehicle, snoring away as if he hadn't a care in the world.

'Hugo!' she yelled, then pushed his leaden body as far as she could across the seat, so that she could get into the car herself.

'There I was, in danger of my life, held at bay by a slavering monster of a dog, and then the police arrived.'

'Wossat?' slurred Hugo, endeavouring to pull his sleep drugged old body into an upright position.

'And it wasn't just any old policeman,' she continued, ignoring the dilapidated state in which he had found himself, at being woken suddenly. 'Oh no, it was Inspector Moody – the charming and polite Inspector Moody!'

'And then what happened?' asked Hugo, his wits reassembling themselves with surprising speed.

'*Then* Beauchamp came along and explained to the kind inspector that I was a loopy old biddy, who couldn't be trusted out on her own. And very convincing he was too, weren't you Beauchamp?'

The sound of a murmured, 'Beecham,' reached them from the driver's seat.

'So now he's had his worst fears confirmed, and he's even asked his constable – one PC Glenister, I believe – to keep his eyes peeled for me, in case I go wandering off again, to try to spy through people's windows, and watch them watching television, and doing other equally exciting things. And that brute with the dog! Why didn't he say anything about coming across us before? That's very suspicious behaviour in my opinion.'

'Cor lummy, Manda! You did get yourself into a pickle, didn't you?' commented Hugo.

'And a great help you were, I must say, staying in the car and having a cosy little nap. Why weren't you at my side, defending my sanity?'

'Would it have done any good if I had been?' he asked, surprising Lady Amanda into a thoughtful silence.

'I don't suppose it would have made the slightest difference,' she eventually admitted.

'Beauchamp told me to stay put, so that I wouldn't be associated with you. I know we were seen together at the funeral, but if I wasn't known to be with you on this illfated little expedition this evening, perhaps I may not automatically be assumed to be your "partner in crime", Hugo explained.

'Cunning old Beauchamp!' she exclaimed. 'That means we can still use you as an agent, Hugo.'

'Not on your life!' he blurted out. 'Not after tonight. Now, tell me all about it; it must have been awful.' Not only did Hugo long for the details of the adventure he had slept through, but he knew, if he got Lady Amanda going, she would talk herself into a better mood, just by stealing the limelight, and telling a story in which she was the central character.

Back at Belchester Towers, Beauchamp efficiently produced mugs of cocoa, and the pair of elderly amateur sleuths made their way to bed, both eager for the oblivion that a good night's sleep would offer them.

Chapter Fourteen

No one in Belchester Towers rose early the next morning, and, as Lady Amanda Holmes and Dr Hugo Watson straggled downstairs, Beauchamp suggested that they lie low for a bit, and quit the sleuthing just for a while. He advised them that the bringing to justice of the evil Moriarty could be delayed, at least until they had their strength back, as Lestrade would never get the thing sorted out on his own. Maybe they could occupy themselves in some other, more innocent, way, as today was Sunday.

Lady Amanda gave the idea her best attention, then nodded her head in decision, and announced, 'I know what we'll do! We'll go over to Enid Tweedie's place and give it that airing I promised myself we'd do, before she returned home. You can come too, Beauchamp, for "the heavy". It wouldn't be right for a batty, fragile old biddy like myself to be taxed too much physically, now would it?'

'No, my lady,' answered Beauchamp, wooden-faced. Would he never be allowed to forget what had been said the previous evening? That the expediency and quick-wittedness that had extracted her from a very uncomfortable position the night before, and had been the only possible means of removing her from a situation that might have ended in her arrest, had not seemed to have occurred to her, yet.

As a sort of apology (although he didn't see what he had to apologise for) he made them a sumptuous breakfast that included such little treats as kidneys and kedgeree, and left them to help themselves. After all, he had saved some for himself, and his portion awaited him in the kitchen, keeping warm in the slowly cooling oven.

At ten o'clock, Lady Amanda presented herself in the kitchen, demanded to be allowed to raid the cupboard of cleaning products and equipment, and ordered him to load the vacuum cleaner into the boot of the Rolls.

When he returned from this errand, he found her in the middle of the kitchen, standing beside a broom, dustpan and brush, and mop and bucket, with a carrier bag clutched in each hand. 'I've gathered up polish, bleach, scouring powder, cloths, air freshener, lavatory cleaner, and that spray stuff that's supposed to eliminate foul odours. That should do us, shouldn't it?' she asked.

'You seem to have covered most things, my lady, but may I suggest a glass cleaner as well, for windows and mirrors?' Beauchamp replied.

'If you must! I'll get some out of your cupboard, and you can start loading this stuff into the boot, while I go and boot Hugo up the backside, to get *his* engine running. The exercise of a bit of cleaning will do his stiff old joints good – get some movement back into them,' she stated, and stumped out of the room, in search of the aforementioned unfortunate Hugo, who didn't know what was about to hit him, and by the time he spotted the whirlwind that was Lady Amanda, would not find himself in a suitable position to escape what was about to happen to him.

Poor Hugo was discovered behind an open copy of a Sunday newspaper, taking a casual look at the main news. Lady Amanda, rather in the manner of Beauchamp, approached him without a sound to alert him, and he suddenly found the newspaper torn from his grasp, and was then hauled unceremoniously to his feet.

'Look lively, Hugo!' she boomed, causing him to shrink away from this virago that had suddenly disturbed his Sunday morning musings. 'We're off to Enid's to get the place ready for her return home. Come on! Chop-chop! Haven't got time to waste!'

'I say, Manda, old bean. Give a chap a chance to digest his breakfast, won't you? The world won't come to an end if we don't go this very minute, will it?'

'It might! You never know. Now, look lively, and get yourself out of the house and into the Rolls. Operation Airing Enid is about to begin!'

It was, of course, useless to try to reason with Lady Amanda, when she was in one of her get-up-and-go moods, and so he trailed listlessly behind her, like a naughty schoolboy, approaching the room used for detention.

Enid Tweedie's tiny house was in a road un-edifyingly named 'Plague Alley', and this name seemed to have shaped her life. She had spent many years of her life in and out of hospital, having this altered or that removed, thus living up to the suffering implied in the name of the street where she lived.

The house fronted straight out on to the pavement, with no front garden dividing it from the narrow walkway. It had two bedrooms upstairs, and only a living room and a kitchen downstairs, a ramshackle bathroom having been tacked on to the back of it, somewhere back in the mists of time. Its number was thirteen, and this seemed appropriate, too, given Enid's unfortunate medical history.

She lived here with her aged mother, and an evil smelling, and even fouler-tempered cat, the name of which, Lady Amanda had never bothered to enquire after, knowing only that Enid loved it dearly, as if it had been one of her own children.

Producing the key that Enid had previously bestowed on her from her handbag, Lady Amanda opened the door, and the three of them backed away, as a foul stench rushed out to engulf them in its greeting.

'What, in the name of all that's holy, is that ghastly smell?' asked Hugo, removing a handkerchief from his trouser pocket, and clasping it to his face. 'I could do with one of those old-fashioned vinaigrette things. We're surely not going in there, are we?'

'I'd forgotten about her mother's cigars,' said Lady Amanda, coughing in a ladylike way, behind her hand. 'The smell, as I understand it,' she went on, 'is comprised of the copious amounts of wee-wee with which Enid's mother generously sprinkles every piece of soft furnishing she comes into contact with.

'There is an additional layer added by that stinky old cat of hers, that not only smells of dead cat, but also pees everywhere, marking its territory, I suppose. The final ingredient is the lingering whiff of the small cigars which Enid's mother has recently taken to smoking. She had decided, apparently, that she wasn't getting the best value out of her old age pension, and took up the foul things to augment the gin she purchased, to make life a bit more bearable for the poor old thing that she considers herself to be.

'I haven't actually been here since she started smoking them, but I shall advise Enid to dissuade her from continuing to do so. The old dear's waited on hand, foot, and finger, and I don't see why she should be allowed to choke her daughter to death, just because she's got nothing better to spend her money on.

'I'll go in first, and open all the windows, and the back door, and then, when it's cleared a bit, you can bring all the gear in, and we can get started,' concluded Lady Amanda Golightly, carer for of old cleaners, and narrator of family histories.

A few minutes later, Beauchamp led the way, discharging a white cloud of air freshener before him, as he made his way into the pungent little dwelling. Hugo followed behind, reluctantly, his handkerchief still held to his nose. Fortunately for him, he still carried on the habit, learnt from his father, of sprinkling his handkerchiefs with cologne, and this scent, clasped to his face as it was, gave him the courage to follow Beauchamp.

Lady Amanda was already busy, throwing the cushions from the sofa and armchairs into the back yard, so that they could take the air. She had also gathered all the dishcloths, tea towels and bathroom towels she could lay her hands on, and the washing machine was already chugging away. With the windows open wide, the place already smelled better, and Beauchamp took charge of the vacuum cleaner, while Lady Amanda sat Hugo down at a small dining table with some brass ornaments, cleaner and a cloth.

'That shouldn't prove too strenuous for you, Hugo, old chum,' she trilled, always happy when she was bossing other people around. 'Get those gleaming, and it'll make all the difference to the end result.'

At one-thirty, they took a break, Beauchamp fetching boxes of sandwiches and flasks of coffee, which he had somehow found the time to prepare before they left, from the boot of the Rolls.

'I don't know how you do it, Beauchamp!' declared Lady Amanda. 'I thought we'd have to send out for fish and chips.'

'No chance of that, on a Sunday, if you don't mind me mentioning it, my lady,' he replied then added, very quietly under his breath, 'and it's Beecham!'

'Oh, smoked salmon and cucumber with horseradish,' declared Hugo, after his first bite. 'My absolute favourite, Beauchamp, you clever old stick. I hope Amanda knows what a treasure you are, and pays you accordingly.'

With as much dignity as he could muster, given that he was covered in dust, his normally immaculate clothing dirt-smeared and begrimed, Beauchamp replied, 'I am perfectly happy with the remuneration that Lady Amanda accords to be my due,' and bridled a little, at so coarse a mention of financial matters while eating.

By four-thirty, they had done as much as their energy would allow, the place was looking sparkling, and smelling much better, and Lady Amanda was having a last spray around with, first the air freshener, then with the fabric freshener.

'That should do!' she declared. 'Enid will be delighted when she gets back, but I'm going to advise her not to let her sister know that she's home. The longer she can keep that evil-smelling old witch of a mother of hers out of this place, the better. I'm going to suggest that she approach the local authority, with a view to getting her into a home. I'd love to see what they made of her at the Birdlings, and I might even get Enid to agree, now that she's stayed there, and found it very accommodating.'

'I say, what a topping idea, old thing,' agreed Hugo. 'If staying in that dreadful place is her idea of heaven, then she surely needs a lucky break in life, don't you agree?'

'I shall do my utmost to persuade her that her mother would be much better off, in the tender care of the place that has so admirably suited her, and I'm pretty certain she'll agree. What do you think, Beauchamp?'

'I,' intoned Beauchamp, 'am not paid to think, my lady.'

On arrival back at Belchester Towers, Beauchamp, usually the most stoic of characters, gave a yelp of alarm, as the car approached the frontage.

'Whatever is it, Beauchamp?' asked Lady Amanda, thoroughly shaken. It must be something dreadful, if Beauchamp had reacted in such an atypical way.

'The front doors are wide open, my lady,' he informed her, a quaver in his voice. 'It would appear that we have, or have had, intruders. Does my lady have her mobile telephone apparatus with her?' he asked, putting the Rolls into reverse, and moving it out of view from the front of the property, sensibly placing it behind a clump of large trees.

'Most certainly, Beauchamp. It's in my handbag.'

'Then may I suggest most respectfully, my lady, that the police are informed?' he advised her.

Of course, it was Inspector Moody who attended the callout, and very scathing he was too, of the circumstances of his summoning.

'Are you sure the silly old biddy didn't just forget to close the doors, when you went out?' he asked Hugo, a malicious gleam in his eye.

'Lady Amanda is not a silly old biddy, and I personally saw Beauchamp both close and lock them, before he got into the Rolls,' Hugo answered, as insolently as he could manage given his innate good manners.

'Does anyone else have a key to the property?' Moody enquired, and was referred by Hugo to Beauchamp, who was waiting in stand-by mode, should he be able to provide any help.

'Lady Amanda has no relatives, and rarely entertains. To my knowledge, no one has keys to the property, except Lady Amanda and myself,' he replied with dignity.

'Has anything been taken – stolen,' the inspector continued.

'Nothing,' confirmed the fount of all wisdom that was Beauchamp, 'but several things have been moved from their usual places.'

'Such as?' Inspector Moody showed a reluctant interest in this piece of information.

'The ormolu clock that you may observe on the mantelpiece,' began Beauchamp, 'was originally on the mantelpiece in the dining room. And here, in the drawing room, the bronze you may observe on the low table was on the mantelpiece in here.

'Similarly, there are things which seem to have been taken from the library and put in the study, and things which have migrated from the study to the library,' he concluded.

'And you're perfectly sure that your employer,' here, Moody gave Lady Amanda a malevolent stare, 'did not move these things without your knowledge, before you left the house this morning?'

'Absolutely sure, Inspector. I was last to leave the property and, if you would take the care to notice the objects which have been moved, they are all too bulky and heavy for Lady Amanda to have moved on her own.'

'Could Mr Chumley-Wumley-Doodle have helped her?' Moody asked, with a sneer in his voice at the complexity and calibre of Hugo's triple-barrelled surname.

'Mr Cholmondley-Crichton-Crump has neither the strength nor the mobility to undertake such an exercise, Inspector,' Beauchamp informed the policeman, pronouncing Hugo's name with absolute precision, maintaining his dignity with difficulty, and fighting a powerful urge to give the inspector the benefit of a 'bunch of fives', Beauchamp-style. He had been a boxing champion in the army, and felt that he would soon show he hadn't lost his touch, if he let fly.

'I should request that you all refrain from touching the objects that have been moved, and I shall send a man along to dust them all for fingerprints. If anyone else has handled them, we'll soon find out who,' he informed them, in the most pompous of voices, and incorrect grammar.

'Not if the person who handled them wore gloves.' Lady Amanda had spoken for the first time since Inspector Moody had arrived, and her voice had a sharp, sarcastic edge to it. Moody chose to ignore her, and instead, warned Beauchamp and Hugo to keep a good eye on old Wandering Winnie, or they'd have him to answer to.

When the door had closed behind him, the two men put their fingers in their ears, in anticipation of Lady Amanda's no doubt violent reaction, to being treated as if she were soft in the head, but were rewarded with an unexpected silence.

'This break-in is Foster's doing,' she declared, in perfectly reasonable tones. 'We've got him rattled, and he's trying to rattle us back. It's as clear as the nose on your face. He's left us a message which he didn't need to write down. "I know who you are and where you live, and I can get at you whenever I want to, so leave me alone, and I'll leave you alone". Don't you agree?' she asked, her head on one side like a bird's, as she awaited an answer.

Beauchamp slowly exhaled, suddenly aware that he had been holding his breath, while awaiting Lady Amanda's response to the policeman's visit, and now chose to hold his peace. Hugo, however, spoke up. 'Do you really think he'd do that sort of thing, Manda?' he asked.

'I expect he'd do that, and a lot more, if he could get away with three killings, scot free, and keep all the money he's inherited, as a result of his murderous misdeeds,' she answered. 'You take my word for it – he's out to scare us.

Well, I don't scare that easily, and I'm not giving up.'

'Well, at least you can keep yourself out of mischief, tomorrow,' declared Hugo. 'We're taking Enid Tweedie back to her own home. A good deed like that, after all the work we've done today, ought to keep you on the straight and narrow for at least a day, and by then, maybe you'll have simmered down.

A few minutes after Lady Amanda went up to her room that night, there was a piercing scream and Beauchamp appeared at the foot of the stairs as if by magic, mounting them as if the house was afire. Hugo made straight for the lift, and set it in painfully slow motion, towards the source of the scream. The lift might be slow, but Hugo was considerably slower, and was aware of this fact. This was his quickest route to his old friend's aid.

When he finally exited the little box and entered Lady Amanda's room, he found her sitting on the stool at her dressing table, wringing her hands, and evidently distraught, Beauchamp standing by her side, waiting to see if there were anything he could fetch for her or do, to make her feel better.

The bedclothes were pulled back, and on the bottom sheet, lay a sheet of paper, with letters cut from newsprint stuck on to it. Hugo approached the bed, and leaned down to read what was spelled out on the sheet of paper, being careful not to touch it. He read: *You won't hear or see me approach, but I shall destroy you with a flick of my finger.*

Beauchamp made his exit before Hugo could react. When he did, it was with horror. 'Manda, this is a death threat! What are you going to do about it? He's killed before, and nobody suspects him of anything. You have to take this to the police.'

'What's the point, Hugo? Inspector Moody already thinks I'm in the throes of Alzheimer's, and won't listen to a word I say. He probably thinks you're in your dotage, too. And as for Beauchamp, he probably believes, and quite rightly so, in my opinion, that he would do anything within his power, to avoid trouble or scandal in The Family.'

Hugo heard the capital letters, and responded, 'You're quite sure of that, are you?'

'Definitely! Beauchamp will be loyal to the end, whether that be my end, or his.'

The speaking of his name appeared to conjure Beauchamp up out of the ether, and he returned to the room with a plastic bag and a pair of silver sugar-nips in his hands. 'I'll just deal with this, my lady, then you can get into bed, and get some rest, after all the physical work you have undertaken today. You must be very tired.'

'Thank you, Beauchamp. It's most thoughtful of you to think of preserving the evidence,' Lady Amanda praised him.

Very quietly; even softer than a whisper, came the words, 'That's *Beecham*!'

Chapter Fifteen

The following morning dawned bright and sunny, but with a stiffening breeze that promised less fair weather later in the day. Beauchamp was up and at his duties at his normal hour, but once again Lady Amanda and Hugo were late to rise.

Lady Amanda had had difficulty sleeping, and so had turned to one of her favourite Conan Doyle books, reading into the small hours, before she finally turned out her light. Hugo had sought no such consolation and calm in books, for that was not his way, and tossed and turned, suffering from nightmares, when he finally dropped off to sleep, about five o'clock.

Both of them looked tired and drawn, when they met for breakfast, and neither of them had much appetite. So concerned was Beauchamp, that he was moved to speech. 'You need to eat. You've got a busy day ahead of you, moving Mrs Tweedie out of the nursing home and back into her own house, and no doubt she'll need some shopping done. How are you going to achieve that, if you don't have a bite inside yourselves?' he asked, with concern.

Lady Amanda was so surprised by this unprecedented show of interest in her well-being, that she was moved to speech. 'Thank you for your concern, Beauchamp. What you say is good advice, and I think we both had better act on it. Come on, Hugo! That's a lovely kipper you've got in front of you. Don't let it go to waste. How are you ever going to get the machine to work, if you have no fuel in the engine? That reminds me, you haven't had the opportunity to have a proper ride on that motorised tricycle, yet, have you? We'll have to get that organised *tout de suite*.'

Hugo, suddenly becoming aware that his personal safety was to be put at risk again, responded with, 'No fear, Manda! You'll not get me on that devil's contraption while I'm feeling like this.'

'Then get that kipper down your neck, and have some toast and marmalade. Beauchamp's put your favourite thick-cut lemon out for you. We've got a job of work to do today and I need you on tip-top form.'

Enid needed to vacate her room at The Birdlings by noon, and thus they set off about eleven o'clock, with a picnic lunch in the boot of the Rolls, so that they should not have to go shopping, until after they'd broken bread with her.

Hugo had eventually given in and eaten a fairly substantial breakfast, feeling much better for his effort. He was quite looking forward to seeing Enid's face, when she saw her clean and tidy (not to mention fresh-smelling) home on her return.

Both of them were silent on the drive into Belchester, each of them lost in thought, going over what had happened, not only in the last couple of days, but in the ten days since Lady Amanda had appeared so unexpectedly and abruptly in Hugo's life, and whisked him off to a completely different existence.

Hugo was not sure what he thought about this rapid change in his circumstances. While he was extremely grateful to be released from his former misery in the home, he was not sure how he felt about the added excitement that Lady Amanda had introduced into his formerly dull existence. He thought he quite liked it, but finally decided not to make up his mind, until time had proved that neither of them were about to be set upon by Mr Derek Foster.

Lady Amanda was having similar thoughts. She was getting used to having Hugo around, but it made a huge difference to her normal behaviour. The excitement, she definitely liked. She assumed that time would provide familiarity with Hugo's constant presence. Whatever happened, at least he had livened her up a bit. What a bit of luck it had been, there being a murder, just when the two of them were reunited, after so many years. Well, not so lucky for poor old Reggie, but it had certainly provided something for them to get their teeth into.

Beauchamp, although one may not have thought so, also had his own opinion on the past ten days. He hadn't seen Lady Amanda so animated for a long time, and she certainly seemed brighter since Mr Cholmondley-Crichton-Crumpmondley-Crichton-CrumpmondleyCrichton-Crump had come to stay. Whether this was because of the murder, or because of Hugo's company, he could not be sure, but he hoped that she would continue to be so animated, and not come to any harm from this situation in which she had involved them all.

Enid Tweedie had her suitcase packed and was sitting on the bed in the room she had occupied for the last week, waiting for them. She looked healthy and happy; hardly recognisable as the Enid Lady Amanda had known for so long.

'Oh, Lady Amanda!' she exclaimed as Lady A and Hugo entered the room. 'I've had such a lovely time here, and made so many new friends. I can't thank you enough for your generosity. I feel like a new woman!'

'You look like one, too. I've never seen your cheeks so rosy, and I do believe you've put on a little bit of weight,' observed Lady Amanda.

'And it's all thanks to you!' the soon-to- be ex-inmate enthused. 'I shall have so much more energy when I get home. I shall be round that house like an electric eel.'

As Hugo gallantly hefted her suitcase, there was a discreet knock at the door, and Nurse Plunkett entered, with another couple of members of staff. 'We're really going to miss you, Enid,' Nurse Plunkett declared, with tears forming in her eyes. 'You've been the life and soul of this place, with all those hilarious tales about your family. We're going to miss you terribly.'

This sentiment was echoed by the other two who had accompanied her, and even Matron made an appearance at the door, to pay her fond farewells. 'Such a surprise to find out what a charming friend you have in Enid,' she declared, still at daggers drawn with Lady Amanda, but delighted with her now-departing patient.

'Do come in to visit us sometime, won't you?' pleaded one of the other nurses, and received a beaming smile from Enid, in return.

'Of course I will, my dear. It will be my pleasure!'

'Come along, Enid!' exhorted Lady Amanda, thoroughly fed-up with all this sloppy sentiment, with Enid Tweedie, of all people, at its centre. She'd always found the woman dull beyond belief, and found it hard to believe her to be a fount of humorous stories and anecdotes. Lady Amanda didn't realise it, but sometimes she was jealous of other people's popularity.

The six people from the room made a gay parade as they passed down the corridor towards the exit, and Lady Amanda wouldn't have been surprised if someone had produced a tambourine, and encouraged them all to skip along and dance. Who would have thought that drab little Enid Tweedie could be cast as a 'Pied Piper' character?

The Rolls drew up in front of Enid's tiny house, nearly as long as the house was broad, its very presence turning the house into the image of a veritable playhouse for children.

As Beauchamp collected her luggage from the boot, Lady Amanda and Hugo accompanied her to the front door, waiting for her to unlock it and see the wonders they had wrought within, especially for her homecoming.

Stepping inside, straight into the living room, there being no space to accommodate an entrance hall, Enid looked around her with tears in her eyes, and said, 'Home, sweet home. There's nowhere like it. And just as I left it when I went into hospital.'

'Not quite!' boomed Lady Amanda's voice. 'We three spent all day yesterday giving it a good "bottoming". Can't you see the difference? Can you not *smell* the difference?'

Enid stood for a moment in thought. 'Yes,' she agreed. 'I can see you've been round with a duster. That was very kind of you, but there's a terrible aroma of cheap scent in here. I wonder where it's come from.'

Lady Amanda rolled her eyes, but stilled her mouth, as both Beauchamp and Hugo gave her the most ferocious glares. Some saints, she thought, would go ever unrewarded, their works unrecognised by those who couldn't see beyond the ends of their noses.

'We've brought a picnic lunch,' she informed Enid, 'then we can make a shopping list and get you in some supplies. What about your mother?'

'Mother's staying where she is!' Enid declared. They've got a big colour telly there, and my sister says her cigar smoke keeps her husband out from under her feet. She says she hasn't had such a peaceful life since before she got married. That only leaves my Oscar to be accounted for.'

'That mangy old cat of yours?' enquired Lady Amanda, wrinkling her nose in disgust.

Here, Beauchamp spoke up. 'Before I brought in the luggage, a lady from the house next door attracted my attention, and informed me that the cat had taken up residence with her, since its owner was away in hospital so much,' he informed them.

'Well, with that smelly old witch of a mother of yours decamped, and that stinking old cat of yours peeing on someone else's furniture for a change, life should take a turn for the better for you, Enid,' Lady Amanda offered, judge and jury on the new circumstances in which Enid found herself.

'But what shall I do all day, without Mother and Oscar?' she wailed.

'Get yourself a life, woman!' Lady Amanda advised her. 'You'll have time for all those things you said you always wanted to do – join the WI, do a cookery course, learn to embroider ... There are heaps of things you've mentioned to me, in the past, that you simply didn't have time for, and longed to do.'

'I did, didn't I?' replied Enid. 'And you're right! I shall start right away.'

'Just don't forget you're due up at The Towers on Friday for the 'heavy', as always.'

'Of course I won't. I love working in such a wonderful old home, and I shall be there on the dot of nine. But it won't be the same.'

'Won't be the same as what?' asked Lady Amanda, not quite catching Enid's line of thought.

'I shan't be an undercover agent any more. I found that very exciting.'

'Well, you never know. You might get to do it again, sometime in the future.'

'I do hope so. You lead such an exciting life.'

'And so shall you now, Enid, my dear,' Lady Amanda assured her, 'now you've got a bit of freedom back.'

'Yes, I expect I shall. Thank you all, for what you've done for me.'

That evening, after a good slug of Strangeways to Oldham, Lady Amanda returned to the subject that had been waiting to infect her mind since the day before. 'I need to get *into* that chap Foster's home,' she declared, apropos of nothing.

'You can't be serious, Manda! Have you forgotten already, that beastly note he left in your bed last night?' asked Hugo, aghast at her bold intention. 'He's already threatened your life, and now you plan to go right into the lion's den?' He could hardly believe his ears.

At that moment the telephone rang, and they could hear Beauchamp answer it in the hall. The instrument seemed to be giving him some trouble, as they could hear him say, 'Hello. Hello. Is there anybody there?' a bit like a quack medium at the end of the pier in a seaside resort.

There was a discreet clatter, as he replaced the receiver of the old-fashioned telephone back in its cradle, and he entered the room to inform them, 'Must have been a wrong number, my lady. There was no one on the other end of the line.'

The phone rang again, and Beauchamp left the room with unhurried steps, to answer it again.

The result was the same as before, and Beauchamp gave it as his solemn opinion that there was something wrong with the line. After all, the wind was getting up, and it seemed that they were in for some stormy weather, in the very near future.

'You're no doubt correct, Beauchamp. A line down, or something. Nothing to bother us, though. If anyone really wants to get in touch, they'll leave it until they can get through properly,' decided Lady Amanda, returning to her abandoned conversation with Hugo.

'There must be some evidence in that house that I could give to Inspector Moody, to make him take me seriously,' she declared, spearing Hugo with a gaze that dared him to disagree.

'What do you expect to find, Manda? A recipe book with Strangeways to Oldham marked, and 'poison' added to the list of ingredients? He's not that stupid. He's been clever enough, so far. Why should he give himself away with something stupid like that?

'He's got your number, Manda, and he's let you know that he knows that you know – blast! That sounded like a riddle, but you know what I mean. You need to face the fact that the man's dangerous, and wouldn't hesitate to make you his next victim.'

'Tosh! He's an amateur!'

'I beg to differ. It's you who are the amateur. He's killed three people. I consider, personally, that that gives him professional status; especially as no one but we two suspect him of any wrongdoing whatsoever.'

The telephone rang again, a further interruption to this, now heated, discussion and, knowing that Beauchamp was in the kitchen preparing dinner, Lady Amanda rose to answer it. Lifting the receiver to her ear, she intoned the number and waited for a reply, but there was nothing but silence on the line. No, hang on a minute! She could just discern the soft susurration of breathing.

'Hello. Hello. Who is this?' she asked, her voice rising with impatience.

'Gonna get you!' The words were barely louder than a breath, but she was sure she heard them, before the connection was broken by whoever was at the other end of the line.

Dropping the handset in her surprise, she called for Hugo, and stood stock still with shock, waiting for her mind to tell her she had imagined it, but it stubbornly refused to try to persuade her that this was the case.

'Whatever's the matter?' asked Hugo solicitously, as he tottered out of the drawing room.

'There was someone on the phone,' she announced starkly.

'There usually is, when it rings,' offered Hugo, with maddening logic.

'I think it was *him*!' She spoke quietly, as if she suspected that they were being eavesdropped on by some unidentified presence.

'Him who?' asked Hugo, ungrammatically.

'Him! Foster!' Lady Amanda replied, in an urgent whisper.

'What did he say?' Hugo continued with his maddeningly calm enquiries.

'He just said, "Gonna get you," but it was barely a whisper. I could hear him breathing down the phone, then he said *that*, and it was so quiet, that for a moment, I thought I'd imagined it. But I didn't Hugo, I really didn't!'

'There, there, old girl,' Hugo soothed, putting his arm around her shoulder in an uncharacteristically affectionate manner. 'We'll let Beauchamp know, at dinner, what's happened, and he can make sure that the house is locked up as tight as a drum tonight – keep us all safe till the morning. Everything always looks better in daylight, don't you think?'

Beauchamp locked every door and window, as soon as he was informed of the incident that had so unsettled Lady Amanda, and suggested that they contact the police in the morning. 'After all, my lady, even if he doesn't intend to carry events any further, he is, at the very least, conducting a campaign of terror against you, and he needs to be stopped, before things get out of hand.'

'Was the house locked up yesterday, Beauchamp?' asked Lady Amanda, timidly.

'It was, indeed, my lady,' Beauchamp assured her.

'Then how the dickens did he get in to leave a note under my bedclothes?' she asked, less timidly, and in a more accusatory tone.

'I have no idea, my lady, but I shall do my utmost to ensure that there is no way into Belchester Towers this night.'

Like a 'B' movie horror, there was a flicker of lightning, and an almighty crash of thunder, and the rain started to pelt down with a real vengeance.

'Oh, good grief!' shrieked Lady Amanda, Hugo was seen visibly to jump in his chair, and even Beauchamp raised an eyebrow in surprise.

'Beauchamp, would you be so kind as to make up a bed for me in the room next to Hugo's? I'm feeling rather nervous tonight, and don't consider that my bedroom is a good place to spend the night. After all, he knows where I usually sleep. He evidently had no trouble finding my room to place that note, and I don't want to spend tonight in the same room – just in case,' she ended rather lamely.

'No sooner said, than done, my lady,' confirmed Beauchamp, and left the room, forgetting, in his genuine concern for her safety, to whisper 'Beecham'.

Chapter Sixteen

The storm worsened, and the wind howled in the multitude of chimneys in the old house, and bent the trees in the grounds, in its strength. It soughed in the eaves, and blew hitherto undisturbed detritus into new life, sending it wheeling and spinning across the lawns like the phantoms of discarded lives.

Thunder rolled round the sky, a tympanic accompaniment to the lightning, providing one of nature's most spectacular examples of *son et lumière*, outperforming anything that man, in his humble place in the great scheme of planetary life, could imitate.

Rain bounced from the ground, to make a second impact a fraction of a second later, and plants were battered by its bullet-like impacts. This was no night to be out and about, for either human or animal. The weather waged a war with the area, its power unchallengeable, its dominance supreme.

Beauchamp systematically did his rounds of all the means of ingress, carefully locking that which was unfastened, and checking that which was already locked. The care with which he disposed of this duty was witness to the anxiety that he was suffering. A man not easily ruffled, his feathers were well and truly fluffed up tonight.

Unfazed by many an event that would have left lesser mortals trembling, he found himself to be strangely unsettled by the silent telephone calls, and even more alarmed by that received by Lady Amanda, when examined together with the note, that had mysteriously appeared in his employer's bed, the previous night.

This task completed to his satisfaction, he adjourned to the kitchen to make a cup of cocoa for them all. Cocoa was the ultimate comfort, at bedtime, especially when one was feeling a little ill at ease. As he approached the drawing room with his tray, the telephone rang again, and Lady Amanda appeared in the hall, to answer its urgent summons.

He halted to listen to what would happen, and observed her listening in silence, a look of undiluted horror spreading across her face. Then she repeated 'hello' thrice over, before taking the receiver from her ear and staring at it suspiciously, and reaching down to press repeatedly on the connection bar, in the manner of someone in the past, trying to attract the attention of the old-fashioned operator service, which used to be the only way to get a call put through.

'Is everything all right, my lady?' he asked, putting down the tray on a half-moon hall table.

Without a word, she held out the receiver in offering, and he took it from her and put it to his own ear. Silence! That's all there was. No dial tone. No furtive breathing. Either the storm had brought down the lines, or they had had their telephone line deliberately cut.

'Did he say anything, my lady?' enquired Beauchamp.

'He – he – he said he could see my house,' she told him, her voice breaking up with fear.

'He s-said he could see m-my h-house, and soon he'd b-be able to s-see *me*,' she informed her intrepid manservant.

Not wishing to alarm Lady Amanda any further, he handed back the receiver, and reassured her that it was probably just a crank, or a crossed line, and the breakage that occurred was, no doubt, due to damage caused by the storm, which was still raging round the countryside. 'Come on back to the dining room, and forget all about it, my lady,' he encouraged her. 'I have a tray of cocoa here, to relax you before you go to bed.'

But Beauchamp was worried. Damned worried!

As Lady Amanda and Hugo repaired to their separate rooms, she asked Hugo if he would mind if she left the adjoining door open for the night. She explained that it would make her feel safer, to know that he would hear her if anything befell her, and she, him. Hugo raised no objection, feeling that, if he should need assistance in the night, it would be easier to rouse her without a sixty-pound lump of oak muffling his voice, and creating a physical barrier between them.

Both of them lay in their separate beds, listening to the ravages of the storm, neither of them in the least inclined to go to sleep, each taunted by worries about their own safety, and that of the other. Beauchamp was an admirable chap, but he couldn't be everywhere at once, and the chances of him being anywhere in the vicinity of their adjoining rooms, should anything untoward occur, were slight indeed.

So, neither of them actively sought sleep, but it hunted them down, and gradually overcame their worries and fears, as it does most nights of one's life. By one o'clock, they were both sleeping peacefully, the only sounds in that part of the house, apart from the storm, being the creaking of old wood, and the steady 'tick-tock' of the long-case clock in the hall, the sound of which had always been particularly penetrating.

At about three o'clock, Lady Amanda suddenly awoke, every nerve in her body tingling, with the absolute certainty that she had been awoken by an alien sound, somewhere within the house. Sitting up cautiously, she strained her ears to listen, and there it was again. There was someone in the cellars. She knew Beauchamp wouldn't be so insensitive as to do something like that, considering the state their nerves were in. They had an intruder. Again!

As quietly as she could, she got out of bed, and crept into Hugo's room. He was lying on his back, snoring gently, as a gentleman should. Approaching his inert body, she shook him gently by the shoulder to wake him.

She shook him again, rather more vigorously this time, and still he did not stir. In one final effort, she put one hand over his mouth, and pinched his nostrils together with her other hand. That always worked, and it proved so in this case, as she had known it would. The feeling of being suffocated was a great aid in waking oneself up.

'Whaaa ...!' gasped Hugo, struggling for breath, and gazing wild-eyed about him, to discover the cause of his discomfort. He had left the curtains undrawn, and was able, instantly, to recognise Lady Amanda's figure, standing at the bedside.

'What's up?' he asked abruptly, cross about having his repose disturbed.

'Shh!' she admonished him. 'I can hear someone in the cellars. We've got to hide.'

'Are you mad, Manda?' he hissed.

'Certainly not! But I am sure that what I've heard, twice now, was someone skulking about in the cellars. We've got to get out of here.'

'Where do you suggest we go?' Hugo was still not quite with it.

'Up, Hugo. Up! I'm not sure whether Beauchamp's on patrol, or fast asleep. All I know is that we've got to find somewhere to hide, before he finds us and does us harm. Come on, get out of bed and follow me.' Unused to having such a new-fangled gadget as a telephone, she often forgot its existence.

With great reluctance, Hugo rose from his bed and put on his slippers but, as he reached for his dressing gown,

Lady Amanda's voice hissed, 'We haven't got time for that, nor for hats, scarves, comforters or gloves. Come on, Hugo. We've got to get out of here now!' and clutching only her handbag, she dragged him out into the hall, and headed for the staircase.

'I can't get upstairs that way,' Hugo whispered urgently. 'I'm not steady enough on my pins.' 'The lift then!' she decided.

'He'll hear us.'

'Yes, but if he's in the cellars, it'll take him some time to get to the hall, and we'll have hidden ourselves by then and, with any luck, the sound of the lift will have woken Beauchamp, and he'll be able to rush to our aid.'

A tremendous crash of thunder, like the crack of doom, broke above the estate, virtually simultaneously with its accompanying vivid flash of lightning, and the two of them scampered for the lift, as quickly as age and infirmity would allow.

As they waddled towards it, full steam ahead, Hugo hissed, 'If Beauchamp can hear us, so can he. He'll guess where we've gone, and come after us.'

'There are acres of space up there. Two more floors, and then the attics,' she hissed back, dragging him into the tiny cage of the lift, and closing the doors as quietly as she could. 'This thing only goes up to the first floor, as you know, but it'll give us a head start. I'll leave the cage doors open at the top, then he can't follow us. He'll probably go straight to my bedroom first, as he knows where it is.'

'If he follows us on foot, he'll be much quicker than if he uses this thing,' opined Hugo mournfully.

'Don't be so negative. If we're up against the wall, we fight, Hugo – like animals, if necessary. Now shut up, and save your breath for escape!'

The ascension of the lift was grindingly, painfully, slow, as well as noisy, exaggerating their anxiety and fear, rather than calming them with the fact that they were already in flight, and hadn't been caught, literally, napping. Sounds, as of someone making a bit of a din in the cellars, made their way up the shaft of the lift, further unsettling them.

At the top, Hugo, in his haste, accidentally pressed the 'down' button again, and it was only the quick-witted action of Lady Amanda, that stopped them arriving back at the point where their flight had started.

Exiting the unsettling little metal cage on the first floor, Lady Amanda espied Hugo's Zimmer frame, and hissed a question at him. 'What's that thing doing up here?' she asked.

'I brought it up in case I fancied a bit of exploration, ferreting around, that sort of thing. I could get to the lift downstairs, but thought I might wear myself out a bit up here, and would need it before I came down again.'

'Just shut up and grab it, NOW, then follow me down this corridor. We've got to be quick. He's much faster than us, and we've lost some of our head start because of that silly stunt of yours, with the lift.'

'It wasn't a stunt! It was a simple mistake. Sometimes you can be very judgemental, Manda,' hissed Hugo.

'Save your breath for fleeing, old stick. Come on, just a little faster.'

Hugo propelled his walker as fast as he could, but could not keep up the speed that Lady Amanda set. Eventually, she went back to where he was, opened a door, and pushed him inside a cupboard, casting his walking frame aside, and pressing her handbag on him, as she did so.

'I'm afraid it's the linen press for you, Hugo old boy,' she informed him, as she manhandled him inside the cupboard. 'They took the shelves out years ago, so there's loads of room. You shouldn't be too squashed. Just stay there nice and quietly until either Beauchamp or I come to fetch you out again. I can get on faster on my own.'

With that, she slammed the door on the highly confused Hugo, and made her way as fast as she could manage, up the staircase to the second floor, this one a little less grand than that from the ground floor to the first.

From there, she supposed she would have to head for the attics, but, for now, she just had ambitions of reaching the next floor. One step at a time was how to achieve anything important. Try to tackle too many things at once and you scuppered your own efforts, and played right into your enemies' hands. She'd learnt that at school. During lacrosse practice!

Meanwhile, Hugo had found himself an old packing case to sit on, located by touch alone, and had settled himself to explore Lady A's handbag. He knew she normally carried a little torch in there, and thought that it might be comforting, just to have a little light in his hidey-hole.

Having located the torch, he used its small light (for its head was only half an inch in diameter) to locate a bag of mint imperials, and popped one into his mouth, to keep body and soul together, until someone turned up to tell him that the hue and cry was over, and it was safe for him to come out, and go back to bed again.

He decided to leave further investigations of the gargantuan handbag for his later entertainment, and sat, torch switched off, sucking his peppermint, perfectly content with life, provided it didn't involve him getting caught up in any actual fisticuffs.

From downstairs, there came a crash, and the sound of muffled swearing. Hugo immediately had a mental picture of the wheelchair that had been delivered for him, and the fact that he had left it just outside the door to the cellar steps. Whoever the intruder was, he must have come up from the cellar and run into it, not expecting something like that to be right across a doorway.

An enormous brattle of thunder sounded, the sliver of light at the foot of the cupboard door flickered, then was extinguished. The storm must have knocked out the electricity supply. That was in Manda's favour, he decided, as she had lived here all her life, and knew this house like the back of her hand.

A noise outside his hideaway implied that Foster, if that is who it was, was tackling the stairs to the first floor with some speed, and heading towards the cupboard. Hugo steeled himself for discovery, but instead, heard a howl of rage, as their pursuer had presumably got himself entangled with Hugo's walking frame now. He must not have noticed it, in the sudden lack of electrical lighting.

A similar crash became audible from the second floor, and the sound of someone swearing loudly and robustly. Golly, he thought, Manda must be terrified out of her mind, if she's cussing like that.

Whoever was outside the door of Hugo's temporary housing must have heard it too, for there were sounds of someone picking themselves up, and stamping towards the staircase to the second floor. He was on his way to get her, and there was no way Hugo could warn her of his approach.

Sunk in misery, he opened the handbag once again, more as something to occupy his mind, as sitting doing nothing would drive him to despair. What was that, down in the corner? Hugo scrabbled down to the bottom of the handbag, on a voyage of discovery.

Upstairs, on the second floor, Lady Amanda had got herself into a tangle with a clothes rail filled with old wire coat-hangers, the sudden loss of light having caused her to make this unfortunate collision. As she wrestled with the wretched things now, she could hear someone charging up the stairs towards the ballroom, where she was currently trying to untangle herself.

As she finally pulled herself free, there was a vivid explosion of light from outside, clearly showing her, standing at the far side of the vast space, and illuminating a crouched figure at the other end, apparently getting his bearings.

Without a moment's hesitation, she was off again, heading for a small, semi-concealed door behind which was the tiny, narrow staircase to the attics. Grabbing a chair that stood forlornly by itself, just this side of the door, she manhandled it through the small opening with her, and jammed it against the wooden door, which opened inwards on to the stairs. That should hold him for long enough for her to get herself hidden.

The attics of Belchester Towers had not been cleared since the house had been built, and consisted of a vast network of inter-connected spaces, housing all manner of discarded furniture, clothing, and general junk. Packing cases were strewn everywhere, a trap for the unwary, and old garments, once special, were suspended on hangers from beams, to wrap themselves round the heads of those who did not observe where they were going.

Lady Amanda knew exactly where she was going, and ducked and wove her way through the maze of detritus like an expert. Little had been added since she used to play up here as a child, and she knew her way through the labyrinth from long experience.

She and her friends used to play hide-and-seek in these attics when she was a youngster, and she knew some of the best places to conceal herself, where even her parents would not have discovered her should they have searched.

As she took herself to a cramped space in the middle of a collection of old tea-chests, she pulled down a curtain that hung from a beam, and draped it over her entire body. On one side of her was a suit of armour that would make a marvellous weapon, should her pursuer find her.

The wind up here was considerable, blowing in through the eaves as it did, and she almost didn't hear the sound of sirens wailing their way up the drive. Suddenly there was hope again, and she remembered, with triumph, that she had left her mobile phone in her handbag. Either Hugo had found it, and summoned help, or Beauchamp had become aware of the intruder, and alerted the authorities. Whichever it was, it didn't matter now, for help was on its way.

Suddenly she felt her bowels clench with fear again. Help might be arriving, but would it be in time to save her? Foster was out to get her, and she couldn't see him mildly surrendering himself, just because the police were outside. After all, he still had time to complete his mission, and goodness knows what story he'd come up with, but it would no doubt be a plausible one.

There was a kicking and scraping noise from the bottom of the little staircase, and she knew he was at the foot of the stairs, and hadn't passed by the door without noticing it, and realising its significance.

She heard the sound of wood giving way. That would be the old chair. It would never have made a successful barrier, but it must have been older than she thought. She had considered that it would last a little longer than it evidently had.

There they were now, footsteps on the staircase, leading right to her place of concealment. The steps, however, were slow, and she imagined him savouring his moment of victory, approaching it at a pace that would allow him maximum enjoyment, at her discovery.

Her heart raced, and she felt her mouth and throat go dry. Should she have wished to scream, she didn't believe she had the ability. Suddenly he spoke into the surrounding darkness.

'I know you're up here,' he murmured, and there was an evil little snickering noise. 'I know where you are,' his voice taunted her. 'And I'm coming to *get you*,' she heard.

Maybe, in his intensity of purpose, he hadn't heard the sirens, which heralded the arrival of the police. 'I've got a flask here, of your favourite cocktail,' he teased again, 'and I'm going to get you to drink it all up, like a good little girl.' His voice was getting closer and closer to her place of concealment.

In a fit of almost fatal folly, she found herself wanting to ask him which cocktail he had considered as her favourite, and had to bite hard on her bottom lip, to stop the words escaping from her mouth. She held her breath, and tried to keep every muscle absolutely still.

'I'm coming to get you, and I'm getting *warmer and warmer*,' the voice crooned on, and it did, indeed seem to be much closer to hand than it had been before. With a glance of absolute horror, she stared down, and saw his feet, just the other side of the suit of armour. What to do? What to do? She had to do something, or she'd be dead!.

Without giving it a conscious thought, she pushed with all her strength against the rusting metal structure and, using her feet as the main force, managed to unseat it and send it falling

THE BELCHESTER CHRONICLES BOOKS 1 - 3   183

away from her. As it landed, she heard a scream close at hand and, suddenly, the lights went back on. She knew this, because light flooded up from the ballroom, along with the sound of running feet.

Inspector Moody tugged at the old-fashioned chain-pull that illuminated this part of the attics, and surveyed what lay before him. A man he recognised as Derek Foster lay on the floor, trying to struggle from beneath the weight of an elderly suit of armour. Lady Amanda Golightly was getting shakily to her feet, with a mouldering curtain over her, like a Regency-striped shroud.

Taking this scene in at a glance, he approached her and said, 'Lady Amanda Golightly, I arrest you for the actual bodily harm of Mr Derek Foster of,' here he stopped and searched his memory, 'number eleven Mogs End,' he concluded, smugly.

This rescue wasn't going at all the way Lady Amanda had planned it.

Circumstances eventually sorted themselves out, Hugo was recovered from the old linen press, whence he had summoned help on the mobile phone he had discovered in Lady Amanda's handbag, and Beauchamp was discovered tied to a chair in his sitting room, a gag in his mouth, and a nasty lump on the head where Foster had used a cosh on him.

Although Moody had difficulty in accepting that Foster was the sinning party, and Lady Amanda the party sinned against, he had no choice but to believe her, when both Hugo and Beauchamp backed up her story.

'I say, Hugo, old chap, guess what I saw in the attics when I was up there?'

'No idea, Manda, but don't leave me in suspenders,' Hugo replied.

'The old Carstairs invalid chair with the cane-work back and seat. It was for Papa's mama. Apparently a few hand-picked officers were allowed to convalesce here, during the First World War, and these were what they used to get around in when they weren't quite the ticket. One of them was requisitioned for family use and, I'm afraid to say, was never handed in, and it's still up there. I thought

we might be able to use that now, and send that newfangled affair back to social services.'

'I shouldn't do anything rash, my lady. Should the seat prove to be perished with age, Mr Hugo might go straight through it, and we should probably come across him, effectively hog-tied, as it were,' Beauchamp felt compelled to suggest.

'Good idea, Beauchamp. I shouldn't like to have you come across me hog-tied by an invalid carriage, either,' concluded Hugo, with feeling.

Before he left, there was one thing Inspector Moody wanted to get to the bottom of. 'Would you care to explain to me why Mr Foster has so many bruises about his person?' he asked, wondering how Lady Amanda was going to talk her way out of that one.

'I'm afraid that's all my doing, Inspector. Terribly sorry,' Hugo apologised shame-facedly.

'Your doing?' Moody almost shouted. There was no way he could see this mild-mannered elderly gentleman inflicting violence on anything other than a wayward pillow in his bed.

'I fear that Mr Foster may have tripped over the modern wheelchair that Lady Amanda just mentioned. I'm afraid I stupidly left it just outside the cellar door. And then, when the lights went out, I believe he became entangled with my walking frame on the first floor landing.'

'He must have come through the wooden doors to the old coal chute. The padlock on those was always dodgy,' Lady Amanda added.

As Foster was led off in handcuffs, Moody turned to his erstwhile thorn-in-the-side, and said, 'I suppose you realise that this means two exhumations? He had his uncle cremated.'

'If justice is to be done, Inspector, they are inevitable. Should you need any more evidence, I have the original cocktail glass out of which Mr Reginald Pagnell took his last drink on this earth. It is currently locked in my safe for security reasons, and if you analyse what it once contained, I think that your laboratory will discover, not only poison, but the traces of a cocktail called Strangeways to Oldham,' she informed him, didactically.

'If you had only listened to me in the first place, maybe two of these three unfortunate deaths could have been avoided.' She was at her most imperious, as she addressed him, and he was suitably chastened by what he had discovered.

That did not, however, make him feel any more kindly disposed towards her, and at her pretty little victory speech, he merely made a sour grimace, and left the premises, promising that she would be required to give evidence, should her speculation about how the three men had died prove to be correct.

He had also had PC Glenister in tow, and as he left, in pursuit of his superior, he looked at Lady Amanda and gave her a huge wink. 'I enjoyed that!' he murmured, as he went out through the door, then looked back over his shoulder and mouthed, 'Nice one, Lady Amanda!'

It was Wednesday evening, and all three of the occupants of Belchester Towers were sufficiently recovered and rested from their ordeal, to consider re-instating cocktail hour, which had been in abeyance for the last couple of days.

'I think we shall have champagne cocktails tonight, Beauchamp,' ordered Lady Amanda, sounding just like an elderly duchess bossing her staff around, so puffed up was she, at her own cleverness, and her triumph over the illmannered Inspector Moody. 'And do have one yourself,' she added magnanimously, as Beauchamp turned to leave the room.

Almost inaudibly, he muttered, 'I always do, my lady. And the name's still Beecham.'

'Well, Hugo,' she said, 'How are you enjoying living here?'

'It can be quite exciting,' replied Hugo diplomatically.

'Is everything to your satisfaction?' she asked, rather overdoing the Lady Bountiful impression.

'Except for the unusual experience of being pursued by a murderer,' he said, nodding his head for emphasis.

'That is not,' she retorted, 'part of the normal routine at The Towers. No, I meant everything else – food, laundry, your room, and so on.'

'Oh, that's all marvellous, and I do seem to be a lot more sprightly than I was, when I arrived here.'

'You must be, Hugo,' Lady Amanda purred, 'if you've been leaving your invalid walker upstairs, and I don't believe we've used that wheelchair since you had that appointment with that rather strange Dr Updyke.' 'No, we haven't,' Hugo concurred.

'Champagne cocktails, my lady, Mr Hugo,' announced Beauchamp, entering the room with his usual silent tread, and making Lady Amanda, whose chair wasn't facing the door, start with surprise.

'Don't do that, Beauchamp. I've told you before. If you must move silently, please cough, or do something else to announce that you are about to appear in our midst without the slightest of warnings.'

'Yes, my lady.'

Lady Amanda and Hugo accepted their drinks, noticing that there was one left on the tray. Lady Amanda lifted her glass and toasted them with, 'Chin-chin,' (but in the French way – 'shin-shin'), which left Hugo staring uncomprehendingly at his lower legs. 'Glad to see you took me at my word, and mixed one for yourself,' she said, but fell silent when there was a ring at the doorbell.

'Who can that be, at this time of night?' asked Lady Amanda, not expecting any answer.

'How can we possibly know that before we open the door?' replied Hugo, his usual common sense making itself known.

'No, I mean, we're having our little drinkies late, tonight. It's nearly ten o'clock. No one should be making house calls at this time of night.'

'Let's all go,' suggested Hugo, and they took him at his word, all three of them heading for the front door, Beauchamp still holding aloft his tray with his drink, as yet un-tasted.

It was Lady Amanda who actually opened the door, peered out into the darkness, then shrieked one word, before clutching her hand to her heart. '*MUMMY!*'

Recovering at lightning speed, she added, 'But it *can't* be you, you're *dead!*'

A voice from out of the darkness, beyond the warm light spilling from the hall, spoke, as its owner took a step forward, to be recognised. 'Hugo, you've become fat. Manda, whatever have you done to the colour of your hair? It looks cheap and nasty! Ah, *Beecham*, a champagne cocktail! My favourite! How thoughtful of you.'

Beauchamp smiled as he held out the tray to her.

THE END

WHITE CHRISTMAS
WITH A
WOBBLY KNEE

A Lady Amanda Golightly Murder Mystery
The Belchester Chronicles: Book Two

ANDREA FRAZER

DRAMATIS PERSONAE

RESIDENT AT BELCHESTER TOWERS

Lady Amanda Golightly – owner

Hugo Cholmondley-Crichton-Crump – her old friend

Beauchamp – manservant and general factotum

Lady Edith Golightly – mother of Lady Amanda, and presumed dead for twenty years

GUESTS

Colonel Henry and Mrs Hilda Heyhoe-Caramac – aka Bonkers and Fluffy

Sir Jolyon and Lady Felicity *ff*olliat DeWinter – aka Blimp and Fifi

Major Montgomery and Mrs Madeleine Mapperley-Minto aka Monty and Maddie

Captain Leslie and Mrs Lesley Barrington-Blyss – aka Popeye and Porky

Sir Montacute and Lady Margaret Fotherington-Flint – aka Cutie and Daisy

Lt Col. Aloysius & Mrs Angelica Featherstonehaugh-Armitage – aka Stinky and Donkey

OTHERS

Enid Tweedie – domestic and occasional waitress

Dr Anstruther – an elderly GP

Dr Campbell Andrew – a younger GP Sundry domestics, etc.

POLICE

Detective Inspector Moody – of the Belchester CID
Police Constable Glenister – of the Belchester Police

Author's note on pronunciation of names

'**Featherstonehaugh**' is pronounced 'Fanshaw'.

'**Bradshaigh**' is pronounced 'Bradshaw'.

Someone really ought to tell Enid Tweedie! She thought she could read English!

Prologue

A Rave from the Grave

The very old lady made herself comfortable in a wingbacked chair, raised her glass, and proposed a toast. 'To the return of the prodigal!' she said, and swallowed her champagne cocktail in one gulp. 'I'll have another, if you please, Beauchamp,' she said, imperiously, handing her glass to the unperturbed manservant.

'Yes, my lady,' he intoned, taking the glass, and making to walk away.

'Hang on, Beauchamp, we have something to sort out here with regard to modes of address. I suggest that, while I'm here, you address me as "your ladyship", and my daughter as "my lady". That should sort out any misunderstandings before they happen.'

Lady Amanda, her hand raised to her cheeks with shock, her eyes staring, said, 'But, Mummy, you've been dead these twenty years. How on earth can you be here? You died in that car crash with Daddy, or am I losing my mind?'

Lady Edith and her husband had been killed in a car accident on the London to Brighton Rally some twenty or so years ago, or so everybody had believed at the time, and Amanda had become Lady Amanda, and chatelaine of Belchester Towers.

Belchester Towers had been in her family since it was built by one of her forefathers. in the early nineteenth century. It was a red-brick structure in the likeness of a castle, even having a moat and drawbridge in its early years, before everything got too difficult with deliveries and the advent of the motor car.

Lady Amanda had taken it over happily, running her estate with only the help of her manservant and general factotum, Beauchamp, and the occasional help of an army of people from nearby Belchester, who came in periodically to give the place a 'good going over'. Beauchamp arranged all this, as he did keeping the grounds mowed and clipped, and in a respectable condition.

The only regular help had been a woman from the windy backstreets of Belchester, by the name of Enid Tweedie, who had become very attached to Lady Amanda, a real friend in times of trouble. And, of trouble, there had been plenty in the recent past. Lady Amanda had not only discovered her old friend Hugo, mouldering away in a Belchester nursing home, but also another old friend, freshly despatched to the Almighty, and by human hand.

The subsequent events, which included getting Hugo moved into Belchester Towers, seeing a proper doctor, instead of the bumbling old fool he had been consulting, the ramifications of the murder, and their investigation into it, had changed her life beyond recognition.

And now, here was Lady Amanda's supposedly long dead mother, actually back in her old surroundings, taking over the situation, as she always had done in life. What had Lady Amanda done to deserve this, she wondered, still unable to believe that this was not a nightmare from which she would soon awake, and laugh off, in the light of day. She waited, in complete disbelief, for her mother's explanation of how events were now flowing, and apparently had been, these last two decades.

'Oh, Manda,' her mother replied, completely unruffled, 'you always were naive and gullible. Somebody died in that car crash, but it certainly wasn't me; was it, Beauchamp?' she added.

'No, your ladyship,' confirmed Beauchamp, without turning a hair.

'You mean you knew about this, Beauchamp: and you never uttered a word to me about it, in all this time?'

'That is correct, my lady,' replied Beauchamp, his face a blank.

'How could you! And just exactly who *did* die in that car, then, because they certainly buried somebody, and everyone – with the exception of secretive old Beauchamp here – thought it was you. I'm losing my mind – I know I am. This is all an hallucination, and I shall wake up in the nut-hut!'

'That was my personal maid, Manda. Didn't you notice how furtive she and Daddy were, when they were in the same room together. They were always sneaking off, too. Oh, I knew they were having an affair. That's why I ran away during the night, before the day of the rally. I'd got wind of the fact – thank you very much for that, Beauchamp – that they were going to run away together on that rally, and I wasn't going to be stuck here, with only that ghastly county set for company.'

'So where have you been all this time?'

'Why, the Riviera, of course, Manda. I'd already salted away a great deal of money on the continent, and I just needed to get out with some of my clothes and my jewels. Your father didn't even notice I'd gone, I'm sure. We had separate bedrooms, after all. I just got someone to drive me to the station in the middle of the night, and I had all my arrangements made by letter and telephone, for the other end. By the way, thank you again, Beauchamp, for your part as secret chauffeur.'

'I simply don't believe this!' Lady Amanda was incensed. 'My own mother and my own manservant, in cahoots, deceiving me for two decades, and I suspected nothing.'

'Well, least said, soonest mended,' commented her mother, playing a new tune on an old saw.

'And, no doubt you'll expect to be known as Lady Edith again?' Manda was catching on fast.

'Well, it is my name, and I'm entitled to use it, as the dowager, now your father's dead.'

'And where exactly does that leave me?' (There may be trouble ahead – cue violins!)

'In just the same place that you are now, and have been for the last twenty years,' said the dowager, giving her daughter the ghost of a smile. She might have known that her daughter's first thought would have been for her own position.

'Well, that's all right then. But how long are you planning to stay? You're not moving in forever, are you?' Thus, Lady Amanda betrayed feelings it would have been better to suppress, but Lady Edith was a thick-skinned woman, and just ignored the slight.

'Only until they've finished renovating my new apartment in Monte Carlo. I've recently moved, you know. It'll only be a few weeks – a few months, at the most.'

Lady Amanda didn't know whether to be relieved or horrified. How would she cope with her mother back here, and no doubt trying to run her life for her again? She must be as old as the hills. What right had she to turn up here from the grave and look so sprightly?

'I think you'd better make that three – no, four – more champagne cocktails, Beauchamp. And tell me, why does Manda insist on calling you Beauchamp? I never did.'

'No, your ladyship, but your husband always insisted on the French pronunciation, so I suppose she just carried on the paternal tradition.'

'Stuff and nonsense. Now, fetch those drinks, there's a good man, before I die of thirst!'

Lady Amanda was sorely tempted by this remark, but with an enormous effort of will, managed to keep her thoughts to herself.

'It's good to see you again, Lady Edith.' Hugo spoke for the first time since Lady Amanda had opened the front door and been confronted with what she at first thought was the shade of her mother. 'I always enjoyed my visits to Belchester Towers.'

'You're here rather late, though, aren't you? When are you going home?' Lady Edith was even more forthright than her daughter, and wasted no time on small talk.

Hugo looked pointedly at Lady Amanda, considering that it should be she who explained the current situation to her mother. 'Hugo lives here now, Mummy,' she said, but got no further.

'What, you two, living "over the brush" at your time of life? You should be ashamed of yourselves.'

This really made her daughter bristle. 'It's nothing like that, Mummy, and I'd have thought you'd have known better than to suggest such a thing. I found Hugo marooned in the most ghastly nursing home, because the arthritis in his hips and knees had got so bad, he couldn't manage at home on his own.

'I rescued him, and brought him here, and he's seen my own doctor, and has had his first appointment with the orthopaedic consultant at the hospital. Hugo and I are platonic friends; have never been, and never will be, anything else.'

'Good girl! Now, have we still got that old Carstairs invalid chair? I shall enjoy the grounds once more, if I can press one of you to take me out in it. And, I can be a little hard of hearing. Is Great-grandmama's ear-trumpet still up in the attics? I'll get Beauchamp to fetch it for me. The battery's gone in my hearing aid, and I'll need something to get me through until I can send you on an errand to fetch me some new ones. Still got my old trikes, have you?'

'Of course, we have, Mummy. I use the black one, and I've been teaching Hugo to ride your red one. I even got *Beauchamp*,' (she pronounce the name with the greatest of emphasis), 'to transfer the motor from Daddy's bicycle to it, and make the necessary alterations.

'*Beauchamp* has also got the old lift working again, so you can have your old room back, on the first floor.'

Beauchamp returned, at this juncture, bearing a freshly laden tray, and Hugo cried out, 'Cocktail time, everybody!'

Chapter One

Settling-in Spats and Other Arguments

Beauchamp made up Lady Edith's bed and prepared her room for her and, after she had creaked her way upstairs in the lift, Lady Amanda and Hugo were left alone together, to contemplate their drastically altered immediate future.

'I don't know how I'm going to cope with her bossiness and interference again,' complained Lady Amanda.

'I know how you feel,' agreed Hugo, but not exactly thinking of those qualities in Lady Edith.

'What am I going to do, Hugo, old thing?' she wailed.

'You've always got me,' Hugo reassured her.

'Yes,' she replied, then sighed heavily. 'I know!'

There were, of course, uncomfortable moments, in this settling-down period.

'It's 'Beauchamp!' pronounced Lady Amanda, with fervour.

'No, it's not. It's 'Beecham'!' argued Lady Edith, with fervour.

'Beauchamp!'
'Beecham!'
'Beauchamp!'

'Beecham. Why do you persist with this ridiculous French pronunciation?' asked Lady Edith, her hackles rising.

'Because Daddy always called him "Beauchamp"!' Lady Amanda's hackles could rise too, and hers were years younger than her mother's.

'Beecham!'

'Beauchamp!'
'Beecham!'

'Yes, my ladies?' replied that named individual, appearing as if by magic by their sides.

'Bugger!' swore Lady Amanda, uncharacteristically, and stomped off to her room to sulk.

'I don't see how you can be standing there, so obviously alive, when I've got your Death Certificate in my bureau.'

'Not worth the paper it's written on!' replied her mother, stubbornly.

'I've still got it, and you'd better watch out, or I might just shop you to the fuzz.'

'Don't use such appalling slang, girl! I'll simply tell them that I remembered nothing since the accident, until recently, suffering from amnesia for all these years, as I have.'

'You wouldn't dare!'
'Just you try me, my girl!'

'How are you going to explain to the Queen that she'll have to send a telegram to a long-dead woman, in a few years' time? She'll probably stick you in the Tower.'

'I shall say that rumours of my death were somewhat exaggerated, but that I'm feeling much better now, thank you.'

'Oh, Mummy, you are absolutely impossible!'

'But you've *got* to go, Mummy. I've got my *own* life to live now that you're dead. And if you don't take yourself back off to the Continent, I shall make public, the fact that you ran a knocking shop here for the American servicemen, during the war. And I shall tell about Daddy and his Black Market deals.

And what if it were to be made known that he had worked as an arms dealer after the War? What would people say to that? If all your secrets came out, apart from the fact that you're simply not DEAD, where would you be?' Lady Amanda was furious, and having one of her tantrums.

'I should be a frail old lady with memory loss, or, if I fled, simply a figment of your imagination. You, however, should all this get to official ears, would be stripped of your title, and I'm sure the tax office would be more than happy to strip your comfortable bank account as well, to cover all the unpaid taxes from Daddy's and my illegal activities. Now, how do you like *them* potatoes?' Lady Edith smiled angelically at her daughter, then licked her right index finger, and drew a vertical line in the air. 'My house-point, I rather think, my dear!'

'I just can't stand it any more, Hugo. Every time someone comes to the house, I have to shove Mama behind a door or into a cupboard, in case someone sees her and rumbles what's going on up here. She seems to think it's a hoot, but it's playing merry hell with my nerves. My life seems to be one endless game of 'Hunt the Slipper', with Mama being the slipper: and she's got wheels too. What if she thinks it's a jolly jape to wheel herself out into open view? The gaff will be well and truly blown, and we shall all end up in gaol – except you, of course – with a list of charges against us as long as your arm. I just can't stand the tension: I'm permanently on an adrenalin overload.'

'May I suggest more cocktails,' suggested Hugo, considering this idea with his head cocked to one side. 'It won't alter the situation at all, of course, but it will probably reduce your ability to fret over it, and give you a calmer and more relaxed view of things.'

'What? And let my mother turn me into a raging alcoholic?'
She thought for a moment, then declared, 'Well, just until she
goes, I suppose it's not a bad idea. Good man, Hugo! Have a
Grasshopper! BEAUCHaaargh!

Dear God, man, my nerves are in shreds already. For the love
of all that's holy, would you please not sneak up on me like that.
In my current condition I'm liable to have a heart attack, and
then where would your job be? Answer me that one! '

'I shall need a bit of cash before I go. You know how
expensive moving ... Of course you don't! You've never lived
anywhere but here, but I can assure you, it's a very costly business,
and I could do with a bit of a top-up, if you'd be so kind,' Lady
Edith asked, one day after afternoon tea.

Delighted at the thought of seeing the back of her mother,
Lady Amanda asked how much she required, while Hugo looked
on with keen interest.

'About a million should do it, I think. For now,' replied the
ancient dowager.

Hugo's mouth fell open with amazement and horror. How
on earth she could have the brass-necked cheek, after all these
years of being dead, to ask her daughter for such an enormous
amount of money, he had no idea.

'I'll just get my cheque book, and I'll give the old boy at the
bank a call in the morning, to let him know that I'm authorising
that sum to leave my account,' said Lady Amanda, and went off,
in pursuit of her cheque book, calling back, 'You'll have to tell
me who to make it out to, as I haven't the faintest idea under
what crass alias you have been living these past twenty years.'

Hugo hadn't realised that his mouth could open any further,
but it did, making him think that if he had another shock, while
in this state, his chin might, literally, hit the floor.

Chapter Two

Problems with Workmen and Post-operation Blues

Hugo's first hip replacement operation had taken place in the autumn. Lady Edith had got her feet well under the table by then and, when Lady Amanda had enquired, as politely as she could, when they would be seeing the back of the old bird, she was always ready with some excuse; for example, 'The plumber's on holiday for three weeks, and the electrician can't get on with his work until the plumber comes back,' or 'The plasterer's in Paris on an urgent job, and he'll be gone for at least a month.'

'You seem to suffer from an awful lot of bad luck with your workmen, Mummy,' Lady Amanda had commented sourly, but to the old lady it was just like water off a duck's back. Her daughter was taking things remarkably well, publicly, considering that, only a few short months ago, she had been 'Queen of the Shit Heap', as Lady Edith coarsely described it, and here she was now, back under her mother's eagle eye, and with Hugo twittering at her all the time; but her outward patience wouldn't last forever.

The priority at the moment, however, was Hugo. Having just been discharged from hospital within only days of his surgery ('We need the beds, sir.') there were certain delicate problems to be sorted out, with regard to his mobility, while he recuperated.

Social Services had kindly sent round a commode for Hugo's use, and it was this that had caused the current outburst of rebellion: that, and the metal crutches that had arrived with it.

'I am NOT using that thing!' Hugo had never expressed himself with such volume and anger before, and he pointed at the object of his anger, the commode, as he shouted. 'I will not have THAT THING in my bedroom, with its potty sticking out through the seat for all to see. I may be old, but I insist on retaining my dignity.'

Wading in, with her fingers crossed behind her back for luck, Lady Amanda made a suggestion. 'We have a very old commode in the attic. It just looks like a cube of carved wood – a bit like a large, ornate box. Nobody would ever guess it was a commode.'

'That sounds more acceptable, but I'll have to see it first,' replied Hugo, slightly mollified, and hoping that, as usual, Lady Amanda would come to his rescue.

'I'll get Beauchamp to fetch it down for you,' she soothed him.

'And I'm not walking with those blasted things, either,' said Hugo, pointing to the crutches.

'Why ever not?' she asked.

'Because they'll make me look like a silly old man, who's fallen over and injured himself. I will not go round looking like a victim of my age! And that's final! I had enough of that with that damned Zimmer frame.'

'Beau ...'

'Already here, my lady.' Beauchamp spoke quietly from just behind her right shoulder.

'Oh, you did give me a fright! I've told you not to creep around like that. It's very unnerving.'

'Yes, my lady. How can I be of assistance?'

'Firstly, you can fetch down the carved commode from the attics, and secondly, have you still got that rack of walking canes in your pantry?'

'I have, indeed, my lady,' the manservant answered.

'Then perhaps you could fetch them along, too? The commode is for Hugo's bedroom, and the walking canes can be brought here, for his inspection. He doesn't like the utilitarian crutches, and would like something a little less "medical" to aid his walking.'

'Very good, my lady.'

Beauchamp really was a peach of an asset to the household, thought Lady Amanda, as he left them to carry out his errand.

A little later, Hugo inspected the many fine walking canes available for his use, with enthusiasm. He'd already okayed the 'po', as Lady Edith vulgarly put it, and was now choosing the canes he would like to 'test-walk'.

'I really like this one, with the silver greyhound's head on it. It's just the right height, it's as straight as a die, and it holds well.'

As he went through the sticks, Lady Edith, who had joined them when she heard Beauchamp transferring them into the drawing room, was giving a running commentary on to whom they had belonged in the past.

'That one was Great Uncle Wilbur's. He used to love going to the dog track. Terrible gambler, you know. Just as well my Jonathan came along when he did in the family. Where would the family fortunes be, if it wasn't for Golightly's Health Products?'

'Oh, shut up, Mummy, for goodness' sake, and let Hugo get on with choosing.' It was amazing how the presence of her mother could turn a woman of her age into the petulant child she once had been.

Hugo now selected one with the head of a bulldog: ivory, with ruby eyes. 'I say, this one's a really fine thing. I think I could cut quite a dash, out and about with this in my hand,' he crowed, examining it for damage and suitability.

'That one was Grandpa Golightly's – your father's father's, Manda, dear,' Lady Edith crowed, delighted to see such an old friend again. 'He bred bulldogs.'

'How do you know it's his? He was already dead when you married Daddy.' Lady Amanda was getting herself into a grand sulk.

'Because your father told me so, my dearest,' replied her mother, with the sweetest of smiles, guaranteed to annoy her daughter, and get under her skin.

'Oh, I've had enough of this! I'm going off to do something else. The sticks are usually in the butler's pantry, should you wish to change either of them, Hugo. I'll just leave you to it with Mummy dearest.'

Chapter Three

New Horizons

Over the period of his convalescence and beyond, Hugo constantly suggested to Lady Amanda that she open up part of the house to the public. He knew she didn't need the money, but she did need something to take her interest – something that she could get her teeth into, and keep both her mind and her body active. Her mother was driving her to distraction, and she had too little to do.

After all the change, with Hugo moving in, and working on solving murders, life, with the exception of the prickle in her side that was her female parent, had settled down to a gnawing boredom.

'Why don't we get this place spruced up a bit – just some of it, you know – and we could do little tours for the public. Someone could take them round the bits you've selected, and give them the history of the place and the Golightly family, and perhaps we could serve cream teas as well; let them walk round the grounds, that sort of thing, don't yer know?' he suggested, one morning after breakfast, when Lady Edith requested that her repast should be served on a tray in her room.

'What?' replied Lady Amanda. 'Fill the place with light-fingered plebs, you mean?'

'Of course not, Manda. If you charge a decent fee for admission, then the plebs won't want to pay to come and look around. If you can manage the guided tours yourself, you could ask a good whack, what with you having a title and everything. It'll give you a purpose in life.'

'I wasn't aware that I needed a purpose in my life, Hugo. What makes you think I do?'

'Well, for one thing, your mother's driving you crazy. You could explain to her that, if she's still here when the tours start, she'll have to keep herself well-hidden, in case someone sees her and recognises her. It's all right her swanning around the Riviera and Monaco. She's unlikely to meet anyone from round here, there, and even if she did, she'd be able to pass it off as a case of mistaken identity.

'If anyone saw her in Belchester Towers itself, she'd have no defence. There's no coincidence that great, that her double should be staying here, so long after your mother's death. She has to remember that she is one of the dear departed, in local eyes, and she has to stay that way until her apartment's ready, and she can go off and leave us in peace.'

'You've certainly got a point there, Hugo. I believe the idea is beginning to grow on me,' she told him. 'Let's have a toddle round the place this morning, and see which bits could be tickled up to show to the paying public. Yes, I'm definitely warming to the idea. When do you think we could be ready?'

'We'll have to see how much needs to be done first, and how much of the place you're willing to show off,' Hugo advised her, not wanting her to make any hasty decisions that would leave them with too much to do, and too little time in which to do it.

'Good idea, old stick! The only thing that would be more fun would be another murder,' 'Heaven forbid!' replied Hugo.

But the gods don't like to be challenged, and can be quite contrary, should they feel in the mood to meddle in human affairs.

Their own personal tour of the house rewarded them with much useful information for their proposed venture into the tourist industry. The structure of the building had been kept in good fettle by Lady Amanda, during her reign here, and there was no visible damp.

'That's the benefit of the place not being a thousand years old,' she told him, as they walked round. 'This was only built two hundred years ago, and I believe no expense was spared in making it impervious to the invasion of damp and general mould. Daddy also did a lot of work when there was a problem in the banqueting hall, and he always kept the roof in good repair, as have I. In fact, it was Daddy who put this family back on its feet again, but

I'll tell you about that some other time.'

Getting back to the subject of the house, Hugo said, happily, 'There's quite a lot you could show then, with the removal of the dust sheets, and a bit of a clean-up.'

'There's actually too much of it to show, in my opinion. I'm absolutely exhausted,' moaned Lady Amanda, as they finally got back to the drawing room, and she could flop down into a chair to rest her feet.

'That's even better, Manda,' commented Hugo, cryptically.

'How is that better? My feet feel like they've been beaten for hours with sticks of bamboo.'

'You could have two or three different tours on offer, for different days, or different weeks. That way you could get people to come here two or three times, paying every time they come back.'

'Hugo, you're a right little entrepreneur, aren't you?'

'Thank you very much, Manda. It's very kind of you to say so.'

'What's that?' quavered a voice from a chair by the door, which they had not noticed was occupied.

'Oh, Mummy, you nearly frightened the life out of me.
You're getting as bad a Beauchamp.'

'Beecham! And I couldn't help overhearing. What are you two up to? Anything exciting?' asked Lady Edith.

'Nothing that involves you, Mummy, or, in fact, could involve you. I'm thinking of opening the house to the public, and we couldn't possibly risk you being seen alive, so you'll just have to keep out of the way whenever we do it, or I shall be compelled to murder you.'

'I say! That's jolly unfair, and not very like you, Manda. I'd have imagined you'd hate the idea of the general public swarming all over your family home, putting their sticky fingerprints all over everything, and nicking the bibelots.'

'Not at all, Mumsy. Hugo's suggested a way we can do it without having to suffer the hoi polloi, and you can just put up with it, or beetle off to your apartment in Monte Carlo, and leave us in peace.'

'That's no way to speak to your poor, aged mother, Manda!' Lady Edith chided her.

'Agreed! But then, I'm not speaking to my poor aged mother, am I? I'm speaking, instead, to my fairly well-off, and soon to be even better-off, *dead* mother and, believe me, that makes a huge difference.'

'That's right! Shut me away in the attics, with only bread and water to live on. Treat me like a prisoner in my own home. Children can be so cruel these days.' Lady Edith was really displaying a wealth of self-pity of which Lady Amanda would not have thought her capable, had she not remembered that her mother had once been part of the Belchester Players, an amateur dramatic group that used to put on plays now and again in the city's theatre.

'Well, yah, boo, and sucks to you!' exclaimed Lady Amanda, very childishly, and promptly left the room, in search of a cocktail, even though it wasn't yet lunchtime.

Enid Tweedie was summoned (of course!) for the preparations for opening the house, and was soon to be found under everyone's feet, with a mop and bucket, singing old Eurovision Song Contest numbers much too loudly, and dramatically out of tune.

This stalwart had worked for Lady Amanda for more years than she cared to count, first as a cleaner who came in to do 'the rough', now rather more in the role of Beauchamp: that of general factotum and friend of convenience. She never felt put upon by Lady Amanda, because she had been treated so well by her, during and after her many trips to hospital for minor operations. The latest one had been for ingrowing toenails, and she was only just back on her feet after that.

Lady Amanda spent the bulk of her time at the library table, covering it with a multitude of sheets of paper, planning the various tours that could be offered, and the commentary that would accompany the proposed guests round the various parts of the house.

Hugo, meanwhile, had had his second hip-replacement operation, and spent a lot of his time reading, with a little gentle exercise every now and then. He'd found some local history books in the library, sadly out of date, but, nonetheless, fascinating (for history tends not to change), and often spent his reading time in a porter's chair in the library, interrupting lady Amanda every few minutes, to read out something to her, or ask her opinion on an item he had just read.

Time passed, Mummy stayed on, like a barnacle on the bottom of a ship, and soon it was approaching December, the clocks gone back, and darkness falling slightly earlier every day, making their daily round almost dream-like. It was definitely time to make something happen to wake them all up, and get the wheels in motion for what they had been planning for months, now.

Even the thought of Christmas approaching could not really motivate Lady A. Life had become too predictable, and she was filled with ennui, wishing that something exciting would happen to liven things up again; not that she wished anyone dead, just to provide her with a murder to investigate. She was just hungry for a more dramatic side to her daily round – anything, to relieve the boredom that she felt she might not be able to shake off before the grave. In her opinion, life had been a bit too SOS (Same Old S**t) for some time now, and it was about time things livened up.

Chapter Four

Planning the Changes

'December, Manda!' exclaimed Hugo, over breakfast on the first of that month. 'If we don't do something soon, it'll be next year in no time at all.'

'I don't see what we can do at this time of year. No one will want to come out in this weather. It's freezing cold, dark, and miserable. I thought we'd probably open in the springtime,' she replied.

'But what about a rehearsal, just to get us in the mood.'

'A rehearsal? Whatever do you mean by that, Hugo?'

'Not sure! But give me this morning to think it over, and I'm sure to come up with something. I'll make some notes, and put it to you at cocktail time, when you're less likely to bite my head off.'

'I do not bite your head off, you old fake,' Lady Amanda denied, then, seeing the expression on her friend's face, flushed a little, and added, 'Well, not often, anyway.'

'There you go, then. We'll have a nice little natter over cocktails, this evening, and my head shall remain safe for the whole day.' 'Hugo!'

At six o'clock that evening, Hugo and Lady Amanda entered the drawing room to find it empty, and Beauchamp hot on their trail with a tray containing only two glasses. 'Where's Mummy?' enquired his employer, wishing her mother to Hell, for a nice little holiday. She should find plenty of like-minded people there that she would get on well with.

'Her ladyship is taking her cocktail and dinner in her room tonight. She has been busy all day, trying to finalise details of the completion of work on her new apartment, and is making haste to arrange travel plans,' replied the dignified Beauchamp.

Waiting until he was out of earshot, Lady A turned to Hugo, and punched a fist in the air. 'Thank goodness for that!' she said, with glee. 'The old witch is back off to the Continent!'

'Jolly D, Manda!' Hugo agreed with her, doing a little dance with his lower legs, as he sat in an armchair. 'Perhaps things can get back to something like normal now, with those murders over and done with, and your mother back amongst the living dead.'

'And we can get on with our plans to open up this place, so that it doesn't seem like quite such a mausoleum,' she suggested.

'I've been thinking about that,' declared Hugo, 'as I said I would this morning, and I believe I've got a jolly good idea for how to have a rehearsal, and spread the word amongst the "right sort" of people, who've always wanted to have a good nose round in here.'

'Shoot!' crowed Lady Amanda, necking her cocktail in one swallow, and ringing the bell to summon Beauchamp, so that she could have another celebratory swallow. She was feeling quite giddy with glee, at the thought of getting rid of her mother, and planned to make sure the giddiness could also be attributed to alcohol.

'They don't hunt any more round these parts, do they, after the ban and everything?' Hugo enquired.

'Oh, how I miss the thrill of the chase. How could they possibly have made it illegal?' wailed Lady Amanda, Hugo having accidentally provided her with one of her favourite soap boxes.

'But you said you hated all that horsey stuff with the girls at school. I didn't know you rode,' Hugo said, perplexed. He clearly remembered her saying how she hated the way the girls were goofy about their ponies.

'That still stands. I couldn't be bothered with all that jumping over fences that were only six inches high, then getting a soppy rosette for it. And I still can't see the point of point-to-point. It's like having a racing car, and only ever driving it at thirty miles an hour.

'But hunting? That's a completely different kettle of horse-flesh. There's nothing like galloping across the countryside astride a fine hunter, sailing over fences and hedges, never knowing whether you're going to come a cropper. Now, that's real riding! And now, alas, it is no more,' she stated, with a tragic note in her voice.

'We did have a drag-hunt for a couple of years, but it just wasn't the same, so, now, we just don't bother. There is a Hunt Ball, but there's no Hunt as such, now. The MFH says it's not the same, now they can't tear an innocent animal to pieces at the end, so he's given up organising anything. And all the hounds have had to be euthanized. I bet people wouldn't be sniffy about hunting if they realised how many hounds had to be murdered, because there was no longer any use for them: but they don't think about that. It's all about the blasted verminous fox!

'So now the farmers have to shoot them, or trap them or use poison. It's taken a lot of the colourful history out of the countryside and, I think, made things worse for the fox, for they can shoot a darned sight more than they could have hunted, and I believe the poor things are having rather a thin time of it.

'I got rid of my hunter, you know, after last year's dreary drag-hunt. Christmas was tedious enough without Mummy and Daddy, but without the Hunt, it's going to be absolutely deathly.'

'Thanks for the potted history. A 'yes' or a 'no' would have sufficed,' scowled Hugo, who was getting a bit fed up with Lady A's mini-lectures. It seemed that he couldn't ask a straight question any more, and receive a straight answer. Everything came with embellishments.

'Why did you ask, then?' enquired Lady Amanda, now looking a little confrontational.

'Only because I've had the most marvellous idea, that won't only cheer up Christmas a good deal, but that could lead to us opening, and making a go of this place.' 'Continue,' was his companion's curt reply.

'Why don't we get the place freshly polished and dusted for the Season of Goodwill, which no doubt would have happened anyway, and invite some of the local nobs round on Boxing Day for a tour of the place and afternoon tea? That'll give you something to look forward to on the twenty-sixth, and take your mind of the fact that there's not even a drag-hunt for you to go galloping off on.

'There'd be no charge, of course, but we could let it be known, when they arrive, that we are trying out the idea which, if it gets good feedback, will be a reality in the spring. If they spread the word for us, we'll not only get the right sort of people, but it will be good for the area in general; bring more people into Belchester and the surrounding countryside.'

'What a topping idea, Hugo! You're a pocket genius, you are! And we've still got a few weeks to organise everything.' Lady Amanda was all smiles now. 'That would definitely give Boxing Day a bit of sparkle, rather than the anti-climax I was dreading.'

It was ages since she had entertained anyone but a few friends for cocktails or a cup of coffee or tea. The thought of having a gathering on Boxing Day seemed a sparkling idea to her. Christmas had been rather a dull affair ever since Mummy and Daddy had gone, and she felt a surge of enthusiasm for showing off the old place, decorated like it should be, and with a bit more life in it.

'And what about the old kitchen and scullery, and all those other
domestic offices? Beauchamp has a thoroughly modern kitchen
and I know he doesn't use the butler's pantry any more, because you keep all the silver in the strong-room', said Hugo, suddenly full of enthusiasm for this new idea.

'What about them? They're antediluvian, so they've all been shut up for donkey's years.'

'Exactly!' yelled Hugo, leaping, in slow motion, out of his chair in his excitement.

'Hugo, either I'm an idiot, or I can't see what you're seeing. Explain yourself.'

'That's all the go, these days, isn't? Looking back into the past, at how things used to be done. There're scads of programmes on the television about just that sort of thing. And what about collectors? They just love what I believe they call 'kitchen-alia'. You could work full-time just doing tours of the old domestic offices, and maybe the servants bedrooms – a "How They Used to Live" sort of tour. It would be a smash-hit! People would love it! And you could even let the plebs come in on that one, because it's not as if you're showing off the family jewels, is it?'

'Is this really true?' asked Lady Amanda, not really believing that people would pay good money to look at some old whisks and hair sieves.

'Of course it is, Manda. Give Enid a ring and ask her what she thinks about the idea, then you'll see.'

Lady Amanda moved over to the old-fashioned telephone – one of those that still had its handset actually attached to the instrument – and dialled Enid Tweedie's number (on the exceedingly old-fashioned round dial).

'Hello, Enid. Lady Amanda here. Tell me what you think of this little idea of Hugo's. He's suggested that ...'

A few minutes later, she replaced the receiver and looked at Hugo with a new respect. 'I don't know how you knew it, but it seems that you're spot on. Let's go and open up the domestic offices now, and see what sort of state they're in. I told Enid we'd have a look, and I'd ring her back if we wanted her to come up here and lend a hand.'

'But it's nearly time for dinner, Manda!'

'Yes, and in the time between now and the gong, I suggest we trot along and make use of what little time we have, and not sit here thinking about our stomachs, even if yours presents itself as a ready subject for conversation.'

'Meow!' was Hugo's only reply, and he struggled out of his chair, grabbed the walking canes he had grown accustomed to using, and began to follow her, as she left the room with one of 'those' looks on her face.

Lady Amanda had to give the door to the old kitchen a bit of a heave-ho with her shoulder before it would yield to her, and what they found revealed to them was an almost perfect Victorian kitchen, the only additions being a great deal of dust, and spiders' webs draped about the room like grey lace. In more than one nook or cranny, there was a furtive scuffling noise as the mice, the only occupants of this hithertofore deserted region of the house, made themselves scarce – race memory, coming down through several generations, warning them of the dangers of traps and cats, and especially the people who allowed these horrors to be inflicted on their species.

'Good grief, Hugo! Just look at this place!' exclaimed Lady Amanda, horrified at the condition of the kitchen. 'It looks like it belongs to Miss Havisham! We'll never get this cleaned up.'

'Don't be such a party-pooper, Manda. You can work miracles with a bit of application and an array of modern cleaning products. Remember how we changed Enid's place for her when she was in hospital? That was almost unrecognisable when we'd finished, and now she's offered to help you if you want her to. I'm sure Beauchamp will throw himself into it with enthusiasm too, if you ask him nicely.'

'I do not ask, Hugo: I command.'

'Well command nicely, then. No one likes a bossyboots,' Hugo reminded her.

'Do you really think this midden will clean up?'

'Of course it will. It just needs time and elbow-grease. Show a bit of enthusiasm for what could be the jewel in
    the crown of your house tours.'

'I'll just call Beau ... Argh!'

'Here, my lady,' said a voice just behind her right shoulder.

'Beauchamp! Don't do that! How can you sneak up on people without them having any idea you're there?' Lady Amanda asked him, her right hand clutched to her left breast, as she recovered from the shock. 'By nature, you're more of a Golightly than I am.'

'I've always been very light on my feet, my lady,' he explained, walking in his usual dignified manner to a space between the two of them. 'How may I be of service?'

'We rather wanted your opinion on whether it would be a good idea to open these old domestic offices to the public, for a guided tour.'

'I should say it needed a little light dusting first, my lady. Old kitchens, coal cellars, stables, and all sorts of sites of bygone domestic slavery are all the go, at the moment, I understand,' was Beauchamp's considered opinion.

'Domestic slavery! Domestic slavery? Is that what you consider yourself to be in, Beauchamp?' she squeaked in indignation.

'Heaven forbid that such a thing should cross my mind. I was, of course, referring to times gone by. And, should you be considering such a venture, may I suggest that the scullery, butler's pantry, the flower room, the boot room, and quite a number of other domestic offices might also prove useful additions to this projected tour of yours.'

'Dashed good idea, Beauchamp! Lead on! Frankly, I've no idea where to locate any of the places you just mentioned, but I'd love to have a little peek.'

Beauchamp led the way, charging stuck doors and pulling down curtains of cobwebs as he went, and the investigation of the domestic quarters was not abandoned until Lady Amanda caught something out of the corner of her eye, turned her head, and espied a large and hairy spider on her shoulder. 'Argh! Aargh! Aaargh! Get it off me! Get it off me! Oh, God, I'm going to faint!' she cried, while trying to run away from it, without thinking that it was firmly lodged on her shoulder and would not move without some help.

Hugo proved his lack of mettle by running into the recently opened pantry and shutting the door behind him, from which hiding place he shouted, 'For God's sake *do* something, somebody. I'm not coming out of here until it's gone.'

It was, of course, Beauchamp, who grabbed the offending arachnid in the soft cotton of his handkerchief, and shooed it out through a window. 'Maybe you might like to delay your return here until I have done a little light cleaning and dusting, my lady,' he suggested, with a very superior expression. 'I'm sure there are many other unwelcome visitors to these quarters, which you would be very unhappy to have to meet. I'll let you know when it is fit for you to get to work on it.

'And may I suggest, now, that you return to the drawing room where I have left a further cocktail to uphold you in your time of shock, and will sound the dinner gong in approximately fifteen minutes.' In these few sentences, Beauchamp went up even further in Lady Amanda's opinion, for not only had he been her saviour, but was willing to rid that part of the house of any other invading horrors before she had to go back for another look.

Back in the drawing room, cocktails awaiting them on the usual silver tray, Hugo took a gulp of his and announced, 'I say, Manda old bean, that was rather hairy, wasn't it?'

'So was that dratted spider,' she replied, draining her glass in one; something that had become a bit of a habit, of late. 'My goodness! That frightened the life out of me. And to think, things like that have been living in there for years. It's about time it was all rooted out and cleaned up.

I'll give Enid a ring after we've eaten.'

Lady Amanda was so taken up with Hugo's plans that she had completely forgotten about the possibility that her mother might leave, and was, therefore, surprised when she came down in the morning to find the hall filled with suitcases and trunks, her mother sitting on the top of one of the latter and looking at her watch.

'You off then, Mummy? So soon? And what's all that stuff you've got in your luggage? You certainly didn't arrive with much.'

'Just a few bits and pieces I couldn't take before, given the circumstances of my departure,' replied Lady Edith, haughtily. 'I could hardly take more than a fraction of my possessions when I had to run away as I did, could I?'

'Well, as long as you haven't half-inched anything of mine,' replied her daughter.

'I have taken what was mine when I lived here. If that should include anything you thought you had subsequently inherited, you will just have to wait until I'm decently dead and buried again, won't you?'

'The second part of that could be arranged first, if you'll pass me a shovel,' replied Lady Amanda, but she said it under her breath, so that her mother couldn't hear her and pick her up on it. 'As long as you haven't taken anything I really like,' she concluded.

'I'm hardly likely to do that, am I, my dearest daughter. You have the most appalling taste, in my opinion, and I should be unlikely to reclaim anything of which you were fond.'

As Lady Amanda's face began to show the unmistakable signs of one of her outbursts, Beauchamp appeared, to defuse the situation, and announced that the taxi had arrived at the door, and the driver was awaiting his fare.

The parting of parent and child was so disgustingly insincere and two-faced that Hugo was lucky not to have witnessed it, and even Beauchamp had to go to have a little sit-down after witnessing it. It was, therefore, to a slightly emptier house that Hugo appeared for breakfast that morning, intrigued by the sight of Lady Amanda apparently dancing a jig just inside the front door, and carolling, 'Ding dong! The wicked witch is gone.'

Then, like a machine which has suddenly been switched off, she paused in mid-jig, her face became a mask of horror, and she rushed up the stairs yelling, 'The ear trumpet! The ear-trumpet! She mustn't have taken that! Oh God, please don't let her have taken the ear trumpet!'

Three minutes later, she descended the staircase at a more ladylike pace, cradling the silver ear trumpet in her arms and gazing at it fondly.

'Was all that fuss about an old ear trumpet?' asked Hugo, perplexed as to her motives for this sudden attachment to an inanimate and not very interesting object.

'Do you know how much these things are worth these days, Hugo?' she asked, looking at him in a pained manner.

'Not a clue. Going to enlighten me, then?'

'In the right auction, the best part of two grand, given the company that produced this one. And it's mine! All mine! And I intend for it to stay that way!'

Chapter Five

Actually Getting Right Down to It

Up in the attics the next morning, Lady Amanda, attempting to bounce on a mattress on one of the longdeparted servants' beds, winced as she predicted a bad case of bruised buttocks.

'Surely they didn't sleep on these things?' she enquired of Hugo.

'Have you really never been up here before?' Hugo asked her, looking scandalised. 'Mind your h ...' But he was too late. Lady Amanda had risen without due care and attention, had not remembered that the bed was tucked into the eaves, and was now rubbing the top of her head, her face crumpled in pain. That's heads and tails for me, and it's only nine fifteen! she thought. Who would have thoughts that servants in this house had such daily dangers to face as giant spiders, mice, rock-hard mattresses and low-flying ceilings?

'I really don't think I'd have liked to have been in service,' she declared, moving to a part of the room that was tall enough for her to stand up properly.

'I don't think anyone would have employed you,' was Hugo's retort.

'Why ever not? I'm strong and hard-working!'

'When it suits you. You wouldn't have survived the daily grind for more than a week. No, make that more than a day,' Hugo added, as Lady Amanda did an unrehearsed little dance routine to avoid some sort of insect or another that had scuttled across the floor.

'I fear you're right, Hugo, but it doesn't mean I can't exploit the past for the profits of the future. Now *that* I will be good at.'

'I don't doubt it, but, as I said before, you'd have been an absolutely useless servant. You'd've been forever swooning and having to have your corsets loosened.' There's no answer to that!

Enid turned up just before lunchtime (quelle surprise!) and graciously accepted Lady Amanda's offer of joining them for a bite. Fortunately Beauchamp usually listened in on all telephone conversations, because his mistress could be a little forgetful at times, and it helped if he had the information with which to prod her memory. He had, therefore, prepared sufficient lunch for three people, and let Lady Amanda suppose that he had forgotten that Lady Edith had already left them.

After coffee, Enid was given a guided tour of the servants' quarters, and expressed shock, not only at how much there was to do, but also at the conditions they had lived in, which was outrageously outspoken for such a timid character.

'Never mind all that weeping and wailing and gnashing of teeth about things that are in the past and can't be changed. Do you think it could be done?' asked Lady Amanda, her foot tapping impatiently, while she waited for Enid to consider this.

'If I called in the Mothers' Union,' she eventually replied. 'They'd be glad to help out, to get some insight into how people used to live without it having to be on the telly. Why don't you see if they'd let you be an honorary
     member, Lady Amanda?'

'I'd rather eat my mother,' was her terse reply.

'Did you never want any children of your own?' asked Enid, puzzled that anyone could survive without the martyrdom of motherhood.

'Now listen to this, Enid, and listen good. When you die, they put you in a box and bury you, don't they? No, no, no! This isn't about cremation or burial. But am I right? Yes? Good!

Now, as far as I'm concerned, when you have children, *they* put you in a box, and you bury *yourself*. Me? I want a life, and an unencumbered one, at that. I'm too selfish for a family, and I'm honest enough to declare it.'

'You don't mean that,' declared Enid emphatically.

'Of course she does,' Hugo gave as his opinion, but with a smile on his face.

'If they'd be happy to muck in, though, I'd be very grateful,' accepted Lady Amanda, in as humble a manner as she could muster up at such short notice, and with the thought of volunteer (free) labour, she could muster up quite a lot of humble.

'We've got our monthly meeting on Friday, and I'll put it to them then. I'm sure they'd love to have a look inside this place. They're always asking me about it,' Enid confirmed with the smug smile of one who is sought out as the fount of all knowledge on Belchester Towers.

On Monday morning, the ladies of the Mothers' Union turned up in their best pinnies, scarves tied around their heads to protect their hair-dos from dust, all of them seeming full of vim and vigour. Lady Amanda was as pleased as punch as she surveyed the eager (and nosy) faces that turned to her as she greeted them. If they were full of vim and vigour, she had just the right cleaning products for them: Vim and (from France) Vigor, a very effective spray liquid cleaner.

She was holding a clipboard as she stood before them in the hall, with all the jobs neatly parcelled out into lots. Having explained the rooms she would like 'bottomed', as Enid referred to the thorough cleansing of a room, she handed the clipboard to Enid, chirped, 'You're in charge,' and made to walk back down the hall.

'Where are you going, Lady Amanda? I thought you were going to lend a hand and supervise; not me,' Enid called after her, her face falling. She had rather been looking forward to showing off to her friends in the MU just how friendly she and Lady Amanda were.

'Too much to do, Enid, my dear. Got to get the Christmas decorations down from the loft, hang the darned things, get the trees sorted out, write the cards, write the invitations for this Boxing Day fling – you won't mind helping out as a waitress, will you?'

'Of course not, it's just that I thought you were going to be working with us.'

'Don't be silly, Enid. I've got much more important things to do,' this called over her shoulder dismissively, as she once more disappeared into the bowels of the house in search of Beauchamp. She'd need him to help with all the boxes and things to be retrieved from the attics. And all the dashing about from floor to floor. After all, why keep a dog and bark yourself?

Hugo was waiting for her on the first floor by the lift, Beauchamp on the second floor landing by the door that led to the attics. Standing half-way between them on the second flight of stairs, she addressed her troops.

'Right! Today is "Operation Christmas Decorations". I shall retrieve them from the attics, as I know exactly where they are all kept. I shall bring them to Beauchamp,' here she nodded at the manservant, like a dowager acknowledging a peasant, 'Beauchamp will take them down to you, Hugo,' (again, the regal nod), 'and Hugo, you will load them into the lift.

'Give us a yell when it's full, and send it downstairs, so that Beauchamp can trot down and unload it, then send it back up to you. It should only take three or four trips, and we shall be done.'

'Three or four lifts' worth? Exactly how many rooms do you decorate at Christmas, Manda?' Hugo called up to her, a look of alarm on his face, at all the work to come.

Finger on forehead to promote thinking, Lady Amanda intoned, 'The drawing room, the dining room, the morning room, the library, the study, the snug, the hall ...'

'OK, Manda. I get the idea. It's lucky you thought to get them down today. It'll take until Christmas Eve to get that lot done.'

'Nonsense, Hugo. We've got our little entertainment to sort out, invitations to send out, cards to write, and food and present shopping to do yet, so you'd better stop wasting time asking silly questions, so that we can get started.' And she whizzed up the final half-flight of stairs and disappeared through the door that led to the attics.

Only half an hour later, she had left the door to the steps to the attic open, and was sitting on the bottom step puffing and blowing like a grampus. Between gasps for air, she complained to Beauchamp, 'I seem to have aged ten years since we did this last year. I don't know where all my energy's gone.'

'May I suggest that my lady has had a rather busy time of it, this year, and that events have somewhat sapped her normal energy levels,' offered Beauchamp, sympathetically.

'Somewhat pompously put, but I do believe you're right. We have had some rather taxing and exciting times.'

'What's going on up there? I've been waiting ages for the next lot,' echoed up the stairwell from the floor below.

Beauchamp took over, knowing that he would have to rearrange things for the sake of efficiency and Lady Amanda's health, and called down, 'We're all going to go downstairs now, and I'll sort out a different team, using a couple of women from the Mothers' Union. We should have it done in no time, and I know you've got lists, and lists of things, to make.

'You've got the invitation list to work out, and you'll have to do a route for the tour, a script for the guide, and menus for those who are staying to tea. That should take at least this afternoon, and be sufficient work for both of you.'

'Beauchamp to the rescue as usual,' puffed Lady Amanda, struggling to rise to her feet. As she clumped heavily down the stairs to meet up with Hugo, a ghostly echo floated down behind her.

'That's Beecham!'

Hugo was more than willing to swap activities, especially since Beauchamp's suggestion involved quite a lot of sitting down. He definitely felt up to that, but he was fed up and aching from moving boxes into the lift and stacking them.

The whole exercise was playing merry hell with his back and joints – one knee in particular was giving him problems – and he knew he would enjoy sitting around planning things, which would go much easier with his arthritis.

With the two of them back in the drawing room again, Lady Amanda got herself a notepad and pencil (so that she could excommunicate with an eraser, any guest she changed her mind about) and they put their minds to those of sufficient social status to be honoured with an invitation to this exclusive gathering.

'You go first, Hugo. You've lived away a good long time, so we'll start with anyone you might like to see again – provided they're still alive, that is,' she offered, knowing that it would be her who had the final say, but she might as well let Hugo feel that he was having it as much his way, as she was, hers.

'What about Bonkers and Fluffy?' he asked, after a few moments of thought.

'Nice one, Hugo! They're connected all over the place. Just the sort of people we want to talk about our new little venture,' and she wrote on her notepad: *Colonel Henry and Mrs Hilda Heyhoe-Caramac*. 'Now, whom shall we have next?'

'Umm. Er. Got it! Blimp and Fifi. They were always good for a laugh.'

'Bulls-eye for the second time. You're good at this,' and she wrote again: *Sir Jolyon and Lady Felicity ffolliat DeWinter*. 'My turn now, I think. What about Monty and Maddie?'

'It would be good to see them again. I haven't seen them for, oh, must be thirty years, now,' Hugo agreed with alacrity, and Lady Amanda's pen moved again, as she wrote: *Major Montgomery and Mrs Madeleine Mapperley-Minto*. 'You can have another go, now, Hugo, old stick.'

Hugo scratched at his forehead, wracking his brains to come up with another name from his past. Finally he looked up and said, 'Popeye and Porky. Not long married when I lost touch with them, as I remember. Rather good to see how that worked out. They any good?'

'I'd say. I didn't even know you knew them. Although there are all those rumours about a book ... No, forget I said that.'

'Met them last time I visited the area, at old Stinky's, but that was an age ago.'

'I'll put them down. I don't know that I trust him very much, but she's all right, and their presence ought to cause a bit of a stir – not the most popular of guests in the area.' Again, she wrote: *Captain Leslie and Mrs Lesley Barrington-Blyss.*

'Why's that?' asked Hugo, curious.

'No idea,' she lied, having listened to all the gossip she found
available to her, 'but I mean to find out, and Boxing Day will give
us the ideal opportunity, won't it? And, as you mentioned him,
what about old Stinky and Donkey?'

'Oh, yes. Hilarious couple! Had a grand time when I last
went to theirs, although, as I said, it was a long time ago.'

'They haven't changed, Hugo: only got a bit older, like we
all have,' Lady Amanda assured him, turning once more to her
list and noting down: *Lt Col. Aloysius and Mrs Angelica
Featherstonehaugh-Armitage.* 'Now, one last couple, and I think
a dozen's enough, don't you?' 'Ra-ther!' agreed Hugo.

Both of them had been lapsing into a state of deep thought
between suggestions, but finally, that splendid chap, Mr
Cholmondley-Crichton-Crump, opened his eyes wide, as if he
had had what one used to think of as 'a lightbulb turning on'
moment but, now, could no longer be pertinent to describe such
an occurrence, what with the time it took to get any light
brighter than a glow-worm's, for what seemed like ages, out of
one those new-fangled energy-efficient jobbies.

'There's always Cutie and Daisy,' he piped up, remembering
this august personage and his rather childlike and over-feminine
wife, of whom he had always been rather in awe.

'Bingo!' she shouted in triumph, adding the final names to
her pad: *Sir Montacute and Lady Margaret
Fotherington-Flint.* 'We've done it, and in record time. I
thought it would take hours to sort out a dozen people, and here
we are, done in not much longer than twenty minutes. Right, I'll
just leave this list, with the draft invitation I've already prepared
– it's in my desk – and put it on the salver in the hall.

'Phew! What a list! I hope the printer's got some really wide invitation cards. I'm just glad I don't have to send you one, Hugo, especially if I'd have to include all your other middle names. Anyway, Beauchamp will know what it's all about, and take it to the printer's. If I put a separate note about Christmas cards, he'll get them to print the same as usual.'

'You get your Christmas cards *printed*?' asked Hugo, aghast.

'You funny old thing! Doesn't everybody? Saves so much time having to write them by hand, and the local printer's even got a facsimile of my signature, so that all I have to do is put them in the envelopes. He even prints the sticky labels for the envelopes. Costs a bit more than buying them in Smith's or somewhere like

that, but it's worth the money to avoid the annual grind.'

'I like writing Christmas cards.'

'Well, nobody's stopping you, but you'd better get on with it, or they'll have to be New Year cards instead. Do you want me to put a PS on my note to Beauchamp to pick some up while he's in Belchester?'

'Please, Manda. I seem to have lost track of the date – not an uncommon occurrence – but a dashed nuisance if it happens when one is writing a cheque. I sent one out the other week, and it was returned to me because I'd dated it for some time in 1955.'

'Hugo! You old duffer!'

At this point a mobile pile of dust, grime and cobwebs entered the room, coughed, more from necessity than manners, and Enid Tweedie's voice issued forth from it. 'Mr Bowchamp asked us if we'd like to have a bite of lunch, to save us going home and having to come back again. He said that if it was all right with you, to tell you that your lunch would be slightly delayed, but that he was sure you wouldn't mind,' and she said this all in one breath, in case Lady Amanda would think it impertinent of her to presume that she and her crew of stout mothers might presume to eat here, as well as have the privilege of cleaning decades of dirt from its back-stairs regions.

'Absolutely no problem, dear Enid.' Lady Amanda beamed at the mobile midden, so pleased was she with the completion of the guest list, which she had considered would be a much more onerous task than it had proved, and good old Hugo had been worth his weight in gold, with the suggestions he had made.

'Hugo and I were just going to plan where to put all the Christmas trees, weren't we, Hugo?'

'All?' queried Hugo, an expression of horror taking possession of his features.

Chapter Six

Right in the Thick of it

'Just how many Christmas trees do you put up every year?' asked Hugo, through a mouthful of cod in parsley sauce. 'We only ever had one really big one in the entrance hall. Drapings of holly, ivy, and mistletoe sufficed for all the other rooms of the house. Of course, the staff had a small one in their sitting room, but we didn't go mad. One was enough for us.'

'Well, it's never been enough for this family. Let me see ...' and she counted silently on her fingers, 'I think it's ten.'

'TEN?'

'And why not? We always liked Christmas to colour every room we used over the yuletide season, and I've seen no good reason to meddle with tradition.'

'*Where?*'

'Entrance hall, drawing room, dining room, breakfast room, study, snug, library, ballroom, morning room and first floor landing, so that the lights shine down on one, out of the darkness. So jolly! Oh, and I nearly forgot – two outside, each side of the entrance, to brighten up leaving or entering the house. And I suspect Beauchamp has at least one, in his own quarters.'

'And all this just for you?' Hugo was astounded.

'I'm worth it, aren't I? And anyway, it makes up for not being surrounded by a large and loving family at that particular time of year, which seems to be tailored for that sort of thing,' she replied, somewhat belligerently.

'But you'd hate that, wouldn't you? Scores of relatives everywhere, running hither and thither, and generally messing up your routines.'

'Of course I would, Hugo, but it'll be an awful lot nicer, having you here, this year.'

This compliment caused Hugo to blush rather, and he looked down at his plate, studying the remaining new potatoes and peas thereon with unwarranted interest.

'Jolly decent of you to say so, old thing.'

'Not at all! Now, eat up, and we'll have our coffee and half an hour to digest, then we'll get going on those trees.'

'Were they up in the loft, too?' asked Hugo, innocently.

This question caused Lady Amanda to burst out laughing. 'You don't think I'd allow an artificial tree house room, do you? No, these were delivered to the stable-yard yesterday afternoon when you were taking your nap, and Beauchamp is going to drag them round to the front door when he's cleared away luncheon. Then we can get on with the fun bit!'

Hugo, who couldn't see where the fun was, trying to hang things on branches that were always just out of reach, and getting oneself covered in spiky needles and, occasionally, resin, the stickiest substance known to man, volunteered for an alternative duty. 'Couldn't I work on the menus for Boxing Day afternoon, instead?'

'No, you certainly cannot! That is something that I'm particularly looking forward to myself, and I don't see why you should have all the fun of that, while I'm doing something else. Besides, you're taller than me, and can reach the higher branches easier.'

'Now, how did I know that that was exactly what you were going to say?' asked Hugo, accepting the inevitable with bad grace, and producing a sulky pout that lasted until Lady Amanda passed her compact mirror over to him, and showed him his face.

Hugo hadn't realised just how big the trees that Lady Amanda had ordered would be, and was horrified to find that most of them were about ten to twelve feet tall, with just two of them being the rather more manageable height of eight feet. When he'd gone outside to take a look, Beauchamp was lugging round a variety of containers in which to plant them, a look of resignation on his face.

As he passed Hugo, he muttered confidentially, 'I don't mind so much getting them inside and in their pots, because you do get the look of them when they're decorated to enjoy, but lugging them out again in New Year is a thankless task, and I absolutely dread it – all those pine needles everywhere, and it doesn't matter how much you clean – they keep turning up till after Easter.'

This cheered Hugo up no end, to realise that he was not the only one in the household that wasn't a hundred per cent enamoured of these seasonal decorations and, having seen the look on Beauchamp's face as he made this confession, decided to throw himself into the activity with all the enthusiasm and energy he could muster, to support the man who had to do what he was told.

It was after Beauchamp had lugged the eight giant trees into the house, only leaving the two relatively shorter ones outside, that Hugo decided to begin his good deed, and bent over to grab hold of the base of the trunk of one of them. That was his first and only mistake. With what he thought must have been an audible 'ping', his back went, and he was stuck fast, bent over the length of evergreen, unable to stand up again.

'Manda!' he cried, all the blood rushing to his head. 'Help!
I'm stuck! Help, Manda! Help me!'

Lady Amanda came scooting out of the house and was
brought up short by the sight of Hugo, bent nearly double, and
shouting his head off. 'Whatever's the matter with you?' she
asked.

'Back's gone!' he explained, using as few words as he was
able, to retain his puff. 'Can't get up! Can't move!' 'Hang on
there a moment, and I'll get you inside,' she instructed him.

'But I can't move!' he reiterated, before noticing that she
had disappeared in the direction of the stables, returning a few
moments later pushing a stout wheelbarrow.

'Lady Amanda to the rescue,' she trilled at him. 'Just stand
there, and go with the flow. Don't resist anything,' she
commanded.

'I can't even stand up, let alone resist any ... whooo!'

Hugo yelled, as the wheelbarrow hit him square behind the
knees, and he fell backwards into the old wooden contraption
which Lady Amanda had thoughtfully filled with straw, before
felling Hugo like a small tree with it.

'That hurt!' he spluttered in indignation, lying on his back
looking up at her.

'Serves you right!' she replied, unsympathetically. 'Silly old
fool, trying to drag that thing indoors. It might not be very
heavy, but you know you're not supple enough to do it. I'll have
to get Beauchamp to give you a good rub with horse liniment.
That ought to do the job!'

At that moment, Enid slipped through the front door for
a few minutes away from the dust-filled air of the domestic
quarters and, looking with amusement at Hugo, overturned like
a stranded tortoise in the wheelbarrow, ,commented, 'He's not

the first prize in the Christmas draw, is he?' before dissolving into giggles.

Lady Amanda explained what a pickle he'd got himself into, and Enid responded immediately. 'One of our retired ladies used to work as a chiropractor. Shall I ask her to get cleaned up and come and have a look at him?'

'If you would, Enid, we'd both be most grateful,' agreed Lady Amanda. Hugo tried to smile but found that hurt too, so just lay there, like the prize pig in a rural raffle, while Enid disappeared into the house again, calling, 'Mrs Hardacre? Mrs Hardacre? Where are you?

Someone has need of your special talents,' while Lady A wandered a short distance away, where she could have a little snort of amusement without hurting Hugo's feelings.

Not only did Mrs Hardacre work wonders on Hugo's locked back, but the ladies of the Mothers' Union returned on Tuesday, to carry on their cleaning work in the attic bedrooms, and again on Wednesday, to help decorate the trees for Lady Amanda and Hugo, whom they viewed as an elderly couple in need of practical help.

By this time, Hugo, with two more treatments from Mrs Hardacre, was more sprightly than he had been before his unfortunate mishap with the tree, and Lady Amanda was busy sliding cards into envelopes, hot from the local printing press, and invitations (marked prominently RSVP ASAP) into rather grander envelopes, for their Boxing Day 'do'.

The sooner she knew how many were coming, the sooner she would be able to sort out the catering, and if they all did answer promptly, then any refusals could be filled with substitutes, with still time to RSVP before the shops closed for the festive season, and she was champing at the bit to get on with things.

Having deposited her tottering piles of envelopes on the hall table for Beauchamp to put in the post box, she sought out Hugo so that they could run through the route of the tour, and discuss any food phobias from which their guests might suffer.

She found him stretched out on a chaise longue in front of the fire, in the library, and his face was wreathed in smiles when he saw her approach. "Lo there, Manda. Come for a li'l chitty-chatty?' he asked, his forehead creased in puzzlement at the indistinct diction he had just demonstrated.

'Are you all right, Hugo?' she asked in concern.

'Think so. Not abs'l'y sure, acksherlly,' he replied, and Amanda went to the other side of him, to see if there was any obvious evidence of what was wrong with him. She hoped to God he hadn't had a stroke. How he (or she) would cope with that, on top of his other medical problems, she didn't dare even to think.

Her fears proved unfounded, however, as she espied at the head of the chaise longue a brandy bottle and balloon, and a box of coproxamol. The silly old bear had just about knocked himself out with strong painkillers and alcohol. 'Have you been drinking, Hugo?' she asked him acidly.

'Just a li'l one. 's only medic-ic-imal!' he stated, with inebriated dignity.

'Just a little half a bottle!' she declared, her voice rising with each word. And how many of these pills did you take?'

'Wha' pills? Don' know nothin' 'bou' no pills,' he stated, ending on a high-pitched fortissimo hiccough.

'BEAUCHAargh!' she shouted, leaping to one side, as the man seemed to emerge from the very floor.

'Yes, my lady?' asked Beauchamp, his usually bland expression somewhat challenged at the sight of Hugo with his thatch of white hair sticking up all over the place, and the idiot smile on his face.

'Mr Hugo is rather tired and emotional, Beauchamp,' Lady A stated, recovering her dignity with amazing alacrity. 'I wonder if you could see him to his room, and make sure he gets to bed without mishap.'

'As you wish, my lady,' agreed Beauchamp, and added quietly, as he turned to his task, 'I'll just get the wheelbarrow, shall I?'

'What was that? I couldn't quite catch it?' asked Lady Amanda, and couldn't understand why Hugo had just started to laugh hysterically.

'Nothing, my lady. Just encouraging Mr Hugo.'

The next day, after Hugo had refused a fried breakfast, and settled instead for some dry toast and black coffee, Lady Amanda suggested that they get on with the menu for the dry run on Boxing Day.

'Manda! Have a heart!' Hugo exclaimed in as loud a whisper as he could. 'I'm not feeling quite the ticket. Must have been something I ate yesterday, although I've no idea what, as we ate exactly the same things.'

'I don't think eating was the problem, Hugo. Tell me, what do you remember of going to bed last night?'

Hugo sat and thought for a while, even though thinking increased the thumping headache he was nursing. 'I don't have any clear memory of going to bed, actually,' he replied, looking a mite puzzled.

'What is your last clear memory?' Lady Amanda was going to let him have the unvarnished truth about the matter, because she didn't want a recurrence, not only over the festive season, but ever.

'I was in the library,' Hugo articulated slowly, a frown creasing his brow. 'I had made the decision to have a tot of brandy, then try a little nap; just to refresh myself, you understand. Then ... well, not a lot.'

'I'm not surprised. You got yourself into a right old state, taking your painkillers and brandy – about half a bottle, I estimated, and BeauchaARGH! I wasn't actually calling you: I was just mentioning your name. Now run along and get back to whatever it was you were doing. I really must get you some shoes with steel heel and toecaps, or bells on them, or something, anything just to warn me of your arrival.'

The manservant left the room, smiling mischievously to himself and stifling a chuckle, as Lady Amanda continued, 'Now, where was I? Oh, yes, you were in fact sozzled! As squiffy as a drunken sailor! As pissed as a newt – if you'll excuse the vernacular. You were, in fact, steaming drunk, Hugo, and Beauchamp,' (she whispered his name this time), 'had to fetch the wheelbarrow and put you to bed to sleep it off.'

'No!' exclaimed Hugo, accidentally raising his voice in surprise, then wishing he hadn't, as all the little men with mattocks started digging away at the bedrock of his brain again.

'Yes, Hugo, and it just won't do. A cocktail or three – fine, no problem. A bucket of spirits, however, is too reminiscent of Grandpapa, who couldn't face the day without a snifter of brandy first thing in the morning.'

'I never knew he was a tippler,' said Hugo with a grimace of effort, as he tried to place Lady A's grandpapa.

'More of a toper, although it was hardly noticeable until he had to write anything, then all he could do was a sort of scribble, because he was too far gone for his coordination to work efficiently. He was known by his contemporaries as Old Scribbler, which is just as well, for in his later years, he was more like Old Dribbler.

'Now, have you taken anything for that birdcage mouth, the little men drilling in your head and the stomach like a stormy sea?'

'No,' he replied, groaning as she reminded him of his individual symptoms, 'And it's not drills, it's mattocks: little men with mattocks,' he informed her for the sake of accuracy.

'What an old-fashioned hangover you're having. And as for the way you're feeling, I'll get Beauchamp to make you one of his prairie oysters – goes down like fire, but cleanses as it goes, and leaves you feeling as right as ninepence.'

'Who's old-fashioned now? That should surely be as right as 4p. Urhhh!'

On queue with the groan, Beauchamp stepped smartly into the room with a tall glass on a small silver salver. 'For you, Mr Hugo,' he intoned, leaning forward to offer the glass. 'I noticed how you looked this morning, and thought you would probably feel a lot more human after one of these.'

Hugo eyed the glass, and it eyed him back. With a start, he asked, 'How can I drink that when it's looking at me?'

'That's only the egg yolk, sir. It'll slip down without you even noticing.'

'And no doubt reappear within a few seconds looking for an encore.' Hugo was very dubious about the contents of the glass.

'Trust me, sir. I have been ministering to hangovers in this house since I was a boy, and I haven't lost a patient yet.'

'Hold your nose while you drink it, Hugo, old bean. It'll make it easier to swallow if you can't taste it.'

With two pairs of eyes scrutinizing him closely as to what he would do next, Hugo pinched his nostrils together with the

forefinger and thumb of his left hand, while lifting the glass to
his lips, and tossing off the contents almost in one swallow.

He sat in silence for a while, colour slowly returning to his
cheeks, then he opened his mouth and made a sound like an
air-raid siren. After this sound had ceased, he sat back in his
chair, ran a hand through his thatch of white hair, and smiled.
'I don't know what you put in that, Beauchamp, but it seems to
have worked a miracle. What was it?'

Lady Amanda butted in as he finished speaking. 'You really
don't want to know Hugo. Just be grateful that you got it down,
and it's staying down. I can see you look better already. Which is
good, because today I wanted to go over the menu with you for
our experimental opening of the house. I suggest, however, that,
given the delicate state of your constitution, we do nothing until
after lunch.'

'Good-oh! I might feel human again, but I think I'll just go
to my room and have a little lie-down. I didn't sleep soundly
last night, as I was haunted by the most peculiar dreams. After
Beauchamp's contribution to my constitution, however, I feel I
shall sleep like the dead. Perhaps you would be so good as to
wake me just before the gong for luncheon.' And with that, he
rose from his place at the table, folded his napkin, and made as
hasty a retreat as he could manage from the room.

'Thank you for your anticipation, Beauchamp. That will be
all for now,' Lady A trilled at her manservant, and was unaware
of the muttered 'Beecham' from him, as he headed back to his
own corner of the house.

Chapter Seven

Reactions and Counter-Reactions

Through letterboxes all over the county were dropping thick white envelopes, containing social dynamite. The postman was delivering the invitations that Lady Amanda had written and caused to be posted the day before.

In the Heyhoe-Caramac residence, it was the housekeeper who delivered the mail to Colonel Henry and Mrs Hilda, when breakfast had been cleared away. Both master and mistress were still sitting at the dining table, enthralled in items in their separate newspapers, when the post was slapped down on the table in front of the colonel.

Without comment about the slapdash way in which their mail had been delivered, as this had become the norm over the last year or so, he picked up the pile of envelopes and went through them, commenting on each one, and making a pile for himself and a separate pile for his wife.

'Christmas card, Christmas card, Christmas card, letter from Letitia,' he began, slapping four envelopes in a pile for his wife's perusal. 'Bill – damn and blast it! Has that tailor no patience? Another bill – damned wine merchant, this time, I suppose. Why he couldn't have waited until the New Year I shall never know.' That was two in his pile, as he continued, 'Readers' Digest – no doubt we're in a draw to win £100,000.' This envelope he tossed towards the fireplace, to be consumed by the hungry flames.

'Bank statement – that's mine. Christmas card, Christmas card, Christmas card – all for you, I presume, my dear. Hello! What's this?' he concluded, holding up the velvety envelope in which their invitation from Lady Amanda was enclosed. 'Don't recognise the handwriting, so we'll both take a look at that.

Three more Christmas cards, and that's it for today. Shall we have a look inside our mystery envelope first, Fluffy?'

'Please, Bonkers. I'm dying to know what it is. Maybe one of our friends is having a New Year's Ball, and we're to be invited,' gushed his wife, always one to live in hope.

Colonel Henry – aka Bonkers – used his thick thumb as a rather inefficient letter-opener, and pulled out the stiff oblong of card from within its folds. His wife Hilda – aka Fluffy – looked on with the face of someone who always sees their glass as half-full rather than half-empty, and chided him to hurry up, as his eyes widened, his nostrils flared, and his mouth fell open. 'Well, what is it, Bonkers? Come on: hurry up and stop teasing me. It's an invitation, isn't it? From whom? To what? When?'

'Damn and blast the woman!' exclaimed her husband, holding the oblong of cream card at arm's length, the better to focus on it. 'Trust her to make us an invitation we couldn't refuse; although we could fake illness, or even death, if we wanted to.'

'What are you babbling about, Bonkers? What woman? Invitation to what? Why can't we refuse? Why should we need to fake illness or death?' This morning was proving to be full of unanswered questions for poor old Fluffy Heyhoe-Caramac, and she could feel her kipper turning sour in her stomach with the upset of it all.

'It's that ghastly Golightly female – dreadful woman ...'

'I rather like her,' interrupted his wife, only to find herself uncharacteristically slapped down for her comment.

'Shut up, woman, and listen to this.'

'There's no need to be so rude about it. Whatever it is, it's not my fault.'

'Sorry, Fluffy. Just got my dander up, that's all. She wants us to go to that fearful fake castle of hers on Boxing Day?'

'What for? What use could we be to her on Boxing Day?'

'There's some blether here about her opening the house for guided tours – stuff and nonsense, if you ask me – and she wants to do a trial run with some of her friends – ha ha! Good one, that! – with afternoon tea thrown in, to see if: a) we would give her some feedback on the quality of the tour and food, and: b) to see if we would recommend it to any of our friends – people of the right background who wouldn't pinch the silver or spill things on the furnishings.'

'Does she actually say that?' asked Fluffy, now fascinated with what she was being told. 'In those exact words?'

'No, silly, she just implies it. I'm perfectly able to read between the lines, and if there's a sub-text to anything, you know I'll find it. She seems to be attempting to break into the lucrative tourist market, using us as guinea-pigs and free advertising.'

'Do we have to pay for the tour and the tea?' asked Fluffy in a more practical vein than her husband.

'No: it's to be free for trial, to a few select friends.'

'Then we'll go,' stated Fluffy, decisively. 'You know how annoyed you always get on Boxing Day, when all the poor relations and local scroungers show up, hoping to be shown a bit of seasonal largesse. Then you get a terrible gastric attack because you're so infuriated, and I hardly see you again till New Year.

'This year we'll be out when they arrive, and they can stay on the doorstep for as much of the day as they care to. We shall be elsewhere, getting a free feed for once, and your digestive system will, no doubt, purr like a cat in consequence. So, let's have no more of this looking a gift horse in the mouth, and accept with a good grace.'

'Do you know, you're a genius, Fluffy? You're absolutely right! Maybe Popeye and Stinky will be there too. It could prove to be a very enjoyable afternoon, being shown behind closed doors, then being waited on and fed like royalty. I'm going to write and accept this very minute. Trust you to find a completely different way of looking at things.'

'That's because I always look on the bright side, Bonkers, unlike you, who would probably have found fault with the Garden of Eden,' she informed him, only for him to score an unexpected point by adding,

'Never did like apples. Now, that would have made a very interesting story.'

She aced his serve, but only in her head by thinking that he only didn't like the woman because she was a better shot than him, and his pride was wounded more often than the game, when he was shooting.

At The Manor, Sir Jolyon *ffolliat* DeWinter – aka Blimp – sniffed suspiciously at the thick expensive envelope that had arrived with that morning's post, wrinkled his nose, and handed the missive to his wife Lady Felicity, with a sound that may only be represented in the written form as 'Hrmph!'

'What's that you're passing to me?' asked Lady Felicity – aka Fifi – suspiciously. Anything not addressed solely to her, that her husband passed over for her to deal with, usually spelled trouble, and the dark side of her curiosity was instantly aroused. 'What horrible nest of vipers are you handing over to me now?' she asked, taking the offered piece of correspondence, and working at it with her marmalade-smeared knife, in order to set loose the snakes.

'Whatever it is, I'm neither giving nor donating anything, taking part, buying anything, or getting involved in any way,' replied her husband, leaving the whole thing to his wife to deal with.

'Oh!' Fifi exclaimed in surprise. 'It's an invitation. Now, let me just look at the details before I tell you about it.'

'I'm not going to any auctions or fund-raising dinners,' stated her husband, his figure swelling with indignation at the very thought, and explaining why, at an early age, he had been nicknamed 'Blimp'. 'I don't want to sponsor anyone or anything, nor do I wish to attend any exhibitions of new and exciting artists, whose work will be a splendid investment for the future. I'm fed up with being rooked and preyed on, and that's all anyone ever wants these days: to dip their hand into my wallet, and leave it a little thinner than it was before they came along.'

'You'll be well-pleased to find out that it's to something that is absolutely scot free, then. It won't cost you a penny, we'll get a little look behind the scenes at a well-known local residence, and fed, into the bargain.'

'I say, Fifi. That sounds more like it. Go on.'

'It's from Lady Amanda Golightly, and invites us to Belchester Towers for a free tour of certain quarters of the property, with a slap-up afternoon tea thrown in. If we're willing to stay behind and give her some feedback on the experience, and maybe dig up a few friends of the right calibre to pay to do the tour in the spring, we can stay to cocktails as well. There! What do you think of that?'

'When is it?' asked her husband, his face beginning to clear like a grey day after rain, his smile representing the sun, which was definitely coming out from behind one of the last clouds.

'Boxing Day,' replied his wife, noting his change of mood. 'What do you think?'

'I think that's rather splendid!' replied her husband. 'I've always hated the twenty-sixth – no character whatsoever, and everyone making do with left-overs from the day before and pretending it's all a jolly jape to be eating food that should have been fed to the pigs before something completely original had been cooked instead. The hunt used to be the only highlight of a rather grim day, and that's gone for ever now, more's the pity.'

'That's a 'yes' then, is it?' Blimp never said one word when ten would do the job just as well.

'It's a splendid idea, and I should love to have a look round that old place. I haven't been there since we were courting. Do you remember that fake priest hole that the original Golightly had constructed when the building was first going up?'

'Yes, to the first question, and how on earth could you remember when the place was first built? You'd have to be over two hundred years old to be able to do that.'

'Family story. Passed down. But, I say, it was rather fun in that old priest hole, wasn't it?'

Fifi blushed, and turned her attention to her other mail. She didn't feel that the breakfast table was a fitting place to remember the follies and indiscretions of youth. 'I'll reply in the affirmative then, shall I?' she asked, opening another envelope which obviously contained a Christmas greeting from one of their friends.

'Definitely! Tally-ho! and all that. Maybe we can raise the ghost of a memory, if the tour visits a certain little cell.'

At The White House, Belchester, a rather more modest residence than the two that had already received their summons, Madeleine Mapperley-Minto usually dealt with the mail, as its contents often had the effect of upsetting her husband to the extent that he had to wander off in search of a little tot of something to soothe his nerves.

She had put this practice into place after one particularly bad week when nothing but bills had arrived, Monty's little tot had turned into a bit of a binge, and she had taken refuge in several bottles of rather bad white wine, not because they usually drank the bad stuff, but because she knew that the way she would throw it down her throat, taste would be the last of her considerations of its quality.

She was, not unnaturally, a little wary, as she knocked discreetly on the door of his study, to apprise him of the arrival of an invitation. 'There's something I need to speak to you about, Monty,' she announced in a firm voice as she entered the room holding the invitation card in her hand.

Monty's eyes fixed on it as if it were a cobra, risen and ready to strike, and she could see him swallow as he started to salivate at the thought of something that annoyed him and sent him into a rage, with the inevitable following administration of a few pegs, to calm his nerves and restore his good humour.

'Now, don't get yourself into a state. Just listen to what I have to say before you even think of going off to empty the decanters. This is a lovely invitation, and I'm sure it will put you in a good mood just hearing about it,' said Maddie, diplomatically and firmly.

'Lady Amanda Golightly has invited us to a rather unusual event which is to take place on Boxing Day and, as it mentions cocktails at the end, I thought you might be tempted to attend.'

'That's a good start. What's she up to?'

'She wants to consult a group of friends – from the right circles, of course – to try out an idea she has, of giving guided tours of certain parts of her residence. There will be afternoon tea afterwards and, for those who don't mind, as I said, staying on to give feedback and, perhaps, recommend her new enterprise to 'suitable' friends, there will be cocktails served.'

'What, no wine with the afternoon rations?' asked her husband, rather churlishly, thought Maddie.

'You know very well that you'll take your hip flask, no matter what, and you also know that I know that you hate Christmas. At least this would get us out of the house, and she's bound to have invited other people that we know, so I think it could turn out to be rather a jolly 'do'.'

'OK, then.'

'What, no argument? No need for me to plead with you?'

'No! I've heard that she's hooked up with old Chummy – you remember Hugo Cholmondley-Crichton-Crump, don't you?'

'I could hardly forget him, with a name like that, could I?' replied Maddie, finding herself unexpectedly smiling. She had thought she faced a much harder task than this had proved to be.

'Fancy a chin-wag with old Chummy. Haven't seen him in donkey's. Thoroughly good chap!'

'That's settled then. I'll drop Lady Amanda a note of acceptance,' said Maddie, hardly believing her luck.

'Splendid!' commented her husband, and returned his attention to the *Financial Times* without a hint of going off in search of alcoholic stimuli.

Captain Leslie (Popeye) Barrington-Blyss of Journey's End, Belchester, would never leave an important task like opening the mail to his meek but solidly built wife, Lesley, whom everyone who knew her well enough addressed affectionately as 'Porky'.

Their long-term nicknames were easily explained by stating that Capt Leslie (he still insisted on his rank being used) had been careless enough to lose an eye and wore, as a consequence, a black eye-patch. Being the sort of man that he was, he wasn't beyond popping out his false eye to frighten both servants and children alike for his own crass amusement. As for Porky, she had been a well-built child who had never lost her puppy fat, later adding the extra weight she had gained by having two children quite late in life, and was now as round and bouncy as a rubber ball.

In the mail this morning, Capt Leslie had received an invitation to Lady Amanda's 'Belchester Towers Tours (with afternoon tea provided)' trial run, and had seized on this as a superb opportunity for him to do a little snooping. He was writing a book – 'County Characters – Unmasked' was its working title – and this would give him carte blanche, not only to poke around a bit in a house he had barely seen for years, but to eavesdrop on the other guests, who would probably be known to him, and thus provide grist for his literary mill.

Without consulting his wife, he penned a reply in the very worst purple prose, and walked down to the post box to send it, before Lesley could offer her opinion, and maybe try to scupper the idea of going at all.

On his return, he threw the information casually into a conversation they were having about Christmas arrangements in general, and waited for her reaction with bated breath.

To his surprise, she seemed utterly enchanted at the idea. 'What a lovely idea! It's about time a few more people got a look at that intriguing house, and you know how boring I find the twenty-sixth. I shall, of course, have to have a new frock though – I've absolutely nothing to wear.'

'That's because you keep growing out of everything in your wardrobe,' said her husband spitefully, but he said it sotto voce, so that she shouldn't hear him and cause a scene. Goodness me, the tent-makers were going to be busy between now and Christmas Day! was his last unkind thought on the matter, before he moved the conversation on to an inquisition on why the house-keeping accounts seemed to be so high over the last month, wanting every last penny accounted for to his satisfaction. This was one of his favourite pastimes, and he enjoyed himself thoroughly for the next hour and a half.

At Squire's Court, Lady Margaret (Daisy) Fotherington-Flint came rushing out of her dressing

room in her lacy dressing-gown, hooting like a siren and making little squeaking noises of happiness and excitement. She headed straight for her husband, Sir Montacute (Cutie)'s dressing room, almost skipping at the pleasant news she had to impart.

Without knocking, she sailed into the room, catching Sir Montacute fighting with his socks, in an effort to be ready for breakfast on time. Looking at him wrestling to catch his feet and capture them in sober black cashmere, she thought how fitting his nickname had been all his life. From photographs, she knew he had been a pretty baby who had grown into a beautiful child, and from this state of development, into a handsome man, as he still was in his later years, and she felt a thrill of pride that she had captured him and that he was still hers.

'What the devil do you think you're doing, bursting in on me like that, without any warning whatsoever?' he asked, a little grumpily. A man should be allowed to dress in privacy, and not be interrupted when he was in the puffing and blowing acrobatic mode that this pastime now represented, now that he was not in his first, or even second, flush of youth. Dressing had become an undignified occupation that should not be viewed by anyone, least of all his wife, for whom the perfection of his daily turnout should not be marred by the exertions needed to achieve that state every day.

'Oh, Cutie, don't be cross with me. I have such exciting news. We've had an invitation to something that sounds fun, fun, fun!' An unbiased observer may have, at this point, wondered how, if this was how Daisy normally behaved, her handsome husband had put up with this sort of girlish behaviour for so many years.

'What's that?' asked her husband, now attempting to put his feet into his shoes, and having quite a time of it with his aim. 'I hope it's not another blasted charity ball. I'm not made of money, you know, and times are hard.'

'It's from Lady Amanda, and it won't cost you a penny, Cutie, my darling,' she cooed back at him, not at all ruffled by his grumpy responses. She had learnt to ignore them years ago, and they hardly registered at all on her consciousness now.

'Damned pleased to hear it! What's the old wind-bag up to now, then?'

'She's planning to do guided tours of The Towers, and she wants us to be guinea pigs.'

'Oh, God! I hope that doesn't mean being dragged from room to room while some wrinkly old worthy spouts on about their boring family history.'

'Nothing of the sort, my sweet. We're to have access to bits of her residence that we've never seen before, and then be provided with afternoon tea – a no doubt splendid affair, given that she only acts mean, and is actually rolling in it.'

'Glad to hear someone is.'

'Do be quiet, Cutie, and let me finish,' she chided him, automatically. 'If we're willing to stay on and give her our opinions, we'll be included in cocktails. She wants this thing up and running by spring, and to have exactly the right sort of clients booking the tours: personal recommendation only, for the first month or so.'

'Well, cocktails sound super. Keeping the old cupboard stocked with the hundreds of bottles that seem to be required to have even a modest cocktail party these days is simply beyond my means. And if it means that I can recommend this tour to all those acquaintances that I thoroughly dislike, that will be the icing on the cake. When's this shindig scheduled to happen?'

'Boxing Day,' replied his wife, pleased with the reaction she had received to the invitation.

'Hallelujah! There is a God after all! I can now cancel my snivelling cousins who always take the trouble to have a good old suck at my wallet on the twenty-sixth. They can go hang, for we have a prior engagement, and cannot be here to receive them this year. I feel so happy about telling them, that I could kiss Lady Amanda's hand. I just hope she doesn't change her mind and cancel at the last minute. The County grapevine is every bit as efficient as the community variety.'

'Well, that's that settled, then. I shall write to accept, straight away.' Skipping like the child she had once been, Lady Margaret returned down the landing to her boudoir, where she sat at a tiny Davenport, extracted her pen and a sheet of paper embossed with her name and address, and began to write, in a beautifully flowing hand.

At the breakfast table in The Old Convent, Lieutenant Colonel Aloysius Featherstonehaugh-Armitage – aka Stinky –

puffed on his after breakfast cigar, perusing the oblong of fine quality card that he held out in front of him, with interest.

'Golly, Stinky, no wonder that's what they called you when you were old enough to smoke those vile things. I do so wish you wouldn't smoke one at the breakfast table, though. Thoroughly bad form, if you ask me,' commented his wife, Angelica, affectionately known by her friends and family as 'Donkey', because she could be a bit slow at times, and as stubborn as her nickname-sake.

'Sorry old girl, but a man's got to be able to do what he wants in his own home, as there's nowhere else he can do it. Why don't you take breakfast in bed? That should solve everything. I could have my morning cigar, and you could have your breakfast in the unpolluted air of the bedroom. What do you say, old thing?'

'The air in there isn't exactly pure when you've spent the night in there.' (Amongst their friends and acquaintances, they were about the only two who still shared a bedroom.) 'I presume they didn't give you your nickname just because you took up smoking those dreadful things. You must have had it from a very early age. I wonder if it's time we had separate rooms, my little snuggle bunny. I know how my tossing and turning, and my snoring disturb you. Maybe you'd like to consider *that* over your breakfast cigar?'

'Sorry,' apologised Stinky. 'Went off into a brown study there. Didn't take in a thing you said.'

'Never mind. I'm sure I shall raise the subject again in the near future, maybe as a New Year's resolution.'

'Jolly good show, Donkey, old girl. Talk to me about it another time, what?'

'Of course, my dear. That invitation's given me an idea, though. Why can't we do the same thing here?'

'What same thing?' Lt Col. Featherstonehaugh-Armitage was still not paying his wife any attention. 'What invitation?'

'Oh, I do wish you'd listen sometimes. We've been invited to Belchester Towers on Boxing Day to do a trial run on a guided tour. We'll get a slap-up afternoon tea afterwards, and if we can be bothered to stay on and tell Lady Amanda what we think of her tour, we'll get cocktails as well,' she explained, speaking in a rush, because she was so fed up with repeating herself. She sometimes wondered whether her husband needed a hearing-aid or a resounding slap.

'Having people round for cocktails, you mean?' Stinky was still rather in the dark.

'No! Oh, I do wish you'd pay attention. Opening up part of this place to the public. Restore some of the nuns' cells, maybe do up the chapel a bit, and offer cream teas – at an extra cost, of course.'

'Ah, got you, Donkey. Go on a reconnaissance mission. Clever old thing. Not like you at all to have a brainwave. Are you feeling quite the ticket today?'

'Don't be so cutting, my dear. I'm not the utter ass you've always assumed I am. I just save my good ideas for really important things, and don't squander them on trivialities.'

'Good girl, good girl!' soothed Stinky, completely immersed in his newspaper. 'I say! Old Binky's getting a new ball-and-chain. Says so right here, in the forthcoming marriages section. At least no one could be more of an old misery-guts than the last one. Always moaning about being ill with something or other.'

'She *did* die, dear, so she must have been right. Don't be so hard on her memory.'

'You're right. Dear old Donkey! Always trying to bring out the best in people. Still, I suppose you've got your work cut out with me. I say, haven't you, old girl? Got your work cut out with me?'

'If you weren't such a fine-looking specimen, I should have poisoned you years ago and gone in search of pastures new,' replied Daisy but, Stinky was oblivious to his wife's words, reading the obituary of an old army comrade-in-arms.

Chapter Eight

Menus and Stockings and Lashings of Good Cheer

While the various invitations were being received and considered, Lady Amanda had encountered Hugo in rather finer fettle than he had been before his first ever encounter with one of Beauchamp's prairie oysters, and had cornered him so that she could bully him into joining her at a little menu planning for Boxing Day.

'Come on Hugo! You know you want to really! You've always loved a party, and you could pack away canapés faster than anyone I knew. I'm sure your educated stomach – and palate, of course – could come up with some wonderful ideas for our little tea party.

'It's got to be special, to get them to tuck in and prolong their stay: then we have to keep them hooked into the occasion long enough for cocktails to be served. That'll get 'em going. Relax them with a shot or two of alcohol, and the truth about what they really think of our enterprise, and this establishment, will come pouring out, and all without any guile whatsoever.'

'Then you don't consider that coercing them to stay for cocktails to loosen their tongues is in any way a use of guile?' asked Hugo, astonished at her attitude.

'Of course not. It's normal social practice, as far as I'm concerned, and the whole bang-shoot of them would agree with me, were they in a similar position. Come along, Hugo! Get your thinking cap on. Let's go and sit in the drawing room and see what we can come up with.'

A few minutes later, Lady A sat with a pad on her lap, a pen in her right hand, waiting for Hugo's first suggestion. 'Come along, old thing. I can't wait forever.'

'You go first,' grumbled Hugo. 'My mind is a complete blank. You'll have to crank it over like we all used to with the old cars.'

'I think you need new batteries, if the truth be told, Chummy. Right, here goes: those lovely little squares of rusked bread with cream cheese and smoked salmon, with a little dollop of caviar on the top.'

'That's pushing the boat out a bit, isn't it?' asked Hugo, surprised at the extravagance of her first suggestion.

'We want to get them relaxed and content, don't we?' she parried.

'S'pose so! What about doing something similar with smoked venison and haggis, with a tiny drop of

Cumberland sauce on top, finished off with just the merest hint of Scottish gravy?' Hugo said, a greedy look entering his eyes. This was one of his favourite nibbles.

'I'm sure the whisky supply will stand up to that. Now, what do you think of anchovy toast?'

'Absolutely topping, Amanda, old bean. Love the stuff. Can we use toasting forks and make our own toast at the fire, so that's it's hot and crispy, and not cold and limp, as it always is when made in the kitchen, then transferred to the table?'

'Superb idea! That will tie in with the tour of the domestic quarters, and let them remember how it had always limped to the table in a parlous state when made in advance.'

Lady Amanda had hardly had time to write down this idea before Hugo had another brilliant idea. 'And we could have some of those prune things wrapped in bacon. The chaps always gobble those down.'

'Better remember to get Beauchamp to de-stone the prunes, then,' remarked Lady A rather sharply, 'or there'll be cracked dentures all over the floor,' then added, 'We could do with some of those little puff pastry case things – damn! I can't remember what they're called, but you can put a variety of fillings in them. Vol-au-vents o – that's the little beggars.

'They're a bit 'Tupperware party'-ish, aren't they?' asked the Educated Stomach.

'Have you ever actually been to a Tupperware party, Hugo?' asked Lady Amanda, skewering him with her eye. 'Well, no ...'

'Then don't talk about things about which you know nothing.'

'I suppose you have been to one, then. Just your sort of thing, I suppose: pieces of plastic for a kitchen you never enter.' Hugo was now feeling quite waspish.

'I have actually,' replied his hostess, with a smile of triumph on her face. 'It was about twenty years ago, at Enid's house, when times were hard and she was trying to make a little extra money.'

'Bet you didn't buy anything.'

'Well, there, you're wrong. I did.' Lady A definitely had the winning hand in this game.

'What?' asked Hugo, mesmerised by the idea of Lady Amanda in Enid's tiny little house in Plague Alley, at something as mundane and common as a Tupperware party.

'Well, the demonstrator, as I think she was called, called it a Yorkshire pudding batter maker, but I think she must not have been trained very well. To my eye, it was a plastic cocktail shaker, for use in dire emergencies, and I immediately entered one on my order form. If one forgets the real thing on picnics, it could be a life-saver, when one is in the middle of the countryside, without a civilised dwelling in sight, and nothing in which to mix the cocktails.'

'By George! I didn't think they sold anything useful,' exclaimed Hugo, and gave her leave to add vol-au-vents to the menu, provided she could come up with some appropriate fillings.

After a few moments of silence in which she contemplated this challenge, she smiled, looked Hugo straight in the eye and said, 'What about a little melted Camembert, topped with a sharp fruit jus? Or chopped game, set in a port aspic, with a crunchy little morsel of green on the top?'

'Manda, I think you just made the vol-au-vent fit for civilised company. Of course, we haven't even started to discuss sandwiches or cakes yet, which are the main components of a good afternoon tea. No plates of bread and butter for us, on such an important occasion, I assume.'

'Absolutely not. I suggest rare beef with horseradish,' replied the hostess, licking her lips in anticipation.

'Thinly sliced pork with an apple and cinnamon sauce,' interjected Hugo, raising his voice just a tad against a tremendous rumble from his stomach. 'Golly, this is making me hungry, Manda. What time is Beauchamp bringing through afternoon tea?'

'Not long! Now think! It's better to think of food when you're hungry, because you have more enthusiasm for it. Smoked salmon and watercress. If there are any vegetarians, and I haven't seen any of these folk for some time, they'll just have to peel away the bread and eat that. Now for cakes. Over to you, Hugo.'

'Walnut and coffee, with a coffee butter cream filling and outside coating. Golly, I feel positively faint with hunger.'

'Double chocolate cake with a fresh whipped cream filling,' continued his partner, 'and I think a good oldfashioned seedcake for those who like a little punishment with their luxuries.'

The door opened soundlessly, and Beauchamp entered the room and slid across the floor as silently as a snake, a large laden tray in his hands. Hugo actually clapped his hands in glee. 'Oh, thank God you're here, Beauchamp. Here we've been discussing the afternoon tea for the twenty-sixth for I don't know how long, and I'm dying of starvation just thinking about all that food.'

As Beauchamp set down the tray, Lady Amanda tore a page out of her notebook and handed it to him. 'Cast your eye over that, will you, and let me know if there are any problems, or if there is anything you would like to add to the list. We must do our guests proud on this occasion, because so much depends on it.'

Beauchamp took a cursory glance at the list and, just before he took his leave of them, murmured, 'Bite-sized lemon meringue pies. Individual treacle tarts with a creme patissiere topping ...'

'Just add them to the list, my good man. I'm sure anything you come up with will be gastronomically excellent.'

The fact that the afternoon tea that had been set before them wasn't of the gourmet quality they had been discussing, made no difference whatsoever, so hungry had their menu-planning session made them, and they fell on the food with gusto, and slightly less good manners than usual.

The next few days saw the arrival of six envelopes, all containing acceptances to Lady Amanda's invitation, and by Christmas Eve, she was literally rubbing her hands together in glee at the thought of her forthcoming advertising campaign, cunningly disguised as a plea to her friends' good taste, and for their generosity in spreading the word of the future opening of the official tours.

'I don't understand why you're so excited at this commercial enterprise, Manda,' stated Hugo during the afternoon. 'I mean, it's not as if you need the money, is it?'

'Of course not! Don't be so coarse! I like people, and I haven't seen enough of them in recent years. Running into you has brought that home to me. Not only have I gladly accepted you into my house and enjoyed your company, but I have also craved more. I thoroughly enjoyed our little adventure earlier in the year, and as something like that isn't likely to land in our laps again, I'm making the effort to be more sociable.

'I'm basically a very nosy person, and have found myself in a position to have no one to be nosy about. If I can get nothing out of this enterprise except the renewing of old friendships, it will be enough. If it actually works, I shall be meeting different people every week, and life will be more fun. Though I did like being a detective! Still, I suppose I shouldn't wish someone dead, just because I want to play at being 'Shirley' Holmes again.'

'Does that mean you don't really want *me* here?' asked Hugo, not quite understanding what she was trying to tell him, with all this talk of meeting different people every week to make life fun again.

'Exactly the opposite. After a few initial hiccoughs, I think we've settled down admirably together. And renewing our friendship has made me hungry for other contact. You've breathed new life into me, Hugo, old boy, and I shall be eternally grateful for that. Now, don't forget to hang up your stocking on the fireplace tonight, will you?'

'Whatever for?' Hugo sounded scornful. 'We're hardly children anymore.'

'Let me tell you a little story, Hugo, old bean. When I first got my state pension, I put the money towards financing the best cocktail cabinet in the county. When I'd done that, I had the money paid into a special account, to which only Beauchamp has access – I trust him implicitly with my funds.

'From this, every Christmas, he buys himself anything he wants, as a gift from me. The remaining funds are to buy me presents. He is my own personal Father Christmas, and it's much more exciting than when I was a child, because he always knows exactly what I want, even if I haven't realised it yet. This year, you're on his present list, too, and as you've been a good boy all year, to my knowledge, you'd better be prepared to hang up that old stocking, and get what's coming to you, in the morning.'

'Why don't you just donate it to charity?' asked Hugo, somewhat ungratefully, she thought.

'Because I already make generous donations to charities throughout the year, and this is my one annual indulgence, to which I feel I'm entitled.'

Hugo sat for a moment, lost in thought, while he digested what she had just told him, then sat bolt upright and looked straight at her. 'You're absolutely right, my dear, as always. And may one ask if there is any limit to the size of the stocking I'm allowed to leave out?'

'A yacht is completely out of the question, but I leave the size to your own discretion. Anything that won't fit will be left by the fireplace, with your name on it.'

'I think I'm going to enjoy this Christmas. You're going to make it just as sparkling and magical as it used to be in the old days, before I got old and crippled and stopped going out. It's not a time of year to be on one's own, and I don't have children to visit or to invite me round. I thank God every time I remember old Reggie, that you were on a mission to cheer up his day, and arrived in that ghastly nursing home while I was in residence.'

They attended Midnight Mass with Beauchamp chauffeuring the Rolls. It was a custom that neither of them liked to miss, although Hugo, of later years, had had to make do with the first Eucharist of Christmas on the television. When they had been younger, it didn't matter how long the party had been going on, they all pulled themselves together to go as a large group for this special service, and managed to behave themselves during its lease.

Tonight was a bit like old times, as they remembered those Christmases of so very long ago, and the people who used to be such good friends, before the war had intervened, and they had either been killed, or been scattered all over the world. They might be old, but at least they had gay and happy memories, and, hopefully, would spend the last years of their lives enjoying each other's company, and not being alone on all the important days throughout the year.

When they arrived back at Belchester Towers after the service, even though it was twelve forty-five, they did not go directly to bed. Old people do not need so much sleep, and they repaired to the drawing room where Beauchamp brought through a tray with three cocktails on it, as he always celebrated the dawn of another Christmas as a member of the family, and not just a hired help. That was how things had always been, and they would not change in Lady Amanda's lifetime.

'Well, what have you cooked up for us this Christmas?' asked Lady Amanda, as Christmas cocktails were always Beauchamp's choice.

'I have provided a 'White Christmas' for you, my lady, as I noticed the first few flakes of snow falling as I put away the Rolls. Mr Hugo, I know, has been having problems with one of his knees, so for him, I have prepared a 'Wobbly Knee', which I thought was very appropriate. And for myself, a new recipe which rejoices in the unusual name of a 'Bumpo'. I have no idea what it means, or even what it tastes like, but I like a surprise. Cheers! Merry Christmas to you both! And to you both, a peaceful New Year!' Beauchamp had no idea how he had tempted fate with his toasts, and this was his second offence.

The next morning reminded Hugo of his childhood Christmases. Strings of white lights had appeared, draped round every room, and every Christmas tree in the house was ablaze with lights. Holly and bright tinsel decorated every picture that hung from the walls, and mistletoe hung at strategic points, throughout their living quarters.

This must be all Beauchamp's doing, but Hugo couldn't work out when the man had found the time and energy to transform the old place so, when he had so much extra work to attend to both today and tomorrow. He quickly abandoned his speculations on this subject when he heard a joyful yell from the drawing room, and found Lady Amanda there, on her knees in front of the fireplace, ripping paper off a large flat parcel.

'Oh, Hugo, just look at this! It's an antique blotter with silver cherubs on the front. I didn't even know Father Christmas was aware of how tatty my old one was getting.

This is beautiful! I can hardly wait to write a letter, so that I can use it. What have you got Hugo? Come along, old chap, get ripping. You've got quite a few parcels to open.'

Hugo's gaze turned to where he had hung his 'stocking' last night; in actuality, a linen pillow slip with a card pinned to it, which bore his name. It was bulging with angled parcels and boxes, and the excitement that he had felt at this season so long ago now filled him again. He had, indeed, been transformed into a little boy.

Taking down the pillow slip and putting it on a sofa, he began to remove gifts from it, and unwrap them; first slowly, as one is taught to do in a polite way, then more vigorously, as one would like to do with every present one is ever given, but forbidden to by the dictates of good manners.

By the time he had a pile of discarded wrapping paper round his feet, the sofa held the components that comprised a complete train set, with all the fun little items that went with it: little signal boxes, a miniature station with its personnel, tiny passengers and sundry suitcases, miniature trees, a humped shape that was a tunnel, a level crossing, complete with gates: there seemed to be endless little bits and pieces with which to construct a railway world.

'How did he know?' asked Hugo, flabbergasted, but hugely impressed.

'How did who know what?' enquired Lady Amanda, holding up a sparkling pair of earrings to the light.

'Beauchamp. And that I never had my own train set. I always had to ask my older brother's permission to use his, and he hardly ever said yes – at least, not until I had agreed to let him give me a Chinese burn, which was horrible.'

At that precise moment, he became aware of Beauchamp at the side of the sofa, and jumped slightly. 'Golly, you're just like a character in a pantomime – rather appropriate at this time of year. What can I do for you, Beauchamp?'

'Nothing. I just wanted to let sir know that I utilised an old wooden table, covered it with baize, and it now resides in the great hall, should you wish to play with your new acquisition.'

'Beauchamp, you are a miracle on two legs. There's nothing I'd like to do more,' replied Hugo, looking quite young again.

'By the way,' interjected Lady A, 'what did I get you for Christmas?' she asked. knowing that he always chose his own present.

'A micro-scooter of the highest quality, my lady. So convenient for getting around all the long corridors in such a substantial residence with efficiency and speed. And jolly good fun it is too,' he replied, with a smile of satisfaction on his lips.

Christmas has the ability to bring out the child in everyone, even someone as stolid and reliable as Beauchamp.

'I believe it would be in order to open the rest of your presents before commencing on setting out your track,' the manservant advised him, disappearing as suddenly as he had arrived, leaving the two elderly children to re-enact their childhoods in peace.

Hugo's next parcel contained a railway guard's hat, and the next one, a whistle on a sturdy piece of cord, so that he could properly control the running of his new railway service. 'I say, Manda! I don't know where you got Beauchamp, but he's an absolute diamond geezer, if you'll excuse my use of the vernacular.'

'I've actually no idea where Mama got him,' she replied, rubbing the material of a cashmere scarf against her cheek with approval. 'He just appeared after I came home from school for the last time; as a boot boy, in those days, and he's just been here ever since. I know we never deserved him, but he's stuck with the family through thick and thin, and I really don't know how I would manage without him. He goes above and beyond the call of duty as a matter of course, and in an emergency, he simply works miracles.'

Enid Tweedie arrived just after they got back from church, a guest for Christmas lunch, as it would give her a change from looking at her sister's miserable face and her mother's evil countenance, both of which she must have had to observe every Christmas of her life so far. She was going to be helping with tomorrow's affair, and Lady Amanda had decided that the only way to say a proper thank you was for her to join them for Christmas lunch.

She arrived in a swirl of snow, the like of which had been gently falling since the early hours, and now had reached a rather respectable two to three inches – enough not to hinder walking too much, but sufficient to proclaim the rare occurrence of a white Christmas. Standing on the doorstep with a sprig of holly (with berries) pinned to the lapel of her best coat, and a sprig of mistletoe attached, in an ambitiously racy way, to her hat, Lady Amanda looked at her old employee and friend as she stood there, snowflakes melting on her coat, and felt a wave of affection wash over her.

This woman too had stuck with her through thick and thin, giving her time generously at the drop of a hat, and had even acted as an undercover detective for her earlier in the year. How much more could you ask of a friend, and yet Lady Amanda had treated her, for most of that time, like a hired dogsbody. Feeling the prickle of a tear at her eye, she decided it must be time for a sherry, to drown this flood of sentimentality that had suddenly overtaken her.

For a moment, she had the revelation that it must be the unusual company of an old friend, in the shape of Hugo, this morning as she opened her presents, sharing her excitement and appreciation, that had made her look on Enid in a new light, but a couple of glasses of sherry would soon cure that, and a couple of cocktails would definitely see her back to normal.

'How did you get here this morning?' she asked, not having seen Enid's bicycle outside.

'Well, I thought you sent him,' she replied, enigmatically.

'Sent whom?' Lady Amanda had done absolutely no 'sending' today whatsoever.

'Beauchamp. He knocked on my door just as I was about to leave, and said he'd come to save me the journey in the snow. He said he didn't want me either slipping off my bicycle, or falling over and hurting myself.'

'Well, I'll be blowed. I simply didn't think about it Enid, but Beauchamp really has been your knight in shining armour this morning, hasn't he?'

At this information, Enid blushed, and slipped the sprig of mistletoe from her hat and popped it into her handbag. Maybe today was her lucky day.

After taking her outer clothes, Lady Amanda led her into the drawing room where, from under the tree, she collected three presents, and thrust them into Enid's arms with a gruff, 'Merry Christmas, old friend.' Enid's face was a picture of surprise and delight, as she viewed the parcels now nestling in her arms.

'You shouldn't have, Lady Amanda,' she exclaimed, with a face that expressed the exact opposite.

'Little thank you for what you did for us when we were tangled up in those murders, earlier in the year. Got to reward our undercover agent for all her hard work,' replied Lady A, looking a little embarrassed. 'Go on, then, open them.'

Enid sat down on a chaise longue and delicately began to remove the wrapping paper, prompting a question from Hugo. 'Why are you doing it so carefully, Enid?'

'So that I can iron it and use it again,' came the automatic reply. Enid was too absorbed in not letting the sticky tape damage the pattern on the paper, even to think what she was saying.

As his mouth opened, to urge her to let herself go and just rip it off, he was stilled by a glare from Lady Amanda, who knew how important little savings like this were to Enid's life. She was not impoverished by any means, but the habits instilled in childhood had not died in Enid's psyche, and it was a matter of pride to her to let nothing go to waste unnecessarily.

From the first parcel she pulled a beautiful Italian leather handbag, exclaiming with delight, and reading out loud from the label. ''From Hugo, with all best wishes.' Why Mr Hugo, what a lovely present, but it looks awfully expensive.'

Hugo's mouth gaped, as he had, until now, had no inkling that such a gift from him existed. Lady Amanda came to his rescue by tipping him a discreet wink and explaining, 'Hugo knows how ladies love their handbags, and he wanted you to have something lovely but practical.'

'How thoughtful. I wouldn't have considered that such a notion would cross a man's mind. It's absolutely lovely, and I shall enjoy using it immensely. Thank you, Mr Hugo.'

'The second gift revealed a pair of silk scarves, one in spring colours, the other in autumn tints. 'Oh, Lady Amanda! You shouldn't have done, but they're beautiful.'

'Get on and open the other one, Enid. I'm dying to see what's in it,' she lied, for she had been the inspiration behind all three of these surprises.

'I'm doing my best, but there seems to be rather a lot of tape on this one, for the size of it. Hang on, there we go,' gushed Enid, now thoroughly enjoying herself with these hitherto fore unheard of seasonal offerings. 'Why, what a beautiful purse! And so practical, with all those sections. And I don't think I've ever felt such soft leather, apart from gloves. But who's it from? *Beauchamp?*' she cried, with surprise, then her face fell, and she added in a small voice, 'But I've brought nothing for any of you.'

'We don't give to receive, Enid, dear. These are a token of our appreciation for all the hard work you do here, without the slightest murmur of complaint, and for the help you gave us in our little adventure. Enjoy them and think of us when you use them. Nobody could ask for more in return, than that.' Lady Amanda really knew how to schmooze when it was necessary.

A gong sounded in the hallway, and the three of them adjourned to the dining room where an impeccably laid table now held the various serving dishes necessary for the meal, and a great carving dish on which nestled a mediumsized turkey, a guinea fowl, a pheasant, and three quail. Beauchamp did like to provide a choice, and was even happier if everyone asked for a little of each, for that meant that he had chosen his viands successfully.

The meal passed with a little more liveliness than it usually did, and this was all down to the presence of Enid.

When she uncovered the parson's nose on her plate – maybe it was the three glasses of wine that she had already consumed that was the cause of her reaction – she laughed so hysterically that she ended up with hiccoughs, and her conversation throughout the rest of the main course was laced with small explosions from her diaphragm, and profuse apologies for the interruptions.

'Ab – hic-solutely deli-hic-ious birds – hic! I don't thhic-ink I've ever ta-hic-sted some of these be-hic-fore. You must let me know wh-hic-at they are-hic.'

This set Lady Amanda and Hugo giggling, mainly at the surprised expression on her face whenever she interrupted her words and, here again, it was probably because, by now, they had caught up with her wine consumption, and all three were neck and neck.

There was an interesting hiatus during the pudding, when Enid started to choke on a silver sixpence; one of many that had graced the Golightly Christmas puddings since these particular coins had been made of sterling silver. Fortunately, Beauchamp knew how to administer the Heimlich manoeuvre, grabbed her swiftly from her seat like a rag doll, and carried out the coup de grace, producing a projectile that bounced across the table and landed back on the pudding plate, a feat so unlikely that none of them could believe it.

So far through the meal (and the wine) were they, however, that no one had the sharpness of mental capacity to calculate the odds of this happening. It also cured Enid's hiccoughs, and she sat down at her place again, grateful for Beauchamp's intervention.

'Nice try!' announced Lady A, swaying contentedly as she sipped from her glass.

'What do you mean, nice try?' asked Enid, unable to follow the thought processes that had produced this incomprehensible statement.

'Well, I thought you were trying for a Christmas Day visit to the hospital, just to wish all the staff you know the complim-iments of the sea-season, 'n-all that,' – a brave attempt by Lady A to keep her speech coherent, but a little unsuccessful towards the end.

This produced more helpless laughter from Enid, and she replied, with difficulty, 'S-silly wo-woman. Anyone would thin-ink I spent ha-ha-ha-half, ha ha ha ha ha, my life in the hostipal. Ooh, whoopsadaisy! Bu' you know wha' I mean, don' you?'

Beauchamp made the brave decision, at that point, to abandon the cheese board and port, and the coffee and liqueurs, and suggested, in quite a forceful way, that they would be better off retiring to their rooms for a little lie down, after all the excitement (wine). Enid was welcome to have a rest in one of the guest rooms that was already made up and ready for occupation, should she agree.

Enid agreed. So did Lady Amanda. And Hugo. With alacrity. To each, the other two appeared blurred, therefore, they concluded, in their fuddled state, that the other two must be drunk, but they wouldn't mind a little time-out themselves. Thus it was agreed, and they left the dining room, Beauchamp supporting Enid on his arm, for the oblivion and recuperative qualities of the small death that is sleep.

At four-thirty, Beauchamp eventually retired to his own quarters to partake of his own Christmas meal, glad of the break and the fact that no one would ring for him for at least an hour. Tomorrow was going to be a very busy day, and he needed any rest he could manage to wangle today, to face the rigours of the Boxing Day experiment.

The rest of the day passed quietly, with only halfhearted nibbles attempted at the Christmas cake produced at teatime, the only liquids consumed during the afternoon and evening being several pots of tea and a large jug of Beauchamp's home-made lemonade. This was just as well, considering what the morrow would bring.

Chapter Nine

The Experiment Ends in Murder

Edith, with the loan of a flannelette nightie and a spare toothbrush (from Beauchamp's supply of same, for emergency use) had stayed the night for the first time in her acquaintance with Lady Amanda, and appeared at the breakfast table the next morning bright and breezy, and ready for whatever the day would bring. She could get to work earlier than if she had had to make the journey from home, as there was no public transport today, and she would have had need of her ancient bicycle to make the journey in the snow.

Lady Amanda, after an early night and a long sleep, was in sparkling form, fairly crackling with anticipation as she considered the task ahead of her. Hugo, on the other hand, was unusually pessimistic, and gave it as his opinion, over the bacon and eggs, that persuading a bunch of people that they had seen little of for quite some time, and didn't regularly socialise with, to support their venture, was a waste of time, energy and money.

'Come on, Hugo! Where's your spirit? Where's your hunger for a challenge? We can do this standing on our heads if we just summon our natural social graces and powers of persuasion. Look at that time you persuaded Daddy to line the parapets with fireworks for New Year's Eve. He was dead against the idea until you'd worked on him for a while.' Lady A had to spark his enthusiasm somehow.

'And regretted it afterwards. It took the fire brigade quite a time to put out all the little fires it started up on the roof, and he took rather a wigging from the chief fire officer afterwards, for doing such a foolish thing during a very dry winter. The fires very nearly broke through to the attics, and then where would you have been? Faced with a huge roofing bill, without their valiant efforts; that's where you would have been.'

'Don't be such a party-pooper, Hugo. It gave Daddy just the opportunity he needed to get that old roof sorted out, and all at the expense of the insurance company. Anyway, he never told you, but he just souped-up a few of those fireworks, so that he would get the desired result.'

Hugo's mouth went slack. 'You mean he used me as a pawn in a game of "fleece the insurance company"?'

'Of course he did. He thought you knew.'

'I had no idea. I've carried the guilt of the damage I thought I'd caused ever since.'

'Silly, silly Hugo. I thought you knew Daddy better than that. Anyway, perk yourself up. We may not have seen these people for a long time, but we used to have some damned fine times with them, and I hope that today will just be the first in another round of fun for all of us.'

'May I see the guest list, please, Lady Amanda?' asked Enid, who always like to know people's names, so that she didn't have to go through the embarrassing procedure of having to ask who they were.

'In my desk, Enid. Top drawer, under my diary. Help yourself. Hang around as I admit them, if you like, and that'll help you when it comes to remembering who's who. There're not coming until two o'clock, so you've got plenty of time to commit their names to memory.'

The morning, not unsurprisingly, was spent rehearsing the tour part of the afternoon's proceedings, and the doors of all the rooms that they were unwilling to have other folk poke around in, were securely locked against any unwelcome invaders.

The plan was to give everyone a drink to welcome them to the establishment, then take them on what Lady Amanda considered to be the 'below stairs' tour, to include the kitchens, scullery, buttery, brewery and wash room, downstairs, then to ascend to the second floor where the servants had their sleeping quarters. Beauchamp, being more familiar with the domestic running of the house during his employment, had volunteered to conduct the tour, pointing out items of interest on the way, and telling stories from the old days which had been passed down to him by long-gone members of staff.

He would leave tea laid out in the library, with the exception of the delicacies which had to be freshly produced, Lady Amanda would accompany him to add her two-penn'orth of interesting figures and facts, and Enid and Hugo would make the tea at a given signal (one bong on the gong on the half-landing to the first floor) to commence this task.

Beauchamp forbade anyone to enter the kitchen during the morning, and flew about its confines like a blue-arsed fly, getting the tasty morsels prepared. Lady Amanda consulted a notebook in which she had noted the 'off-thecuff' stories with which she would flesh-out the bones of Beauchamp's prose, and with this, she prowled her kingdom (or queendom, which may be more apt, but isn't actually a real word), mouthing the tales she would tell, with appropriate facial expressions and arm and body movements, even going so far as to feign laughter in complete silence, at a joke she would make at a certain point in the proceedings..

Enid armed herself with a long-handled feather duster and a polishing cloth, and prowled every available room with this weapon, fighting a last-minute war with dust and the like, so that no one should get the impression that the household was slovenly in its care of the house. She was deadly with a duster, and nothing escaped her eagle eye, so long had she been eradicating this particular arch-enemy.

While this hive of activity swarmed around him, Hugo took himself off to the library, selected a book from the more modern shelves of the room's contents, and settled down, contentedly, to read. His excuse was that his knee was giving him particular trouble, and as he did not have an appointment to see the orthopaedic consultant until after the New Year, nobody could question the veracity of his tale.

At seven minutes to two, all three of them stood in the entrance hall, like sprinters at the start of the race of their lives. The whole house stood in silence, holding its breath for the moment where it would be put to the test.

At the sound of a car backfiring a good quarter of a mile away on the main road, they all visibly started, Enid going so far as to issue a squeak of surprise. 'Calm, troops,' ordered Lady Amanda, who was steeling herself to be nice to people. 'Best smiles to the fore, small-talk loaded and ready to fire.'

The sound of the bell ringing, at two minutes to the hour, almost caused the timid Enid to faint clean away, but Lady Amanda trod on her foot (accidentally on purpose) in her anxiety to be the first to greet her guests, and that brought her back to a state of being fully alert and ready for anything, including taking particular care where she put her feet. Lady Amanda was no slip of a girl, and she didn't want to spend the rest of the busy afternoon with a broken toe or two.

Lt Col. Aloysius Featherstonehaugh-Armitage and his wife Angelica were the first to arrive and Lady Amanda, in her excitement at the commencement of her battle plan, forgot to address them formally for Enid's benefit, and merely bade them welcome with the words, 'How lovely to see you again after such a long time, Stinky. How's the family, Donkey? All prospering, I trust?'

As they crossed the threshold, Beauchamp stepped forward to take their coats, hats, and gloves, and the residents of Belchester Towers had their first opportunity to take a look at what had happened to the grounds since they had last been outside. Lady Amanda opened the large doors wide and surveyed the iced lawns and bedecked shrubs and trees, as her guests stamped their feet on the (fortunately large) doormat to rid themselves of the encrustations of snow they had gathered on their walk from their car.

'Can't remember when we last had a white Christmas,' exclaimed Lady Amanda, clapping her hands together with glee. 'Perhaps we could all have a snowball fight on the lawn after tea.'

Totally ignoring the scandalised expressions on her first two guests' faces, she turned to them with a winning smile and urged Beauchamp to accompany them to the drawing room where a large fire burned, so that they could defrost before they had a little drink. She had obviously made up for her gaffe about snowballs by this remark, and Stinky and Donkey smiled in approval at the idea of a winter warmer at such an early hour. It was, after all, a bank holiday, and the sun and the yard-arm would have nothing to do with protocol today.

As all the clocks in the house chimed the hour, there was another smart knock on the door, which opened this time to admit Sir Jolyon and Lady Felicity ffolliat DeWinter. Sir Jolyon was red of face, even from the short walk he had taken from the car to the front door, and his complexion wasn't aided by the air temperature. Although the sun was shining, it was bitterly cold, with a slow lazy north wind that sliced at one like knives.

Lady Felicity merely looked like a child wearing an older person's skin, and skipped into the house babbling happily about how delighted they had been to receive Lady Amanda's invitation, and how much they had been looking forward to such an unusual experience. Beauchamp relieved her of her mink coat, hat, and fur-trimmed gloves, scandalised to hear Sir Jolyon call after him, 'You make sure you take care of that coat. It's not ranch mink, my man; it's the real wild article. Just make sure it doesn't bite you!' The manservant bore them away, with a scowl of fury at being so addressed, to some below-stairs region where such things resided while guests were in occupation. "My man"! Whatever next? 'Oi, buddy', perhaps?

Search as she might, over the years, Lady Amanda had never been able to solve the mystery of what Beauchamp did with all the coats, and had finally given up the impossible task of discovering his hiding place. Maybe the man had access to another dimension, where all menservants hid such bulky items during family entertainments. She just hoped he didn't decide to stay there, today, after such a blow to his dignity and elevated position.

Blimp escorted himself to the drawing room, anxious as he was to warm his backside at the fire, and when Beauchamp returned to accompany Fifi, she was still prattling away happily to herself about how lovely everything was, and how much she was looking forward to seeing the others invited for the occasion, hoping that she would already know some of them. The manservant at her side nodded his head in attentive agreement with much that she said, without even being aware that he was doing it. Such a habit had it become, that his mind was in the kitchen, running over all the preparations, to check that nothing had been neglected.

'Henry! Hilda! What a pleasure to see you again!' trilled Lady Amanda as a third couple arrived on the doorstep. She had picked up her game, and was using their real names now, so that Enid could chalk-up a house-point by addressing them as such, without having to be introduced. Although she wasn't using their full names, she was at least giving Enid sufficient evidence to work out who was who, and had only blundered over the first arrivals.

Cutie and Daisy were next, and each received a warm handshake and a kiss on the cheek, as Lady Amanda chortled, 'Sir Montacute! Lady Margaret! How delightful that you could attend our little entertainment this afternoon.'

The penultimate couple to enter Belchester Towers that afternoon was the Mapperley-Mintos, who actually commented on Lady Amanda using their given names. 'Given up on Monty and Maddie then, have you, Manda? Too grown-up for all that stuff, now, eh?'

'Not at all,' gushed Lady Amanda. 'I just thought that you might think it childish of me to use the diminutives of so long ago.'

'Not at all,' growled Monty. 'Still use them ourselves, as a matter of fact. Go back to that now, shall we?'

'With pleasure, Monty,' replied their hostess, noticing out of the corner of her eye that Enid had placed herself just out of the arriving guests' sightline, and was making copious notes on her list of those invited for the occasion. She'd get it right. She'd cudgel them into her memory, until she couldn't get it wrong if she tried. Very tenacious, was Enid.

Last to arrive by a good five minutes, and causing some little consternation in the troops that manned the line by the front door, were Capt Leslie and Mrs Lesley

Barrington-Blyss, the former looking a tad out of sorts, the latter, with a worried smile on her face. Porky, as Mrs B-B was known, made profuse apologies for their tardy arrival, citing a domestic staff crisis just before they had left. While she did this, she kept one hand behind her back, her stout fingers crossed to negate the lie.

Beauchamp took their outer clothes, while Porky clung possessively to a large tapestry handbag. 'Why on earth have you brought that monstrosity with you? Surely you haven't brought your knitting?' her husband asked, glaring at the bag with disgust, as she opened it to insert her gloves for safe-keeping. 'Why don't you go the whole hog, Porky, and wear a damned rucksack, but I can assure you'll be walking alone, for I won't be seen with you' he concluded, in withering tones,' then added, 'Whole hog – Porky! I say, that was rather a good one, wasn't it? Haha! Hahahahaha!'

Neither Beauchamp nor Lady A, though, seemed amused by this comment, made in extremely dubious taste, but, instead of an angry retort from Porky, a small smile of triumph appeared on her face. Why, though, she should be so pleased that she had annoyed him in front of others, was inexplicable. Maybe it was the sour look that she, Amanda, had bestowed upon him that had pleased Porky, thought Lady A. Popeye wasn't the most popular man in the county, nor ever would be, but he'd better tread carefully – Porky was his only ally at the moment, God bless her, and she'd stuck with him through thick and thin, even with this awful book business. She really was a good and loyal soul.

What she didn't know, however, was that Porky and Popeye had, in fact, had a rather heated discussion – row – about whether to attend at all. Popeye had stated categorically that he wanted to stay in his study and work on his book, which was nearly ready for publication. His publisher had sent him a series of instructions for where he wanted changes made, and small rewrites, and he wanted to get it finished as soon as possible, to get the book hurried on to the bookshelves. Never mind how much embarrassment and trouble he caused for others; he just wanted the notoriety.

The money would be damned useful too, for he was sick of penny-pinching in these hard times, even though he'd had to pursue a less than traditional route to get his work before the public gaze, and he just hoped that the risk would pay off. He'd warned her that, should it not sell extremely well, they might have to consider moving to a smaller property and dispensing with what little domestic help they currently enjoyed, and this had left Porky in a cleft stick.

She had finally justified putting her rather pudgy foot down over the matter by telling him that he might make some very useful contacts from the afternoon, as they had no idea who else had been invited, and that, furthermore, if he didn't comply, he'd become known as an untrustworthy, ill-mannered cur, throughout the County set. She'd make sure of that!

All her guinea pigs safely gathered in, Lady Amanda escorted the late-comers into the drawing room where she was pleased to find that Beauchamp had already taken orders for drinks and was, at this very moment, handing them round to those who had arrived more promptly. The man was a veritable gem.

'... hook from which the meat hung, behind this sheet of semi-circular metal ... a device for cutting the Seville oranges for marmalade-making ... a wash-dolly with which the laundry maid would agitate the clothes ... copper moulds for all sorts of puddings, both shapes, custards and ices ... the hard wooden beds on which the servants slept ... the wooden staircase which the female staff ascended to their rooms ... the marble washstands where they had to wash in cold water every morning ...'

Beauchamp led the party into the library at the end of the tour, looking as fresh as the proverbial daisy. Lady Amanda brought up the rear, looking as if she had been into battle, but quickly pushed her hair back into place, fixed a big social smile on her face, and entered the room which was now scented with some of the delights of which they were about to partake.

Not even a torturer from the Inquisition could make her confess how exhausted she felt, traipsing round the unfamiliar quarters that had been occupied, in her childhood and for many years before, by the staff, nor the horror she had felt when she had taken a good, hard look at how they had lived. Cleaning the quarters up had not done this for her, but today had, and she thanked her lucky stars that she had been born into the layer of society that she had.

Beauchamp had disappeared as soon as he had reached the library, now at work in the kitchen, no doubt on the things that had to be served either fresh, or warm, and her guests were gathered round the big library table helping themselves to delicate morsels of food. Enid and Hugo had done their job as promised, and two large silver teapots, one each of Indian and China, stood on mats on the table, to assuage their guests' thirst after their portion of enforced education for the day.

Lady Amanda sank into the confines of a porter's chair, and hid herself for a moment, to give herself a few seconds to summon up fresh energy and enthusiasm. That they enjoyed their afternoon tea was tantamount to the success of her venture, but that they felt relaxed enough to stay on for cocktails and give her some decent feedback was just as vital, and she must remain the perfect hostess, throughout the experience.

Finally rising from her hideaway, she poured a cup of the restoring Indian infusion for herself, put some choice morsels on her plate and began to circulate amongst her guests. No one seemed at all put out by anything, and they looked as if they were having a jolly time of snooping round a neighbour's home. Well, she had an extra card up her sleeve that would make their day.

'Excuse me, everyone,' she announced after about twenty minutes. 'Today my home is at your service. Should any of you wish to explore its other rooms, those that constitute, I suppose, upstairs, please feel free to do so over the next hour or so. Beauchamp will be your guide, should you require him. At that point, I should be grateful for any comment on what I propose to do, and you will all be very welcome to stay on for cocktails.'

Hugo, suddenly coming to life, called out, 'Why don't we get Beauchamp to light a yule log in the great hall and turn this occasion into an out-and-out party, everyone? He's a domestic marvel, and I'm sure he could rustle up enough grub for us all. A bowl of punch and a bit of music would liven us all up a bit, and we could make this a redletter day. After all, we haven't seen each other in an absolute age, have we?'

Enthusiastic mutterings greeted this suggestion, and as the guests made themselves ready to vacate the library, discarding cups and saucers, and plates empty of everything except a few crumbs, in preparation for having a good old nose around Belchester Towers, Hugo was unaware of Lady Amanda's approach until she suddenly landed next to him on the sofa, making him squeal in pain as the jolt shuddered through the joints he was still waiting to have replaced.

'I say, old thing, that was a bit rough, wasn't it?' he asked, trying to draw himself away from her encroaching bulk, as all the bits of her settled into place with a little help from gravity.

'And throwing my home open to this bunch of social vultures for a full-blown party isn't? Really, Hugo, I don't know how you have the bare-faced cheek to do something like that, when I've been running around like a headless chicken all day, and all you've done is sit around on your bum and rest your poor old joints. Making extra work for other people on a day like today is just beyond the pale, and you know it.'

Hugo had the grace to look shame-faced, but defended himself by saying, 'I thought everyone was having such a jolly good time that it would be just like the old days, with some of the old crowd here to recreate the atmosphere.'

'Do you actually remember "carriages at three"? It was deadly! One hardly ever saw daylight, and entered a twilight existence that was just one round of parties. A single one of those would be the death of me now. I just hope that a good snoop round, followed by a few drinks and a good old bitch about our set-up here will be enough for all of them. I forbid you to tell Beauchamp to light a yule log in the great hall, or forage around for enough food for well over a dozen people.'

'Sorry, Manda. I must have been temporarily astray from my wits. I had forgotten that morning-after feeling, and I think the consequences would be much greater at my age. If anyone says anything, I'll tell them I'm getting a bit senile. Will that do you?'

'Just be honest, and say that your enthusiasm carried you away for a moment. We don't need them spreading the news around the county that Hugo Cholmondley-Crichton-Crump is going off his chump, now do we?'

'You're right, as always. Shall we retire to the drawing room for a little peace and quiet, while they're all off moaning that they can't get access to our underwear drawers?'

'Just a minute,' she requested, and, turning from Hugo, she called in a very loud voice, 'If you would all follow Beauchamp, he will do the rounds of the tour with you, as he knows so much more of all the interesting nooks and crannies of this place than I do. When the tour is finished, feel free to take yourselves where you will and have a good old explore. I'll be very interested to hear what you have to say later, when I ask you for some feedback. And don't forget the cocktails! Have a good time!'

'Now,' she turned back to her house-mate. 'You had just made a most excellent suggestion, and one I think we ought to act on, on the instant. What about you, Enid?' she called, seeing her house-guest enter the library to carry away some of the crockery and the few morsels of uneaten food out to the kitchen.

'I'm fine, Lady Amanda. I'll just finish this clearing away, while Beauchamp is conducting everyone round the nooks and crannies, and when he gets back from showing them the public and family rooms, I shall help him with the washing up, then I expect we'll have a nice cup of tea at the kitchen table. I seem to have upset one of your guests, however,' she concluded.

'How on earth could you have done that?' asked Lady Amanda, surprised that such a well-mannered and mild woman as Enid could make any impression on the elephants' hides that her old friends possessed.

'I think, although I'm not quite sure, that I had a bit of a 'Chumley' moment with that old army man with the moustache.'

'What on earth did you say to him?' asked Lady Amanda, wondering what sort of gaffe Enid had managed to make.

'I asked him if he was enjoying himself. I'd worked out who he was from my list, although I think you called him 'Stinky' when you let him in.'

'Yes, sorry about that. I was a little over-excited, and forgot that I was giving you clues to everyone's identity.'

'I addressed him by what I had assumed was his name, but when I used it he looked at me as if I were a snake ready to strike, and went off muttering to himself and snorting.'

'What did you call him, Enid?' asked Lady Amanda, knowing exactly what her friend was about to say.

'Lt Col. Featherstonehaugh-Armitage, of course.'

'And I suppose he went off muttering 'Fanshaw', did he?'

'That's exactly right, Lady Amanda. How on earth did you know? Although I think I already know the answer.'

'Because that's how his name's pronounced: Fanshaw-Armitage.'

Enid sighed the sigh of someone tried beyond endurance. 'Well, I just wish he'd spell it that way then. What is it with your lot – sorry to sound coarse – that they can't just spell their names how they sound?'

'Sheer bloody-mindedness, I expect,' was the answer she received, and she must have been satisfied with it, because she trotted off to the kitchen, perfectly happy once more.

Lady Amanda and Hugo had had barely an hour of peace and quiet in which to snatch forty-winks, when a shriek, as piercing as that of a banshee, suddenly shattered the silence of the house.

Lady Amanda awoke with a 'Whaah!' of surprise, only to find that she had dribbled all down her cardigan while she had been 'resting her eyes'. Hugo, not so tired from the day's exertions, as there hadn't been any for him, was already up and heading for the door before she shook herself fully awake. 'What the hell's going on?' she asked, rubbing discreetly at her front with her handkerchief.

The screaming carried on, occasionally interspersed with the long drawn-out wail of 'Muuurdeeer!'

With Hugo now at her heels, having been overtaken, she sped towards the source of the distress calls, when Beauchamp suddenly appeared in front of her and uttered the words, 'I'm sorry to inform you, my lady, that there is a body in the library.

I'm afraid that one of your guests has been the victim of a murderous attack.'

Heading directly to the library, without stopping to pass 'Go' or collecting £200, Lady Amanda punched a fist in the air and called over her shoulder, 'Yes, Virginia, there is a Santa Claus!' Hugo, who had not watched the right films to explain what she was talking about, merely limped along in her wake, trying to summon up sufficient energy to keep up with her.

Chapter Ten

An Inspector Calls

Inspector Moody was not in the best of moods. In fact, it would be more accurate to state that Inspector Moody was in an absolutely diabolical mood. There he had been, his sister and family gathered round his dining table playing their annual game of Monopoly, his wife struggling in the kitchen to assemble enough turkey sandwiches for the whole brood of them, when his telephone had shrilled, and extinguished the flame of pride that always burned in his heart when he put up Susan and her brood, and treated them to the benefit of his entertaining expertise.

The call had come out of the blue, and when the nature of the crime had been partnered with the residence of Lady Amanda Golightly, Moody had turned a very odd colour. Mrs Moody would not have been surprised to see smoke issuing from his ears. She knew that expression very well, and was always grateful when she was not on the receiving end of it.

He was still grinding his teeth when PC Glenister arrived at the house to collect him, and his whole family gave a collective sigh of relief and gratitude when he disappeared through the door, informing them that he had no idea when he would be back, and hoped that he made it back home without committing murder himself. That certainly left them with something to chew over in his absence.

Now, he found himself in the library at Belchester Towers, staring down at the lifeless body of Capt Leslie Barrington-Blyss, his head slumped forward on the library table. 'So, what did this poor chap do? Criticise your mince pies?' he asked, throwing a glare in Lady Amanda's direction.

'I had nothing whatsoever to do with this, Inspector. He was perfectly all right when I last saw him about an hour and a half ago. There must be a maniac on the loose. Have you had any reports of someone wandering off from Speedwell?'

This, as Inspector Moody was well aware, was the local psychiatric hospital, and he wasn't going to let this new sparring partner get away with blaming a perfectly respectable mental health facility, that did a very sound job of securing the establishment and its grounds, for something that she was obviously responsible for.

'There have been no such reports. And don't you think this is a gross case of overkill? Are any of your guests out of their minds, or subject to psychotic episodes?' If she could besmirch Speedwell, then he could return the slur, by implicating one of this bunch of Hooray Henrys and Henriettas.

'Overkill, Inspector? Would you kindly explain yourself this instant? I have no idea what you are babbling about, and how dare you insult my guests!'

'Have you taken a close look at the deceased ... m' lady?' he asked, the last one and a half words nearly choking him, and causing his face to empurple quite alarmingly. He didn't see why he should kowtow to this interfering old windbag, just because she had some sort of minor title. She had been a thorn in his side once, and he didn't want to find himself worrying at the same spot again, at the end of the year.

'I have been too busy summoning you, comforting his widow, and dissipating the air of panic that was present when he was discovered. Pray, share your more intimate knowledge with me, so that I may render a proper opinion.' She could be haughty when she chose, and she wasn't going to be intimidated by this lump of a man, whom she considered had the intellect of a flagstone.

'If you would care to take a closer visual evaluation, you may note that a blow to the back of the head seems to have been administered – note the bloody wound. An examination of his neck will show signs of a garrotte having being used on him, as it is still in place, and if you examine his throat, you will notice that, just below the still present garrotte, it has been cut from ear to ear. Anyone who wasn't half-blind would notice the knife sticking out between his shoulder blades, and from the colour of his lips and the slight odour issuing from his mouth, I would hazard a fairly confident guess that he has been poisoned as well.

'Is this some sort of Christmas joke that you're all playing, because if it is, not only is it not funny and in the most appalling taste, but someone is going to spend an awfully long time in prison for what has happened here today. I will not be taunted like this!'

As the inspector came to the end of his descriptive accusation, he had worked himself up into such a state of fury that spittle had gathered at the corners of his mouth, and collected in a very unpleasant and not at all refined fine froth. Beauchamp handed him a tissue without a word.

'I thoroughly resent what you're implying about my old friends here. Murder is no joking matter, and should not be treated as such. I'm sure that each and every one of us is willing to co-operate to the fullest with your enquiries, to bring whoever did this to justice. Now, if you could just act like a gentleman for a moment, and not carry on like an hysterical teenager, maybe we can begin this investigation.'

'Are you implying that I am not acting in a professional manner?' asked Moody, looking as if he could turn nasty again.

'If the shoe fits, Inspector ...' Lady Amanda let this hang in the air, and saw PC Glenister trying to suppress a smile. As he caught her gaze, he winked at her, and she suspected that she had an ally in the making in this young man.

Remembering the first foray into murder investigation that she and Hugo had made when the latter had moved into Belchester Towers, she reckoned that with this chap 'on side' they had a far better chance of beating Moody to the solution.

At last she had admitted why things had seemed so humdrum. She had been longing for the excitement of detecting again, the call of adventure, and the investigation of the unknown. It had added a liberal sprinkling of spice to her existence, and now she felt she couldn't live without it.

She and Hugo would tackle this murder and, come hell or high water, they would identify the murderer before that small-minded little inverted snob could even scratch the surface of the truth. And if Hugo didn't want to play, he could stay behind in his playpen, while she went hither and thither searching for clues.

'I shall conduct my guests to the drawing room, Inspector Moody, while you seek to gather together your manners, and you may interview us one by one in the dining room. The table in there should prove perfect for taking notes. I shall also alert my manservant to expect a team of what I believe you call SOCOs, to take samples and suchlike from the scene, for forensic analysis.

'Should you or your men require any refreshments, just ring for Beauchamp, and he will oblige. Now, if you will excuse me, I must accompany my guests to less distressing surroundings.' With a strong sense of having put the man in his place, she gathered her old friends round her, and set off for the drawing room, requesting Beauchamp to bring them all a nice pot of tea, to settle everyone's nerves.

Inspector Moody, more out of spite than from any other motive, apprehended Beauchamp on his way to the kitchen to carry out his mission of mercy before he could obtain access to his over-sized kettle, and informed him that he would like to question him first.

'But I'm ordered to provide tea to soothe the guests' nerves. Some of them are undoubtedly suffering from shock,' he retorted, and got it; both barrels.

'I don't care if her ladyship has asked you to provide a priest for a dying child, matey. You're going nowhere until I've questioned you, and you can argue until you're blue in the face, and it won't make any difference. At the moment, I'm in charge, and I'd like that to be clear to everyone in this house this afternoon, including you, Jeeves. And if you refuse to co-operate, I shall arrest you for obstructing a policeman in the execution of his duty. Got that?

'Lady high-and-mighty Golightly might think herself mistress of all she surveys, but she, like every citizen of this country, is not above the law of the land, and today, I represent that law. What I say, goes, without question. Now, put that in your pipe and smoke it. And if Lady Muck doesn't like it, she can whistle! Comprende? Good! Now, siddown, and don't you dare to look down your nose at me, or I'll find something to charge you with; you see if I don't.'

'Very well, Inspector,' replied Beauchamp, with his very best manners polished to perfection. 'How may I be of assistance?'

PC Glenister was already seated at the dining room table, his notebook out, his pen poised, resembling nothing more than an eager puppy waiting for a stick to be thrown for him. He hadn't long come out of training and Belchester was his first posting. He'd thought it would be all lost dogs and cats, with perhaps a few pairs of knickers being stolen from clothes-lines thrown in, for a bit of spice, but it had not proved to be so.

In his first month as a fully-fledged police constable, Lady Amanda had whirled into the station with a tale of murder in a nursing home, and had beaten his boss to the finishing line, while Inspector Moody still thought there was no case to investigate. Now, here he was again, embroiled with the same energetic and enthusiastic old lady, and there had been another murder.

He suspected he was going to really enjoy this posting, and had a feeling that he would be working more closely with his current hostess than with his boss. Moody's name suited him, and anything a humble PC could do to solve a mysterious death in semi-aristocratic surroundings couldn't do said PC's career a jot of harm.

Beauchamp, another who was no fan of the inspector, extracted great enjoyment from informing that officer that during the time when the murder could have taken place, i.e. after the tour during the period when everyone was wandering around alone, he had spent the whole time in the kitchen with Enid Tweedie, dealing with the domestic fall-out caused by the rather large number of persons for afternoon tea, and, resentfully and reluctantly, the inspector had to let him go about his duty of providing tea for the drawing room.

PC Glenister was dispatched to fetch Lady Amanda, and when she entered the dining room, the inspector had daggers in his eyes. This overweight – fat, actually – old windbag with all her airs and graces, had defeated him once, and he was determined not to let that happen again. She might be a Lady, but he wasn't inclined to be a gentleman when dealing with this case. He would use every low-down trick he could think of to get to the perpetrator first. He would not be humiliated a second time by this bumbling old amateur.

'Sit down and let's get this over with,' he said in a commanding voice, his eyes as cold and hard as flints, as he gazed at this infuriating woman.

'So kind, Inspector,' she replied, giving him one of her most open smiles, and pulling out a dining chair. 'Will you and your constable be in need of any refreshment?'

PC Glenister's eyes lit up, but Moody merely glared at his hostess and declined the offer, without even the manners to have declared it a kind one.

'I want you to give me the goods on this lot you've got here. I want to know everything about them that may have given them a motive, and I don't want you to pull any punches. And if you don't co-operate, I'm going to have you down the station so fast, your feet won't touch the ground. A night in the cells will soon loosen your tongue,' he spat at her.

'How frightfully amusing of you, Inspector. I must tell the Chief Constable about your talent for doing impressions of a detective from a B-movie. Now, from what I understood of what you just said, you would like me to tell you anything about my friends that might be construed as a motive for murder. Is that correct?'

Moody was shocked into silence by what she had just declared, and merely nodded his head to the final part of it, while enquiring, 'You actually know the Chief Constable, then?'

'Of course I know old Roland. We've served on several committees together over the years. He can't be far off retirement now. I know he'll fight that tooth and nail. Very dedicated man. But as for my house guests, I haven't known them well since we were all much younger. We used to go around in a group with a few others. You know the sort of thing? Everyone invited to the same balls and dinners, you sort of end up as a little gang.'

Moody, of course, knew nothing of the sort. The only balls he had ever had anything to do with were footballs, and he had what he called his 'dinner' in the station canteen, at what he called dinnertime – about one p.m. His upbringing had been so different from hers that he might as well have been brought up on another planet, and he resented this deeply. She belonged to a world, part of which it was impossible for him to become. How dare she! He refused to feel inferior!

'I know Maddie used to smuggle bottles of sherry into her dorm – that's Mrs Madeleine Mapperley-Minto, PC Glenister. And, of course, there was that time – actually, I think it was twice – that Bonkers was caught raiding the jam cupboard at school; hand actually in the jar when he was busted by Mato. That's Col. Henry Heyhoe-Caramac, if you're taking notes. I don't think I've even been custodian of the knowledge of anything that has occurred, of a criminal nature, in their adult lives, however.

'I know I'm not being particularly helpful, but they're mostly a bunch of jolly good chaps, and I can't see any of them having a reason to commit murder, and in my house, too. I still stick to the theory that it was an escaped psychopath from the mad house up the road.'

'You must know something. Come on, spit it out, or I'll have to get tough with you.' Moody had temporarily forgotten about the Chief Constable.

'I can assure you that you could torture me with red-hot pokers, and I would not be able to deliver any further knowledge than I've already given you. You don't still do that, do you? I don't think I should like it very much.'

The woman was toying with him, and he'd gone as far as he could with his rudeness. There was nothing else to do but dismiss her from his sight, and hope that one of the other nobs would know more than she did about this whole sorry crew. Moody could be a very jealous man when he chose to be.

Hugo, on the other hand, had nearly driven the inspector into a state where he would have admitted himself as a voluntary patient at the local mental institution, with his tales about pranks and larks they had all got up to as teenagers, stopping to indulge in a wheezy laugh, as he got to the end of each story. He had managed to bumble on for about fifteen precious minutes of the 'golden time' after a murder, before Moody had actually stood up and held up his hand to halt the flow.

Without a word of explanation, he had merely said, in a strangled voice, 'Goodbye, sir. Send in the widow next!' and Hugo left feeling puzzled and unappreciated. Had he not unearthed every little episode of their early years that could have landed them in quite a lot of hot water? How ungrateful he had seemed, and he'd hardly paid attention at all. The PC, on the other hand, had scribbled away like nobody's business, sometimes smiling to himself as he struggled to keep up with the flow of anecdotes. Nice young man, that, he concluded, and went off to ask Porky to attend at the inspector's pleasure.

Mrs Lesley Barrington-Blyss arrived with a handkerchief clasped to her face to staunch the tears that sprang from her eyes. A bonny baby, she had grown into a chubby child, then a tubby teenager. Her weight had made her self-conscious, and meeting Capt Leslie when she had been a portly and definitely on-the-shelf adult, had been the only thing in her life that allowed her not to be distressed about how she looked.

She had never minded being called Porky, because she knew that her husband loved her just the way she was. She was now a majestically large woman, although light on her feet, and seemed to float along the ground rather than walk.

This afternoon she floated into the dining room, weeping copiously, and threw herself down into a dining chair which creaked ominously as she landed. 'Whatever am I going to do without my Popeye?' she hooted in distress, like a ship that has been holed below the waterline, and sending the inspector into a panic. What on earth was a 'Popeye'? As far as he was concerned, it was a sailor man, whose girlfriend was called Olive Oyl.

'Popeye?' he queried, wondering if the woman was crackers.

'My husband,' she replied through the cotton of her handkerchief. 'Leslie.'

She was at it again! Surely *her* name was Lesley. Inspector Moody cleared his throat self-consciously. He was already in the dark as to what a Popeye was, and now she was introducing herself as if she were a separate person from herself, as it were. And where on earth did her husband fit into all this gibberish? His thoughts may have been muddled, and he knew what he meant, but he had no idea what this lady was talking about? 'Lesley?' he queried, in a rather worried voice.

'My husband. We shared the same name, but spelled differently,' Mrs Barrington-Blyss explained, as if to a fool, without losing her place in her handkerchief.

Now Moody really was flummoxed. Of course they shared the same name. They were married. What in the name of God did Popeye and this other Lesley have to do with the dead man? Maybe she was on some sort of medication and hallucinated, or made up things that couldn't possibly be true.

He was just about to send her away until she was less hysterical, when Glenister approached him from behind and whispered in his ear, 'I think you'll find that they shared the same forename, and that he was called Popeye because he wore an eye-patch, and only had one eye. You may have noticed the patch in the library when we examined the body.'

Moody had done nothing of the sort in his fury at being summoned to Belchester Towers on Boxing Day, but in the situation in which he thought he had been embroiled, this information shone a great light on the events since

Mrs Barrington-Blyss had entered the room. He glowered instinctively at Glenister, for having the temerity to interrupt him when he was questioning a possible suspect, but he was nevertheless intensely grateful for this enlightenment, although he would never admit it.

'I'm very sorry for your loss,' Moody began again, only to produce a fresh howl from the recent widow. 'And I should be very grateful if you would pull yourself together for a few minutes so that I can question you. I'm sure you want your husband's murderer caught as much as, if not even more than, I do.'

At the mention of the murder, Mrs Barrington-Blyss's sobs rose to a howl that suddenly transformed into hysterical laughter. Pulling the handkerchief from her face, she screamed with mirth, rocking backwards and forwards in her chair, tears shooting from her eyes as she did so. Moody was scandalised and not a little nonplussed. What on earth was he to do with a woman who appeared to find her husband's murder so highly amusing?

Louder sounds penetrated through to the drawing room, the door of which was not completely closed, and her laughter reached the others, foregathered there. 'I'd better go and give that ghastly little man a hand. He hasn't the nous to know what to do in a situation like this,' announced Lady A, rising from her seated position.

In the dining room, the door was suddenly flung open, Lady Amanda marched smartly into the room, stopping by Mrs B-B's chair, raised a hand and slapped her soundly on her left cheek. The ensuing silence was deafening. 'This woman is in no condition to be questioned. I am going to summon my own doctor, who can administer a sedative. Your constable here can take her home, and you can question her when she is in a fit state to think straight. Her husband's body is barely cold, and you expect her to be able to answer questions about it? Disgraceful, I call it!

'Constable Glenister, I should be grateful if you would drive Mrs Barrington-Blyss home, and I shall get Beauchamp to follow you in the Rolls. He can then bring you back when the doctor has arrived to take care of her. I believe she has a housekeeper, so I assume she will not be alone tonight. Her health and mental state are more important, at the moment, than answering a few silly questions from the inspector here. Follow me, both of you,' she concluded, and led the way from the room, Constable Glenister and Lesley Barrington-Blyss following meekly in her wake, leaving Moody to twiddle his thumbs in solemn solitude.

Lady Amanda deposited the emotionally charged widow in Hugo's room, and moved to the hall to call Dr Campbell Andrew away from his Boxing Day festivities. This done, she found Beauchamp, as usual, at her shoulder when she wanted him, and explained the situation to him. All the while, Constable Glenister had stood by, a grin on his face at the way she had bested Moody, without even seeming to try, and in such a situation, that the inspector could hardly argue. What a woman!

As the door of Hugo's ground-floor bedroom shut behind Lady Amanda, Moody left the dining room and burst in on the rest of the party, demanding to speak to each of the other guests in turn. She could hardly ruin all of his attempts at questioning his prime suspects in the case.

Sir Jolyon ffolliat DeWinter took the lead, and rose to follow the man into the next room. Someone, after all, had to set an

example and, most probably, put this uppity oik in his place.
Sir Jolyon had gained the impression that the inspector suffered
from a shortage of good manners, and anyone who could reduce
good old Porky to such a pitiable condition needed to be taught
a lesson, in his opinion, but he'd treat him as he found him – for
now.

After the preliminary enquiries concerning name, address
and contact numbers, of which Moody had, himself, to take
note, as Glenister would obviously be gone for some time, the
inspector began his questioning with, 'Have you any idea who
may have had a motive for this murder?'

'Absolutely none,' replied Sir Jolyon. (*The subject answered in
the negative,* scribbled Moody.)

'Can you tell me what you were doing at the time of the
murder?' he continued.

'What time, exactly, would that be, old man?' queried Sir
Jolyon, not being in possession of this snippet of information.

'Between the time the official guided tour ended, and the
time Capt. Barrington-Blyss was discovered in a lifedeprived
condition in the library,' replied Moody, beginning to let his
language blossom into purple blooms, and suspecting that Sir
Jolyon was being purposely obstructive and time-wasting.

'Life-deprived – ha! Is that new police-speak, then? What's
wrong with good old "dead"? And to answer your question, I
went to the old ballroom where I spent many a happy hour in my
youth. This time of year, and all that, can get one a bit nostalgic
and sentimental, and I just wanted to bring back some of the
sweet old memories.'

'I am reliably informed that the free time available to the
group of guests was something in the order of an hour. Do you
expect me to believe that you stood in an old ballroom

reminiscing for a full sixty minutes?' Moody was well on the way to living up to his name.

'Believe what you like, old chap. That's what I did, and whether you choose to accept it as the truth, is neither here nor there. I'm not going to invent things just to make your job more interesting.'

'Can you produce any witnesses to this pensive period in the afternoon?' Moody was definitely up for a bit of a rumble with this pompous old twit.

'NO!' roared Sir Jolyon. 'Neither can I produce rabbits out of hats, nor doves out of handkerchiefs. I stood there for an hour recalling the past, and if my word's not good enough for you, you can take a running jump. You've already had poor Porky in hysterics, and now you're trying to goad me beyond endurance.

'I've know the deceased since Porky married him. We have never been close friends and I know little about him. Why on earth, that being the case, should I want to murder him; and so comprehensively, I might add?'

'My investigations will reveal anything that you do not admit to me during questioning.' Moody didn't think he was winning, but was willing to get a little heavier.

'You jumped-up little jobsworth! Your threats don't frighten me! As far as I'm concerned, you can stick your questioning where the monkey sticks his nuts, and bloody good luck to you. I'm going back to the drawing room, and, should you wish to speak to me again, I shall insist on my solicitor being present, if only to restrain me from committing common assault on a very common little man.'

After this uncompromising outburst, Sir Jolyon extracted a fat cigar from the inside pocket of his jacket, clipped the end, and lit it, blowing his first inhalation of smoke across the table, straight into the inspector's face. Then, without a by-your-leave, he stood up and left the room, his face a picture of someone who is having problems with his haemorrhoids, leaving the inspector unexpectedly alone, without even having been given the opportunity to demand that Sir Jolyon request his wife to attend next for interrogation.

Once more, he betook himself to the drawing room, this time looking cautiously round the door, to make sure that there was no Sir Jolyon there waiting to ambush him, and relieved, to find that there wasn't, asked Lady Amanda, who had returned to her guests, now that Porky was on her way home, to accompany him into the hall for a moment, where he cravenly asked her for a list of her guests, so that at least he could address, by name, the person to whom he wanted to speak next.

Re-entering the drawing room, a reluctant Moody behind her, Lady Amanda obligingly borrowed Enid's list, handed it over, and left it to him to make his choice, in front of everyone else. It was sheer bad luck that Lt Col. Aloysius Featherstonehaugh-Armitage was at the top of the list, and Moody's pronunciation of the name, as it was spelled, earned him a round of hearty laughter from his merry little group of suspects, thus further reducing his self-esteem.

By the time he left Belchester Towers that evening with his newly returned PC, Moody was in a steaming fury at the lack of respect that had been shown him during the afternoon. In fact, had there been a broom handy, he'd have grabbed it and swept out of the property in a demonstration of his state of anger and high dudgeon. He was now determined to take it out on his family when he got home, just by way of re-asserting his authority on his world and making himself feel better. He was a man who, if bested, always looked for someone further down the pecking order to kick, to ease his frustration and rebuild his self-esteem.

Chapter Eleven

Plotting

When the police presence had removed itself, Lady Amanda courteously showed out her guests, and promised to call on them all to get the feedback from their tour, if they would be so kind as to let her. No one demurred, and she felt it was best to leave this part of what she had wanted to achieve for another day, especially as she felt so excited about being involved with another murder, and was doing her damndest not to show it.

Once back in the drawing room with a cocktail apiece, she began to show the true colours of her mood. 'We're in business again, Hugo! We've got a new investigation, and we've really got a head start on Moody, because we know the world these people move in. We're going detecting tomorrow and I can hardly wait! What say you, old thing?'

'Oh no!' exclaimed Hugo, who had forgotten her comment about the mysterious Virginia and Santa Claus, dismissing it as just a throw-away line, and had hoped she could keep her nose out of police affairs this time. If Moody went digging about in the past for motives, Manda's family had quite a lot of closets absolutely bursting with skeletons.

'Oh, yes, Hugo! I'll bet my shirt that it was something to do with that blasted book he's said to have been writing. If he's going to blow the lid on the County Set, no wonder someone had it in for him. He was just a social climber, after all's said and done. That's the only reason he married Porky when no one else would have her.'

'But, Manda, if he's been poking and prying into everyone's past, has it not crossed your mind that you'll be a really prominent suspect?'

'What are you talking about, Hugo?'

Lowering his voice, Hugo hissed, 'One: your mother not being dead, two: her running a knocking-shop here for the GIs in the war, three: your daddy's trade on the Black Market, and four: his arms deals after hostilities had ceased.' This statement of facts was greeted with quite a long silence.

'Bum!' said Lady Amanda. 'I hadn't thought about any of that. But that's even more reason for us to get at the truth before Moody. If we can provide him with a murderer, maybe we can get Porky to suppress the book, or take it out of the publisher's hands or something. What you've just said makes it even more urgent that we get on to this murderer's trail before the police. It's not just me that will be in deep doo-doos, it's all my friends as well, and you can bet that their families aren't all sea-green incorruptible.

'We've got to solve this to save the family honour, not only of the Golightlys, of all our friends, Hugo. Don't you see that? It's imperative that we beat that ratty little muffball to the solution, for all our sakes. And don't get all holier-than-thou about your own kin. Daddy used to tell stories about your father that would make your hair stand on end.'

'What stories?' Hugo was horrified at the very suggestion that his father had not been the honourable man he remembered and had so much admired and loved.

'You'll have to wait until all this is solved. If keeping you in the dark is the only way I can ensure your help, then keep you in the dark I shall,' said Lady A, with a wicked little smile with which anyone who has ever been emotionally blackmailed would be familiar.

'And what about your lot, Manda?' asked Hugo, a twinkle of triumph in his eyes.

'My lot? What have I got to hide? Apart from what you've already pointed out,' she added, looking rather shame-faced at the embarrassment of riches that Hugo had just listed.

'Surely you haven't forgotten so soon the main reason you used to send your mother back to her apartment in Monte Carlo? What a great potential for current scandal instead of old news: that fatal car crash, after which they buried a woman who wasn't dead, under an erroneous name, while the real Lady E made off to foreign climes, to live out the rest of her years under a false name,' Hugo reminded her. If she could use this fact to send her mother scuttling off back to the continent, then someone else could get considerable mileage out of it in a sensational tell-all book.

'Oh my giddy aunt! None of those things entered my mind, so used to them was I, as part of my own family history. If he breathes a word, not only will the family name be ruined, but Mummy will be extradited and tried for faking her own death, and no doubt there'll be something they can prosecute me for, for using a title to which I'm not entitled, even though I didn't know she wasn't dead. And as for the shares in the family pharmaceutical company – we'll be wiped off the stock exchange.

'Bum!' She declared this last word again with enormous feeling, then followed it with, 'Double bum!' After a few minutes with her chin in one hand, hand balanced on her knee, she looked at Hugo with enormous frightened eyes and intoned soulfully, 'What am I going to *do*, Hugo? They're sure to suspect *me* as it was in *my* house that the murder was committed.'

'Well, I suppose we'll just have to take on the case and expose the real murderer before that chap Moody has time to uncover what old Popeye had included in his book,' replied Hugo, with a long-suffering face.

'Did you say "we", Hugo? Are you really prepared to help me on this one?' she asked, hope dawning on her face.

'Well, I suppose I'd better, old thing, if those stories about my father were as hair-raising as you seem to think they are. Anyway, these people are our friends, and we don't want their reputations to go down the plug-hole just because old Popeye fancied making a bob or two, do we?'

'He never really fitted in, did he? I mean, Porky didn't marry until she was absolutely the last thing left on the shelf, and she didn't exactly do herself proud. He was only a captain, and then insisted that he use the rank socially. I rather thought, at the time, that that was a bit beyond the pale.'

'Me too, Manda! He's not what my papa would have called a pukkah sahib. There's definitely a whiff of the common about him, and I, for one, was never comfortable in his company. He always seemed to be trying to worm information out of one, about one's finances and connections. Definitely not cricket, if you ask me!'

'And he wormed his way into invitations to things to which nobody would normally have dreamed of inviting him. Dolly Pargeter got waylaid by him at some cocktail party or other, she was telling me in the spring, when she suddenly realised he'd smarmed her into inviting him to her spring ball. That wouldn't have been so bad, but when he did turn up, he wasn't wearing white tie, as had been specified, and then he tried to borrow fifty quid from the butler.'

'Shocking! How did Porky put up with him?' barked Hugo, getting quite het-up about these reports of insupportable behaviour on the part of the corpse, then added, 'I suppose we're acting like insufferable snobs, discussing him like this.'

'That's why people like us were put on this earth, Hugo: to be superior. Porky, though, never was a very bright old thing,

I suppose. As long as he kept the compliments flowing, she probably just turned a blind eye to his social indiscretions and faux pas, glad to have a man on her arm at long last.'

'So how are we going to go about our investigation, Manda? Have you had any bright ideas?' Hugo wasn't great in the bright ideas department, and usually left all that to someone else with a quicker intellect than his.

'It's so obvious, it's staring us right in the face, Chummy, old stick,' she declared, bounding upright and beginning to pace the room, lost in thought, as the plan developed in her brain.

'It might be to you, but I'm afraid I haven't the faintest idea what it is you plan to do.'

'We visit them all, one by one, and do as much subtle questioning as we can. We never did get to the bit about feedback from my tour, and I think I've a right, having fed them a top-notch afternoon tea, to expect something back in repayment. We'll just call round like I threatened to do, and do some pumping, while we're finding out how they enjoyed their time here.'

'Do you really think we'll get anywhere? If that book of Popeye's is full of stuff that they've been keeping quiet, surely a little discreet questioning isn't going to get them to spill their guts to us?'

'Oh, Hugo, how you are getting into the role! But you're perfectly right. You and I are a good team, but we mustn't forget that we have two other members on our strength. I'm going to send Enid undercover again, and I think I have a role for Beauchamp as well. And don't forget, they're much more likely to confide in us than they would have been to tell all to old Popeye.'

'If they want to have anything to do with it, considering what happened during their tour.' Hugo was highly dubious about their consent to participate in a little feedback session.

It was nearly midnight at the end of a very long Boxing Day, and as Hugo and Lady A sat in the drawing room where Enid had finally joined them, Beauchamp came in with four cocktails on a silver tray, although there were five glasses. He had deemed it socially acceptable that he join in the final discussion of the day, as he had been responsible for so much of its content, murder excepted.

Hugo had his game leg up on a footstool, so that he could rest the knee that had been giving him so much trouble over the last few weeks. Enid was just finishing off her tale of what she had seen and heard that day.

'Ah, Beauchamp, splendid! Just pop the tray on the credenza for a moment will you? I've been waiting for all four of us to be together, for I have something to ask both of you. Hugo and I have been discussing what to do about today's unfortunate event, and have decided that it is our social and moral duty to investigate.

'Both of you were involved in our last investigation, and I would like to ask if I may count on your support for a second outing of the Famous Four? What about it, eh?'

'Will I have to be undercover again, a spy, like last time?' asked Enid.

'Will you be putting yourself in physical danger again, my lady?' asked Beauchamp.

'Hmm. How shall I put this? Yes to your question, Enid, and probably, to yours, Beauchamp.

'Yes, please,' squeaked Enid Tweedie, her eyes sparkling at the thought of her life being elevated above the humdrum for a second time.

'Provided we can miss out the bit where I get knocked on the head and tied to a chair, with sticky tape across my mouth, you can count me in, too,' agreed Beauchamp, in his haughtiest voice.

'Bungo-ho!' cried Hugo, unable to believe that they wanted to play private detectives again with Lady Amanda, and clapped his hands in his enthusiasm.

'So, what drinks have you brought us, to end such an unexpectedly eventful day, Beauchamp?'

The manservant retrieved his tray and, starting with Lady Amanda, began to offload his cargo of colourful glasses. 'A White Christmas for you, my lady: a Wobbly

Knee again, for Mr Hugo: and for Mrs Tweedie ...'

'Do call me Enid.'

'How kind. Thank you. For Enid, a Waste of Time – you get two glasses with this, my dear, and their contents might explain the cocktail's name; and a Hopeless Case, for myself.'

'Are you being facetious, Beauchamp?' asked Lady Amanda, as the last two drinks were named and distributed.

'I wouldn't know how to, my lady,' he replied, with the ghost of a twinkle in his eye.

'Before draining her glass in one swallow, Lady Amanda held it aloft and proposed a toast. 'To the Belchester Towers Irregulars! And bugger Baker Street!'

'And then I really must be off, if you would be so kind as to allow Beauchamp to escort me home in the Rolls,' added Enid, totally pricking the balloon of Lady A's mood, with her down-to-earth practicality.

Chapter Twelve

The Belchester Towers Irregulars Strut their Funky Stuff

Hugo awoke at nine o'clock the next morning, because the sound of a human voice, apparently in endless monologue, had insinuated itself into his dream and was drowning out what Carmen Miranda had been trying to whisper in his ear. He would have been quite happy to let things be, but her mangoes were bobbing about on his head to a tango rhythm, and he yielded, eventually, to the inevitable separation from such a lovely scenario, and woke up.

The voice, however, continued, and proved to be coming from the hall, where Lady Amanda was just coming to the end of a telephone marathon in pursuit of the naked truth (and some feedback on her tour).

Pulling on his comfy old dressing gown and stepping into his slippers, he went out into the corridor and walked down to where the instrument lived, only to find her in the action of hanging up for the final time. 'Whatever have you been doing?' he asked, still chagrined about his loss of Carmen Miranda, even if she had assaulted him with her mangoes, 'Filling in for the speaking clock?' His white hair stood up in stiff meringue peaks, and his unshaven face gave him a slightly sleazy look that Carmen Miranda would probably have loved.

'I've been arranging our covert interrogations,' she answered brightly, as if she had been up for hours, which she had, but had not dared to use the instrument until eight o'clock when, even if the object of her call was still dead to the world, a member of staff would be available to note down the time of her visit, and her excuse for paying a call – spurious now of course, as there was something much more enticing afoot.

'I've spoken to Dr Andrew, in the strictest confidence, of course, and he confirmed exactly what I hoped he might: that Porky shouldn't be left alone at the moment, because of the shock she has suffered. I, of course, offered Enid as a live-in nurse for her, until she is feeling herself again, at no cost whatsoever to Porky, as a sort of apology for her husband being murdered under my roof.

'I left him to put the proposal to her, giving him my permission to say that it was all his idea, and then phoned

Enid to get her ready to go to work.'

'But I thought she had a live-in maid.'

'Gone to daily, I'm afraid, and refuses to stay overnight any more.'

'How you do wrap people around your little finger. I simply don't know how you do it. Is it because you charm them? Because they're terrified of you? Or are you really a witch?'

'Don't be silly, Hugo. It's because they trust and respect me. Now, where was I? Oh, yes: I've made appointments for one of us to call at some of the households, to talk to them about yesterday, including Porky's.'

'Hey, that's a bit like asking Mrs Lincoln how, apart from the assassination of her husband, she enjoyed the play!' Hugo looked scandalised for a moment.

'Don't be such an old woman, Hugo. It's got to be done. Now, hurry off and get dressed, and get some breakfast down you, so that we can get on with the investigation.'

'What else have you done? I can see something in your eyes that you're not telling me.'

'I've sent Beauchamp out on a little errand, that's all.' Lady Amanda was at her most dangerous when she was playing the innocent.

'And what little errand would that be, then?' Hugo knew her too well.

'I've just asked him to ask a few people a couple of questions.'

'What people and what questions?' Hugo was not going to be fobbed off on this one.

'I've sort of decided, maybe, to have a servants' ball here in the great hall, and I've sent Beauchamp out to question one or two domestic staff as to what they would like to do and to eat at the event. Although, of course, I might not be able to manage it this year, at all.'

'You've sent him round to all the houses of yesterday's guests, to pump their staff, haven't you?'

'I might have.'

'Manda, you are just about the end. I'd hate to be on your hit list: I wouldn't stand a chance,' with which opinion, Hugo toddled off to the dining room, limping slightly, in search of sustenance with which to break his fast.

Luckily, there had been a bit of a thaw overnight, so that Enid Tweedie was able to accomplish her mission of getting to Porky's residence on her bicycle, without the necessity of Beauchamp having to collect and deliver her in the Rolls – which was just as well, as that gentleman had been sent about other business. Her pump primed with instructions, she rang the doorbell of Journey's End at ten o'clock exactly, dressed in what she considered a lady's companion/nurse should wear.

Her sensible tweed coat covered a white blouse with no frills or fussy bits, and a comfortable old tweed skirt that looked as though it had been inhabited by several governesses or nannies in the past. On her feet were sensible lace-up shoes, and her head was protected from the wind by a headscarf which friends had assured her looked very like one that the Queen had worn when filmed out and about at Balmoral.

Her sensible large black handbag held a roll of freezer bags with which to protect any evidence she should find it necessary to 'acquire', and a notebook and several pens (in case one ran out) with which to make notes, during her stay. Enid's overnight bag would be delivered later, when Beauchamp was once again free to carry out this task, as she could hardly have managed the cycle with a suitcase in the wicker basket on her handlebars.

The door was answered by Mrs Twigger, a rotund figure with her hair rolled up underneath a (rather inferior, Enid thought) headscarf, and a button-up overall, for she was just a daily, now, and only worked three hours a day.

'Cor! Am I glad you've got 'ere!' Mrs Twigger exclaimed, looking at Enid as if she were the Archangel Gabriel himself. 'She's in a right old state. I can't do anything with 'er, and I'm not even supposed to be 'ere today. Supposed to 'ave a week orf, I am, and 'ere's me, only two days in me own 'ome, and 'ere I am again. Well, it's not good enough. If I 'adn't known you was comin', I'd 'ave given me notice in there and then, when I got 'ere, what with 'er weepin' an' wailin' all over the place.'

'Never fear! I am here to take the load off your shoulders,' announced Enid, in what she thought of as a confident and trustworthy voice. 'You may go as soon as I've had a word with you about Mrs Barrington-Blyss. I understand she's suffering from severe shock, and I'd like to know everything that's happened since you arrived, so that I can assess what treatment is needed.' Enid Tweedie would never have used the word 'bullshit', but she sure knew how to utilise it.

'I'll tell you what: I'll make us a nice cuppa, and we can sit in the kitchen for a bit, and I'll give you the whole story. What a ghastly thing to 'appen when yer out visitin'.'

Enid trotted into the house and followed the ample behind of the 'daily', with great hopes of what she would find out.

Beauchamp, meanwhile, was sitting at the huge kitchen table at The Manor, the residence of Sir Jolyon and Lady Felicity *ff*olliat DeWinter, being treated like minor royalty. He had a very charming way to him, when given the chance, and he'd certainly done a number on the female staff of the house. They buzzed round him like flies, offering him more tea or another slice of cake, checking to see if his chair was comfortable enough, or would he, perhaps, like another cushion?

One can only state that the manservant, who spent most of his time at the beck and call of Lady Amanda, was in his element. If he couldn't get any sniff of a suppressed scandal from these eager females, then his name wasn't Beauchamp! And he had brought tidings of a possible free knees-up. How popular could a man get?

Although it was nice to be treated like a lord, it wasn't until he was issued with an invitation into the butler's private sitting room that anything in the nature of scandal was to come to light.

Fustion, who had once been valet to The Manor's late master, and had seen the staff of the establishment dwindle until he was the only indoor manservant left, had leaned forward in his chair with a very malicious gleam in his eye, when Beauchamp mentioned the suspicious death at Belchester Towers the day before.

Lifting his right index finger, with which to either conduct or punctuate what he was about to say, he launched into his exact feelings about the deceased. 'That man was an absolute cad. How he ever managed to deceive dear Miss Lesley into marrying him, I will never know.

'He might have fooled some people, but he never fooled me. A gold-digger and a social climber he was, and it looks like he got his just desserts. Always sniffing around, he was, for any little snippet of gossip he could pick up. I heard he was writing a book about the county folks hereabouts, and that it was to be a right nasty one.

'Miss Lesley was a lovely girl in her youth, if you didn't mind a nice roundness to the figure. I've always liked plump women, myself, but she had a real down on her figure, and then found she couldn't stick to no diet sheet for more than a day or two. Many's the time, during a party or a ball here, I've found her sitting all alone in some dark corner, just feeding her face and looking miserable.

'I used to tell her that the right chap would come along one day and sweep her off her feet, but I never thought it'd be that bounder Barrington-Blyss. Right wrong 'un he was. I could tell from the word go. And she was never what you'd call happy. Still went on stuffing her face with anything she could lay her hands on. If she'd met the right chap that would never have been the case.'

'I did hear he'd got a publishing deal, and that his book was due out soon. Just between you, me and the gatepost, do you suppose there's anything about your household in it?' Beauchamp had worded his question carefully, using language that would cunningly persuade Fustion that he was of paramount importance in the ffolliat DeWinter household, and it worked.

'I don't know as there's anything that could be proved or not, but there was some sort of monkey business going on when Sir Jolyon's father – the late master, as it were – died – that, I do know for a fact, for it's had me puzzled ever since.'

At this, Beauchamp pricked up his ears and, trying not to look too eager, he leant forward in his chair and encouraged Fustion with a mildly curious look, hoping that he would spill the beans in an effort to appear all-knowing.

I was valeting the old gentleman at the time, you understand, this place having a much bigger staff. The old master had terrible trouble with his breathing towards the end, probably because he was never to be seen without a cigar sticking out of the side of his mouth.

'Anyway, he eventually took to his bed one winter: didn't even have the puff to go up and down the stairs but, being a cantankerous old bug ... soul, he sent me downstairs when he'd been in bed about a week, saying that he felt well enough to have a little puff, and asking me to fetch him his cigar case from his desk drawer in his study.

'It simply wasn't my case to argue, so off I went, trotting down to the ground floor to fetch him his dratted cigars, but when I got close to the study door, I realised it was ajar, and there was someone on the telephone inside the room. Well, I knew my place, same as everybody else in this household did, so I stopped, waiting for the call to finish, as anyone would've done, if they'd had any manners at all.'

Beauchamp recognised this for what it was: an invitation for him to sanction something that was nothing more nor less than out-and-out eavesdropping. 'That must have left you in a very difficult position, Fustion. If you walked away, whoever it was would have heard you, and you couldn't just walk in on a private telephone call without seeming terribly rude.'

'Exactly, Mr Beauchamp. So I thought the best thing to do would be to stand my ground, wait for whoever it was to finish the call, then tap gently on the door as the call ended; which is exactly what I did do.' The bait had been enticingly dangled again.

'So, who was it, making telephone calls from your late master's study?' Beauchamp was taking the softly-softly approach.

'It was the present Sir Jolyon, Mr Beauchamp, and what I heard – completely reluctantly, you understand – was a man pleading for more time to clear his gambling debts.'

'No! I had no idea Sir Jolyon was a gambling man.' Lady Amanda would have been proud of her manservant. He was reeling in his fish with enormous skill and dexterity.

'He isn't any more, I can tell you; but back then he was going through a bad time, and was heavily into cards, not to mention debt. He sounded desperate on the telephone, and was begging to be given just a few more days to get the money together.'

'And?' enquired Beauchamp, looking eagerly at the older man, who looked just as keen to tell his story as Beauchamp was to hear it.

'And, I didn't think anything more about it at the time, but the next morning, when I went up to the master to set about washing and shaving him, I was to get the surprise of my life. The maid had been in with his early morning tea, but she'd said he was still asleep, so she'd just left it on the side; he had a foul temper if woken, and she didn't want to catch the rough side of his tongue so early in the morning. He could be a right tartar at times.

'I went up about fifteen minutes later and drew the curtains, and when I turned to wake the old man, I got the shock of my life. There was nothing on this earth that would ever wake my master again, except for, perhaps, the last trump. He was stone cold dead. I can tell you, I nearly passed out cold when I saw him lying there, with no more breaths left to draw. He'd had his last cigar, and I think I rather imagined that that had sent him off to the other side, and I felt so responsible; as if I'd killed him myself.'

'How ghastly for you, Fustion. You must have been riddled with guilt,' interjected Beauchamp, just to keep the story flowing, for he was certain that it hadn't, yet, reached its conclusion.

I hardly knew what to do next, and I went into what I think is called a sort of auto-pilot mode. I tidied the bed sheets, thinking that he hadn't gone as peacefully as I'd have liked, They were in a fair old mess, as if he'd tossed and turned half the night. I also picked up a pillow from the floor, never thinking how it might have got there, except through his restlessness. I remember standing and staring at it, as if it might hold the solution to my problem of how to inform the household of what had occurred, and the only thing I recall, is looking at the material and thinking the old fellow must have dribbled a lot in the night, for there were quite a few saliva stains on it.' 'Go on,' Beauchamp encouraged him.

'Well, I put the pillow back on the bed, and took myself off downstairs to inform the new master and his wife, who were early risers, and would be at breakfast by now. I'd had such a shock, that I was very conscious of the fact that I would upset their meal, but I had no choice, and went straight in to them. That was when I felt they weren't acting quite right, but I don't really know how to explain it.

'She already looked as if she'd been crying, which I thought rather odd, as they weren't a quarrelsome couple, and when I entered the room, Sir Jolyon jumped up, as if someone had pulled a gun on him. His eyes were round and fearful, and yet I hadn't said a word to them about what had happened.'

'That is odd. Almost as if they already knew, you mean?'

'That's precisely it, Mr Beauchamp, and when I finally did blurt out my news, it had very little effect on either of them. To my mind, they acted very uncharacteristically. On the way down the stairs, you see, I'd already played out the scene in my mind.

'Sir Jolyon isn't a man to use two words when twenty will do, and I thought he'd go off into a right old rant about how the old man didn't deserve to go, and would still be here now if he'd followed medical advice, instead of being bloody-minded and doing exactly as he pleased, blaming me for getting him that last cigar without consulting him. I thought Lady Felicity would burst into tears and have a hysterical turn, weeping and wailing that she never had time to say goodbye properly, and now it was too late.'

'And they did nothing of the sort?'

'You're right about that, Beauchamp. Sir Jolyon himself just blustered something like, 'the old man had to go sometime' and perhaps I would sort out the undertaker, as the doctor had been in recent attendance. Lady Felicity merely said what a relief it was to know that he was no longer suffering, and then I was dismissed.'

'Didn't it play on your mind that something was out of kilter, Fustion?'

'It wasn't my place to say anything. I could've lost my position, and it wasn't really any of my business. I dismissed it from my mind, until that gentleman, who is no gentleman, came snooping around here a few months ago, asking impertinent questions and generally upsetting the staff.'

'I'm assuming you're referring to Barrington-Blyss?' Beauchamp wanted all the 'i's dotted and all the 't's crossed, and would chance to presume nothing.

'That's the feller. Got himself knocked off at your place, yesterday, I hear. Can't say as he'll be missed. From what I've heard. I never could put up with him, as I've already made clear. He was never what you'd call a popular man – more someone who was tolerated because of who he'd married, if you get my drift.'

'Oh, I do, indeed, Fustion. Least said, soonest mended, eh?'

'That's it in a nutshell, Mr Beauchamp. Now, would you like any more refreshments?'

I have had an adequate sufficiency, thank you. My compliments to the cook on her baking, and I must take my leave now. Thank you so much for sparing the time to talk to me.'

'Is your old gal playing detective again?' asked Fustion as Beauchamp rose from his chair.

'I shall tell her ladyship that you asked after her,' he replied, and winked at the old keeper of secrets at The Manor. They were two of a kind, and they both recognised this fact.

After morning coffee, Hugo had been surprised and delighted to find out that he would be responsible for a fact-finding mission on his own, and not under the beady eye of Lady Amanda.

'Hugo,' she trilled, as he set his empty cup back in its saucer. I want you to go out on reconnaissance for me, this morning.'

'You'll be coming too, though, won't you?'

'No. This is a mission strictly for you. I want you to go over to the Heyhoe-Caramacs' and ask if it's possible to speak to their gardener. His name's Grundle, I believe.'

'What's gardening got to do with the murder?' asked Hugo, perplexed at this request.

'If I remember correctly, he was Col. Henry's father's man, when the colonel was in the army. He must know an awful lot about the old fellow and the household's history, right up to date. If there's anyone at that house who can give us a pointer or two in the right direction, it's Grundle. He's a bit of a grumpy old curmudgeon, but I'll give you a bottle of whisky to take with you as a peace-offering.'

'What shall I tell him I'm there for? I can't just turn up without a reason,' Hugo asked plaintively.

'Tell him I want him to do me some cuttings from all his honeysuckles and clematis. I've complimented him on his climbers in the past, so he'll have no reason to doubt the veracity of the request.'

'Righty-ho, Manda. Where do they live?'

'At a place called The Grange. It's only a few hundred yards up the Belchester Road, so you might as well take the tricycle.'

'In this weather?'

'Hugo, a man has lost his life, and you complain about getting a bit chilly? What are you, a man or a mouse?'

'Squeak,' was Hugo's inevitable answer, but Lady Amanda informed him that Beauchamp had taken the Rolls and would not be back until it was time to prepare luncheon. With that, she bundled him into the hall, handed him his top coat, his hat and gloves, and offered a long stripy scarf to protect his face against the wind. Then, when she had him suitably bundled up, like a rather colourful Egyptian mummy, she whizzed off to the stables and rode the motorised trike round to the front of the house, and helped him on to it. She had left it running, and her last act in seeing him off was to release the brake, giving him a rather unexpectedly wobbly start to his first mission for the day.

Hugo sputtered haphazardly down the drive, muttering insults into the wool of his scarf, containing words such as 'dictator', 'control-freak', and 'blasted Little Miss BossyBoots'.

The road had been cleared, so he had little difficulty with snow or ice, and he eventually found it quite revivifying to be puttering along in the bright sunshine under a powder-blue sky, on such a crisp and beautiful day. His spirits rose as he rode, and by the time he'd reached The Grange, he was in a fine mood.

Stopping only to open the gate to admit himself and his machine, he turned the handle-bars towards the greenhouse, in which he could detect a fine clouding of smoke; a sure sign that the old man was in there with his pipe going full blast. Hugo had met him once before, but

only in passing, but was sure he could hold his own, on this mission. He liked people and, in general, they like him. It might not be such a bad morning after all.

Meanwhile, shortly after Hugo's reluctant departure, Lady Amanda had been surprised to receive a visitor in the guise of PC Glenister, who stood on the front step and twinkled at her. 'Morning, ma'am,' he greeted her, and gave her a dazzling smile with just a hint of conspiracy in it. 'I thought I'd pop round and keep you up to date with events relating to yesterday's suspicious death.'

'That's very kind of you, young man, er, Constable. Do, please, come in and warm yourself. Tell me, has Inspector Moody sent you?"

'Absolutely not, ma'am. I just thought you'd like to be kept abreast of what the police have turned up.'

'Are you conspiring with me, Constable?'

'Oh, absolutely, ma'am. I saw that look in your eyes yesterday and, as I'd rather get the case wrapped up before New Year when I'm off to visit my family, I thought I'd back you as the winning horse.'

'How very charming and astute of you. So you're proposing to be my police mole, is that it?'

PC Glenister squeezed his eyes nearly shut and made vague clawing motions with his fingers.

'Jolly good impression. Perhaps it might be more comfortable for us, if we're to collaborate, if I called you something less formal than PC Glenister. What is your Christian name?'

'I believe the politically correct expression now is "forename",' he informed her, as a corner of his mouth twitched.

This was a test, she felt, and replied, 'Christian name was good enough for my parents, and it's always been good enough for me, so I repeat, what is your Christian name, PC Glenister?'

'Call me Adrian, ma'am.'

'And you may call me Lady Amanda. Now, what have you got for me? Has old Mouldy-Wump got anything to go on yet?'

'I'm very much afraid he has. That's why I'm here, really. I couldn't bear to see him steal a march on you. Oh, and if anyone should ever find me here when we're consulting, I wonder if you'd be so good as to say that I'm just here on some routine follow-up questions.'

'Excellent idea!' Lady Amanda agreed. 'Now, what's the old windbag got?'

'I'm sorry to have to tell you that he obtained a search warrant this morning, for the deceased's house, having got wind of a book he was writing, that might leave a number of members of the County Set right in the proverbial poo,' he informed her.

'Damn!' swore Lady Amanda. 'And did he find it?'

'I'm afraid so, and there's no point in asking me if I can get access to it, because he's got it locked up in the evidence room with instructions that no one's allowed to retrieve it except himself. That is, he found a paper copy, and confiscated the deceased's computer.'

'Blasted dog-in-a-manger!'

'Exactly! That was the final straw that made me decide to throw my lot in with yours. I think I've got him pretty well summed up now, and I don't want to be working on this case until I draw my pension.'

'Good lad! Stick with Auntie Amanda, and you won't go far wrong. Now, has the book got him any further forward?'

'He was reading it when I left the station, and making some very excited noises. I've got a nasty feeling that he's got his hands on the goods, but he's bound to bungle it somehow. From what I've seen of him, he couldn't detect the location of his own backside with both hands and a mirror. And by the way, there were absolutely no fingerprints to be found on any of the weapons. I thought you'd be pleased to hear that, so at least he's got nothing to go on in that department.'

'Okay, Adrian. You've been up-front with me. I'll now be up-front with you. I've managed to get one of my friends – not a classy one, you understand, just to make that clear – installed in the widow's house as a companion/nurse while she's coming to terms with the shock. So, I've now got someone on the inside, and I intend to use her.'

'Nice one, Lady Amanda. You've stolen a march on him there. He hasn't even thought of putting a WPC in the property, in case Mrs Barrington-Blyss's life is in danger as well.'

'Well, if he does, she'll have good old Enid Tweedie to contend with, and I hear she's pretty good with a loaded handbag.'

Back at the greenhouse, in the gardens of The Grange, Hugo was perched on an old tea chest, drinking whisky laden tea strong enough to flatten a stevedore, and was well into worming his way into Grundle's confidence.

'... and I know he doesn't really like Manda, because she's so much better a shot than he is. He really resents the fact that a woman should be so good with guns.'

'Well, he certainly doesn't take after his father, that's all I can say.'

'His father was a good man with a gun?'

'I'll say! We had a bit of an adventure during the war, and it was his shooting kept us going until we could get ourselves back to Blighty.' Grundle's rheumy eyes were misted with memories, as they gazed back down the long tunnel to his youth.

'We both went over with the British Expeditionary Force, him and me. I was only a private, you understand, and he was the major, so we weren't buddies, or even on a level where we'd even pass the time of day. Then all hell broke loose, and we found ourselves on our own, cut off from our own lads, and surrounded by bloody Jerries.

'I was a gibbering wreck, with what I'd seen on the beaches, but the major shook me back to my senses and told me that if I wanted to live, I'd have to pull myself together, and listen to him. We weren't going to be able to leave northern France with all this hoo-ha going on, so we'd better get ourselves down south a bit more, and see if we could contact the Resistance.

'I was that shocked that I'd have done anything he told me to do, but he played a cool hand. We travelled only at night. We slept under hedges and in barns at off the beaten track farmhouses. We stole eggs and chickens. We foraged for food as best we could, and it took us a while, but we finally got somewhere where we managed to pick up on the local Resistance fighters.

'Stupid, it seems, looking back on it, now. There we were, being so clever and underhand, moving about the countryside by night, then we got busted for having a whispered chat in one of them 'piss-whar' things. Thank God the Froggy who heard us was on our side.

'He bundled us out of that little stink-hole and into the back of a truck, where he covered us in sacks and drove us off God knows where. In the middle of nowhere we were, when he signalled us to get out. He'd taken us to what looked like the middle of a blasted forest, and suddenly we weren't sure whether to trust him or not. I expected him to hand us straight over to the enemy, but he just stood there whistling a little tune, and soon other men began to materialise out of the trees.

'We'd really landed on our feet, and we knew we were in safe hands. They took us off to an old farmhouse with no neighbour within seeing distance, and gave us some old French clothes to wear, putting our uniforms below the floor in a secret compartment, which I could see already had guns in it. Then they put this heavy old sideboard over the stash. If Jerry came visiting, he would go through the whole place, but they'd got so complacent, those dratted Huns, that they weren't going to move the furniture around looking for secret compartments.'

'You sound like you had quite an adventurous time in La Belle France, what?' Hugo commented, seeing the story in his mind's eye, and turning it into the sort of romantic tale that would have scandalised the old gardener, were he able to read Hugo's thoughts.

'Oh, we worked. It was no holiday camp. We had to sleep in the back of the chicken house, and work in the fields during the day, so we didn't stick out, but they fed us well, and after a couple of days, there was a meeting in this little restaurant nearby. Shutters all closed, closed sign on the door and, inside, all oil lamps and candles, and cloak and dagger.

'They had plans to seriously disrupt the Jerries thereabouts, and we were to be a part of it. Life sort of took on a different rhythm then, if you know what I mean. Working on the land was what I was used to, and a bit of a song and dance, getting up Jerry's nose was fine by me.'

'You must have been very brave, both of you. I hope you were well decorated for your efforts for your country in a foreign land.' Hugo was trying to change up a gear to find out if he was on the right track. This must lead back to Col. Henry at some point, but they were still stuck in the war, when the colonel would have been a mere infant.

'To cut a long story short ...'

'Thank God for that,' murmured Hugo under his breath, under the camouflage of nipping at his eye wateringly alcoholic cup of tea.

'What I couldn't understand was, several times, seeing the major yammering away with them Jerries, out in the forest where no one could see them. I thought he was gathering information for the Resistance lads, so we could make more of a nuisance of ourselves, but he never said nothing about it afterwards, not even to me.

'We must've been there about a month when this started, and, only a few days later, one of our young Frogs was shot as he left the restaurant. The first shot missed, and he made for the barn over the road, and took one in the shoulder there. He managed to get out and hared off down the road as if all the hounds of hell were after him, but Jerry got his aim together, and he put one through his head, that dropped him like a stone.

'They got us out of there the next day, in case we drew unwanted attention, and passed us on to another group travelling north, to see if they could get us back to Blighty somehow; perhaps on a fishing boat, over the Channel.'

'So, did you ask him what he was chatting so earnestly about with the enemy?'

'I did, Mr Hugo. I waited until we were completely on our own, and I put it to him that I'd seen him talking to them, and he said he'd just been passing the time of day in German, to sort of keep his hand in with the language. A couple of days later, just when we were about to try to get back home, we heard through the unit we were now with, that the unit that had looked after us had been carrying out a raid on a railway line, trying to de-rail a Jerry train, when the Jerries appeared out of nowhere, and just fired until they were all dead. Ten men from the little village we were staying near were killed that night, and the Jerries went back there and shot all the males that were left: old men and teenagers, some of them; even kiddies.'

'What did your major have to say about that?' Hugo had half an idea he was on to something here, and ought to stick it out to the bitter end.

'I thought he'd be devastated, like I was. They were people we'd got to know. In fact, if we'd stayed on, we would have been in that raiding party with all the rest of them. But, that was the funny thing: he didn't seem to give a damn. Just said it was part of the price of warfare, and that we should just forget it and get on with what we were posted to do.'

'I say! That was a bit cold of him, wasn't it?' asked Hugo.

'Cold weren't the word for it. We went our separate ways, though, having got back, and I didn't see him again until near the end of the war. We met again in a convalescent home. We'd both got a Blighty shot, and it was the end of our service for that war. He'd taken a hit to the shoulder that had done a lot of damage to the bones, and I was left with a game leg.

'We got talking, one day, and I suppose I was a little down, what with thinking what on earth I was going to do when the show was over. I mean, how much chance does a man with a game leg have against fit candidates, for a physical job? I reckoned I'd end up in the gutter, and that's when he turned up trumps. He gave me his card and said to get in touch with him when I was de-mobbed, and he'd take me on as his gardener. And here I am, still working on the same garden I came back from the war to.'

'Wonderful story, old man. Been most interesting talking to you. I'd better be off, though. I was only sent here to ask you about those cuttings,' Hugo said, his head full of enough food for thought for a cranial banquet.

'Tell her ladyship that, as soon as they've struck, I'll bring them over and hand them over to Beauchamp. He'll know what to do with them. Grand fellow! And give old Grundle's regards to her ladyship. Fine figure of a woman, she is. If I was only a few years younger ...' The old man trailed off, a leering smile forming fleetingly on his lips.

Hugo entangled himself with his coat and scarf in an effort to re-don them, and generally made himself ready for the return journey. Old Grundle had to give him a hand with his gloves, as he'd managed to get them on the wrong hands and then stood helplessly, wondering how on earth he could right the situation.

With a final twist of the scarf round his neck, he headed, rather haphazardly, towards the tricycle, mounted it, started the engine, released the brake. And drove straight into the pile of manure that was quietly and warmly steaming in the cold, as it rotted at the end of the garden.

When Lady Amanda opened the doors, slightly later in the afternoon, Hugo entered at a staggering run, turned a full three-hundred-and-sixty degree circle, staggered to his left, and ended up hugging the newel post at the bottom of the stairs, several feet of scarf draped in his wake, like the trail of a giant snail, and his hat down over his eyes at a very jaunty angle. 'H'llo, Manda,' he intoned, joyfully and slowly, taking great care with what enunciation he could muster.

Still on the step, she found Grundle, his hat held respectfully in his hands. 'I'm terribly sorry to bring Mr Hugo back like this, your ladyship, but he seemed to be having a bit of trouble with his old pins.'

'But, how on earth did you get him back here? And where's the tricycle?' Although Lady Amanda cared very much about Hugo's welfare, there was an expensive tricycle in this equation to consider as well. Hugo would, no doubt, be sober in the morning, but a new tricycle cost money.

'Down by my greenhouse, your ladyship. I loaded him into the bucket of the digging machine and drove him here by the back route. My digger's just across there, near the stables. I hope you don't mind.'

'I am most pleased with your ingenuity, Grundle, and I shall tell Col. Henry so, when I see him.'

'Thank you very much, your ladyship. I'll be taking my leave of you then. Good day!'

As Lady Amanda closed the door, she discovered that Beauchamp must have helped Hugo to a more comfortable position, and opened her mouth to locate him. 'Hugo! HUGO! Where the devil are you?'

A groan answered her from the direction of the library, and she turned and headed in that direction. She knew Grundle of old, and Hugo had probably fallen for the offer of a nice cup of tea. Nice cup of tea, be damned! It was nearly neat whisky, the way that old rascal served it.

Well, he'd better be feeling tiptop by the witching hour. She had work planned for them that night, in the wee, small hours, and she didn't want him blundering around giving away what they were up to.

After a late and solitary luncheon, Lady Amanda decided to leave Hugo to sleep off his excesses, for he had, seemingly, dispatched himself to bed in the library, not only without any supper, but without several more meal stops along the day's menu. As 'it' had happened in her residence, she thought she'd pay a courtesy call on Porky, to see how the old thing was doing. If, during that time, she had the opportunity to conspire with Enid, then so much the better. Before she left, she dropped a small brown bottle into her handbag, and smiled to herself. Some people didn't need official search warrants.

When Enid saw who was on the doorstep, her face became a mask of misery. 'Oh, Lady Amanda, I don't know how to break this to you,' she began.

'I know what you're going to say, Enid, but I already know about the police search. Never fear, there's bound to be more than one copy. No one puts all that effort into writing a book and then only keeps one copy of it. There'll be at least one more copy, or an earlier version of it around. The original notes are still probably tucked away somewhere, too. How hard did they search?'

'They were only here a few minutes. They found a manuscript on his computer and took that away with them, saying that the book would probably contain the motive for the captain's murder, and would be stored and given in evidence in any subsequent trial. They also found a copy for proofing in paper and took that as well.'

'How did poor old Porky take it?' They were speaking in whispers, but poor old Porky was obviously aware of their conversation, and her voice called out to Enid plaintively, 'Who's that, Mrs Tweedie? I don't want any visitors at the moment, not while I'm feeling like this.'

Before the lady of the house had time to draw breath, Lady Amanda was bustling into the drawing room, all smiles, pulling a pile of ladies' magazines and a small box of chocolates from her capacious handbag, and asking after the welfare of the recent widow. 'Poor, poor Porky,' she crooned, sitting down beside the woman and asking,

'How are you going to manage without Popeye?'

'I don't know how I shall manage,' Lesley BarringtonBlyss replied. 'Popeye did all the household accounts and managed all the bills and his own business affairs, and I haven't the faintest idea where to start with all that paperwork, let alone arranging a funeral for him. It might have been I who had all the money, but I had nothing whatsoever to do with the handling of it, and now I'm all at sea. I've no idea how to go about managing my own affairs.'

She spoke in a voice that gave the impression of husky grief, but Lady A noticed that her fingers were working on the cellophane round the chocolate box in an effort to get at the contents as she spoke, an independent action that said more about the way she really felt than any words could.

'Let me help you with that, old girl,' offered Lady Amanda, reaching forward, but Porky merely looked down into her lap with surprise. 'I had no idea I was doing that!' she stated. 'It must be one of those automatic reactions that people speak of.'

'I'll just get them open for you and then I'll go. You need everything from which you can derive comfort at a time like this, as well as a lot of time on your own to reflect on what has evidently caused an enormous upheaval in your life. There you go, my dear. I hope you enjoy them.'

With that, she left the room and sought out Enid in the kitchen, who was forward thinking, and was already making a pot of tea. 'Psst! Enid!' she hissed, opening her bag once more, as Enid poured the amber cascade into three cups. 'I've got something here for you, and I want you to do exactly as I tell you to do with them.'

'What are you scrabbling about looking for?' asked Enid, whispering again, in the conspiratorial way they had spoken in the hall.

'Aha! There it is!' said the older woman, and produced a small brown bottle from her bag, opened it, and placed two tiny white tablets in the palm of Enid's hand. 'Take these, crush them between two spoons, dissolve them in a little water, and then sneak them into anything in which she might not notice a slightly bitter aftertaste.'

'Like what?' Enid had only been there a few hours, and knew nothing of Mrs Barrington-Blyss's daily habits.

'She always has coffee after dinner, and she has it black and strong, with no sugar. Slip it into her coffee, and make sure you manage to get her upstairs as quickly as possible.' 'What on earth are they?'

'Sleeping tablets. And they work like magic. Don't ask any more questions. Just make sure you get her to swallow them,' ordered Lady Amanda.

'Why? I expect the doctor's left something for her anyway.'

'Because, when Hugo and I get here about midnight, we're going to turn this place upside down, looking for another copy of Popeye's book. I don't know what he's put in it, but I can't just see my friends socially ruined. I heard he had been boasting about absolute dynamite, and I don't want it to blow up in the face of anyone I know.'

'But we're sure to get caught,' Enid squeaked, starting to shake.

'How? Even if she wakes up, she will be too dopy to remember anything in the morning, and if there's anyone who can see lights on in the house, they'll know there's been a recent bereavement. That sort of thing sparks all sorts of out of character behaviour, such as roaming around the house at night.'

'I don't like this at all, lady Amanda,' Enid opined, looking anxious.

'I didn't ask you to like it Enid, I asked you to do it. Those are two totally different things. Got it?'

'Got it.'

Back at Belchester Towers, Lady Amanda went straight to her desk, having made sure the doors to the library and her study were shut. Hugo was making a hell of a racket in there, mumbling to himself, snoring and even once breaking into song. She needed to gather her thoughts and make some notes. There was work she knew she would have to conduct on the computer, but she needed to see her thoughts in writing first, so that they would gel in a comprehensible way.

After a moment of contemplation, she began to write. *Same one-shouldered shrug.* Then followed that with *Head on one side when asking a question to which the expected answer is 'no'.* Here, she paused for a moment and mumbled, 'But couples do get very alike when they've been together for a long time. Might be nothing at all.'

She then gnawed on her pen for a couple of minutes, before jotting down, *Auction catalogues – sales during the two years prior to five years ago. Ring Lady Mumbles! Births, marriages and deaths. What is Somerset House called now? Use search engine!*

Lord above, she was thirsty. That tea with Enid had disappeared without trace. Putting down her pen, she called, 'Beauchaargh!' The man was already behind her. She'd never known a man so cat-like, and was wondering if he led a double life as a cat burglar. His sudden appearances must have taken months, if not years, off her life.

'I didn't want you to wake Mr Hugo,' Beauchamp informed her in a low voice.

'I don't think a cannon would wake him, at the moment. You've had a mug of Grundle's tea before, haven't you?'

'Oh, no! Not the tea!'
'I'm afraid so,' she confirmed.

'Well, what may I get you, my lady?' asked the manservant, at a more normal volume. 'If he actually drank that witches' brew, he'll be out for hours yet.'

'I think I'll take my afternoon tea a little early, if you don't mind, Beauchamp. Then I'm going to do a little more research on the computer, before going to bed for a few hours. I have a little investigation to carry out tonight, and I want to be as alert as possible for it.'

'Very good, my lady,' answered that good man, not batting an eyelid at what his employer had just told him. 'Do you wish me to be in attendance in case there's any, er, bother?'

'I think that might be a very good idea. I don't want to involve you in anything criminal, but we might need to make a quick getaway.'

'How jolly invigorating. I shall look forward to it with enormous anticipation.'

'I somehow thought you would,' replied Lady A, dropping him a half-wink.

After taking her tea, her ladyship spent two hours surfing the net, tutting and expostulating in a genteelly mild way at what she read. Her notepad beside her, she jotted down what she considered important from her searches, then left it to ferment in her subconscious. She wouldn't think about any of this until the morrow, for there were other plans afoot before then.

At six-thirty, she rang for Beauchamp and asked him if he would be so good as to make sandwiches and coffee for eleven o'clock, and to rouse her and Hugo when all was ready. It wasn't a long drive to Journey's End, and they'd have time to assemble some sort of plan for the search.

'I suggest that you awaken Mr Hugo as well, and get him properly settled in his own bed. If we suddenly spring coffee and sandwiches on him, on top of the fact that we're going out to make an illegal entry to one of our friend's houses, he won't be too pleased, if he wakens in the library, wondering what on earth happened to the rest of his day.'

'Very good, my lady,' spake Beauchamp, and went off in the direction of the library on his unenviable mission.

Chapter Thirteen

A Midnight Misadventure

Hugo hadn't just been grumpy when woken from his alcohol-induced sleep in the library; he was pretty tetchy when he was woken again at eleven o'clock, grumbling about madcap schemes and batty old women. He then informed them that he'd been so bucked about by the tricycle and had lain at such an awkward angle while he was sleeping off his 'tea' that he could barely walk, and would have to take his sticks with him or he wouldn't be able to come at all.

'Hugo, how on earth do you think we can go off on this mission with you clumping along with two walking sticks? Are you mad, man?' asked Lady Amanda.

'Take it or leave it. I'd be quite happy to go straight back to bed.'

'Oh, no you don't! I need you there. I need all the eyes we can get, to get this search done, and you don't get out of it that easily. Buck up, man! Where's your sense of adventure?'

'Back in my bed, where I ought to be too,' he replied, poking his tongue out at her, as he had done as a youngster.

'Put that thing away and pull yourself together. You're probably just suffering from low blood sugar, and here's good old Beauchamp with coffee and sandwiches for us. That'll put some lead in your pencil.'

'Should I need to make any notes, I shall use my trusty fountain pen,' replied Hugo in a huffy voice, but he was reaching for a sandwich as he said it. It would be as pointless to try to hold Lady Amanda back as it would be to try to halt the sea in its progress inland, and he, unlike King Canute, knew when he was beaten.

At eleven-thirty, Lady Amanda hooshed him along to get ready to go, as she had arranged for Enid to let them into Journey's End at midnight, a suitable time for an illicit adventure in her opinion, then wished she hadn't, as he appeared wearing so many layers of clothes that his movement was restricted.

'What on earth do you think you're doing, Hugo? What, exactly, are you wearing for this forbidden little outing?'

Hugo looked down at himself and explained totally ingenuously that he had on his usual pullover, over which he had added a quilted button-in lining under his overcoat, a scarf, mittens, and his trilby. 'It is rather late and the weather has been inclement. After what happened this morning, I want to be adequately dressed to cope with the night temperature.'

'But we're going house-breaking! How on earth do you expect to be able to search in silence and move about the house with stealth, when you look like a Michelin man, and with only half the limited mobility you usually have?' asked Lady Amanda in exasperation.

'Don't know,' replied Hugo, not really getting the point at all. 'What on earth do you think you're doing?'

Lady Amanda was, in fact, pulling off Hugo's hat and scarf, and had already started undoing the buttons of his overcoat as he asked his question. 'You're not going out in all those layers. You'll give the game away before we've even got out of the hall, blundering around in half a wardrobe's worth of clothes. There, that's better!'

Hugo was now stripped down to his indoor pullover again. 'But, I don't understand. I thought you told me to get ready. That's all I've done.'

'I asked you to get ready for entering somebody's house without their permission, and giving it a jolly good search. Stand there and wait for me, and I'll get you what you need.'

'Hang on! Can't I at least have my scarf back?'

'Absolutely not!' she called over her shoulder. 'You'd only knock over something with it or, knowing you, trip over it and make a hell of a row.'

Lady Amanda joined him shortly with a navy blue balaclava helmet, hand-knitted by her mother during the war. 'Here you are, Hugo. Put that on. The moth doesn't seem to have got at it,' she instructed him, mirroring his action with the twin of his headgear.

'Now, take these,' she told him, holding out a torch and a pair of horribly pink rubber gloves.'

'What on earth do I need these for?' he asked.

'Well, you don't suppose we can just stroll in and turn lights on willy-nilly, do you? And I don't want you leaving any fingerprints. If it's suspected that the place has been turned over, that ferret-faced Moody will be in there like a shot, looking for traces of whoever it was who had been searching. I don't want him to come sniffing round here because you haven't had the sense to wear gloves.'

'But I look like I'm about to do the washing up, Manda. And I'm going to catch my death without at least a coat on.'

'Firstly, this is not a fashion parade. We're looking for evidence in a case of murder, and secondly, we'll be in the Rolls for most of the journey. I don't know if you've noticed, but it is adequately heated, and I'm sure Porky doesn't keep her house at sub-zero temperatures, even at night. When you're not in one, you'll be in the other, so stop whingeing, and let's get off, or Enid will wonder where we've got to.'

'But surely Porky will hear us.' Hugo thought he had a good point here, as he'd certainly know if someone was rummaging about near his bedroom.

'Not a problem, Hugo. I've got Enid to drug her.' Lady A's face betrayed not a shred of conscience.

'You've done what?' Hugo's mouth was agape at what he'd just heard.

'I just slipped a couple of sleeping tablets to Enid and gave her instructions for administering them. By the time we get there, Porky should be sleeping the sleep of the dead.'

'Manda! That's hardly cricket, is it?' Hugo was appalled.

'No, but then, neither is murdering a man in my home, and I am determined to get to the bottom of it, and see the murderer put behind bars. Popeye may not have been the easiest man to like, but he didn't deserve to be murdered, and that's that! So let's be off! Hugo, what the Christopher Columbus are you doing with those walking sticks?'

'I've been trying to get through to you that my knee's been giving me severe gyp, but you've either not taken it in, or ignored me completely.'

'But you can't go round a house in the middle of the night with two sticks and a torch. How are you going to hold the torch?'

'Don't you worry about that, Manda: I shall sort out how to do it when we get there. It's a bit late now to be worried about the sticks. A little more sympathy and care when I first mentioned it, might have negated the need to use them at all.'

'Hugo Cholmondley-Crichton- Crump, I shall swing for you one of these days. Put your Marigolds in one trouser pocket, the torch in the other, and let's get out of here before dawn breaks and finds us still standing here bickering.'

'Will Beauchamp be coming in with us?' asked Hugo, knowing he was pushing his luck.

'No he certainly will not. He has to stay with the car in case we need to make an emergency get-away. Now get yourself through that door before I lose my temper with you.'

At Journey's End, Beauchamp dropped them off at a pedestrian side-entrance, well screened by trees, and switched off the engine. 'Remember,' he said, 'just push the call button on your mobile phone, and I'll start the engine, ready to make a break for it. The phone's already programmed with my number, so all you've got to do is push 'send'.'

'Walk on the grass, Hugo, not on the path,' directed Lady A, remembering that the path was gravel, and walking on it would be the night-time equivalent of having a brass band escort them to the dwelling.

'But the grass is crunchy with frost, and my feet'll get frozen,' Hugo moaned.

'You can put them in a mustard bath when we get back,' whispered his companion.

'But I'll get chilblains,' he went on.

'Hugo?'

'Yes, Manda?'

'Would you like a smack in the mouth?'

'No, thank you. I feel I shall be just fine if I walk on the grass, and a mustard bath would be very soothing.'

'Good boy, Hugo!'

There was no need for torches, as the bitterly cold night boasted a clear sky, and moonlight lit their way adequately, and might prove of some use in helping them navigate their way around the house.

'Manda?'

'What now?' Lady Amanda was getting a bit fed up with the peevish note in Hugo's voice.

'My sticks are slipping in the frost.'

'Then take my arm until we get to the front door. Really! It's like taking a five-year-old to the dentist, taking you anywhere.'

'I just don't want a broken hip,' Hugo whispered plaintively.

'You'll get a split lip, if you moan any more. Now, pull yourself together and ... oh, my God!' Lady Amanda had abruptly halted and frozen in position, a condition that had nothing whatsoever to do with the cold.

'What is it, Manda?' asked Hugo, his blood suddenly running colder than the outside temperature could possibly be responsible for.

'There's a policeman on guard outside the house. Don't move! We'll have to wait until he does a circuit of the property, before we can give Enid the signal to let us in.'

They stood in silence for exactly two minutes, before Hugo said, with an element of urgency in his voice, 'Manda?'

'What is it this time, Hugo?' she answered, wondering what he was going to complain about next.

'Manda, I need to *go*. Now!'

'Just like a man!' she hissed angrily. 'Out of the house for five minutes, and you need to use the lavatory. Well, you'll just have to hang on until we can get inside, or go behind one of the bushes.'

'I can't 'go' outside. I was very strenuously pottytrained, you know,' he replied, a note of anguish entering his voice.

'Look, he's going!' Lady Amanda cut in. 'The policeman! He's off on a tour round the house, probably to check all the doors and windows. Now's our chance. Run!'

'!'

'Make a noise like an owl, Hugo, like you used to, when we were young. That's our signal to Enid to get the front door open.'

Lady Amanda remembered well the realistic owl hoots that Hugo used to produce, cupping his hands together and blowing expertly through his thumbs but, tonight, his hands stayed firmly at his sides on his sticks. '*Toowittoowoo*,' Hugo warbled, giving it his best shot, but sounding more like a lame sound-effect in a very cheap and amateur production.

Lady A stood rooted to the spot with horror, her fond memories scattered by this parody of his old skill. 'What on earth do you think you're playing at?' she hissed, sounding like an angry snake. 'You used to do it with your *hands*, Hugo! I could've *said* 'toowit-toowoo'. You were supposed to blow through your thumbs and make a noise that at least sounded like an owl, and not some old man trying, and clearly failing, to sound like one.'

Still holding firmly to his sticks, Hugo gave a shrug, almost Gallic in its expressiveness. 'I can't do that any more, Manda. Arthritis! My hands just aren't the same shape as they were. Tempus has fugit-ed, and all that, and I can't make a silk purse out of a sow's ear, even for you and for old times' sake. Sorry!'

'Miss Marple never had this sort of trouble!' she retorted, knowing that comparisons with Agatha Christie's heroine would come into play at some part of the investigation. 'Look, Enid must have heard you anyway. She's opening the door. Quick!'

'!' Once again, Hugo was speechless at her hopeless command. The only 'quick' he could manage was being alive, and when he stopped being able to do that any more, he would be so slow, he would be dead.

At the door, Enid was hopping up and down with nerves, and scooped them through the entrance as if she were a human ladle. 'Thank goodness you're here at last,' she said, 'I've been tiptoeing to this door and opening it at the sound of every owl for the last hour. My nerves are shredded, because, every time I came to open it, there was that PC Glenister.

'My heart was in my mouth, I can tell you, but each time, he just bade me a polite 'good evening', smiled and touched his helmet in greeting, as if it were nothing out of the ordinary for an elderly woman to be running to the front door every five minutes, at this time of night. I felt I should die of embarrassment after the last time, for I'm almost sure I heard him say, 'They'll be here soon.' But at least, thank God, I knew *that* one was Mr Hugo's,' she concluded with relief, only to have her complaint cut short by Hugo's urgent whispering.

'Where's the lavatory? Tell me quickly! Cold weather always does this to me,' he explained, shooting a look full of daggers at his partner in crime. 'Urine contains DNA – even I know that – and I don't want us to be arrested because of the presence of my 'doings' on the hall carpet!'

As Hugo unburdened himself (as quietly as possible, to avoid any one of them suffering unnecessary embarrassment – oh! how he missed the bees or the flowers on the old Victorian lavatory pans, which at least gave a man something to aim at) in a small cubicle just off the hall, Lady Amanda explained, as if to a child, why Enid had been wasting her time for the last fruitless sixty minutes. 'My dear woman, to arrive early is as badmannered as to arrive late so, of course, we're here at the exact hour. What else did you expect of us?'

Ignoring this finer point of etiquette, so as to waste no more time, Enid explained that she'd done exactly as she'd been asked, and administered the drug in a cup of cocoa, which Porky, unexpectedly for her, took without sugar. 'She didn't notice a thing, then said she felt absolutely exhausted, and I helped her up to bed. That was about three hours ago, but I don't know how long the tablets will work for.'

'Why did you give them to her so early?' asked Lady Amanda, frowning crossly. She'd hoped that they would be slipped to her about eleven o'clock.

'Because I always go to bed at about half-past nine,' replied Enid, without a thought to her lack of logic.

'You blasted idiot, Enid. You knew you were going to let us in at midnight, so why didn't you wait a couple of hours?'

Enid's hands flew to her mouth. 'Oh, Lady Amanda, I just didn't think. I could have stayed up later, couldn't I?'

'Of course, you blithering idiot, but we must just make the best of things. You're going to have to be on guard on the landing now, in case she wakes and tries to leave her bedroom. Take a glass of water up with you, then you've got an excuse to be out of your room. You can either say you went to get it for yourself, or you went to get it for her, but, whatever you do, don't let her come out of her room.'

'Of course. Of course. Anything you say. I'm *so* sorry.' 'First things first,' said Lady A, ignoring her apologies. 'Where's Popeye's study?'

'Upstairs in the box-room,' Enid informed them, steeling herself for Lady Amanda's reaction to this unhappy news.

'Upstairs? God deliver me!' She sighed deeply, as if the world were full of fools, and she the only sensible one in existence.

'Well, we've no choice. You go up to the landing and keep an eye on her door, and Hugo and I will follow you up to search. We'll just have to play this one by ear. Now, off you go!'

Enid tiptoed up the stairs, her legs trembling with fear and adrenalin. Hugo went next, placing his sticks with care as he slowly climbed. Lady Amanda followed behind – just in case Hugo fell, and she had to catch him.

All went well until Hugo reached the half-landing, when one of his sticks slipped on the wood at the edge of the carpet of the stair he was just mounting. It shot sideways, and he was unable to do anything about it as it hit the dinner gong on the half-landing with a sonorous and echoing 'bong'.

The three of them became a frozen tableau, each arrested mid-action, as if part of a paused film. Amanda was the first to react, hearing movement from Porky's bedroom and a series of short moans. She fled back down the stairs, dragging a bewildered Hugo in her wake, his sticks in one hand, as Enid rushed to the bedroom door to prevent Porky coming out on to the landing to find her house invaded by midnight friends.

Hugo did his best to dismount as rapidly as he could manage, given the state of his joints, and the vigour with which he was being pulled, but was given a jolt of unexpected haste as he heard a key turn in the front door, and a voice call out, 'Is everything all right in there?' The last things he remembered before he was in darkness, were a hearty shove between the shoulder blades and the sound of a door slamming shut behind him.

PC Glenister entered the darkened hallway of Journey's End, having heard the sounding of the gong, and wondering if it was a distress call from one of the ladies inside. 'Is everybody okay?'

he called, shining his torch around in an effort to locate whoever had instigated the metallic 'bong'.

'I'm up here,' called Enid, desperate to distract him from looking around too rigorously downstairs. 'Mrs Barrington-Blyss needs putting back to bed. There's nothing to worry about,' she reassured him, keeping the fingers of both hands crossed. 'I'll be down in a minute.'

'I'll just take a quick look around down here then,' he replied, and headed for the drawing room door. Being about his lawful business, he had no hesitation in switching on the light before checking the room and, behind the largest of the sofas, discovered Lady Amanda stretched out flat on the floor, Hugo's sticks, one each side of her, aligned tidily with her body.,

Giving her a smile and a polite wave, he switched off the light and left the room, checking next, the dining room. The most convenient (in more ways than one) door was that of the downstairs lavatory, and, on opening that, he found Hugo standing with his back to him, his hands on the low cistern and his head turned over his shoulder with the most innocent of expressions on his face.

'Not interrupting, am I?' asked the young policeman, in embarrassment.

'Not at all,' replied Hugo. 'I'm just hiding in here.'

'Good idea, sir. Wish I'd thought of it first,' was PC Glenister's somewhat puzzling answer.

At that moment, Enid could be heard tripping down the stairs, her head a whirl of anxiety about being caught redhanded like this. Her look of inquisition at the PC was one that said she was about to face the rest of her life with a criminal record. 'Everything all right?' she croaked, almost cringing away from him as she awaited the arrests that would surely follow.

'Everything's absolutely dandy down here. Got her back to bed?' he enquired, a hopeful expression on his face.

'Sleeping like a baby again,' Enid replied, wondering why events were not unrolling according to the doomladen script she had written in her head.

'I'll get back outside then,' he informed her, then let a small smile curve his lips. 'If you're looking for the others, you'll find Lady Amanda behind the sofa in the drawing room, and Mr Hugo in the downstairs cloakroom. Very fastidious man, Mr Hugo. Even wears rubber gloves to go to the lavatory, I noticed,' he joked.

Enid ignored this seemingly inexplicable remark, and merely looked relieved. In fact, her whole body slumped as she received the somewhat inexplicable news that he knew the others were there, but planned to do nothing about it. She might not be able to explain his reaction, but she could certainly appreciate it, and saw him out of the door with a feeling of disbelief. They were going to get away with it after all!

Chapter Fourteen

A Bit More Pumping is Required

Breakfast was cancelled the next day at Belchester Towers, as was lunch, and brunch was declared to be the most appropriate meal, after such a late night and all the trauma that it had involved. They had managed to make a search of the house, with Hugo safely tucked away in the drawing room, keeping out from under Lady Amanda's feet. Enid had even been able to join in, but, of a copy of the manuscript, or even notes pertaining to it, they had found no sign, and the night's adventure had not even been discussed in the car back to the Towers.

They all three retired straight to bed after arriving home, an air of dejection about the trio, who had had such high hopes of that night's clandestine activities, so the first chance there was of any discussion, was at the brunch table the next day, and very late in the day, it was, too.

'Why on earth didn't we get carted off in handcuffs last night? We were caught red-handed, in someone else's house, at an un-Godly hour, and we could have been up to anything. That young constable just made the most extraordinary comment, and treated it like it was an everyday thing for him, to find interlopers in strangers' lavatories.'

'He's one of *us*, Hugo,' explained Lady Amanda, with a rather smug smile.

'What do you mean, *one of us*? Are you sure you don't mean *one of them*, breaking in on a man when he's in the lavatory?'

'Were you actually conducting any business, Hugo? And don't be so bigoted!'

'No, I was just hiding. And I'm not! Bigoted, that is.'

'Well, there you are then. That proves it, doesn't it?'

'Proves what?'

'That he's one of *us*. He came to see me yesterday, you know.'

'When?' asked Hugo, his voice high with indignation that he had not been apprised of this visit.

'When you were off drinking toxic tea with that old devil Grundle.'

'You could still have told me when I got back.' Hugo felt quite huffy about this clandestine visit, and his total lack of knowledge of it.

'Oh, no, I couldn't. If you remember, you spent the afternoon sleeping off your cup of 'tea', snoring like a grampus in the library, until I got Beauchamp to put you to bed.'

'You could've told me when I woke up,' he challenged her.

'Well, I didn't. You were too grumpy. Now, shut up, and let's work out today's plan of action. We've only got the afternoon and evening left, and three other households to infiltrate.'

'At least we won't be sneaking about like thieves in the night again.'

'Thieves in the night do *not* bang gongs with their walking sticks, Hugo.'

'Fair point, Manda. Fair point.'

After a lot of discussion, which necessitated Beauchamp joining them at table, it was decided to split the work up thus: Hugo was to go off into the woods and 'pump' Sir Montacute Fotherington-Flint's gamekeeper, hoping that he wouldn't be off in the family's woods somewhere doing something incomprehensible and gamekeeper-ish.

'As a boy, when he first started there as a boot-boy, he was a favourite of the housekeeper, so it would be a good idea to see if you can get him reminiscing about when he first came to the house. He, no doubt, picked up endless bits and pieces of household gossip, just because he was so unimportant,' she informed him.

'Beauchamp, I'd like you to just drop in for a chat with Major Mapperley-Minto's man. Old Monty likes a drink or ten, and he can be very confiding when he's in his cups. It will have been his man's duty to make sure he got to bed safely, and many a confidence has been shared after dark with a close member of one's staff, with a bellyful of booze.'

'Very good, my lady, and that's Beecham, if you don't mind,' chanced the manservant.

'It's Beauchamp, or I'm a Chinaman, and I don't speak a word of Mandarin. Now, I, meanwhile,' she swept on, without a second thought for her manservant, who was standing directly behind her, repeatedly mouthing 'Beecham' silently to the back of her head, 'shall pay a polite call on the Featherstonehaugh-Armitages. Stinky and Donkey,' she clarified, as Hugo was not very good at remembering names, which was ironic, considering the clunking great moniker he himself possessed, 'and I have a few other little calls to make, before the afternoon is out. All clear about what you're doing?'

'Yes, Manda,' agreed Hugo, nodding his head in a vague way.

'Yes, my lady,' concurred Beauchamp, and turned to leave the room.

'One moment, Beauchamp. Just a word before you go.'

'Yes, my lady?'

'I presume you had forgotten about the mirror facing where I was sitting, when you were behind me.'

'I had, indeed, my lady,' said Beauchamp. 'Very remiss of me,' he added, turning a nice shade of pink.

'Dis-missed!' The troops were dispatched.

Beauchamp needed no excuse to call at The White House, as he often dropped in to see the valet/butler, Mr Tinker, when he had a half-day free, and was, therefore, welcomed without question, and shown into Tinker's sitting room.

'Hey, there, Beechy! How are you doing?' he was hailed, before he was fully through the door.

'I'm doing fine, Tinker. How are you? I haven't seen you since well before Christmas,' replied Beauchamp, suddenly coming over all 'hail fellow, well met'.

'All the better for seeing your smiling face. Now, what can I do for you, or have you just come over for one of our little chats?'

'On the button, as usual, Tinker. At this time of year I find I get very nostalgic, and I thought, if there's another man in Belchester who would understand how I feel, it's good old Tinker at The White House.' Lady Amanda would not have recognised this Beauchamp.

'I know just what you mean. You get to thinking about all those other Christmases and New Years you've spent in the same place, and it really does get you remembering old times, doesn't it?'

Accepting a tankard of ale, Beauchamp prepared to steer the conversation around to the possibility of dark doings in the household, way back in the past.

Tinker had, to a certain extent, picked up some of his habits from his employer, and it was while he was pouring Beauchamp's second pint, and his own fourth, that he came over all confidential, and told the other a story that he had heard no hint of in any of the other residences of quality in the county.

'My two are getting on a bit, just like yours. Funny the way your old lady just ran into old Chummy, wasn't it? There's some tales I could tell you, though, that have never passed these lips before, and would make your hair curl.'

'Really, Tinker? Like what?' asked Beauchamp, flashing his hip flask for the fourth time and obligingly pouring a little soupcon – quite a large soupcon, actually – into Tinker's tankard, then waving it over his own, so that he served himself nothing more substantial than fumes.

'Very hospitable of you, Beechy. Wait up there!' the other requested, and toddled, slightly drunkenly, over to the door, to make sure that no one was eavesdropping. 'Can't be too careful, these days,' he added, and tapped the side of his nose with his right forefinger in a knowing gesture.

'There's a story about this fambly would fair knock you out, old son, an' I'm gonna share it with you today, cos you're my bes' mate, and I'm thinkin' of retiring' soon, so it don't matter a flyin' fig ter me wot anyone finks.' Tinker's speech was becoming a little slurred, not only because of the strength of the beer, but because of the constant addition of large measures of brandy to his drinking vessel.

'It 'appened when I was but a bit of a boy, 'ere, long, long ago.' A tear of alcohol-inspired emotion quivered at the corner of one eye, as he said this. 'It was when the major was only a captain, and 'e was posted abroad, but the missus wouldn't go wiv 'im. Don' know if you remem-em-ember tha''

'Of course I do, but you weren't quite a boy were you, because I'd just started as boot boy at Belchester Towers, and you're a good bit older than me,' replied Beauchamp, unable to completely stop himself from aiming for some accuracy.

'Wha'ever! Nearly two years, 'e was gorn, and 'er all alone 'ere. I got called out to do for 'im after only a coupla months – 'e 'ad a sort of local bungalow-y building 'e lived in by then – and you couldn't even make up what I saw when I was out there, with 'im, in forrin parts.'

'Only went and got 'isself married again, di'n't 'e. To a native girl wot wasn't more 'n seventeen years old. Would you believe it, ol' son, ol' Beechy, ol' friend?'

'He didn't, Tinker! So what happened to her, this little foreign stunner?'

'She only went an' 'ad 'is baby, di'n't she.'

'Good grief!' exclaimed Beauchamp, trying not to let his voice boom out in his astonishment.

Tinker merely nodded sagely and drunkenly. 'Bigigamy, tha's wha' i' was. Big-ig-igamy!'

'So what did he do? Just leave her there when he got posted back to Blighty?' Beauchamp really was all ears. He'd never expected anything of this magnitude to come of his visit to see his old friend. What a motive for murder!

'Nuffink! Di'n't 'ave to. Arter she 'ad the nipper, 'er fambly sent 'er orf into the mountains, too ashamed to look their friends in the face again, what wiv 'er avin' a forrin baby an' all tha'. An' 'e just came swannin' back 'ere like nothin's 'appened. I reckon 'e was a right Pinkerton, don't you, Beechy?'

Beauchamp, who knew his *Madama Butterfly* but was surprised that Tinker did, nodded his head sagely in agreement, thinking that that little bombshell could be alive and well, and liable to burst on to the scene at any time, with no warning whatsoever. 'And has he never looked for them?' he asked, listening as intently as an Archers fan for the next instalment of the story.

'Nah! Said it was just a forrin bint, and that the marriage was a sham anyway, not bein' in English, like.'

'Well, bless my soul!' ejaculated Beauchamp, shocked to his very roots. This would make Lady Amanda's hair stand on end, when he told her later. 'I won't divulge this to another living soul,' he promised earnestly, his fingers crossed behind his back. And if Popeye had got wind of this, he wouldn't have to watch his tongue for much longer. That book really could be dynamite!

Hugo was also to be offered the roots of a family scandal by the wily old gamekeeper on the FotheringtonFlint land, but had a harder time finding his quarry. He knew where the gamekeeper's hut in the woods was, but, after squelching through the mud created by the thaw, earning himself boots that felt like they belonged in the Somme, so heavy were their soles, he found no one at home.

He stood rather disconsolately, as the trees dripped on him, calling out in his loudest voice, 'Rodgers! Rodgers!' that being the gamekeeper's name, but answer was there none. After a few efforts in this manner, with no answer whatsoever, he decided he'd better make for the house, but when he tried to walk, he found he couldn't get his shoes out of the ground. The thick covering of mud on the soles had melded into the mud below them, and stuck him faster than he had the strength to fight.

At this point, he changed tactics slightly, and began to shout, 'Help! Help!' Within less than a minute, a man had materialised like magic from a clump of trees and was walking towards him calling out, 'Hang on in there. I'm just coming.'

'Are you Rodgers?' asked Hugo, of this newly arrived stranger.

'I am, that,' replied the man, taking a good look at Hugo's predicament. 'You stay there a moment, and I'll just go and get something to release you. Very clayey, is this ground,' and disappeared off into the trees again.

By the time that Hugo had begun to wonder if the man had
been a mirage born of panic, he returned with a spade in an old
wheelbarrow. 'Soon have you out of there, old man. I'll take you
back to the house, and we'll get your shoes cleaned up. Who have
you come to see?'

'You actually,' answered Hugo, eyeing up the wheelbarrow
suspiciously. He had a nasty idea that he knew what it was for.

'Deftly sliding the spade under Hugo's feet, one at a time, and
trying to keep it as close to the actual sole as possible, Rodgers
manage to break the suction and, having given Hugo a freedom
of sorts, put the wheelbarrow behind him and gave him a deft
little shove in the chest, so that he collapsed neatly into its
interior.

'Quickest way, old man,' he consoled the humiliated Hugo,
who merely sat in his new place of imprisonment, sighing and
tutting. This was the second time he'd taken an undignified ride
in a wheelbarrow this December, not to mention a barely
remembered trip in the bucket of a mechanical digger, and it had
to stop. He was feeling distinctly like a potato!

Lady Amanda, meanwhile, had tried to contact old Lady
Mumbles, who had once been a big noise in the county before
her husband lost everything gambling. She had had to sell up
eventually, but made a game attempt to keep her property going
by selling off the contents, bit by bit, and now lived with her
niece just outside Belchester.

She was very chagrined indeed to find out, when she
telephoned, that Lady Mumbles had, in fact, succumbed to an
attack of influenza at the end of November, and had not survived
the experience. She did find out from the niece, however, that
her aunt had sold a lot of her possessions to F A Antiques in
Belchester itself.

Thanking the niece and passing on her condolences, Lady Amanda ended the call and sat tapping a pen on the top of her desk, as she let her memory go for a stroll down its own personal lane. The name she wanted was in there somewhere; she just had to wait for it to surface before she could do anything else.

After a quarter of an hour of tapping and waiting, she suddenly shouted, 'Aha!' and dialled the number for Directory Enquiries. Within less than five minutes she was in contact with an auction house about a hundred and twenty-five miles from Belchester and, within another ten minutes, was in possession of the information that confirmed her, up to then, unsubstantiated suspicions.

Her next move would be to casually drop in on Donkey, on the pretext of seeking some feedback about the house tour that now seemed like years ago, instead of only a few days.

Hugo found himself in the pleasant fug of a large kitchen in the throes of baking day, and had gladly swapped his clay-caked shoes for a cup of (non-alcoholic) tea and a plate of chocolate biscuits – to raise his spirits after his unfortunate mishap, Mrs Hipkiss, the elderly housekeeper had said, as she set them before him on the kitchen table.

Hugo decided to play this hand perfectly straight, and he laid his cards on the table without a qualm. 'I'll be perfectly honest with you, Rodgers, Mrs Hipkiss, I am here to see if you have any knowledge whatsoever of a family scandal that would be ruinous, should it ever be made public.

'I don't do this alone. Lady Amanda and I are checking out several families of good name and status, because that wretched Capt Leslie Barrington-Blyss has written a book that he claimed would blow the lids off many of the families of this type.'

'As you know, he was murdered on Boxing Day in Lady
Amanda's library, and we have taken it upon ourselves, now that
he's dead, to try to uncover what he might have found out. We
are absolutely certain that his widow will halt publication. What
we would like to do, however, as the only known copy of it, other
than the one with his erstwhile publisher, is in the hands of the
police, is to get there first, as it were, as any information you may
be able to impart may be instrumental in uncovering the identity
of his murderer.

'We don't want to leave Inspector Moody, whom we
consider to be incompetent, to muddle the case up, then let
out details of what is contained in the book, to try to uncover
the murderer. It would be advantageous to everyone if we could
solve the case first, and save many families untold
embarrassment. At the very least, it will give those involved
sufficient time to take out an injunction against the contents of
this execrable tome being made public.'

Hugo finished his speech just before the point where he
talked himself into a state in which he didn't understand, any
more, what he was talking about, and was surprised when his
audience of two began to clap their hand in appreciation.

'Noble words! Fine fellow! And Lady Amanda, too!'
Rodgers congratulated Hugo's sentiments.

'May God bless you, Mr Hugo!' added Mrs Hipkiss, before
looking at Rodgers to see if he had anything to offer.

'Sorry,' the gamekeeper apologised. 'I'm afraid I can't think
of anything that would count as a big scandal likely to do damage
to the Fotherington-Flint name. I wish I could help you, but I
can't.'

Hugo sighed, and transferred his gaze to Mrs Hipkiss, who
was looking doubtful. 'Well,' she mused, 'there's nothing in my
time, and I'm as old as Mrs Methuselah; but my mother worked

here before I did, and I think, if you give me a minute or two to get my head together about it, I might – I just might – nothing definite – have something for you.'

Hugo, ever a patient soul, dunked his biscuits happily, and accepted a refill of his teacup, as Mrs Hipkiss wracked her brains to recall a tale told to her decades ago, and which she hadn't thought much about since. Eventually, she gave a yell of, 'Got it!' and pulled up a chair opposite the unexpected visitor to her kitchen.

'Oh, it was donkey's years ago, ducky,' she began, 'and it wasn't to do with the present Sir Montacute, but his parents, young lovers that they were, then. Still teenagers, and not married, although betrothed and properly engaged, his mother-to-be suddenly disappeared from sight. She never left her parents' house for months on end, and a story was circulated that she was gravely ill.

'Meanwhile, the wedding was planned, but there were those that believed she'd never be well enough to attend the ceremony.' Hugo was already enthralled, and sat with his chin in one hand, his mouth slightly open, with what Lady A referred to as his 'catching flies' face.

'My mother was good friends with her mother's maid at the time – they used to spend all their half-days together – and her friend told her of the awful weeping and screaming that had gone on about a week before that girl was seen in public once more. Her friend had been convinced that she was in her death throes.

'My mother, she was altogether more sceptical, and she remembered how that girl's mother had called at this house the same night that her friend reported the weeping and screaming, and my mother distinctly heard her mother say just a few words. 'It's a girl. It's already gone for private adoption.

'Well, I can tell you what my mother deduced. That the young couple had put the cart before the horse, and now the mess was being sorted out for them by their parents. The wedding went ahead about three months later, and it was less than a year before they produced our own Sir Montacute, but none of this has got anything to do with him. He wasn't even born at the time.'

'Eh?' grunted Hugo. 'Is that the end of the story? Couldn't you tell me another one, please? I was really enjoying myself there.'

Lady Amanda was shown through immediately to the drawing room of The Old Convent, where she found Angelica Featherstonehaugh-Armitage already in the arms of a cocktail, and thoroughly enjoying the experience.

'Manda! How lovely to see you again!' she brayed, putting down her glass and coming forward to embrace her unexpected guest fondly. 'Take a seat and I'll get you a dry martini. I know how you love your cocktails.'

'Please don't bother on my account,' countered Lady Amanda. 'Got to watch the old digestion after all that rich food over the festive season, but don't let me stop you.'

Taking this as an invitation, Angelica swayed over to the cocktail cabinet and fixed herself another drink, calling over her shoulder, 'And to what do I owe the honour of this visit?'

'Just thought I'd drop in and see what you thought of the old tour of the Towers, you know. Stinky not about?'

'Absolutely not! He went up to his club for a couple of days after that dreadful incident in your library, but I'm expecting him back tonight.'

A voice in Lady Amanda's head yelled, 'Yippee!' although she wasn't quite sure why this part of her mind was so pleased.

She'd ask it later. Instead, adopting a very casual air, she enquired after the antiques business that the lieutenant colonel used to run.

'I never did ask you why Stinky relinquished the old antiques game in North Street. Wanted to retire, did he, and just gave it up?' she purred casually.

'Not a bit of it,' replied Angelica, absorbing her dry martini in the manner of a parched sponge. 'It was more like *it* gave *him* up. Dammit! Empty glass again! I was sure I'd just mixed myself one.'

As her host returned to the cocktail shaker (for, like James Bond, she preferred hers shaken, not stirred) Lady Amanda cast her bread upon the waters and asked temptingly, 'Whatever do you mean? I can't see how that can have happened,' then added, 'It's so rare that you and I get the chance to have a good old girlie chinwag, Donkey old sport.'

'You're right, there,' replied Donkey, the bread and hook firmly in her mouth. 'I'll tell you all about it, and you can see how it went from fabulously profitable to absolute zilch in just a few short years.'

With an internal grin of triumph, Lady Amanda relaxed back in her armchair and prepared to make mental notes.

'When he first started in the business – that was when he took over from his father, and he himself had just come out of the army – things were selling like hot cakes. Whatever he bought was snapped up in the craze for Victoriana. I remember, in particular, that even a broken gout stool and a dilapidated fire-screen fetched unheard-of sums.

'Then the bottom fell out of Victoriana, so he turned to Georgian and Regency items, specialising in furniture and pictures – he isn't really a bibelot man, as I'm sure you can appreciate. Then we hit the present, seemingly endless, slump,

and the bottom fell out of brown furniture.' At this point, she
went off into screeches of hysterical laughter at her own humour,
calming down again only to return to mix herself another
martini, muttering, 'Bottom fell out – heehee. Clunk, ouch!
Heeheehee!'

'So how did you manage?' asked Lady Amanda, determined
to get her on to more solid ground, and not let her disappear
with a bad case of barman's elbow.

'Couldn't believe it myself, but, for a while, it was horrible
old pictures. Stinky had quite a lot of luck with them. Filthy old
daubs, they looked to me, but he'd go off to a country auction or
whatever, and come back with these horrible things, and the next
thing we knew, one or two of them had sold for a fabulous sum
at auction. Boy, did that man have an eye.'

'To the main chance,' muttered Lady Amanda inaudibly.
This was what she'd come to hear, having spoken to the niece of
the poor, dear, departed Lady Mumbles, and the auction house.
That man had an eye, all right, but it wasn't for a picture, it was
for a sucker, and one who trusted him because of who he was.
He'd out-and-out swindled old Lady Mumbles in her hour of
need, and, no doubt, she wasn't his only victim.

When Lady A looked across at Donkey, after this
momentary pause for thought, she saw her eyes droop, and her
martini glass along with it. Quietly removing the latter and
placing it on a handy side-table, she tiptoed from the room and
left the house. It was lucky she had caught Donkey in a 'relaxed'
mood, as it had saved her the bother of being too wily in her
quest to loosen the woman's tongue – so naive, and so trusting,
that she was.

Back at 'the ranch', all three of its occupants had tales to tell
and, checking that she wouldn't disturb any plans for dinner,

Lady Amanda convened a meeting to share the intelligence they had gathered that day, and requested that Beauchamp might like to join them in a cocktail for this gathering.

Beauchamp arrived promptly with the drinks tray, but Hugo was tardy by a good two minutes. 'Sorry!' he called as he came through the door, having been taken short unexpectedly again, by a call of nature on his amble along from his bedroom, then went flying across the carpet, as he tripped, just inside the doorway.

Beauchamp rushed to his rescue, ascertaining that he was uninjured, just rather surprised and shaken. As he helped the man to his feet, Hugo said accusingly, 'I fell over your blasted handbag, Manda. What do you think you're doing just dropping it on the floor where anyone could fall over it?'

'I'm so sorry,' she replied, real chagrin in her voice. 'It's just that I've learnt some things that I'm finding it hard to come to terms with, and I suppose I just abandoned it without thinking. My apologies, old stick.'

'Well, be more careful in future. Thing like that could kill a man.'

'I know, Hugo, and I'm so pleased you haven't broken anything,' she replied.

'You should take a look at my dignity. It's shattered into a thousand pieces on the floor. What on earth do you keep in the thing, bricks? It weighs a ton.'

'Only what I deem absolutely essential,' she replied with dignity.

'And why would you carry around a couple of house bricks? Come on, what have you really got in it. Show me.' Hugo had never examined the contents of a lady's handbag before, and was now genuinely interested.

'Pass it here,' she asked, then began to intone, as she removed items from it, 'Lipstick, mirror, face powder, small bottle of perfume, address book, mobile phone, house keys, screwdriver, apple corer, wire cutters, scissors, sewing kit, fifteen metre metal tape-measure, crochet hook, pen, pencil, cross-hatch screwdriver, small hacksaw, paint brush, nail polish, manicure set ...'

'Manda!' Hugo exclaimed, although there were still items left in the bag. 'Are you sure you haven't got a cement mixer in there too? It's as well-equipped as a tool box. Why on earth do you carry all that stuff around with you?'

'Because it's all very useful stuff, and I never know when I might need a hacksaw or a screwdriver. The applecorer I use all the time. So useful for a healthy snack if one is on the move.'

'Well, I have to hand it to you; you would have made a marvellous boy scout. Be prepared? You're more than that, but I don't think I could be bothered lugging such a heavy receptacle around with me wherever I go.'

'That's the difference between men and women, Hugo. When a woman needs something unexpectedly, she can usually find it in her handbag. When a man wants something unexpectedly, he usually asks his lady companion if she's got such a thing in her bag.'

'Touché! I surrender!' Hugo retired from the battlefield with a good grace, nursing his wounds without rancour.

'Any luck, chaps?' she asked, when they were all settled round the fire with a drink apiece. Receiving a pair of answers in the affirmative, she told them to fire away, and listened with round eyes to what they had gleaned from their visits.

At the end of it, she availed herself of a, 'Well, I'll be blowed,' then set out to summarize what they had learned so far. 'Let's start with the Heyhoe-Caramacs. We'd all heard about his father being a war hero and his work with the Resistance in France, but from what has been turned up, it would seem that there is a strong possibility that he collaborated with the Germans, and was the cause of several civilian deaths. Unbelievable!' she added, 'but probably absolutely true. Unsubstantiated rumours are often disproved as merely malicious, while the guilty truth is guarded like Fort Knox.

'Next, we'll look at what we've discovered about the *ff*olliat DeWinters – good work there, Beauchamp, with old Fustion. No one ever suspected there was anything suspect about *ff*olliat DeWinter senior's death, because he had been so ill, was a reckless old fool with his health, and would heed advice from no one.

'Now, it would seem, that he was given a helping hand into the afterlife by his loving son and daughter-in-law. Of course, there's nothing to disprove that he wouldn't have popped off that very day, but the old fellow, knowing how stubborn he was, might have hung about for years, and those two obviously had pressing financial problems that couldn't wait.

'Mapperley-Minto's behaviour while abroad seems to be completely beyond the pale, and if that book were published, it was more than likely that the tale would be examined in minute detail, and his 'not-wife' and illegitimate child traced. Utter disgrace!

'Still, at least it kept him out of Maddy's bed for more than a twelve-month. I did hear that he was a real old lecher when he'd had a few drinks to relax him, and she really couldn't be doing with that sort of thing.'

'Manda!' exclaimed Hugo, at this, in his opinion, totally unnecessary foray into bedroom habits.

'It's true! She told me once! First time I've ever mentioned it, though,' pleaded Lady Amanda, in her own defence. With a regal shake of her head, to clarify her thoughts after this interruption, she went on, 'Next, we come to the Fotherington-Flints, and that's where I've been doing some investigation, with a little help from our friendly neighbourhood policeman, PC Glenister, who was able to obtain access that was denied to me, to certain records.'

'But I did that one!' cried Hugo, in distress. 'It was me – I – who found out that Sir Montacute's parents had an illegitimate baby and gave it away to private adoption.' He felt righteously indignant that Manda should steal his thunder so.

'I know, Hugo, but it was I who found out that fate conspired for them to meet years later and marry.'

'No!'
'Impossible!'

'I know how you both feel. The machinations of a malevolent fate make my toes curl, but that's the truth of the matter. I don't think they found out until long after their marriage, but old sins have long shadows, and there's always someone, somewhere, who knows the truth. I have a feeling that they've been living in a brother/sister relationship for a very long time, dreading the truth coming out.

'No wonder Daisy tries to act younger than her years, being, in fact, older than him, and that Cutie has grown so grumpy in his later years, learning the truth about his wife's parentage, having believed she was a product of the parents who had adopted her.

'That only leaves us with the Featherstonehaugh-Armitages, and I confirmed the goods on old Stinky today. He was swindling trusting customers who came to him to sell some of their heirlooms when their circumstances became straitened. They trusted him because of where he stood in society, and he let them down completely, telling them that their pictures were copies, or their precious pieces of furniture were reproductions, and that their jewellery was paste.

'When confronted with their disbelief, he told the old story; that their forebears had only done what they were attempting to do now, but actually replacing the originals with copies, so that they wouldn't lose any face to the world at large. Isn't that beastly, to cheat your own kind?' she asked, then concluded with, 'Well, that's the lot of them, and I bet Mouldy Moody's having a field day, running his grubby little eyes over that lot!'

'It's not quite all, Manda,' said Hugo, softly.

'What do you mean, not all. Isn't that enough to be going on with?' What else could there possibly be?'

'You!' he said, looking her sorrowfully in the face. 'What about all the goings on in this family over the years? If Popeye got wind of that, he'd have thought he'd won the football pools.'

'I think you'll find it's the Lottery, these days, Mr Hugo,' interjected Beauchamp, but with his face creased with anxiety.

'Don't forget,' Hugo went on, 'Your mother's still alive and living in Monte Carlo, and she's living proof of all that went on in this family.'

'Oh, my God!' whispered Lady Amanda, more to herself than to her two companions.

'So who did it, Manda? Which one of them killed Popeye?'

'I haven't the faintest idea,' she replied. 'All I know is that it wasn't me.'

The sombre mood was broken at that juncture by a heavy knocking at the front door, and the sound of someone pulling frantically at the bell-pull, and Beauchamp left the room in thoughtful mood to answer the summons.

Inspector Moody stood in front of the fire unashamedly warming his buttocks as he addressed them, PC Glenister standing just inside the door, in the remote case that one of them would make a run for it. Moody wasn't taking any chances with his run-in with a higher social circle: he didn't trust them further than he could throw his car.

'I don't care if you find it distasteful. I insist that it be done. If anyone can blag their way through a believable tale, it's you,' he said, fixing Lady Amanda with a gimlet eye. 'I want the whole lot reassembled in the library tomorrow, so that I can say my piece.' And what a piece it was too. He was almost bursting with pride at his deductions, as well as his literary knowledge. He'd always wanted to gather the suspects in a case in a library, and give it to them with both barrels.

'If you won't comply with my request, I shall arrest the lot of you, and do it down the station,' he threatened, intoning the last three words in a sepulchral voice, to emphasize the gravity of the situation.

After the departure of the two representatives of the law, Lady Amanda went to the telephone and consulted her address book. If it had to be done, it had to be done, and there wasn't a thing she could do to prevent it.

Chapter Fifteen

Hugo Pulls it Off

The following afternoon, with the exception of Capt. Leslie Barrington-Blyss, the same guests who had assembled so hopefully on Boxing Day gathered again at Belchester Towers, but this time they were a subdued crowd, with hardly a word to say to each other. There was the smell of fear in the air, as they moved, for the second time that Christmastide, through to the library. Enid Tweedie, too, was in attendance, and in charge of refreshments, but these were simple today, as Beauchamp had thought that nobody would feel much like eating and drinking.

When they had all settled in seats, an utter silence filled the room as Lady Amanda announced that Inspector Moody would be joining them, as she had explained on the telephone the night before. There had been several cases of insomnia in and around Belchester the night before, at the prospect of what this little gathering would reveal.

PC Glenister, as usual, was in the background, as Moody began pompously, perhaps imagining himself to be Hercule Poirot, 'I have asked you to return to the scene of the recent murder of one of your number, because I have several things to say which will, I am sure, lead to the unmasking of whoever committed this terrible crime.'

'I have read Captain Barrington-Blyss's book in its entirety, and, in that manuscript, I have found several motives for murder, should certain things be made public. 'You!' he suddenly shouted, pointing at Lt Col. Featherstonehaugh-Armitage. 'You borrowed money from your father's business before he died, and I know you didn't have permission. How would that look to the public eye, stealing from a sick old man? Eh? Eh?'

Stinky and Donkey merely looked at each other and smiled, shrugging their shoulders as they did so. 'If you say so,' retorted Stinky, looking more cheerful than he had since he arrived, and causing Moody to crease his brow in puzzlement. This wasn't how it was supposed to happen. They were supposed to look scared and guilty.

He ploughed on, nevertheless, turning his attention, next, to Sir Montacute Fotherington-Flint. 'You, sir, used to poach on your father's land, and sell the valuable game birds to a restaurant thirty miles away, under a false name. Not only is poaching illegal, but what you did was out and out theft, then you fenced the proceeds to a restaurant.'

Cutie managed a wry smile, and invited the inspector to 'pick the bones out of that one'. This laid-back attitude to criminal accusations was anathema to Moody. They should be quaking in their boots at the thought of prosecution, not to mention what else he had up his sleeve, not treating his statements as if they were an everyday occurrence, and of no consequence whatsoever. His lawabiding soul was scandalised.

'And you!' he suddenly roared, this time indicating Major Mapperley-Minto. You cheated at cards. I have it all in black and white that you were a card cheat, and you can't deny it.'

'I don't propose to do so,' replied Monty coolly, his face a mask of relief. 'But I had my reasons.'

'There's no excuse for what you did!' roared Moody, now beginning to feel his ship, which had just come in for him, beginning to sink beneath his feet. His voice rising a little as he lost a bit of nerve, he next singled out Sir Jolyon ffolliat DeWinter. 'You were caught out having forged your father's signature on a cheque. A more despic ...'

At this point Hugo, feeling vastly relieved, began to tune out the hysterical accusations of the inspector. Old Popeye may have thought he had social dynamite between the covers of his book, but all he'd really had were a few damp squibs. He'd never really got down to the real dirt, to reveal the skeletons in the family closets, and Moody was ranting and railing to no avail. He'd get no change out of that lot.

As he mused to himself, he found his eyes lighting on a black patent leather handbag, sitting at the feet of Fifi and, given his uncommonly close encounter with one of those contraptions, and Manda's revealing tour of the contents of hers, he wondered what weird and wonderful things she carried around with her. It wasn't as big as Manda's, but he had realised, the day before, that handbags were invariably bigger on the inside than they were on the outside, a fact that had escaped his notice all these years.

His eyes moved on to Maddie M-M's, and found it to be roughly the same size as that of Fifi's. This one was red suede, with little flowers embroidered on it, and he wondered that he had never looked at these everyday workhorses before, in all their various guises.

Becoming thoroughly interested, now, he carried on moving his eyes from woman to woman, taking notice of their taste in such receptacles, and idly musing what one would find, should one venture to open them.

Moody had not noticed that Hugo had fallen into a brown study, and was carrying on with his tirade. 'And as for you,' he shouted, pointing at Col. Heyhoe-Caramac. 'What sort of man beats his dog? I shall be informing the RSPCA about what I've learnt of your behaviour towards animals.'

At this point, now wild-eyed, as he slowly became aware that nobody was listening to him any more, and had begun to talk amongst themselves, he raised his voice as loud as he could and yelled, 'I know who killed the captain!'

This certainly drew attention back to him as, his face red, his hair rumpled where he had run his hands through it at the thought that they could have ignored him at such an important part of this denouement, he prepared to *reveal all*. His mouth wide open, he declared in a bellow, 'It was all of you! Every single one of you, or at least in pairs. Did you think I didn't notice what a case of overkill it was? He was poisoned! He was stabbed! He was garrotted! He was hit over the head! And his throat was cut!

'Do you honestly think that I never read *Murder on the Orient Express*? Did you think you could fool me that easily? You all had adequate motive to do away with him, and I think you got together and planned the whole thing. Do you know how long you can get in prison for conspiracy? And I haven't finished yet, not by a long chalk!' He now looked and sounded like a raving lunatic.

Hugo, meanwhile, had continued his visual examination of the various handbags in laps and on the floor of the library, and was just beginning to appreciate how much better than pockets they were. One could carry so much in them without disturbing the line of the cut of one's clothes. One could simply put them down, without having to go around with a load of clunky things in one's pockets.

He had just decided what a jolly good idea they were, and was quite chagrined that men could not use them, when his eyes fell on Porky's bag, and a small light went on at the back of his mind, accompanied by the almost inaudible tinkle of a very small bell.

The bag was so small that he had hardly noticed it, propped up against an ankle: what he thought was referred to as a clutch bag, which could contain little more than keys and a lipstick. On Boxing Day, he had been impressed by the size of the tapestry bag she toted around with her, thinking it as big as Manda's, and here she was today, with something in which it would be impossible to keep even something as bulky as a hair brush.

All around him, Inspector Moody was being conspicuously ignored as the guests lost themselves in happy chatter. When Enid had gone round earlier with sausage rolls and mince pies, she had received a universal refusal. As she circulated, once more, in this vastly relieved atmosphere, with her little snacks, the uptake was a hundred per cent, as was Beauchamp's offer of glasses of sherry. Both snacks and drinks were being relished as the babble of conversation rose in volume, to the 'rhubarb, rhubarb' chorus present in any parliamentary broadcast, and Moody was on his feet now, about to explode with wrath at this disrespectful attitude to one of his rank.

The light at the back of Hugo's brain suddenly glowed like phosphorus, and the bell rang with the sonorous tones of its campanological brother, Big Ben. It was all to do with handbags! The book was involved in there somewhere, but the clue to the murderer was a handbag, and he believed he had just had a revelation.

As Moody called for silence, Hugo sprang, as quickly as he could manage, from a sitting position, and yelled, 'It's her!'

All eyes were swivelled to look in the direction in which he was pointing, to reveal Porky, her face as white as a sheet, and opening and closing her mouth like a landed fish.

'What the hell do you think you're saying, you doddering old fart?' spat Moody, as Lady Amanda called out, 'Explain yourself, Hugo! What was Porky? What are you saying? Tell me this instant.'

'Not until I've asked a couple of questions first,' replied Hugo rebelliously. He would not have his thunder stolen; no one was going to rain on his parade today. The library, now, was absolutely silent as he spoke. 'Porky, I would like to know the name of the publishing house with which Popeye was dealing,' he demanded in a much more forceful voice than was usual for him.

'That's none of your damned business, Chummy!' she retorted, looking daggers at him.

'And how are your finances at the moment? I would have thought that Popeye would have had a rather plump advance from a publisher who thought he was exploding a social bomb.'

'That's none of your damned business either, you nosy old fool.'

'What are you talking about, Hugo?' asked Lady Amanda, not having caught the direction of his thoughts yet.

'We've heard, courtesy of the well-read inspector here today, about the sensitive information that was in Popeye's book, and from the attitude in this room now, I think that we can take it that it's not worth a penny.'

'Hear, hear!' shouted Major Mapperley-Minto. 'I admit that I did cheat at cards, but only when I was playing with her husband. I spotted him first off as a card-sharp, and I was determined to play him at his own game. Apart from the few games we played together, and he soon stopped asking me if I fancied a hand, I have never cheated at cards in my life.'

Everyone was clamouring to have their say now, and it was Sir Jolyon ffolliat DeWinter who wrested the floor from the others, next. 'As for that signature on my father's cheque, it was one he had meant to sign before he went away on business for a couple of days, but if I hadn't settled the debt, I would have been in real trouble. I was only a young stripling, and when the bank questioned the signature, my father backed me to the hilt, and said he had been feeling rather shaky that day, and the signature was, in fact, his.'

'And with reference to my poaching, my father knew what I was up to, but never said anything until years later, when he explained he had kept quiet because he didn't want me to end up a rotten shot like old Bonkers.'

At this moment, Colonel Henry Heyhoe-Caramac shot him an evil glance, and rose to his feet for his moment of justification. 'I may have been a bit rough when I trained the dog to which you were referring, but only with a rolled up newspaper, and that training wasn't a waste of time. When I fell off the barn roof, it was dear old Stumpy who went back to the house and barked his head off until someone would follow him. I'd gashed my leg badly on the way down, and if it hadn't been for that dog, I'd have bled to death. So there!'

Lt Col. Featherstonehaugh-Armitage now stood, taking his turn in the limelight. If everyone else was going to explain away their apparent misdemeanours, he didn't see why he shouldn't have his turn too.

'My father had no idea that I'd 'borrowed' money from the family business, for the simple reason that he had what we refer to now as Alzheimer's, but in those days, was referred to as 'senile dementia'. My mother wanted it kept as quiet as possible, because she felt it would bring shame on the family – you know how people used to think in those days.

'Anyway, as co-signatory on the account, she very kindly loaned me the money until I could pay it back, which was something my father never could have done, because he didn't even know who I was, by that time. Does that satisfy you, Inspector bloody Moody?'

In the meantime, Lady Amanda had made her way across to the unpopular policeman, and in the guise of offering him some words of comfort at this sudden implosion of his multiple-murderer theory, whispered in his ear, 'If you say one word about the Golightly family, I shall have you in court so quickly on a defamation of character and slander charge that your feet won't touch the ground, sonny!'

She then went to the middle of the room and requested that Hugo go on with his accusation.

Hugo, in fine form now, took the floor once more and declared, as if in court, 'It is my belief that Porky brought that huge handbag with her on Boxing Day because of financial irregularities on the part of her husband, and that, in it, she had secreted all the weapons that were used on her husband in his murder.

'Her intention was to confuse and confound, for she knew how unpopular he was. She relied on this unpopularity, so that some dolt,' at this point, he looked at Moody, 'would come to the conclusion that all the guests were in collusion, and had conspired to kill him.

'I expect that you will find something in her house – maybe a bronze, or something of that sort – with which she brained him. He was garrotted, and the cord or wire, or whatever was used, must have been cut from somewhere. I suggest her garden shed be examined in minute detail. His throat was also cut. I put it to you,' he was in fine courtroom drama form now, 'that he was stabbed with the knife that also cut his throat, and that that knife was none other than the one he used at his own desk for opening mail. I'm sure I've seen it somewhere before, and I'm fairly certain it was in his house.'

At this, there was a general murmur of agreement, which really gratified Hugo, as he hadn't been in Popeye's house for a very long time, and was actually winging it now. 'As for the poison, may I suggest a thorough rummage through the greenhouse might throw up an old week-killing product that contains something now banned?'

Porky raised her considerable bulk from the chair and spat across the room, 'You foul old fiend. How did you know all that?'

'Because you've just confirmed it for me, thank you very much,' replied Hugo, not forgetting his manners, even in the face of melodrama.

PC Glenister moved unobtrusively from his position in the background and slickly applied handcuffs to Porky's wrists, before looking towards his superior for instructions as to how he should proceed.

Moody had grabbed a sherry with each hand from Beauchamp's beckoning tray, and was too busy pouring them down his throat to even acknowledge that he had noticed what Glenister had done.

It was, or course, Lady Amanda who took charge of the situation, nodding to Beauchamp to stay where he was, while the inspector quenched his thirst at his leisure, although it seemed a pity to see such a fine old sherry being downed as if it were cordial.

'Come on, Porky, spill the beans. Why did you really do it? Was it all down to money? I thought you were loaded. In fact, I thought that was why Popeye married you in the first place,' she asked baldly.

'I was loaded. Back then. But I had no idea how Popeye had been getting through the money, and when I went Christmas shopping just a while ago, I had my bank card refused in two shops before I thought to call into the bank to see what the problem was. The problem was that there was next to nothing left in our account, because Popeye had spent it all. And he'd always been so mean and frugal with me.

'I went off home in a rage, and on the way I thought that all he could talk about for months had been this bloody book of his, so I thought I'd have a little rifle through his drawers when he next went out, so that I could work out if he'd just borrowed a chunk of it temporarily, while waiting for his advance cheque to arrive.

'Boy, was I a sucker! There was no advance cheque. All I found in his desk were rejection letters from over a score of publishers. The only contract I could lay my hands on was from a vanity publishing house, which he was actually paying to print the bloody thing, and he'd ordered thousands and thousands of copies, as if he wanted to stock every book shop in the country. That's where the last of the money went!

'I was in such a rage that I felt almost calm. I opened up the computer and began to read what he had written – something of which he probably didn't think I was capable – and it was absolutely terrible. It wasn't just that he didn't have enough dynamite to blow his own nose, it was the grammar and the spelling too. And talk about purple prose. If he paid for that to be published – and with my money, I might add – he'd be a laughing stock, and a broke one at that.

'I rang the publishing house after checking the cheque book, and told them I'd put a stop on the cheque, and they weren't to go ahead with anything until I said so, and if they didn't do what I asked, I'd go to the papers about them publishing a book that was likely to attract some notoriety in the courts, because all those mentioned in it would sue the pants off both the author and his publisher. I was absolutely incandescent with fury.

'And, I wasn't quite prepared to face poverty without even the company of my old friends, and he had some hefty insurance policies on his life, so I just thought, why not? Why not remove the only fly in the ointment of my life, and at least preserve what little money I had left and collect on the insurance?'

There was a general chorus of, 'Porky!'

'Don't you dare look down your noses at me! What was I supposed to do? Take it all in good part and put my name on the list for social housing? I'd certainly no hopes of maintenance if I divorced him, so the only way out I could see was to do away with him completely. Why are you all looking so shocked? None of you liked him!'

Constable Glenister helped Porky to her feet, moved over to where Inspector Moody was sitting and pulled him by the shoulder of his mackintosh until he stood up. He turned briefly towards the assembled company and wished them a cheery 'good day' before making his exit, on his return journey back to the police station. Once outside, he unlocked the car, ushered his prisoner into the back seat, then opened the passenger door for the inspector.

'I think I'd better drive, don't you, sir?' he asked, removing his helmet before assisting the broken man into the car.

Chapter Sixteen

OMG – Again!

After seeing the thunderstruck guests off the premises, Lady Amanda, Hugo and Enid gathered in the drawing room, waiting for Beauchamp to join them with a tray of cocktails, not only because it was 'cocktail o'clock', but because they had had a very trying afternoon, and needed a little kick to revive them.

'I say, Manda, who would have thought it of poor old Porky?' declared Hugo, a smile of victory hovering around his lips.

'Well, *you* obviously, you cunning old bloodhound, you. How on earth did you work it out?' retorted Lady Amanda, looking a shade jealous of Hugo's revelations in the library.

'I wouldn't have given it a thought, if I hadn't tripped over your handbag, old thing. Sort of put the things in my mind, so to speak, and when that dreary little inspector was droning on about the pathetic contents of Popeye's book, I just let my eyes and mind wander, examining the women's bags and comparing them.

'Yours had contained what appeared to be the entire contents of a garden shed and make-up counter combined, and I wondered how much stuff other women carried round with them. I thought I was getting quite a feel for colour and style, when my eyes lit on Porky's bag. I don't know if you noticed it, but it was one of those tiny things that you can tuck under one arm. Is it a clutch bag?' he asked.

'Where on earth did you learn so much about ladies' handbags, Hugo?' Enid asked, making him blush.

'Just the sort of thing that one picks up, you know? Anyway, there was something at the back of my head that said that bag was somehow wrong, and I didn't have the faintest idea why

I should think such a thing, when I had a vision of this vast tapestry bag, and realised that when she was here on Boxing Day, she had had an absolutely enormous specimen with her. Then I suddenly lighted on why she needed such a big one.'

'To carry all the necessary weapons to make it look like a crowd of people had murdered her husband,' supplied Lady Amanda. 'And I actually saw her put her gloves into it when she arrived, so now we know why there were no fingerprints on anything. It did fleetingly cross my mind, with them being so obviously at loggerheads with each other, that she might have chosen that one just to annoy him, but then I thought no more of it, with so much going on. Clever old Hugo!

'I must say, I've heard of crowds of people being massacred by a lunatic individual, and an individual being massacred by a crowd, but a massacre being committed by one person on only one other is really bizarre. But how ingenious of her to think of it in the first place!'

'Manda!' Hugo admonished her. 'The poor woman's going to prison for murder. Have you no sympathy?'

'Not really. She should have kept a closer eye on her finances if they had joint accounts. She was the one who had the money when they married, and she should have been more aware of what was going on; and made regular checks. Anyway, as Popeye's book hasn't already flooded the market, she can claim that his death nullifies the contract, and will have no problem with the cancelled cheque, although I suppose that's the least of her worries at the moment. Now, where's that man? BEAUCHaargh! There you are! You nearly scared the life out of me, Beauchamp.'

'That's Beecham, my lady!' the manservant retorted softly.

'No it's not, and I'm not deaf, you know. Not yet, anyway. I heard exactly what you said. So, what have you got for us tonight, then? Something appropriate, I hope,' she asked, rubbing her hands together in anticipation.

'I have a White Christmas for you again, my lady and a Wobbly Knee for Mr Hugo, as he's still suffering. It might, perhaps, have been more appropriate to serve him with a Little White Lie, but I don't think the police suspected anything when he said he'd seen the knife on the captain's desk.'

Hugo turned red and smiled at the same time. 'First time for everything, what?' he retorted.

'And for Mrs Enid and myself, I have made a Best Year, and I think I can say that, with all the changes that have taken place this year, it has been the best for a very long time.'

'Well said, Beauchamp! Here's to the Fearless Four, and to more detecting. It's certainly put a spring in my step and some zest in my life! Cheers!'

As they drank, there came a loud knocking on the front door, and Lady Amanda looked at the clock with astonishment. She had issued no other invitations for the day, and she was sure that Inspector Moody was probably still breaking pencils and climbing the walls in his frustration, at this very moment. Who on earth could it be?

'I'll get it,' volunteered Enid. 'You stay here and enjoy your cocktail, Beau ... Beech ... ham,' she compromised on his name, not daring to choose one body of opinion over the other.

At the door she found an elderly moustachioed gentleman in a bowler hat and camel hair coat who thrust a business card at her, and apologised for arriving without an appointment, but that he had to see Lady Amanda with the utmost urgency.

Enid took the card, held it at arm's length to read it, and said, 'Do come in, Mr Bradshaigh.'

'That's Bradshaw!' the man retorted, slightly miffed at this pronunciation. 'Can't you read, woman?'

'I certainly can, Mr Bradshaigh, and 'Bradshaigh' it says on this card,' and then she lost her temper. 'I've had Cholmondley that's pronounced Chummley, Crichton that's pronounced Cryton, Featherstonehaugh that's pronounced Fanshaw, and now you say you're Bradshaigh, pronounced Bradshaw. What sort of schools did your forebears go to? I ask myself. Mine went to a place that taught them to read what was in front of them, and not miss out half the syllables, and then just make up the rest of them!' and she stamped her foot in exasperation before she recovered her manners.

'Follow me into the drawing room where I'm sure everybody will be able to read your name with complete accuracy,' she replied in high dudgeon, and stomped off, a rather surprised Mr Bradshaigh trailing in her wake, totally flummoxed by Enid's spirited outburst of confusion and anger.

At the door, she announced, 'There's a Mr Bradshaigh who says his name's pronounced Bradshaw, to see you. Here is his card,' and with that, she sat down again and threw the rest of her cocktail down her throat defiantly.

'Mr Bradshaigh,' Lady Amanda welcomed him, with perfect pronunciation. 'How nice to see you again, but it must be twenty years since we last met. What brings you here so unexpectedly? Mama's solicitor,' she added, so that the other three knew who he was.

'It's about your mother,' he began, but was stopped in his tracks as Lady Amanda interrupted him.

'But Mama's been dead these twenty years. What business can you have, concerning her affairs?'

'I know she's not dead, Lady Amanda. I was in on the plot. How could she live abroad under another name without someone to manage her finances for her? I've been in the background all this time, quietly working away at her behest. But, to cut a long story short,' he said, noting that Lady Amanda's mouth was hanging open at the thought of someone else (other than Beauchamp) who had known about her mother faking her own death, when she herself knew nothing.

'Whatever's the man talking ...' began Enid, but was immediately silenced by one of Lady A's glares, and her almost spat instruction.

'Enid, you will repeat nothing whatsoever that is taking place in this room now, to another living soul, and if you do, I know where you live, and I will hunt you down and kill you like a dog. Do I make myself crystal clear?'

'Absolutely, Lady Amanda. No word shall ever pass my lips. I swear on my mother's life that I shall be mute for the rest of my life.' Enid felt a shiver of genuine fear move through her body at Lady Amanda's vehemence.

Mr Bradshaigh, having remained silent while Lady Amanda set out her absolute demand for silence, continued without turning a hair, 'To cut a long story short, your mother is on her deathbed with pneumonia and a chest infection, and I had a call from the hospital on my mobile to tell me that she was fading fast. If you want to see her again, alive, you'll have to move quickly.'

The mood in the drawing room grew sombre, as Lady Amanda asked, 'Is that all you know?'

'I know that she's written a letter for you, in case you're too late, and that she asked that you be informed that you're not an only child. Either she, or her letter, will explain, when you get there.'

'WHAT?' Lady Amanda was on her feet. '*Not an only child*? I've *always* been an only child. Ever since I was *born*! Has the woman *finally* lost her marbles? Where's the *proof*? Inventing phantom children like that! Well, it simply won't *do*! I *demand* to know what's happening!'

THE END

Read on for cocktail recipes from this story!

AFTERWORD
<u>**Cocktail Recipes**</u>

White Christmas

1 measure crème de banana
1 measure white crème de cacao
1 measure scotch whisky
1measure double cream
Shake and strain, sprinkle with grated chocolate

Wobbly Knee

1 measure Amaretto di Saronno
1 measure Kahlua
1/2 measure vodka
3/4 measure coconut cream
1 measure double cream
Blend briefly with a glassful of crushed ice, sprinkle with grated chocolate

Bumpo

2 measures golden rum
1 measure lime juice

1. tsp caster sugar
2. measures hot water

Add to glass, dissolve the sugar. Dust with nutmeg

Hopeless Case

1 measure sloe gin
1/2 measure peppermint schnapps

3 measures cold cola
Add to ice-filled glass. Garnish: lime slice

Best Year

1 measure vodka
  1/2 measure blue curacao
  1/2 measure Licor 43
  11/2 measures pineapple juice
  1/2 measure Rose's Lime Cordial
  Shake and strain into glass filled with broken ice

Waste of Time

1 measure Midori

1. measure white rum

1/2 measure amaretto

1. measures pineapple juice

Prepare 2 glasses
Glass 1: rim with grenadine/caster sugar,add cherry on stick.
Garnish: fruit in season.
Glass 2: plain, ungarnished. Shake and strain into glass 2.
Serve both!

SNOWBALLS AND SCOTCH MIST

A Lady Amanda Golightly Murder Mystery
The Belchester Chronicles: Book Three

ANDREA FRAZER

DRAMATIS PERSONAE
& PRONUNCIATION GUIDE
(for budding Enid Tweedies)

Guests at Rumdrummond Castle

Lady Amanda Golightly and Hugo Cholmondley-Crichton-Crump – from Belchester Towers; Hugo's names pronounced Chumley-Cryten-Crump

Sir Cardew and Lady Siobhan McKinley-Mackintosh – host and hostess; Lady M-M's name pronounced 'Shevawn'

St John Bagehot – pronounced Sinjen Badgitt

Ralf Colcolough – pronounced Raif Koukli

Wallace Menzies – pronounced Ming-is

Drew and Moira Ruthven – pronounced Riven

Iain and Elspeth Smellie – pronounced Smiley

Quinton Wriothesley – pronounced Rizzly

Staff at Rumdrummond Castle

Evelyn Awlle – lady's maid to Lady Siobhan, hostess

Walter Waule – valet-cum-butler to Sir Cardew, host

Angus Hamilton – chauffeur at the castle

Janet MacTavish – cook at the castle

Jock Macleod – piper at the castle

Sarah Fraser – lady's maid to Moira Ruthven (guest staff)

Mary Campbell – lady's maid to Elspeth Smellie (guest staff)

Duncan Macdonald – head gamekeeper and ghillie

Sandy Gunn – piper

Beauchamp – pronounced Beecham by everybody, with the exception of Lady A, who favours the original French pronunciation – valet to Hugo Cholmondley-Crichton-Crump (guest staff)

Enid Tweedie – lady's maid to Lady Amanda Golightly (guest staff)

Police Officers

DI Glenister

PC MacDuff

Prologue New Year's Eve

Lady Amanda Golightly, together with her dear friend Hugo Cholmondley-Crichton-Crump, entered the hospital in Monte Carlo where her mother, Lady Edith, lay gravely ill, at the fag-end of her life. Hugo's face was full of concern, but Lady A's was set in grim determination. As they reached Lady Edith's hospital bed, the nurse slipped discreetly from the room, closing the door softly behind her. Lady Edith, who had faked her own death twenty years earlier, smiled up at her only daughter beatifically, sighed, and departed this world to a place where it would be a very long time before her only offspring could find her again.

'I think she's gone, old girl,' Hugo said, keeping his voice soft and solicitous. He didn't like overt displays of emotion and he hoped Lady Amanda would be able to act with dignity, given the circumstances. She didn't!

'Wake up, you evil old witch!' she hissed, grabbing her mother's nightie and lifting her bodily from the bed to give her a good shaking. 'You can't just send me a message that I'm not an only child, then pop off. I need to know what the hell you meant by that message. How could I not be an only child? I always have been. What did you mean, you secretive old hag?'

'Manda, I think you'd better put your mother down. She's passed over: she's not going to tell you anything now.'

'She's gone on purpose, just to spite me. I need to know what she meant. How am I not an only child?' Lady Amanda's voice had risen in volume, and attracted the attention of the nurse who had just left.

Hearing footsteps, Hugo pulled at her fingers to release their grip on her mother's nightgown, and led her away from the bed. 'There's someone coming, old thing. Best to act with dignity, in the face of tragedy,' he counselled her.

'Tragedy?' she said in a furious whisper. 'If I don't find out what the old bag meant, I'll kill the messenger and consult a medium to confront her; you see if I don't. I must know!'

'I have a letter here that your mother requested be given to you, should you arrive too late to speak to her. I don't know if she's up to conversation,' said the nurse, from just inside the door, an envelope in her hand.

'The only conversation she'll be having is with St Peter, trying to persuade him to let her through the pearly gates, after everything she's done in her devious life,' spat Lady Amanda, still in a fury. 'She's dead!'

'My sincerest condolences on the loss of your mother, Lady Amanda. We've all become very fond of Lady Edith in the short time she has been with us,' intoned the nurse in a sepulchral tone.

'Condolences be damned! Give me that blasted letter, and get on with making the funeral arrangements. I shan't need her body repatriated, as that would make life rather complicated for me, so if you'd just kindly arrange a cremation and send me on her ashes along with your bill, I should be very grateful.'

Lady A's mood had tempered slightly at the sight of the envelope which would, no doubt, contain the information on why she wasn't an only child. With her hand held out, she tried an ingratiating smile, but in Hugo's opinion, it didn't come off, and looked more like an evil leer.

Hugo decided it was time he took over. 'If you would just give Lady Amanda the envelope, we'll get out of your hair. I have a card here, with the details of where we're staying, but I expect we'll be off to good old Blighty tomorrow, so I'd better give you details of how to contact her there.'

'Blighty? Where is this place called Blighty? I have never heard of it.' The nurse was confused. Some words are inexplicable, if one doesn't know the root or the usage.

'We'll be in England,' Hugo added, hoping this was explanation enough and, grabbing Lady Amanda's handbag, which she had dropped on the bed in her fight to resuscitate her mother, he extracted a card and handed it over, along with the one he had picked up before they'd left the hotel.

Back in Lady Amanda's hotel room, she sat and fumed on the bed, as she re-read the letter her mother had left for her, for the fifth time.

'I simply can't believe it!' she stormed. 'It can't be true! It's impossible! This must be some kind of a last sick joke on her part.'

'There are details in there that tell you how to get a copy of the birth certificate. If there's a birth certificate, then it must be true and you're going to have to believe it, whether you want to or not,' Hugo told her, getting a little fed up with her raging at what was obviously the truth.

'But Hugo,' she countered, 'How the hell am I going to live with the fact that Beauchamp is my brother – or, at least, my half-brother? That's just mad!'

'Mad, but true. You'll have to tell him, of course, although knowing Beauchamp, he'll already know all about it.'

'Bugger!' snorted Lady A and went over to the drinks cabinet to pour herself a very large brandy.

Chapter One Two weeks later

'Oh, Lord!' exclaimed Lady Amanda Golightly, holding a stiff invitation card that had just arrived in the post, in her hand. 'Blast! Damn! Poo! Well, I simply shan't go. I can't face it again, so I shall refuse.'

'What's that, Manda?' asked Hugo Cholmondley-Crichton-Crump, her elderly friend. 'Where do you refuse to go? What can't you face?'

'It's the blasted McKinley-Mackintoshes. They've invited me for Burns' Night. I don't know; my grandmother's sister marries into the family, then her daughter marries one of her McKinley-Mackintosh cousins, and suddenly we're close kin. My mother put up with it, but I never have, and I won't now.

'I haven't been up there since before Mama died for the first time, and I'll be damned if I'll go again – not to that draughty old castle right in the middle of hundreds of acres of Mac-nowhere.'

'Is that the Mac-nowhere in Scotland?'

'Where else?' asked Lady A, crossly.

'And for Burns' Night, you say?'

'Are you getting hard of hearing, Hugo? Of course it's for Burns' Night.'

'So you've been invited to a castle in Scotland for Burns' Night?' Hugo persisted.

'How many times do I have to tell you? That's what I've been complaining about, isn't it? Are you sure you're not losing your marbles?'

Ignoring this last disparaging remark, Hugo replied, 'Oh, Manda; I've never spent a Burns' Night actually in Scotland. And in a castle too. Please say yes and take me with you as your guest. Please, please say you'll accept.' Hugo had always been very susceptible to the skirl of the pipes.

'Oh, really, Hugo, you can't be serious! You want to go all that way, in January, to the wilds of Scotland, just for a haggis dinner?'

'Pretty please, Manda. I'm getting on a bit now, and if they invite you again next year, I might be dead, and never get the chance to do it.' Hugo was adept at emotional blackmail when he wanted something badly enough.

'Don't say that, Hugo! And you really want to go, do you?' Lady Amanda was astounded by the light of enthusiasm in his eyes, and not willing to contemplate a life without his company now, decided she'd better think twice.

'More than anything. For me. Just this once.'

'I capitulate, but you'll owe me big time for this one,' she replied, with a wince at what now lay ahead of them.

'Will there be a piper? And an address to the haggis? And Scottish country dancing? And ... maybe some sword dancing?' he asked, as eager as a child promised an esoteric treat.

'Oh, there'll be all of that, and more. There'll be long, cold, stone passageways with real torches flaring along their length, and deerstalking, although the only thing shooting these days are cameras. There'll be gamekeepers and ghillies all over the place, and absolutely everything will be covered in tartan, both dress and hunting.'

Hugo rubbed his hands together with glee, just before Lady A exclaimed, 'Damn and blast!'

'What is it now, Manda?'

'We've apparently got to bring our own butler/valet and lady's maid. Whatever am I going to do about a lady's maid? I've never had one, and I don't intend to start a habit like that so late in life.'

Hugo, noting the 'we've' with satisfaction, suggested, 'What about roping in Enid? She'd probably be game for it. Get it? Game? Scotland? Deerstalking?'

'Hugo?'

'Yes, Manda?'

'Shut up! But you're right. She'd be perfect. I'll get Beauchamp to collect her, so that I can get her exact measurements, then I'll make a call to Harrods and have them send something down. Beauch ... aargh!'

'Yes, your ladyship?' A tall, impeccably garbed figure had suddenly appeared at her side like magic. It was taking some time to get used to the fact that her butler and general factotum was also her half-brother, but she was dealing with it as best as she could.

Neither could see any good reason to change the status quo, as they were both perfectly content with the way their lives ran, but sometimes it gave Lady A a strange feeling, when she asked – or told – him to do something, then remembered that he was, in actual fact, kin.

'I've told you before not to pad about like a cat. You must've taken years off my life over the years, just turning up like that, when I'm about to call you.'

'Sorry, your ladyship. What can I get you?' Beauchamp's voice was exactly as it had been before Lady A had known about their blood kinship, but that was probably because he had known the truth for most of his life, and had just kept it to himself.

'Enid, is what you can get me. Could you just run into Belchester and bring her up here? I want to measure her for a lady's maid's uniform.'

'Is she by any chance going into service, your ladyship?' Beauchamp asked, a little perplexed at this request.

'Sort of, but I'll explain all when she gets here. If she asks, just tell her there's a little holiday in the offing.'

'Yes, your ladyship. Will there be anything else?'

'Not for now, but when you get back, we'll all have a little cocktail to give us a chance to discuss arrangements.'

'The McKinley-Mackintoshes' for Burns' Night?' queried the manservant, a knowing glint in his eye.

'No names, no pack-drill, my man. Now, the sooner you go, the sooner you'll be back, and we can all have a lovely little chinwag about it. But not a word to Enid until she gets here. I don't want her to get wind of what's in the air until it's a fait accompli.'

'You mean you don't want her to suddenly have another engagement that makes it possible for her to wriggle out of it. You just want a chance to bully her before she knows what's coming,' commented Hugo, tapping one side of his nose with a forefinger.

'Exactly!'

When Beauchamp had gone off on his mission, Hugo became lively again, and asked, 'Can we have tartan, Manda? Please. I've always fancied myself in a kilt.'

'We can, but you'll have trews and be done with. I have no desire whatsoever to be faced with your scrawny old legs every hour of the day,' she replied, waspishly. 'And I shall have a long skirt and one of those over-the-shoulder shoulder sash-cum-shawl thingies. I can order those, with accurate measurements, from a little place my old friend, Ida Campbell, uses in Scotland. She's so clan-crazy she's even got tartan carpet; makes me feel quite ill after a while, so I don't visit often.'

'But I don't want trews,' Hugo wailed in disappointment.

'Do you know what's actually worn under a kilt, Hugo? Nothing: absolutely nothing. You'll freeze your wrinkly bits beyond recovery. Do you really want to do that?' 'Not really? Is it so very cold there?'

'Hugo, it's January. It's in the north of Scotland. There'll probably be feet of snow, and the only heating in that humongous stone castle is from log fires, which may look huge, but, if I remember correctly, the heat never reaches further than two feet away from the seat of the fire, and the rest of the space might as well be outside, as far as temperature goes.'

'Hmm.' Hugo took a moment lost in thought. 'I think trews might be a better idea. I don't suppose I can wear a sporran with them.'

'Absolutely not! That would look, to my mind, rather obscene, as if you were ... hm-hm,' she cleared her throat self-consciously, 'flying without a licence.' This description gave Lady A a flush of embarrassment, and she hurried on with, 'I'd suggest you pack lots of warm jumpers and your winter underwear, and we'll discuss it further when Enid arrives.'

Enid joined them about half an hour later, and Beauchamp immediately went off to mix some cocktails of sufficient strength to persuade their poor guest that she really wanted to stay in a draughty old Scottish pile, not as an invited guest, but as a lady's maid.

Enid was all of a flutter, wondering why she had been summoned at such short notice, delaying the explanation even further by divesting herself of several layers of clothing before settling on a sofa, eager to hear what was afoot.

Before any explanation could be made, Beauchamp returned bearing a tray with four double tulip glasses on it, handed it round with his usual air of formality, then announced, 'I made Frozen Melon Balls, which seemed rather appropriate, but I used the larger glasses, as the usual size seemed a little – shall we say, unpersuasive.'

'Quite right, too, Beauchamp, and it'll give Hugo pause for thought on the subject of kilts,' Lady A intoned, puzzling the two who had not been party to the conversation about the merits of trews over kilts, then she came over all embarrassed again, as did Hugo himself, at the name of the cocktail, and the thought that they might begin to discuss his private parts as if they were an everyday subject of conversation.

Enid broke the impasse by raising her glass and twittering, 'Chin-chin, everybody, now what am I here for?'

'Chin-chin,' they all repeated automatically, and Lady A, recovering her aplomb, speared her with a steely gaze, smiled a wolfish smile, then asked her how she would like to celebrates Burns' Night in a castle in Scotland where they had their own piper.

Cunning old vixen, her words had Enid hooked immediately, and imagining all sorts of romantic images of what it would be like. 'Oh, I'd love to, Amanda.' For she had been invited to drop the 'Lady' when addressing someone who was now more of a friend than an employer, but that was not to last for long.

'Excellent, but you'll have to start referring to me as Lady Amanda again, and after we've had this drink, I must get you measured for some lady's maid's outfits, if they're to be here before we leave. I'll measure you later, Hugo, so we can get the trews exactly right.'

She had successfully changed the subject, as Hugo declared that he knew his own measurements, and would verify them himself, in private. This was getting a bit near the knuckle again, and he willed Enid to butt in and ask some questions.

She obliged exactly on cue, having sat with a bewildered expression on her face, as Hugo protested about letting Lady Amanda at him with a tape-measure. 'What exactly are you trying to inveigle me into, now? I don't think I like the sound of lady's maid's uniforms. What's going on? What are you planning?'

'I've been invited – it's all right, Hugo, it does say 'and guest' – for Burns' Night, to Castle Rumdrummond. You know, the McKinley-Mackintoshes' pile in the north of Scotland? That invitation I've been turning down every year since Mama and Papa died.

'Well, Hugo really wants to go, as he's never been in Scotland for Burns' Night before. I usually just refuse out of hand, but I've capitulated this year because of Hugo's heart-rending plea. However, the invitation insists that I bring my own butler/valet and lady's maid. And I thought it would give you a nice little holiday, and a change of scenery.'

'Waiting on you hand, foot, and finger. Yes, that really would make a lovely change for me. Just what I've always wanted, to be a skivvy in a cold and draughty building in the middle of nowhere, somewhere in the north of Scotland,' Enid replied, a positive sting in her voice.

'It won't be anything like that, I promise you. You're only going as a maid to help me out, not to actually carry out the duties of a maid,' Lady A told her in her most persuasive voice, before turning to Beauchamp and asking him to refresh the cocktails. He rose, with a knowing wink, collected the glasses, and disappeared into the interstices of Belchester Towers to make fresh drinks.

Unlike Castle Rumdrummond, Belchester Towers was not a magnificent ancient pile, but had been built by one of Lady Amanda Golightly's forebears, early in the nineteenth century, to incorporate every luxury of the day, being updated, as new-fangled domestic fashions became popular, including a rope-pulled lift, when Queen Victoria had such a thing installed in her newly built Isle of Wight home.

This fad of modernisation continued, so that, when Lady Amanda was born, the imposing building boasted electric lighting, central heating and the luxury of several bathrooms, each with its own hot water supply. The fabric of the building had not been neglected either, and it had been kept in good order, unlike Castle Rumdrummond, which had spent a century or more crumbling around its owners' ears, they being landed gentry, and unlike the Golightly family, merely nouveau riche, and therefore more financially stable.

Belchester Towers was of red-brick construction, with a tower at each corner, and had three floors and extensive cellarage. The original folly of a real moat with drawbridge had been done away with long since, and it now boasted a rather more conventional means of entry.

Its current owner was a short, portly woman past retirement age, with startlingly bright green eyes, suicide blonde hair, and a positive mania for good manners, except when it applied to her. She spoke as she found, always telling the truth and shaming the devil.

She had found her friend Hugo mouldering in a local nursing home the previous year. A man whose family friendship dated back to her childhood, Lady Amanda immediately rescued him from his depressing and utterly boring existence, and installed him in Belchester Towers as a permanent resident.

She then set about solving the mobility problems which had been the cause of his original incarceration in such a demotivating dump, arranging appointments with an orthopaedic surgeon, to set in place a plan to replace both his hips and his knees, and relieving him of the financial burden of living alone.

After some initial difficulties, they had settled well together, and Hugo, after the first two operations of the planned surgery, had progressed from a walking frame to a pair of walking sticks, and was much livelier than he had been when she had first come across him again. Their shared younger years rejuvenated both of them, and they were better for each other than any therapy or medicine that could be offered to them.

Enid Tweedie, at one time an occasional cleaner at the Towers, had become more of a friend, and her life had become spiced with excitement in the process. Prior to this change in status, she had been a frequent visitor to the local hospital, always having some procedure or another done. Now she had little time to consider her health, she was much the better for it. She had, as the modern saying goes, 'got a life'.

Beauchamp, whom Lady Amanda insisted on calling 'Bo-sham', declared, equally strongly, that the name in England was pronounced 'Beecham', and this was a constant running battle between them, and had been for decades, for Beauchamp had spent his entire working life at the Towers, employed first by her parents, and now, by her.

During the last, eventful year, a few family skeletons had been evicted from the closet, revealing that Lady Edith, Lady A's mother, had not died in a car crash some twenty years before, but had, in fact, faked her own death and spent the intervening two decades on the Riviera, then finally, in Monte Carlo, where she had died at New Year.

Lady Edith's final revelation had been to reveal that Beauchamp was Lady Amanda's half-brother, courtesy of her late father, and that had really thrown the cat among the pigeons. But they were working it out, slowly adjusting a now very ambiguous relationship, with regards to status, but it would be some time before life returned to anything that resembled the norm and, when it did, it would be a completely different norm from before these unsettling facts had emerged.

Lady Amanda had considered this when Hugo had made his heartfelt plea to be taken to Scotland. Maybe a break in a really dysfunctional household would do them the world of good. Only the truly grotesque could make the merely ugly look beautiful.

The next morning, about ten-thirty, Lady A telephoned Enid's measurements to Harrods, the exact model having been chosen the evening before on the Internet site, with a request for express delivery.

Another phone call connected her to the little shop that provided anything in tartan, right down to tea cosies and tea towels. She gave the measurements for herself and Hugo, with those needed for Beauchamp to have a matching waistcoat, all of the garments to be in the Rumdrummond tartan – dress of course, not hunting. These items would be sent, from stock, by courier, the same day as ordered.

Within forty-eight hours, they were all in these strange garments, admiring themselves and each other, ready to set off for what were, to them, foreign climes. 'Well, I don't think we look too shabby,' exclaimed Lady A, looking round at her little clan. 'What does everyone else think?'

'I still think I should have had a kilt,' sulked Hugo, returning to his previous theme. 'I mean, they do wear such long, thick socks, I don't see how I would have been too cold.'

'You would, if you'd ever felt the draught in their dining hall. It just whistles along at floor level, and blows up whatever you happen to be wearing,' Lady A told him.

'And these trews cut a bit underneath, if you know what I mean,' Hugo continued.

'Take off your jacket and come here,' Lady A ordered him. 'It's only your braces. I don't know, Hugo; why do you find it necessary to haul your trousers up to your armpits, when they're supposed to sit at waist level. I realise how difficult it must be to determine exactly where your waist used to be ...'

'I say. Manda! That was a bit below the belt, wasn't it?'

'In your case, that's almost just under your ears,' she informed him, not in the least repentant about her remark, working, the while, on setting his braces at a sensible length, so that his suffering was eased, and he looked a little less like a tartan clown.

'I feel like a cross between a refugee from *Upstairs Downstairs* and a loose woman who does 'thing' for money,' commented Enid, rather grumpily, joining in the round of general ingratitude.

'You'll soon get used to it. You need to be more open to change,' her friend advised her.

All eyes turned to Beauchamp, in his bright waistcoat. Eventually he pronounced on his new image. 'I feel like a right tit,' he pronounced. 'I suppose you're going to tell me that I'll fit in just fine,' he said, turning to his halfsister.

'I think you look darkly romantic,' offered Enid boldly, with an attractive flush to her cheeks, at this unusually forward remark.

'He does, indeed,' agreed her friend, and smirked at her butler, soon to be Hugo's valet.

'How are we going to get there? What are the travel arrangements?' Beauchamp asked, a mistrusting expression on his face.

Lady Amanda took a deep breath and said, 'Hugo and I will fly up on Friday, while you two take the Rolls for us. I'm sure we'll be well looked after while we wait for you, and I can't presume to be lent transport when we get there. Expecting to be provided with a car would be too much of a liberty.'

'And sending us up by car isn't?' Beauchamp's worst fears had been fulfilled.

'It'll be an adventure, and think of all that beautiful countryside you'll pass through.'

'You've only arranged this so that Enid and I can take the huge amount of luggage you want to take.'

'That's simply not true,' his half-sister argued, noticing how much more like siblings they were becoming.

'Liar!'

That confirmed it, but she managed to rake up sufficient grace to ask him, 'You don't really mind, do you? You do love driving so, and you can stop off overnight where ever you choose. I can't go up without a change of clothes twice a day, and I don't want to wear anything twice, or they'll think I'm too old to care.'

'What do you say, Enid?' Beauchamp asked his proposed travel companion.

'Oh, I don't like flying, but a long journey by car will be a treat for me,' she replied, smiling shyly.

'Well, that's all settled then, isn't it? I suggest you go and mix us four Highlanders, and we can all toast our proposed little holiday,' trumpeted Lady Amanda, a smile of triumph splitting her face in two.

Chapter Two

Lady Amanda and Hugo's flight was as uneventful as any other plane journey that doesn't include the unexpected excitement of a crash landing, or a collision with mountains or sea.

The food provided en route was more easily identified by colour, than by taste, and when their bland meal was offered, Lady A ignored what the flight attendant had told her about the two choices on offer, and turned to Hugo, who had insisted on a window seat, and asked him, 'Do you want brown lumps or white lumps?' They'd both taste of nothing, so it was probably best to choose by eye.

'I beg your pardon?' queried Hugo, not used to flying, and in a very excitable mood.

With a sigh, she replied, 'It is alleged that the choice is between chicken supreme and beef stew, but they'll both taste of nothing, so it's just as easy to choose by colour. What may be pleasing on the eye will certainly not be pleasing to the taste buds.'

'I'll have whatever you're having,' he decided distractedly, looking out of the window again, through a break in the clouds.

She had already had to dissuade her travelling companion from having a practice run with his life-jacket, and had rescued him from the lavatory, where he was unable to work out which way the door opened, and had cried plaintively for help, like one of the three old ladies in the 'Oh dear, what can the matter be?' children's song, so she was just pleased that he had found something on the ground to hold his attention.

The brown lumps also distracted him for a while, but she was mightily relieved when the plane landed, feeling great sympathy for mothers who had to travel with small children.

They were met at the airport by an ancient Bentley and an even older chauffeur, a bent old man whose face was as creased as that of a monkey, his head proving to be covered with only tiny wisps of white hair, when he doffed his cap. He introduced himself as Angus Hamilton, tottered around in a haphazard manner while Hugo loaded the bags into the boot, then fussed around them with fluffy blankets, when they were finally settled in the rear of the car.

'How long is the drive?' asked Lady A through the ancient speaking tube, raising her voice sufficiently for it to carry without the tube's aid, as their chauffeur had not proved to have the acutest hearing during their short acquaintance.

After three repetitions of her question, Hamilton considered for a moment or two, then said, 'It should take about an hour and a half, but with the snow, it'll take a wee bitty longer, ye ken.'

There was quite a bit of snow lying around, and although this proved a very pretty prospect through the windows, it was obvious how detrimental to driving it was, as the car slipped and slid in an alarming manner, while Hamilton fought to control the wheel, sitting so low, that he could barely see over the steering wheel.

'The gritters couldnae get oot the mornin', because their diesel was frozen solid,' he informed them in a cheerful voice.

It was a tense drive, Lady A resorting to silent prayers, while Hugo cowered under his blanket like an ostrich burying its head in the sand, and took, not an hour and a half, but nearer four hours. The heater in the car worked in only a half-hearted way, and they were frozen stiff by the time the vehicle crawled up the long drive to Castle Rumdrummond, which had, fortunately, been gritted by the estate workers.

Hamilton seemed not a jot affected by the bitter temperatures, both inside and outside the car, and ,dismissing them as poncy Sassenachs, wheezed his way up to the front door to get someone to help with the bags. As far as he was concerned, his duty was done for he would have no truck with heaving around luggage,.

A suitably attired member of the household staff came out to their aid, and introduced himself as Walter Waule, butler-cum-valet to Sir Cardew McKinley-Mackintosh. 'We dinnae hae a great number of workers in the Castle, so we all double up, as it were,' he explained, rolling his 'r's ferociously. 'Hae ye any staff with ye?'

'We've got a valet and lady's maid arriving by car sometime tomorrow,' Lady A explained.

'That's vera well, as some of the guests seemed tae hae forgotten to bring staff wi' them, and we cannae cope withoot help.'

He showed them to their rooms, explaining that the booming sound they heard as they entered was the dressing bell. The two Sassenachs had hoped to arrive in time for afternoon tea, well over by now, but it was only six o'clock, and surely far too early to be dressing for dinner.

'Dinner will be served at six-thirty,' explained Hamilton. 'The master and mistress like to dine early, so they can get to bed by nine. No need to change t'night, as ye've on'y just arrived.'

Lady Amanda bit her knuckles with distress at this news, and Hugo's face was so long, he was almost trailing it up the stone staircase, as he plodded in Waule's wake. They exchanged a look that said all too obviously: what the hell have we let ourselves in for?

Their rooms proved to be next to each other and had an adjoining door, through which Hugo wandered after only a few minutes on the other side of it. 'I say, Manda! You might have explained exactly what you were getting me into,' he complained.

'Me getting you into? It was you who pleaded like a petulant child to be allowed to come here. I told you I'd much rather have stayed at home. If that man Waule and the chauffeur are anything to go by, the members of staff are going to drive me mad with their accent. That's the Scots all over, though. If they're not rolling their 'r's at you, they're rolling their eyes. It's not easy being a Sassenach up here.

'And it's a dry house. That's not to say that some of the walls aren't running with moisture, but don't expect any cocktails, or wine with dinner. You'll get a thimbleful of scotch on your haggis tomorrow, but apart from that, the only other drink they ever indulge in is a wee tot of whisky at Hogmanay, and then only the one.'

'What?' Hugo was horrified. 'How shall we survive?'

'Don't worry, help is at hand,' announced Lady A, producing a silver hip flask from her capacious handbag along with two small silver beakers. I have brought us enough for two Scotch Mists apiece, and when Beauchamp arrives he has with him a hamper with the necessary ingredients to provide us with cocktails as usual, and a few bottles of wine with which to while away the time between dinner and a decent bedtime.'

'You genius woman,' exclaimed Hugo, eagerly accepting his beaker. 'And we shan't need any ice because this place is absolutely freezing. I shall be surprised if I sleep a wink in this temperature. Hang on a minute, though. If we have no ice and no lemon, that means that the only ingredient left for a Scotch Mist is the whisky. You can hardly call that anything but a straight scotch.'

'Oh, use your imagination, Hugo, and be grateful that I brought anything at all. It'll be the essence of a Scotch Mist, and we shall just have to pretend. Never fear about the night-time temperature, though. I have four hot water bottles in my case;

two each. You can have one at your feet, and cuddle the other. With a little nightcap, you should go off splendidly.'

'You have been here before, haven't you?'

'In spades, Hugo. And, like an elephant, I never forget, especially if my home comforts are threatened. What do you think of your room?'

'More of a dungeon, if you ask me. Tiny windows like slits, so it's probably in permanent twilight even in full daylight. Everything's stone, except for the furniture. The bed's old enough to have had Bonnie Prince Charlie sleep in it, and the draughts – they seem to come from all directions at once. I'm really grateful that you thought to bring hot water bottles.'

Lady Amanda looked towards her bed, a tiny half-tester that must once have been the property of either a midget or a child. 'If I don't lie still in that thing, I'm going to roll off and get a concussion on this stone floor.'

'My bed's so big you could get lost in it. I'll never get the whole bed warmed up in a million years. Just as well you brought your hip flask.'

'I've got another in my luggage with cognac in it, so that we can warm our insides before turning in for the night. There's also a pack of cards and a set of dominoes, so that we don't die of boredom.'

'You might have said it was going to be this grim,' Hugo grumbled.

'I did!' barked Lady A, in self-justification. 'You just saw the romantic side of staying in a Scottish castle for Burns' Night, and never examined the impracticalities. I did say: be it on your own head, but did you listen? No, you bally well didn't!'

'I suppose we'd better go down,' he sighed, using his sticks to turn towards the door.

'Yes,' sighed his companion. 'Don't want to miss the non-alcoholic cocktails, now do we?'

'Dear Lord!' was Hugo's reply. 'What a beastly thought!'

Pre-dinner drinks turned out to be a variety of very unpleasant vegetable juices, all originating from produce grown on the estate. 'I think mine's sprout,' hissed Hugo, grimacing as he tried the contents of his glass.

'Shhh! Here come our host and hostess. Don't let them hear you maligning their hospitality. Here, she broke off and turned to her right. 'Good evening, Cardew. Lovely to see you again, Siobhan. This is a friend of mine, Hugo Cholmondley-Crichton-Crump. Hugo, please allow me to introduce you to Sir Cardew and Lady Siobhan McKinley-Mackintosh.'

'Room all right?' asked Sir Cardew, shaking hands vigorously with Hugo.

'Comfortable enough?' queried his wife, offering him a hand as limp as a wet fish.

'Thank you very much,' Hugo replied, being careful not to utter the out-and-out lie, 'yes'.

The dining room proved to be a cavernous hall lit by huge flickering chandeliers, a fire burning at each end, but totally failing to project the heat as far as the ends of the long table, some of its length having been removed for the relatively modest house party of just ten guests, no doubt more than just two of them in torment, due to the Spartan state of their accommodation.

'Who are all these people?' Hugo whispered sibilantly into Lady A's ear.

Keeping her voice down, she murmured, 'The names here are going to give Enid forty fits.'

'Go on, then,' ordered Hugo, sounding a bit more enthusiastic than he had since their arrival.

'Well, you've already been introduced to Sir Cardew,' she reiterated, nodding her head to one end of the table where their elderly host sat, his bald head gleaming in the light from the chandeliers, a moustache of immense proportions helping itself, along with its owner, to the Cullen skink they were currently consuming, 'and his wife Siobhan.' She nodded at the other end of the table where their hostess sat, her hair ruthlessly tinted and backcombed into a style reminiscent of the sixties, her face a thick mask of make-up totally inappropriate to one of her years.

'On Sir Cardew's left is St John Bagehot,' she informed him, impelling him to take a quick peek at a terribly refined-looking man who brayed like a donkey when he spoke. 'And he's next to Ralf Colcolough. He's a rather 'naice' young man who's come in place of his parents this year, because the poor old things are both in bed with flu, but he'd no doubt have tagged along anyway.

'Then there're Elspeth and Iain Smellie.' Iain was a small man with a fiercely thick black beard and a mop of similarly-coloured hair. His wife – goodness gracious, Hugo! – was a delicious half-caste, he thought, and whom he would later learn had a Bahamian father. Her wiry hair was caught at the back of her head and held there with a hair clip that looked suspiciously as if it had been made out of knitting needles.

'Next, you'll find Wallace Menzies, making up that side of the table. Siobhan thinks he's hot, so she arranges to have him sitting next to her whenever possible.' Menzies had the almost-black hair and piercing blue eyes of that particular sort of Celt, and was, indeed, capable of being described as almost beautiful. He also wore full Scottish regalia, which the ladies thought enhanced his appearance immeasurably.

'On this side, starting on Sir Cardew's right, is Quinton Wriothesley, known, behind his back, as Grizzly Rizzly – one look should explain that one. On his right, next to you, is Moira Ruthven, and on mine is her husband, Drew, and that's the lot.'

Moira was a small grey-haired woman who knew exactly how to apply make-up suitable for her age group, and her husband was a tall man with what hair he had buzz-cut to a brutal number one, thus giving the impression of almost complete baldness. He, too, wore full dress tartan, and his sporran gave Hugo a start, as, at first glance, he thought the man had a cat on his lap.

'I shall introduce you to Moira, then I'm going to have a good old catch up with Drew,' she told him, thinking that it was time Hugo let go of Nanny's hand and acted with a little more independence.

'Manda, can I just ask you a quick question? Why do all the guests, with the exception of that charming coffee coloured lady across the table, speak with upper-class accents? Are they all English?'

'Indeed they are not, Hugo, my dear little innocent. They were all sent to good English public schools exactly so that they would talk like that, and not with the accent of their birth country. Think about it. If you wanted little sonny boy to, one day, have a career in the Foreign Office or the Diplomatic Service, would you choose for him to adopt a Scottish accent, or would an upper-class English one seem preferable?'

'I see what you mean. So what about the little lovely over there?' he asked. 'She sounds decidedly Scottish, although she certainly doesn't look it,' he concluded, indicating Elspeth Smellie with a barely discernible nod of his head.

'That's because she was brought up in Edinburgh, although she did go to a good school, and Iain met her and fell in love with her. Nothing his parents could say or do could sway his opinion, so in the end, they had to give in and give their blessing for the marriage. I rather think her colouring and the accent make a delightfully enigmatic mix.

'Now, may I introduce you to Drew Ruthven, who is the son of a bishop, but still retains an incorrigible sense of humour? Drew, may I introduce a very old friend of mine, Hugo Cholmondley-Crichton-Crump?'

'Crikey, Manda, that's a bit of a mouthful,' he replied, and then turned to Mr-C-C, 'Do you mind if I just call you Hugo? We often use surnames for male guests, but if there was a fire and I had to call you – Fire, Cholmondley-Crichton-Crump! – you'd be burnt to a crisp before I got to the end of your name.'

'See what you mean,' replied Hugo with a smile. 'That's perfectly all right, provided I'm allowed to call you Drew, otherwise I'll sound like I was your fag at school.'

'Heaven forfend. Hugo and Drew it is, then,' agreed his new acquaintance, and they fell into easy conversation about what they could expect from their visit.

Lady A, meanwhile, was gossiping eagerly with Moira, leaning right across Hugo in a most unmannered way, to catch up on news of old friends, and friends who had gone to that great yearbook in the sky. It was as well to know who one could cross off one's Christmas card list, as it was such a waste of a card and stamp, if the recipient were deceased.

As it was announced that coffee would be served in the library – there was no need for the ladies to depart while the gentlemen partook of port, as it was a 'dry' house – Lady Amanda grabbed Hugo by the arm and whispered, her lips not moving, giving a good impression of a ventriloquist, with Hugo as her dummy, 'We'll try the coffee once, but it used to be dreadful. If it hasn't improved, I've got something a little more palatable upstairs and, by tomorrow night, Beauchamp will have arrived with full supplies for us.'

The library was as depressingly stony as the dining hall, with little in the way of comfortable furniture to lighten its atmosphere: what furniture there was being of the hard, lumpy variety that never encouraged one to linger for longer than a few minutes.

Coffee was duly served in plain white, chunky cups and saucers that looked as if they had been lifted, wholesale, from a 'greasy spoon', and the coffee itself dribbled feebly from an urn that had been pushed in on a trolley by one of the castle's staff.

Hugo sipped tentatively at the turgid liquid at the bottom of his cup, thinking that generosity with any sort of fluid wasn't the norm in this household, then his face crumpled with disgust as the liquid hit his taste buds. With a tremendous effort of will, he managed not to spit it back into the cup, but instead, removed a handkerchief from his pocket and delicately coughed into it, thus expelling the dribble of foul stuff from his mouth without losing face.

It had tasted strongly of chicory, with only the barest hint of coffee, and the texture was disconcertingly muddy, reminding him of the old joke that the coffee must be fresh, because it was 'ground' only half an hour ago.

Halfway through coffee, Sir Cardew disappeared and Siobhan explained to the gathered guests that he always went outside after dinner for a little quiet contemplation. It was a habit that he had acquired shortly after they took over the castle following her mother's death, and she was glad of it, in that it gave her time to take in the fact that she was an orphan, and had climbed another rung higher up the mortality ladder.

She also took time to look back at the strange custom of her family, in that inheritance went down the female line, with the husband of the first daughter of the family always having to change his name to Rum Drummond, instead of the wife taking her husband's name. The entail of the estate had insisted upon this practice until she had challenged it when she married Cardew, and had won the battle to have this name-change clause revoked, leaving her husband free to retain his birth surname.

Taking a further sip of the execrable coffee, to ascertain whether it was as ghastly as he had first thought, Hugo took a quick glance in Lady Amanda's direction, as he heard her delicately clear her throat, and noticed that she, similarly, had a handkerchief pressed to her mouth, a frowning forehead showing above its material. Meeting his eyes, as if she could feel him looking at her, she removed the handkerchief and announced that they would be off to bed, now, if nobody objected, as they always retired early at Belchester Towers.

The others could think what they liked about the two of them retiring at the same time. After that explosion of filth in her mouth, she didn't give a damn, and needed something to wash the gritty aftertaste away, as soon as possible.

Hugo trotted along behind her, his sticks almost a blur in his haste to retreat to the tiny corner of Castle Rumdrummond that had become their temporary haven, away from both their hosts, and the rest of the guests staying there. He felt that he might have missed his way in the time/space continuum, and found himself in the middle of a Vincent Price film, where he had no business to be at his age.

Outside, at the base of the west tower, stood Sir Cardew, contentedly puffing his cigar. This was one of the pleasures of his day, and he liked this quiet place. The west tower was the highest of the castle's look-outs, and it had the best view over the most vulnerable flank of the stronghold.

From there, even at ground level, he had a view across rough pasture to the beginnings of the pine forest to the west. To the north he could see the steep climb of the hills, ascending towards the heather of a high moor and, to the south, the land sloped gently down to a river valley studded with little clusters of stone dwellings, their lums reeking tonight in straight spires rising to the heavens, undisturbed by any breath of wind.

The weather was in a state of uneasy calm but, when he was full and contented after his evening meal, this surveying of his land lifted his spirits, and he firmly believed that this aided his digestion and relaxed him before retiring for the night.

Back in Lady Amanda's room, she took the hot water bottles into the bathroom and filled them from the tap, knowing that the hot water could inflict serious burns in the evening, but chill to the marrow in the morning.

A fire had been lit in both rooms, and they moved the one hard chair that each bedroom contained over to the fire in Lady A's room. The clock on the mantelpiece showed that it was only eight o'clock, and Hugo sighed, as he read the story its hands told. 'A few days here is going to seem like a lifetime,' he commented glumly.

'But you'll be able to dine out on the stories for years to come,' Lady A soothed him, 'And tomorrow night, Beauchamp and Enid will be here, and maybe we can make a four at bridge. That'll help to pass the time, although, tomorrow being The Night, there'll be piping and dancing, so perhaps we won't be confined to our chambers so early.'

Before Hugo could unburden himself of a cheery comment at this prospect, the wind suddenly made itself felt by belching smoke from the fire into the room, and he collapsed back in his chair in a fit of coughing. 'Listen to that wind,' Lady A said in surprise, suddenly becoming aware that the noise that had been niggling at her thoughts as they chatted was actually the narrow windows shaking in their frames. 'It's getting wild out there. I'll just take a look out,' she said, putting her head the other side of the curtains.

A few dim lights shone out from the mean castle windows but, apart from that, it was pitch dark, with no starlight and no sign of the moon. 'Thick cloud cover, by the looks of it,' she pronounced, withdrawing from her draughty position next to the glass. 'I shouldn't be surprised if there's snow on the way.'

'Oh, great! There's no way I could face being holed up here for weeks on end,' Hugo grumbled.

'And the castle is said to be haunted,' the bad-news bringer added. 'Did I tell you about the ghosts?'

'No you blasted well didn't, but I suppose you're going to, as now's the perfect moment, with us marooned here at night, and snow on the way. Go on, do your worst!' he challenged her.

'This place is at least seven hundred years old, and has known a lot of history. Over the centuries, several spectral figures have been reported within its confines. There is a lady dressed all in grey who is purported to walk through the dining hall, but at a slightly higher level than the present floor, and leave the vast room through a door that isn't there any more.

'The bedrooms in this wing ...' but Hugo interrupted her with a little yelp.

'Surely you don't mean these bedrooms?'

'They're exactly the bedrooms to which I am referring. Anyway, to continue: apparently the corridor outside the rooms used to be a good deal wider. It was narrowed in works carried out in the eighteenth century, which was probably the last time anyone really worked on this place, with the exception of the sanitary facilities.

'There is a page who is supposed to walk the length of the old corridor, said to be in search of his master. The corridor now being narrower, means that his route is through all the bedrooms, walking through the stone walls between each, as if they weren't there.'

A howl of anguish sounded from Hugo. 'You know I've got this *thing* about the supernatural. Why did you bring me here, when you knew it was reputed to be haunted?'

'I didn't realise you felt that strongly about it,' Lady Amanda replied, with surprise in her voice. 'I just thought it was one of your little idiosyncrasies.'

'What idiosyncrasies?' Hugo exclaimed, startled that she could think he had anything of the sort.

'Well, I've heard you say 'white rabbits' on the first of every month since you've moved in. If you spill salt, you always make sure to dispose of it over your left shoulder; you never walk under Beauchamp's ladder, and I have noticed that you sleep with a night light on. I thought your disapproval of "ghoulies and ghosties and things that go bump in the night" was like those: just things that you'd always done habitually, but nothing serious. You surely don't believe in ghosts, do you?'

'I'll let you know when I see one,' he replied, inching closer to the fire and carelessly tossing on another log. 'Have you ever seen anything here?'

'Of course I haven't. I'm far too pragmatic to be seeing ghosts. They'd be wasting their time showing themselves to me, and they probably know that, and just don't waste their psychic energy. But my mother always claimed she'd seen every ghost supposed to walk this castle.'

'Thanks a bunch. I was just calming down a bit because you'd never had a sighting, and then you have to go and tell me about your blasted mother.'

'But she would say anything to get attention, and you know that, because you knew her.' Lady A was perplexed by what seemed to be a real fear.

'To tell the truth,' Hugo offered in explanation, 'I've never really recovered from a trip on the ghost train at the seaside, when I was a child. I'll admit to you, as I know it will go no further, that I messed my pants on that ride, and it seems to have scared me for life. I did think I'd got over it, but it would seem not.'

'Come on – let's have some of that cognac. A few nips of that, and you'll sleep like a baby, and if you don't think that's enough, I've got a rather drinkable bottle of red wine that I secreted in my hold luggage, and a corkscrew in my handbag.'

'Manda, you really do think of everything.

Chapter Three

Hugo woke several times in the night, but for a variety of reasons. A nightmare about ghostly apparitions had him awake in a cold sweat; the howling of the wind outside and the resultant smoke from the chimney woke him up coughing; finally, an urgent need to empty his bladder drove him from beneath the covers at five o'clock, giving him just enough time to contemplate the folly of drinking half a bottle of wine, as well as three cognacs, immediately before retiring.

At seven o'clock, he was roused again, this time by the family piper marching up and down outside, playing his bagpipes with infuriating enthusiasm. Hugo took a sudden and instant dislike to the pipe music that had always stirred his blood in the past, when he realised it was not just a quick rousing blast, but a performance that eventually lasted for a full half hour.

Exasperated beyond endurance, he made his way groggily to the bathroom in his dressing gown, and drowned out some of the volume of the music (!) with the running of water and the gurgles and bangs that the ancient water pipes made as they delivered the medium in which he would bathe. He could, after all, stick his head completely under the water, thus deafening himself to everything but the noise of the workings of his own body.

The hot water ran cold sooner than he expected, however, and he remembered Manda's declaration of the night before, that the water was only scaldingly hot in the evening, and was determined, thereafter, to bathe before he went to bed. Maybe the warmth of the water would soothe him into the right state to get a good night's sleep, if the piping devil was going to ply his anti-social trade right outside his bedroom window at the same time every morning during his stay here.

There had been no hot soothing cup of English Breakfast tea brought to their beds, as Beauchamp had not yet arrived, and the tea at breakfast proved as unedifying as the muddy coffee, being both lukewarm and almost too weak to be identified as tea. When Hugo tasted his, then looked at Lady Amanda in accusation, she stated bluntly, 'Be careful what you ask for, Hugo, because you might just get it.'

The meal itself was of a similar quality. The bacon was fatty and over-cooked, the tomatoes from a tin, the eggs with yolks as hard as bullets, and the toast both dry and at the same time limp. There were no sausages or mushrooms, and what there was was offered in chafing dishes that completely lacked the ability to keep food warm.

At the breakfast table, his plate loaded with a selection of the poor fare on offer because he couldn't bear the thought of being hungry as well as cold, Hugo noticed that he wasn't the only one looking groggy from lack of sleep. Others, too, were gazing with bloodshot eyes at the other guests to check their condition, bags appending below their lower lids in protest at the lack of any real rest. Others, however, looked as fresh as a daisy, and this wide difference in the others' appearance led him to ask Lady A about it.

'The ones that have been here before use either earplugs, sleeping tablets, or both. I didn't like to offer you any sleeping pills last night, as you always moan so much about the drugs you have to take for the pain in your joints.' Lady A spoke roughly, her conscience troubled that she had not even thought of offering him some of her pills.

'I say, that's a bit unfair, when you knew how scared I was when I went to bed. You could've said something,' Hugo replied, his voice like that of a petulant child.

'I'm so sorry, old chap. I'll let you have some of my sleep bombs tonight. I've brought plenty with me, and if they don't agree with you, you can have my spare pair of ear-plugs for the night after.'

'That's more like it, although I'd like to strangle that damned piper,' he retorted.

'You won't want to, after the hoolie we'll be having tonight. He plays like a dream for the reels and other dances. He's played for the Queen, you know. There aren't many as good as him in the whole of Scotland.'

'Then I shall beg to borrow your earplugs for the occasion. He's very loud. Although, I suppose if I didn't wear them, I might go to bed quite deaf, and then nothing could disturb me.'

'Except for the glowing figure of a spectre leaning over you,' Lady A retorted, with conscious cruelty. It was time Hugo got over his childhood scare, and faced up to his fear like a man, albeit an old one.

Beauchamp and Enid arrived halfway through the afternoon, Beauchamp not a jot worried about the snowfall, which had not been heavy, his companion, Enid, totally relaxed as she had complete confidence in his driving skills, and the weight of the old car to keep them from skidding too much.

Angus Hamilton tottered out to relieve them of the car, and directed them round to the servants' entrance, which was to the east side of the castle, and both of them surveyed the monstrous edifice of the place, both having fairly accurate thoughts as to the level of comfort offered by this huge pile of forbidding stone.

They let themselves in carrying only their suitcases; everything else could wait a while before Beauchamp transferred it to his quarters. There was not much activity at this time of day, because luncheon was over, and it was not quite time to start the preparation of the evening meal. Afternoon tea in this household was only a broken dream confined to the past.

They located the servants' hall by the sound of two female voices raised in anger, and followed this to find a large room with a small number of staff sitting about taking no notice whatsoever of the row, which had now progressed past the insults and curses stage to hair-pulling and scratching.

Taking a look round at the others, who still ignored the fight and the new arrivals, Beauchamp strode across to the two women, now locked in the throes of a bitch-fight, and pulled them apart, holding each at arm's length, until he could extract what the cause of this unseemly behaviour was.

'Behave yourselves, ladies!' he ordered them, his voice slightly raised to gain their attention. 'What has driven you to such disgraceful behaviour? I insist that you explain yourselves.'

An extremely fat woman, who had been sitting quietly knitting, slowly turned round, laying her needlework on her lap, to see who owned this unfamiliar voice, and was intervening on what she considered to be her territory. 'And who might you be?' she asked, looking daggers at the two interlopers, one of which had definitely trodden on her toes, metaphorically. She was the one who meted out discipline, as and when she thought it necessary.

Rising from her seat, she hollered, 'Who the hell do you think you are, molesting those girls like that?'

'And who the hell do you think you are, not intervening in what was becoming a very unpleasant fight?'

Beauchamp yelled back at her. It wasn't often that he lost his temper, but the way the two girls were clawing at each other, without a soul to come to their aid, had really riled him.

'I am the cook in this household, and responsible for staff discipline,' she answered, red in the face from the sudden flood of anger at his transgression on to her territory.

'And I am a peaceable visiting valet,' he replied, his dignity recovered. 'I'm with Lady Amanda Golightly and Mr Hugo Cholmondley-Crichton-Crump. And this is Mrs Enid Tweedie, lady's maid to her ladyship.'

He still had both girls at arms' length, and he surveyed them now, as they calmed down. 'Is it safe for me to put you two down?' he asked, 'or will you start up again where you left off?'

'I'll see to them,' replied the obese woman, who certainly looked like a woman who was in charge of all the household food. 'I'm Mrs MacTavish,' she informed him, her own temper also reined in. 'Mary, Sarah: wait in my parlour, and I'll deal with you later when I've welcomed these two to our establishment,' she ordered the two combatants, rolling her 'r's at them, like marbles across the stone floor.

Approaching Beauchamp and Enid, she held out a work-roughened red hand, and greeted them both with, 'Please call me Janet, and I hope we haven't got off on the wrong footing.'

'What was all that about?' Beauchamp asked, curiosity getting the better of him.

'Both visiting, like yourselves. They've been here before, and they always go on like that, so we just ignore them now. Sarah, the big one and lady's maid to Mrs Ruthven, is a Fraser. Mary, the little one, who's lady's maid to Mrs Smellie, is a Campbell. Fraser's always taunting her by saying it was the Campbells who betrayed her family, and therefore they're mortal enemies.

'Mary defends her name by pleading that it was all hundreds of years ago, and nothing to do with her, as well Sarah knows, but that doesn't discourage her from starting a fight whenever she can. Sarah's impossible, dwelling too much on the past and old grudges, and doesn't seem capable of understanding that it's wrong of her to persecute Mary so, so I just leave them to it. They'll be gone in a couple of days, and peace will return – until their next visit, which I hope is a vera long time in the future.'

'I can see now how tedious it must seem to you all,' admitted Beauchamp. 'Perhaps you would be kind enough to introduce us to the other staff, before someone tells us where our rooms are.'

'Of course. I was distracted by the circumstances under which you arrived. Mary and Sarah you've already had a run-in with. The lady sitting by the fire reading is Evelyn Awlle, lady's maid to Lady Siobhan, although why her mother gave the mistress an Irish name, I've never understood.

'The gentleman leaning on the fireplace cleaning out his pipe is Walter Waule, the master's valet and butler, should the occasion arise when he needs both. The gent sitting at the table tying flies for fishing is Jock Macleod, the piper, and – ah, here he comes now,' she said, as the elderly man who had taken charge of the Rolls entered the room.

'This,' she said, 'is Angus Hamilton, chauffeur of this establishment. Everybody, may I introduce you to Beauchamp and Enid Tweedie, who will be joining us for the duration of the Burns' Night visit.'

'Is this all the staff?' asked Beauchamp, looking around him in wonder at the sparse number of bodies.

'It's Sir Cardew's doing,' she told him. 'He went on an economy drive about two years ago, and got rid of a deal of bodies from the inside staff, and it's been vera difficult to cope ever since. That's why folks ha to bring their aen staff this past two years,' she explained briefly.

There was much shaking of hands for introduction, before Janet told them where their rooms were, and asked Evelyn if she would be good enough to show them the way, as she was based in the castle. 'And if you would be good enough to direct me to where the car is kept, I have some things to transfer to my room,' Beauchamp requested.

'Angus,' Janet named her victim. Please go out to Mr Beauchamp's car and transfer the contents up to his room, while Evelyn shows them their quarters. They'll need some time to unpack, so I think that's the least you could do for them.'

With a muttered, 'Havers, woman!' Angus vacated the seat he had just taken, and tottered off to do Cook's bidding.

Evelyn led them from the servants' hall down a long corridor, and then up the twisting spiral of an ancient and worn stone staircase, which enjoyed virtually no natural light. Enid squeaked with anxiety, but Evelyn merely said, 'Don't worry, dearie. You'll soon get used to it. You'll probably be up and down enough to have learnt it before tomorrow bedtime.' Her accent was not quite as strong as Cook's.

Enid squeaked again, this time with trepidation, at this awful prediction.

At a quarter to four, a discreet knock on the door of Lady Amanda's bedroom produced a squeal of delight from within, and she hurried away from the hand of whist which she and Hugo were playing, to answer the familiar knock. 'Beauchamp!' she cried, as if she hadn't seen him in years. 'Enid! How lovely to see you. Do come in.'

They entered, Beauchamp carrying a large tea tray which he had filched from the kitchen, the rest of the ingredients necessary to providing afternoon tea now being safely established in his room, including a small camping stove. 'I've taken the liberty of choosing Earl Grey – I have lemon, should you require it – and Enid has the biscuit barrel with some of your favourite thin arrowroot biscuits.'

'Oh, Beauchamp, Enid, seeing you here is like a castaway sighting a ship,' said Lady Amanda with real sincerity.

'Hear hear!' added Hugo. 'This is an absolutely ghastly place, and I can't believe I let Manda talk me into this trip. I can see why she's always been unavailable in the past.'

Lady A gave him an old-fashioned look, but did not defend herself, all present knowing the real reason they had come all this way. Instead, she said, 'Would you please be mother, Enid, dear?' the wording of this request enough to convince anyone of how genuinely pleased she was to see the new arrivals.

Halfway through tea, Lady A, dunking her biscuits in a most vulgar manner, explained, 'As tonight is the big celebration, and they seem to be a bit short of staff, here, since I last visited, I expect you'll both be asked to help out in the dining room. Beauchamp, you'll probably have to take the part of a footman, because of your height, and I expect you'll be asked to aid with the serving, Enid.'

Enid squeaked again. It was beginning to herald the forming of a habit. 'But I've never served at table before in a place like this,' she piped, her voice shrill with anxiety. 'I've never even been in a place like this before.'

'Don't worry about a thing. It's the same as serving at much less grand tables. Just serve everything from the left, and try not to drop any 'neeps' or tatties down any of the ladies' décolletages.'

'Great! Now you've said that, I'm probably going to do it. And what the heck are 'neeps' and 'tatties'?' she asked, wondering what exotic ingredients these could be. She had led a sheltered English life in Belchester.

'Turnips and potatoes, Enid. The Scots have little imagination when it comes to food,' replied Lady A, with a sweeping denunciation of Scottish cuisine in its entirety.

'I won't have to serve the haggis, will I?' she almost squealed, just thinking about the accidents that could happen.

'Absolutely not!' Lady A assured her. 'Cardew always does that. Just don't worry about it and everything will be fine.'

'That's easy for you to say.' Enid would not let herself be reassured.

'Yes, it is, isn't it,' replied Lady A, unsympathetically.

The dressing gong boomed dismally at six o'clock, and the guests departed for their rooms to dress for this, the object of their visit. At least the food would be edible, Burns' Night always considered one of the great celebration days, in this household.

Beauchamp and Enid had been requested not to help them dress, as they had been perfectly capable of carrying out this personal task since they had been children. Lady A and Hugo would be dressing in their new tartan finery, and both paid special attention to their appearances for the occasion. At least the huge grim wardrobes boasted full length mirrors on the interior of their doors.

At six-twenty, the discreet knock on Lady A's door heralded the arrival of Beauchamp and his silver tray, holding only two glasses this evening. Enid floated behind him like a little cloud, a small ice-bucket held with two tea-cloths, to stop her freezing her fingertips. 'What, no cocktail for you two tonight?' queried Lady Amanda. 'And why's Enid carrying a blasted bucket?'

'All will be revealed in due course. I'm afraid we're both on duty, your ladyship, and it would not be seemly for us to appear with alcohol on our breath,' he replied, with dignity.

'I suppose you're right, but there you go 'your ladyshipping' me, again. I am not my mother, you know, and never will be.' Until her mother's death, he had always addressed her as 'my lady'.

'I'm afraid you'll have to accept that form of address, now your dear mother is no longer with us.'

'But you never used it before, when she was supposed to have been killed in that car crash two decades ago,' she challenged him.

'That is because I knew all along that Lady Edith had not died, and that form of address would be wholly inappropriate. Now that we know she is really deceased, I'm afraid I can't help it,' Beauchamp defended himself.

'I suppose it doesn't really matter, if it carries connotations of seniority, in your eyes. Now, what have we got tonight?' she asked, eyeing the contents of the glasses on the tray greedily.

'A snowball for you, m'lady, although, before you protest,' he said, holding up one hand as a look of horror crossed her face, 'it is my own creation, which I have privately named "a turbo-charged Snowball",' he concluded, causing Her Ladyship's face to dissolve into a smile of quiet gratification. 'And for Mr Hugo, I have a Scotch Mist, which I understand is the best medium in which to see ghosts,' he added, with a smug little smile.

'I nearly had one of those last night,' Hugo mumbled.

How on earth did Beauchamp do it? thought Lady Amanda. He couldn't have been aware of a conversation to which he was not privy, but he'd already got to the heart of Hugo's fears about the castle. 'Well done! Beauchamp to the rescue, again,' she said, reaching eagerly for her glass.

'You two look very Scotch, I must say,' commented Enid, eyeing the pair up and down, totally unaware of her pun.

With a sharp intake of breath, Lady A exclaimed, 'Don't you ever use that word downstairs with the staff.' She'd almost said 'other' staff, but had managed to stop herself just in time.

'Why not?' asked Enid, puzzled.

'Use Scots or Scottish. There's nothing the Scots like less than being described as "Scotch". It's all right as a name for their national drink, but not for anything else. Try not to get yourself in hot water. They've a fierce temper.'

'We've already discovered that, Lady Amanda. There were two visiting maids fighting like alley cats when we arrived, and Beauchamp had to separate them.'

'Really? How exciting! What were they fighting about?'

'One was a Campbell and the other was a Fraser.'

Lady A held up a hand to halt Enid's narrative. ''Nough said,' she grinned. 'That old grudge will never be forgotten. If it happens again, take no notice, unless they seem about to break anything other than each other's faces.'

The dinner gong sounded its sinister metal voice once more, and Beauchamp withdrew a slim silver hip flask from an inner pocket. 'That was your summons to dinner, as you are no doubt aware,' he informed them, 'but I have a little corpse-reviver here – a full flask of Frozen Spirits, in fact – in case you are in need of a little tipple before turning in.

'Enid, here, has a small bucket of ice, to keep it at the optimum temperature, and I shall place the two over here, in the draught from the window, to achieve that aim. I, of course, will make sure that your hot water bottles are in your bed at a decent time, and I wish you a very good evening.'

Draining her glass at a swallow, then gasping as the turbo-charged ingredient of the cocktail hit her, she summoned Hugo to join her on their descent to dinner. She had high hopes of this evening, and wished that he would enjoy himself too.

Back in the servants' quarters, there was a state of panic reigning over the absence of Beauchamp and Enid, and their reappearance heralded sighs of relief from all sides. Cook fixed them with a beady eye, and informed them, 'You're on wine duty,

Beauchamp, and you're serving at table, Mrs Tweedie.' Enid was too flustered even to attempt to ask her to call her Enid.

'Evelyn and Walter will show you the way to the dining hall, and we all wear sashes on Burns' Night, to show that we're celebrating. Here are yours,' she concluded, handing them the aforementioned garments, which sported a Scottish saltire on both front and back. Beauchamp was already wearing his tartan waistcoat, and felt like a Christmas tree in the process of being decorated, as Enid reached up and dropped it over his head with a little snicker.

The dining hall had been draped with winter greenery, the fires stuffed with logs large enough to completely fill the width of the vast grates, and flaming torches adorned the walls, making the room quite bright and light, and giving it a definite air of being en fete.

As Walter Waule went through the drinks to be served, which, of course, proved not to be wine at all, Beauchamp looked on in disbelief. There was to be a dandelion and burdock to go with the first course, Lucozade to go with the main, and lemonade to help down the dessert.

'What is the first course?' he asked, not quite satisfied with what he saw in front of him.

'Cullen skink,' replied his educator, 'same as last night.'

Beauchamp thought for half a minute, and then suggested, 'Do you not think that orangeade would complement the soup better?'

Walter also stood for a while, lost in consideration, then said, 'I ken you're right, Mr Beauchamp. I'll get it changed right away.'

Beauchamp raised his eyes heavenwards and sighed. He'd be glad to be back in Belchester Towers, where life was reasonably sane – some of the time, at least!

When Lady A and Hugo left their rooms to go down for dinner, they were surprised and delighted to find that the whole length of the corridor to the staircase had been lined with the flares of real torches, much more in keeping with the age of the castle, than the weak electric lights that had guided them to dinner the previous night.

'This is better!' exclaimed Hugo, admiring his trews in the light of the flickering flames. 'I hope the improvement goes on for the rest of the evening, and, if it doesn't, we've always got that flask of cocktail to see us off into the Land of Morpheus.'

'You keep on hoping, Hugo,' Lady A advised him. 'If my memory serves me correctly, the dining hall will be unrecognisable from yesterday evening.'

'Oh, goody!' piped Hugo, his eyes beginning to glow with excitement, and when they reached the dining hall, his eyes and mouth were a trio of 'o's at the transformation that had been wrought since yesterday. It was even warm, the fires being constantly stocked with fresh wood laid in high heaps in the grates, and pumping forth a most gratifying amount of heat.

They took the same places at table as they had before, and Hugo whispered into his companion's ear, 'Why no piper? Seems a bit odd, tonight of all nights.'

'He doesn't appear until he pipes in the haggis, after the first course, but you won't be disappointed.'

'At least he won't be waking me up this time,' Hugo observed, looking smug at this conclusion.

With everyone feeling warm, and delighted in the change in the grim old hall, conversation hummed throughout the first course, not a soul complaining that it was the same as they had been offered the evening before.

The haggis was to be the delight of the evening, followed by dancing.

Lady Amanda and Hugo had quite an audience as the details of their two previous brushes with murder were teased out of them, both adopting a coy attitude and, therefore, making their fellow diners even more eager for details.

When the first course had been cleared, the sound of distant piping was discernible, no doubt emanating from the kitchen, whence the haggis was conveyed to table, and a hush descended on the diners. Lady Amanda took this opportunity to draw Hugo's discreet attention to something she had secreted into her handbag before they left their rooms.

'Oh,' whispered Hugo, his face a mask of delight. 'How sneaky of you,' he commented as his eyes caught sight of the hip flask full of what, no doubt, was cognac. 'I hope it's not lemonade with the main course, or we won't get away with a little slug in our glasses.'

'If I remember aright, it'll be Lucozade, Sir Cardew's favourite tipple, and nobody will suspect a thing, if we add a little extra ingredient, surreptitiously.'

The music grew louder as the piper and haggis grew closer, and the atmosphere of anticipation was palpable. Closer and closer it came, until Jock Macleod entered, his face purple with his efforts, his complexion clashing horribly with his red hair and beard. Behind him waddled Cook, who would not let the honour of carrying the haggis go to anyone but herself. Her face was also a fiery red from her efforts in the kitchen.

Behind her, Enid carried a huge tureen of what Hugo presumed were neeps and tatties, and, behind her, Evelyn Awlle bore a small glass jug of what, he supposed, was the minute ration of whisky, known here as Scottish gravy, for adorning the haggis.

The sound of the pipes was almost unbearable when the piper was so close to them, but they bore up without complaint, as the haggis was set before Sir Cardew, the neeps and tatties in the middle of the table, and the little jug to the right of the master. An intricately decorated short sword was passed to their host by Walter Waule, and Sir Cardew stood, gazing first at the haggis, then round the table at his guests.

The piping ceased, and the hall was completely silent, waiting for the address that would follow, and really start the celebrations. He took a deep breath, puffing out his chest like a pouter pigeon, and launched into the traditional verse, his voice strong and full of emotion, as he began to recite the age-old words of the Scottish bard, Rabbie Burns.

'Fair fa' your honest, sonsie face, Great chieftain o' the pudding-race! Aboon them a' yet tak your place, Painch, tripe, or thairm: Weel are ye wordy o'a grace As lang's my arm.

'I'm glad that's ...' whispered Hugo, not getting a chance to get to the word 'over'.

'Shhh!' Lady Amanda hissed. 'He's only just started.'

'The groaning trencher there ye fill,
Your hurdies like a distant hill,
Your pin was help to mend a mill
In time o'need,
While thro' your pores the dews distil Like amber bead.

'Is that it?' Hugo enquired again, rather fed up with all this stuff he couldn't understand.

'No it is not! Now hush up!'

'His knife see rustic Labour dight,
An' cut you up wi' ready sleight,
Trenching your gushing entrails bright,
Like ony ditch;
And then, O what a glorious sight, Warm-reekin', rich!

'Is there much more of this?' hissed Hugo, through the side of his mouth. 'I'm beginning to feel that Rabbie was short for Rabid.

'Shut up, Hugo! This is almost sacred in Scotland. It'll be over in a minute, and you'll get to stuff your face to your heart's content.'

'Then, horn for horn, they stretch an' strive:
Deil tak the hindmost! on they drive,
Till a' their weel-swall'd kytes belyve
Are bent like drums;
Then auld Guidman, maist like to rive, Bethankit! hums.

'I'm considering suicide, Manda.'

'Then commit it quietly, so the rest of us can hear.' Eyes were beginning to turn in their direction, and Lady A was frantic not to be tarred with the brush of someone who chattered all the way through the almost sacred address to the haggis.

'Is there that owre his French ragout
Or olio that wad staw a sow,
Or fricassee wad make her spew
Wi' perfect sconner,
Looks down wi' sneering, scornfu' view On sic a dinner?

'Oh, come on, this is turning into a joke. And these trews do chafe so, with no underwear.'

'Be quiet, do! You'll upset everyone.' Pause. 'What, Hugo? You mean you're not wearing any drawers? You fool! That only applies to kilts, not to trews. Really, you are the end. No wonder the seams rub. Now, shut up!

Sorry, Moira. Sorry, Drew.'

Poor devil! see him owre his trash,
As feckles as wither'd rash,
His spindle shank, a guid whip-lash;
His nieve a nit;
Thro' blody flood or field to dash, O how unfit!

'Manda?' Hugo hissed again. 'I can't understand a blasted word the man's saying. What heathen language is he speaking?'

'It's old Scots vernacular English. Now, shhh! If Cardew notices us talking, he'll get himself into a fearful bate.' Another 'shhh' came from across the table, and two Sassenach faces blushed at their overheard interruptions.

'But mark the Rustic, haggis-fed, The trembling earth resounds his tread.

Clap in his walie nieve a blade,
He'll mak it whissle;
An' legs an' arms, an' hands will sned, Like taps o' trissle.

'Manda.'

'What now?'

'I need to go. It's urgent. And I really haven't got any knickers on.'

'This is the last verse just coming up, so shut up and hold on to it.'

'But Manda, it's worse than you think. I don't want to do number twos in my trews and besmirch the noble tartan.'

'Then clench your buttocks and pray, for there's no way I can help you. Now zip it! Your mouth, that is.'

'Ye Pow'rs, wha mak mankind your care,
And dish them out their bill o' fare,
Auld Scotland wants nae skinking ware
That jaups in luggies;
But, if ye wish her gratefu' prayer
Gie her a haggis!'

For a few seconds, silence once more reigned, before Sir Cardew made a slashing cut in the skin of the haggis with the short sword, immediately followed by a further burst of enthusiastic piping. 'Can I go, now?' asked Hugo. 'I really don't think I can wait much longer without doing something very childish on the floor.'

'Be off with you, but get back as quick as you can. Cardew likes everyone present to receive gratefully their plateful of Highland *haute cuisine*.'

Hugo unhooked his sticks from the back of his chair and made off as fast as his arthritic old joints would allow him, while warm plates were provided by Mary Campbell, newly arrived from the kitchen, lest her plates cool too much while waiting for the address to the haggis to finish.

These she placed in front of Sir Cardew, dropping a ghost of a curtsey as she did so, and their host began to spoon the spicy delicacy on to plates, which Walter Waule conveyed down the table to the guests.

It was Enid's job to serve everyone with neeps and tatties from the vast tureen she had carried in. Nervous as a kitten, her hand shook as she spooned the savoury lumps onto the plates, anxiety writ large on her face. She started well, however, and the smiles of gratitude as she heaped plate after plate soon helped her to relax a little.

Everything went well until she came to Lady Amanda and Hugo, as maybe she had relaxed just a little too much by them. As she lifted the large serving spoon to serve Hugo, who had now returned, very much relieved, serving from the left as she had been advised, her arm gave a sudden involuntary jerk, and a large piece of potato shot from her spoon, and for the next few seconds, everything happened in slow motion, in her mind's perception.

She saw the potato sail slowly and gracefully through the air across the front of Hugo's chest. With an almost languid gesture, he reached out a hand, infinitely slowly, and clasped the fingers of his right hand deliberately and almost sluggishly around the loose vegetable cannon.

That was the point where the flow of time returned to normal for her, the spell broken by Hugo's scream of, 'Yow!' as he instinctively got rid of this searing object as quickly as was humanly possible; back the way it came, propelled now by considerable force, coming to rest squarely in Moira Ruthven's cleavage, visible this evening due to her low-cut gown.

She, too, gave a screech of pain, but her quick thinking drove her to pierce it with her fork, before throwing it down on her plate where it lay, innocent and mute. Both ladies at table sat with eyes front, innocently, as Hugo attempted to adopt the same expression, as all eyes were now on them.

Enid, however, did not possess such well-bred 'front' and began to gibber and wail, eventually being led away by Evelyn, to the kitchen, where Sarah Fraser was sent to take her place. Cook was very kind to her, explaining that when she had first waited at table, she had had a similar accident, but hers had involved a whole tureen of scalding soup.

'Dunnae fret, pet,' she advised Enid. 'Anyone can make a mistake, if they're nervous. Now, ye'll take a cuppa tea wi' me, and you can go back after the meal to watch the dancing. It'll all be forgotten by then, ye ken. And the lady will dine oot on the story for years to come, ma girl.'

'What, with only Lucozade to lubricate their throats and tempers?' Enid was near tears at the thought, too mortified to ever look any of the guests in the face again.

Cook winked, and told her, 'They've all got a wee flask aboot them, don't ye worry. There's not a guest here who doesnae ken that if they want a wee tipple, they've to bring their own, and be secretive aboot it. The master may claim this is a dry hoose, but behind his back, it's awash with booze.'

After the meal, the piper moved off into the huge main entrance hall, where the dancing was to take place, while coffee was served at table. Lady Amanda and Hugo refused, on the grounds that it would keep them awake, and shortly all twelve diners followed where Jock the piper had gone before them, Lady A and Hugo lagging a little behind, as they took a sneaky sip each from the flask. They weren't the only ones doing this, as they would discover before the evening was over.

When the company was again assembled, Jock struck a lively reel, in which all but Hugo joined in, Lady Amanda being popular as a partner due to the lack of ladies in the party. There were only four present, and Ralf Colcolough unashamedly claimed St John Bagehot for his partner, neither looking particularly put out by the situation, Colcolough taking the woman's part, while Cook, returning to collect her precious haggis tray, was claimed by the master himself, evening things up considerably, with twelve dancers whirling around the floor to the almost tribal, primitive summons of the pipes.

The rest of the staff arrived and were urged to join in, making four more couples, as a grizzled old man who was the head gamekeeper, and not usually inside the castle, joined in. Only Sarah Fraser stood on the side-lines, but she was a big lump of a woman, with a scowling face, who, therefore, attracted no invitations to dance.

The climax of the evening was to be sword dancing, with Sir Cardew taking on the crossed, gleaming blades. Both guests and staff crowded round as he commenced to fling himself around between the knife-like edges of the swords, and all went well until someone gave Hugo a tiny push in the back, he involuntarily moved forward to preserve his balance, and stepped on the tip of one of the blades.

This dislodged the point at which the two swords crossed, and lifted one of them, Sir Cardew lost his timing, and suffered a nasty cut on the ankle as a consequence. As the blood ran down from his wound, the piper stopped playing, and all eyes were on their bloodied host.

'It was nobody's fault,' Cardew admitted gracefully, nevertheless fixing Hugo with an accusatory stare. 'I'll get it fixed up and be as right as rain.'

This seemed to be the signal for the party to break up, as it was already nearly ten o'clock, and well after the household's usual retiring time. As people began to shuffle around preparatory to going to bed, and Sir Cardew staunched the blood from his wound with a handkerchief, Hugo noticed several people taking nips from flasks, their backs to their host in case they were caught out.

'Come on,' urged Lady Amanda. 'Let's get back upstairs and see what Beauchamp's left for us.'

'?'

'I do hope it's champagne,' she answered Hugo's mute question.

As they mounted the stairs, he asked, 'About that poem thingy – did that lot understand it all, or was it just me being ignorant?'

'They were all in the same boat as you, dear Hugo. When Siobhan's father died and he had to take over the address to the haggis, he was in a muck sweat, for he'd never paid it any attention over the years. It was Cook who taught it to him, word for word, by rote.

'Oh, and don't be fooled by Cook. She's a lot older than she looks, her wrinkles being filled out with fat, and charmingly dimpled she appears too, but she's been here since the year dot, and has been the greatest influence over Cardew as to his occasional Scottishness.

'When he came back here, when his wife's father was gravely ill, he hadn't an idea about anything Scottish, with the exception of Hogmanay. Remember, he was brought through the nursery by a nanny, went off to prep school at eight, ended up in an English university, and came home, eventually, to find himself a complete stranger in the land of his birth.

'Then he married Siobhan, and they eventually moved here. That's when Cook took charge of him and gave him Scots lessons, so he didn't look a complete fool, and the old head gamekeeper took him on for hunting, shooting and fishing, so that he could keep his end up with country pursuits. Her father had been the real thing, being educated at home, and never getting as far as university, but Cardew's father wanted his son to have a better education and not appear overtly Scots.'

'What about the rest of the guests?'

'Exactly the same: part-time Scots, to a man, or woman, with the exception of Elspeth.' Here she gave a little giggle, attributable solely to their pre-dinner cocktail and the wee nips they had had during the course of the evening. 'Look around, Hugo, everyone's as staggery as we are, after all their shifty little nips, for they didn't get like that on Lucozade,' and there was, indeed, a sway to the column of guests mounting the stairs in their wake.

'Oh, excellent! It is champagne,' she declared, throwing open the door of her room and seeing the large ice bucket with the top of a bottle of Veuve Clicquot sticking out of it.

A tray held four glasses, but they had not noticed Beauchamp or Enid, because they had been behind the curtains, looking out at the landscape through the tiny slit of a window. Hearing voices, they withdrew from their semi-hidden position and joined the other two, currently taking seats by the fire, which was burning much brighter than the previous evening, for it had been tended, sporadically although this had been, during the last couple of hours, by Beauchamp, who was a wizard when it came to making and maintaining a fire.

'I took the liberty of requesting an extra load of wood, for what was left in here, and in Mr Hugo's room, was certainly nowhere near adequate to provide enough heat to see you through until the end of the evening, let alone the morning.'

'Jolly good show, Beauchamp,' bellowed Lady A in delight.

As Beauchamp dealt with the champagne's cork, his voice barely mouthed the word, 'Beecham,' but he was heard, nevertheless.

'You'll always be Beauchamp to me,' his half-sister retorted, not able to see his mouth, which formed, but did not enunciate, the words, 'I'm Beecham to everybody else, though.'

'It's snowing again, you know,' interjected Enid, in an effort to dispel an atmosphere before it had sufficient time to form. 'It's heavy, too. If it carries on like this, we'll probably have a foot or so by morning.'

This certainly distracted Lady A, for she replied, somewhat imperiously, 'I certainly hope that will not be the case, as we plan to leave tomorrow, and I will not be imprisoned within these ancient walls any longer.'

'Well, as you're not God, you'll just have to accept what you're given, like the rest of us,' replied Hugo waspishly. The thought of staying where they were any longer than necessary had been the reason for this sharp comment, and he followed it with, 'No offence, Manda.

Just stating the obvious. You know what I mean.'

Hugo didn't sleep well that night. His room was undoubtedly warmer, and his hot water bottles well up to temperature, but he only managed to doze fitfully for some hours. At one point he awoke with a start, and fancied he saw a white female face, veiled in black lace, leaning over his bed, like the dead, about to kiss him, then lure him to the other side of the valle lacrimarum.

He became fully awake with a high-pitched scream, a noise loud enough to pierce even Lady Amanda's snores, and bring her to his side, to see if he had suffered some medical problem, or maybe even a fall. She entered through the adjoining door to find him sitting bolt upright in bed, his mop of white hair sticking out in all directions, a look of absolute horror on his face.

'Hugo, you look as if you've seen a ghost,' she declared, taking one look at him and deciding he must have had some sort of a fright, even if it was just a nightmare.

'But I did! I did see a ghost!' he almost shouted. 'It was leaning over me, probably trying to devour me.'

'Stuff and nonsense!'

'No, I tell you, it's true! Take a look out of the door and see if you can see anyone disappearing down the passageway. If you can't, it was definitely a ghost,' he replied, and on this point, he was adamant.

Lady Amanda did as she was requested, but caught no sight of any figure hurrying away from Hugo's room.

As she closed the door again, Hugo had managed to mount his high horse without any help from a leg-up. 'It was a pale woman wearing a black veil over her face,' he stated doggedly, folding his arms to emphasise the point,

'and I definitely wasn't dreaming.'

Seeing his stubborn expression, Lady Amanda didn't try to dissuade him, merely offering to leave the adjoining door open, so that she could listen out for any monkey business.

'You can't hear ghosts,' he declared, 'unless they choose to rattle their chains.'

'Well at least this one didn't do that. If she had have done, of course, I might have heard her, and come rushing to your rescue.'

'There's no point in patronising me. I know what I saw.'

'Of course you do, Hugo. Would you like one of my sleeping tablets? I always get a few from Dr Andrew if I know I'm going somewhere noisy, and I think the seven o'clock alarm-piper's enough to waken the dead.'

'I think I'll take you up on that offer. If she comes back, I'll be sleeping the sleep of the just, and, without chains, she can't possibly wake me for another dose of the supernatural.'

'That's the ticket, old man. I'll just go and get you one. You said you dreamt about ghosts last night, so it's probably just a slightly more realistic attack of that feather.'

Before the sleeping tablet had had time to do its job, however, Hugo let out another high-pitched scream which had Lady Amanda back in his room at the double. 'What is it now?' she fog-horned. 'Another blasted ghost?'

Hugo's face was a mask of terror, as he pointed across to the adjoining wall, his bottom lip trembling with fear. 'There!' he whispered. 'There on the wall! Can't you see it?'

'Can't I see what?' she queried, squinting at the wall in an endeavour to see what had inspired so much terror in her old friend.

Hugo took a deep breath before he could utter the word. 'Spider!' he whispered, beginning to gibber. 'Huge! Monster!'

Lady A removed her slipper and made a pantomime of creeping up on the unsuspecting arachnid. *Splat!* 'There you are, my lad, the nasty monster's gone to the big web in the sky. Just you hope that it doesn't come back and haunt you for I don't have a ghost slipper with which to hit it. Or its mother comes looking for you,' she added, with a modicum of spite, 'Now go to sleep and let me get some rest myself, or I'll be a wreck in the morning.'

Chapter Four

The next morning both Hugo and Lady Amanda were totally undisturbed by the piper, surprising though this seemed when they awoke. They made their way downstairs to break their fast and, shortly afterwards, the breakfast table was a babble of voices discussing the overnight weather. About eighteen inches of snow had fallen, and Sir Cardew had set the estate's small snowplough out to clear the long driveway to the main road, such as it was.

'We've all been asked to stay on, you know.'

'We've no choice. We'll never get out of here at the moment.'

'Don't tell me! The main road's what we'd consider a lane in England.'

'I can't see a gritter coming out this far on such a tiny road.'

'Did you know the phones are out? And I can never get a signal on my mobile, here.'

'Cardew's got a CB radio, so at least he can order rations to be dropped in by helicopter, if need be.'

'Surely it won't come to that? I've got a very important meeting the day after tomorrow.'

'I should give up hope on that, old fellow.'

A loud shout from the old head gamekeeper, now named as Duncan Macdonald and standing in the doorway, drew everybody's attention. Instead of making an announcement, however, he went over to Sir Cardew and whispered something in his ear, discretion having got the better of him at the last minute.

Their host rose from the table, asking to be excused for a few minutes, as something had come up concerning the estate work. 'I wonder what that's all about,' Hugo said to Moira Ruthven, his table companion to the left.

ANDREA FRAZER

'Probably something to do with deer stalking. There's nothing he likes better than a good tramp through the snow, with the possibility of seeing some wildlife, although Duncan thinks he's soft in the head, only shooting them with a camera. Says that's not what he trained him for, and that he'd never educated a sissy before.'

'I say, that's a bit harsh, isn't it? Not everybody's infused with bloodthirstiness.'

When he turned back to his place, he noticed that Lady Amanda was no longer at table, and he wondered idly where she had gone, deciding that it was probably a trip to the Jacques, of which she wouldn't encourage discussion on her return, so he just got on with his breakfast, poor fare though it was.

When she returned a very short while later, she had that expression on her face that said: 'I know something you don't'. 'What's going on? What's happened?' asked Hugo, eager for news, but she rebuffed him, merely saying, 'It's not my business to say,' squeezing this out between clenched teeth and pursed lips.

'Come on, Manda. I can keep a secret.'

'Can't tell you.'

Before Hugo had time to go into a huff, Sir Cardew returned with a grim face, called the diners to attention, and said bleakly, 'It is my misfortune to have to inform you that this house is now without a piper.' At that, he turned on his heel and left them with no more explanation of this cryptic comment.

'Manda!' Hugo hissed fiercely. 'You can't just leave it like that! Has the piper resigned? Been fired? Run away? What the hell's happened to him?'

'Shhh!' she hissed. 'Pipie's dead. The snow plough guys just found his body, covered with snow, on the drive.'

Lady Amanda had wasted no time in dragging Hugo from the table of now dispersing guests and steering him, sticks and all, outside, where they discovered an abandoned small snow plough, and an unpleasant hump of bloodstained snow, Duncan Macdonald guarding it from unnecessary disturbance. At what appeared to be the top end of the hump, the snow had been cleared away to reveal the piper's face, blue and frozen from its icy covering.

'What the hell's wrong with his face?' she demanded to know, for there was a bulldog clip on his nose, and his mouth was filled with something currently unidentifiable.

'He seems to have a grand load of haggis in his mooth, and I think it'll be found to be up his nose as well. His mooth had a wee bitty tape over it when I found it, but I pulled it off to restore a wee bit of the puir man's dignity.'

'You shouldn't have done that, Macdonald,' stated Lady A with her innate air of authority. 'He should have been left exactly as he was found. Have you still got the tape?'

'I dropped it there in the snow,' he said, sulky at having been upbraided so.

Picking it up with her gloves, Lady Amanda popped it into her handkerchief and placed it safely in a pocket. Turning back to Hugo, she found him blanching a bit at the blood staining the snow, and she then demanded of Macdonald to know if any injury had been uncovered.

The answer was more unpleasant than they had expected, as Macdonald told them that the plough had only stopped when the driver had become aware of an obstruction on the normally clear drive, and that the maw of the plough had 'done a wee bitty damage' to the body, lying in such a vulnerable position.

'Yuk!' exclaimed Hugo, imagining mangled arms and legs.

'Havers, man! It's only a wee taste of blood. Sure the man was deid when the plough hit him, so he wouldnae bleed like a stuck pig, now would he?' Macdonald said with disgust at such squeamishness.

'Then get the whole man uncovered, Macdonald. How can you tell what did for him if he's still covered in snow?' Lady Amanda was taking charge of things just as she always did, without a thought for whose responsibility it actually was.

'I cannae do that! Whatever would the master say?' Macdonald was scandalised.

'Do as you're bid, Macdonald. It could be a case of bloody murder. How can the authorities be alerted if no one knows how he died? Do as I say and get that snow off the man's body.'

Macdonald, recognising the air of authority in her voice, did as he was bid, and soon they could see the whole length of the piper, stretched out in the snow, the mortal wound that had felled him now visible to the naked eye.

'There's a clear wound in the abdominal area,' stated Lady A, in a steady and unsentimental voice. 'Just turn him on his side, Macdonald – yes, I thought so. The man's been run through with a sword, by the looks of it. It was no knife that made that wound, because it has both an entry and an exit wound, so the blade was long.

'Can you just have a rumble around in his sporran, Macdonald? It seems to have something in it, as it has a bulge, and is not lying flat, the way it would if it were empty.'

Again Macdonald recognised the voice of authority and opened the sporran, but rolled his eyes at her, first, at this unwarranted intrusion into what he considered to be the master's territory. He removed a silver hip flask of what proved to be whisky, with a note taped to it, and looked at his finds quizzically. Already wearing gloves against the cold, Lady A had no compunction whatsoever about asking him to hand over his finds, so that she could examine them.

'Whisky!' she exclaimed. 'And that's my hip flask. Look! It's got my initials engraved on the cartouche! What a damned cheek! Someone's been in my room! What a blasted cheek! But what the devil does the note say? 'A wee dram afore ye go.' What in blue blazes does that mean? Was it a gift, or did the murderer plant it there? And if he did, why? This'll take some investigating, Hugo. We'll have to get together, the four of us, and see what we can come up with. I'll not have my name blackened with the suspicion of murder. Damned brass neck, trying to fit me up.'

Apart from 'yuk', Hugo had not uttered a word, and Macdonald had only reacted to orders due to his innate recognition of, and reaction to, the voice of authority. He now spoke, however, giving it as his opinion that the master should be out here assessing the situation, rather than a couple of his Sassenach guests, giving Lady A a dark look, which she interpreted as due to the discovery of her hip flask in the dead man's sporran.

'Nonsense, man,' Lady Amanda upbraided him. 'Hugo and I have had experience of this sort of thing before, and we know what we're doing. Do you know if Sir Cardew has spoken to the Procurator Fiscal and organised a doctor and police presence?' For a moment she had pleasant visions of solving this crime all on her own in the snowbound castle, emerging as the heroine of the hour.

'He has, aye,' replied Macdonald. 'He has one o' they CB radio jobbies, and he did some speakin' on that afore he told everyone in the dining room. Walter from the indoor staff'll be comin' oot here when the breakfast's done with, to take my place.'

I'm to round up the outdoor staff so we can clear some o' the ground for the big machine.'

'What big machine's that, Macdonald?' Hugo had finally found his voice.

'Tae bring the doctor and the police, sir,' replied Macdonald, pronouncing 'police' as 'po-liss'. 'They're travelling here by helicopter. It's the only way, when the weather's like this, and ye cannae use the roads.'

'And you're sure you didnae do this? I don't see you running for the hills.'

Lady Amanda treated this last remark with the contempt it deserved, and left him to it, her ears ringing with his broad Scots accent, which seemed, to her ears, ridiculously exaggerated. 'I don't know, Hugo,' she said, as they walked back towards the relative warmth of the castle, 'That's the Scots all over. If they're not rolling their 'r's at you, they're rolling their eyes.

'But who the hell stole my hip flask to use to plant on the piper's body? Someone unauthorised has been in my room, and I intend to find out who that was. If that doesn't turn up the actual murderer, it will probably turn up an accomplice. Hmph!'

They entered through the staff door to alert Beauchamp and Enid that they would be needed for a consultation, and found the staff in little huddles, whispering, conspiratorially, it seemed to them.

The news had also curdled the social order with the guests, and they, too, were sitting about in pairs and trios, muttering to each other. As the quartet headed up the stairs, Lady Amanda commented, 'That's killed the conviviality as well as the piper, hasn't it? I've never seen a bunch of people look so guilty in my life.

'I know people react unnaturally to something like this, Beauchamp, before you remind me of it, but there really is an atmosphere of furtiveness in the air, not just with the guests, but with the staff as well. Is it only an exaggerated reaction to Pipie's death, or is there more to it than that?'

After all the busyness of preparing for and executing the Burns' Night dinner, and their stay being such a short one, Beauchamp did not think he would need to transfer the cocktail ingredients he had kept in his room since his arrival, but with the heavy fall of snow, he had managed to bring them all up to Lady Amanda's room, as she and Hugo were obviously going nowhere fast.

He felt, after even such a short time since his real identity had been revealed, less embarrassed if asked to sit down and join his half-sister for a cocktail or afternoon tea, the feeling of guilt being replaced with one of contentment: that he at last belonged where he lived, and there would be no more secrets or pretence on his part.

He had, however, moved the things for afternoon tea into Mr Hugo's room shortly after they arrived, as he didn't want any of the staff tampering with his cake tin or his supply of biscuits, let alone his half-sister's precious supplies of Earl Grey and Darjeeling, and it was a pot of this latter that he brewed for them, to oil the wheels of speculation, as they discussed what might have happened to the unfortunate piper.

Hugo threw a couple more logs on to the fire, now that they had a decent supply, and the four of them gathered round the hearth with their steaming cups and plates. 'There's one thing to be said about cold temperatures,' ventured Hugo. 'They really stimulate the appetite. I suppose that's because the body has to work so much harder to keep warm, and I've got plenty of body working on that, as have you, Manda.'

'Hugo! Is that a reference to my weight?' barked Lady A, an indignant frown crossing her face.

'I'm only stating that neither of us is emaciated. You never looked like Twiggy, even in your youth; you have to admit that, and I could never have been described as tall, slim, and elegant. We're a couple of "portlies", and nothing can disguise that.'

'I really don't think this is the time or the place to be discussing our body shapes, Hugo. We have a murder to solve, and I've been mulling things over about this place. I haven't been here for some years, of course, but the atmosphere just isn't the same. It used to be a very friendly household. The members of staff – of whom, I might point out, there used to be considerably more – as well as the guests, were always convivial, but there seems to be some tension in the air.

'I know we were all focussed on Burns' Night, but beneath that there was a reserve I've never been aware of in the past. The only people I've really spoken to are Drew and Moira, who were placed with us at table.

'Of course, I've known them for an age, but I've met all the other guests before, with the exception of Menzies, on whom Siobhan seems to have rather a crush, and they've been, on the whole, standoffish. I don't know how you feel about how things are at the moment, Beauchamp. Do you detect a difference from when you last came? I know that was before Mama died the first time, but I missed quite a few visits before that, and you and my parents came on their own. Is it me, or is it the place?'

'I can definitely detect a change in atmosphere, especially if you remember that, when Enid and I arrived, there were two maids trying to tear each other's hair out downstairs, and not a soul made an effort to separate them.

'Cook would never have tolerated that in the past. She'd have given them a severe reprimand, and reported their behaviour to their respective employers. Had they worked here, not only would they have been reprimanded, but would have had their employment terminated, as well. Now, she doesn't seem to care much about anything.'

'Everyone seemed really happy when they were dancing last night,' interjected Enid, innocently.

'Did you see the dead look in that maid's eyes?' asked Beauchamp, who was very observant. 'That big lump of a girl that no one seemed of a mind to dance with?' he clarified, with an interrogatory inflexion in his voice. 'Well, that's the look that a lot of the residents of this house seem to possess at the moment, so I definitely think there's something amiss here.'

'The food's certainly not as good as it was before, and I can't be sure whether that's down to the staff, or the quality of the ingredients, but the place is definitely less convivial than it used to be. Although many of the staff have changed, that never seemed to matter before. Cook would wear her bonhomie like a crown, and radiated it over everyone within reach of her. Now, she seems more introverted. I think I'll try to get her on her own and ask her what's happened to alter things.'

'You could have a "wee chat" with Macdonald, too. I don't think he's comfortable in the company of women,' suggested Lady A. 'Enid, you can do your worst with the rest of them, and Hugo and I will make great efforts to ingratiate ourselves with the guests, as we're all stuck here for a while, and not just because of the murder.

'Oh, by the way, when Hugo and I were outside ...' Here, she gave an account of her and Hugo's discoveries out at the scene of the crime, concluding with, 'And they've notified the Procurator Fiscal, and a doctor and a representative of the police will be arriving by helicopter. The outside staff have been summoned to clear a piece of ground for it to land.

'I just wish we had dear old PC Glenister here. I'm really going to miss his inside information and cooperation. He's become quite one of the gang, even if he does work for that sour-faced Inspector Moody, and he always used to tip us the wink if we needed to know anything.'

'Just be pleased it's not old Lemon-Chops who'll be working on this murder,' Hugo exhorted her.

'No,' she said. 'With our luck we'll probably get Inspector McLemon-Chops, his Scottish cousin, or something similar. But let's lighten the atmosphere a little. I have, in my handbag, a list of the current guests, and I'm sure we'd all enjoy it immensely if Enid would care to attempt to read it to us.'

'That's me,' Enid declared, 'always the clown,' and she prepared to be ribbed mercilessly when she couldn't decipher, with any accuracy, all the ridiculous names that people of Lady A's acquaintance seemed to own.

The sound of an approaching helicopter was discernible just before noon, and a landing place had been prepared for it in an area of pasture not far from the castle. A route to the castle already existed, in the form of the track that had been cleared by the estate workers to access the landing area so that they could remove the snow, so Macdonald was sent up there in a decrepit Land Rover to meet both medical man and representatives of the law.

Lady Amanda, eager to get a head start, in case the Scottish lawmen were resistant to her charms, began to infiltrate the cliques that had formed, dragging the hapless Hugo in her wake for, although she knew Moira and Drew Ruthven, and had kept in rather sketchy touch with them, there were those in attendance that she had not seen for two decades, and one she had never met before.

She proceeded on the assumption that, if she spent some time working on her acquaintanceship with Moira, she could subtly coerce her into introducing her round those she had not met for so long, and provide introductions to Menzies, whom she had never met.

Moira, pleased with the attention, picked up the subliminal message that Lady A was furiously beaming at her, and proceeded to do just as it was hoped she would, starting with Wallace Menzies, who was sitting chatting in the cathedral-like space for which drawing room seemed such an inadequate description, with the Smellies, the room providing many groupings of seating to fill its vastness.

Elspeth announced that this was the first time they had attended for many a year, but they'd just felt like a little break after the hectic chaos that was Christmas with their large family. She, too, was of the opinion that the atmosphere had changed in some subtle way since they had last attended.

Although her husband seemed to be in agreement with this opinion, saying that some of the conviviality had gone out of it, Menzies, who claimed – untruthfully, in Lady A's opinion, otherwise why didn't she recognise him – that he had not missed a Burns' Night since he was a 'wee laddie', opined that it seemed exactly the same as it always had done, to him.

Lady A immediately concluded that a change would not be noted, if it were subtle, by someone who never missed the January visit, if that were true, but was much more likely to be apparent to someone, like herself, who had not been for several years, and she made a mental note to seek out the Smellies later, to have a chat about how they thought things had changed, in the specific.

Seeing that they were on the move again, Moira materialised at their side and steered them over to a trio speaking in low tones, away from the fire and the rest of the others. Here, she and Hugo were formally introduced to Quinton Wriothesley (Grizzly Rizzly, when he was the subject of a conversation in

which he was not involved), Ralf Colcolough (Kooky Koukli –
ditto) and St John Bagehot (Bedbug Bedsit – ditto).

Lady A learnt within minutes that two of them had some
sort of tenuous connection with the estate, but having made her
a gift of that nugget of information, they then turned the subject
to the death of the piper.

'Damned rum thing to happen when one is visiting, I must
say, knocking off the household piper,' Bagehot opened the
subject, his eyes darting round his little group as if he harboured
suspicions that one of them might be responsible for the deed.

Hugo picked up on this, and his face became an indignant
mask. 'Surely it must have been some outsider who had a grudge
against him.'

'Who says it might not just have been a heart attack?'
interjected Moira, re-joining the group. 'Playing the pipes is not
easy. It required a lot of strength and energy just to get a note out
of the beastie. I know: I've tried.'

'Because we've seen the body,' Lady Amanda informed her,
'and he'd been run through with a sharp implement. Of course,
this being a castle, with weaponry displayed all over the walls, the
first supposition is that it was a sword, but I might be wrong.'
She wasn't needlessly giving away inside information; more, she
wanted to see what effect this titbit had on those present which,
with the addition to Moira, had become the main group in the
room.

'And there was something rather odd in his sporran,' she
added, wickedly, then nodded to Hugo as she observed the faces
around her.

Hugo took his cue with a smile of gratitude on his face. He
didn't often get to impart information of this import. 'There was
a small flask of whisky in it, and a piece of paper with 'a wee dram

afore ye go' written on it. God knows what that means, but the police might be able to make something of it.'

'And it was handwritten, not printed,' added his partner in sleuthing, just to get things nicely stirred, 'So I expect they'll bring in a handwriting expert.'

'I don't think we should let any of that worry us,' soothed Moira. 'It must be some sort of falling out he had with one of the estate staff, or someone from the local town. It can't be one of us; we're all civilised people, with impeccable upbringings and backgrounds, and all that good stuff.'

'Hear hear!' added Drew, in support of his wife's irrefutable logic, and the group began to melt away and glide into other formations and combinations.

When there were just the two of them again, Hugo asked Lady A if she had learnt anything from their little bombshells. 'Only that there are a good few poker faces around here,' she replied, as someone tapped her on the shoulder.

It was their hostess, Lady Siobhan, just bursting with news. 'Spit it out, old girl,' urged Lady A, as the other woman looked like she might burst if she didn't speak soon.

'There's to be a wake,' she announced. 'I know that nobody's going to be allowed to leave until the police are satisfied, so we're going to have a wake for our poor, dear piper, the day after tomorrow. It's going to be for staff and guests. We'll have it in here, with whisky and a buffet.

'Oh, don't worry,' she reassured them, as Hugo's face had taken on a stricken look. 'It won't be rowdy. There'll be dancing, of course, and stories about him told, but there'll be another wake for him with all his family. This is just a gesture to show how much we appreciated him, and mourn his passing.'

'But I haven't a black tie with me,' bleated Hugo, feeling seriously underprepared for an event such as this.

'No need for anything like that, Hugo, dear. This will be in full highland gear, and what you wore for Burns' Night will be absolutely perfect. It's just a celebration of his life, and having a last good time for him.

'And as for tomorrow, do, please take advantage of any of the facilities offered by the estate. There'll be deer stalking, if anyone's interested, a horse-drawn sleigh ride for the less energetic, and even skiing lessons, should anyone feel the urge. There's a great piece of ground at the back of the castle that makes a perfect nursery slope.

'I'll put three pieces of paper on the dining table so that people can put their names down for what they'd like to do, then I'll liaise with the policemen, so that we can coordinate keeping him happy with interviews, and keeping everybody else busy and amused.'

'Have you met the policeman who's going to be in charge of this case?' asked Lady A, thinking: know thine enemy.

'No yet. He and the medical chappie are ensconced in Cardew's study as we speak, but, thank God the phones are on again, so we're back in touch with the outside world again. It's such a bore, only being able to speak to people with CB radios – all that 'breaker, breaker' nonsense, you know. They're a bunch of nuts, in my opinion. Oh, by the way, I think he wants to speak to you first, Manda, due to it being your hip flask found in Pipie's sporran,' Siobhan finished before wandering off to see to her lists.

'I do wish she wouldn't plaster her face with so much make-up or wear her hair in that ridiculously out-of-date fashion,' she said to Hugo. 'She'd look ten years younger if she just got a decent haircut and applied just the teeniest smear of make-up. She's got no chance with our handsome Menzies, looking the way she does: although Cardew's probably quite happy about that.'

An hour later, in Lady Amanda's room, a fierce argument was raging, Beauchamp and Enid both in attendance, but keeping well out of it. 'I want to do a sleigh ride, Manda,' wailed Hugo.

'You can want as much as you like, Hugo. You're going skiing, and that's that,' countered Lady Amanda, her hands on her hips and her head raised autocratically.

'And do I get little skis for my walking sticks?'

'You get ski sticks, you silly old fusspot.'

'But, why can't I go on the sleigh ride? I bet you're going to.'

'I certainly am not. I'm going deer stalking.'

'You're what?' cried Hugo, aghast.

'I've got a fair idea of who's going on the sleigh ride, and the interesting ones will be either deer stalking or skiing. The sleigh won't be out for long, and Enid and Beauchamp can do their darndest to find out about the ones who have selected the sedate option, whom I think will be Siobhan, Drew and Moira.'

'Surely, between the two of us, we can get in a few pertinent questions on our excursions?'

'On the way to hospital, you mean?'

'Hugo, don't be such a wet blanket. They know what they're doing. I should think everyone on this estate can ski, given the weather conditions in these parts, and the number of years most of them have been coming here.'

'If I break a leg, I shall find some way of suing you.'

'Hugo, you won't even break one of your beautifully trimmed nails,' she informed him, in the tone of voice that brooked no more argument.

A discreet knock at the door revealed Walter Waule, who requested that Lady Amanda accompany him to Sir Cardew's study, where the inspector was waiting to question her. Hugo was to go down when she returned, followed by Beauchamp and

Enid, the four people most likely to have placed the hip flask
where it had been found.

It was, at the moment, a very incriminating object.

Lady Amanda's knock on the study door was bold, as
befitted an innocent person whom someone was trying to frame
for a murder. A not-too-strongly accented voice bade her enter,
and she went in and was waved to a chair. 'Lady Amanda
Golightly?' enquired the broad-shouldered man sitting behind
Cardew's desk, a notepad sitting before him, and Lady A was
glad there were no 'r's in her name for him to mangle.

'That is correct.'

He rose and held out a hand, saying in his soft Scottish lilt,
'Pleased to meet you. I'm Inspector Glenister, here to find the
murderous cur who made away with Jock Macleod ...'

She held up a hand to stop him and asked, 'I don't suppose
you're any relation to a young PC of my acquaintance, in
Belchester. I know the odds against it being a close relation are
pretty long, but I have to ask.'

'That'll be my nephew Adrian, if I'm not mistaken.'

'Nooo! What a coincidence! We've worked on two cases
together so far – unofficially, of course,' she informed the
inspector.

'Aye, I know. He's told me all about you. Apparently you
give him a little light relief from that miserable lump Inspector
Moody.'

Lady Amanda sighed deeply with relief. 'Then you'll know
that I'm simply not the murdering kind,' she said, relaxing a little.

'Aye, that is so. And now I'll share a little secret with you.
My PC MacDuff is such a miserable and sulky soul that we refer
to him at the station as PC Moody, so my nephew and I have a
matching pair, as it were.'

'Is he here with you?' she asked, staring round the room, as a knock sounded on the door, which she had thoughtfully closed behind her, to ensure privacy.

'That'll be him now. Come in, MacDuff!'

A portly young man in uniform entered the room, his face a picture of misery. Even his uniform seemed to droop in sympathy with him. He sidled across the study, avoiding making eye contact with Lady A, and sat himself in a chair away from the desk, with his own notebook at the ready.

'Before we start,' began Lady A, relaxed now she knew she was in safe hands, 'Is Glenister a Scottish name?'

'It certainly is, m'lady.'

'Do call me Manda. It'll make things so much smoother. Now, what do you want to know?'

'I want to know when you last saw the deceased. I want to know how your hip flask got into his sporran, and I need to ascertain that you are not, in fact, a killer,' he told her, smiling broadly at the thought of his interviewee wielding a sword.

'To your first enquiry, I hadn't seen Jock since last night, when he piped for the haggis and the dancing. About the hip flask, I haven't the faintest idea. I do know that it means someone's been going through my room, and that makes me feel cold all over. As to the third piece of information you require, I can definitely confirm that I am not the murderer. Gosh! This is beginning to feel a bit like a game of Cluedo. Lady Amanda – in the snow – with something very long and sharp. Wrong!'

'Do you know of anyone who had a grudge against, or harboured any bad feeling, towards Jock?'

'Not if you don't count the number of guests here who were not over fond of his seven o'clock reveille on his pipes, no,' she replied. 'The last time I was here, his father was the piper, Jock

Senior, so this is the first time I'd come across him. I say, have you found the weapon yet?'

'Aye. It was taken from a wall display, used on Macleod, wiped, rather inexpertly I might add, as we found blood on the wall where it was hung, having been replaced whence it had come. I got MacDuff to bag it up, and it's gone off in the helicopter with your hip flask.'

'Oh, by the way,' she informed him, 'Did you sort out the bulldog clip and the haggis?'

'Naturally. This is not my first murder investigation,' he replied with a smile.

'I'm perfectly sure of that, but did Macdonald tell you that there was tape over his mouth when he uncovered the poor man's face?'

'No, he didnae. This is news tae me. And what exactly happened to this piece of what might be vital evidence?'

Lady A was grateful for a short speech that contained no evidence of 'r's. Putting her hand carefully into the handbag that she had, naturally, brought with her, for no lady goes anywhere without her handbag, she removed her handkerchief, within which the incriminating piece of tape rested.

'I think this is what you require,' she announced, with a smug little smile. 'Be careful. I know Macdonald just pulled it off, but I lifted it by a corner while wearing gloves, and immediately placed it in my handkerchief for safety. You never know, it might still contain some useful fingerprints.'

'Ye're a marvellous woman! Adrian was right about you. And we've got a murder bag with us, so we can test for fingerprints right here in the castle,' he crowed, taking the proffered square of material, and handing it to MacDuff, to place in an evidence bag.

'Tell me, Inspector, how come your nephew has no trace of a Scottish accent?'

'My brother moved south not long after I joined the police force. He said it was not a fit job for a red-blooded Scotsman. Adrian was born down in England, and was fascinated with mystery stories when he was a child, and murder stories as a teenager.

'With an uncle already in the police force, it gave him, I think, the extra push to do what he wanted to do, which was join the force himself. He'd been having a bit of a hard time of it with yon Inspector Moody, until he met you, but he says you've brightened up his working life no end. He phones regularly, to let me know how he's getting on.'

'Ah, so he was brought up in England. That explains it. Now, if you've finished with me, shall I send down Mr Hugo Cholmondley-Crichton-Crump?'

Oh, that is his name. I was wondering if it was a bit of a misprint, it was so long. And dinnae fash yersel'. There's no reason why MacDuff here can't go and fetch him. And when I've spoken to your party, which I believe consists of four persons, then MacDuff here will be well practised for the rest of the summoning. Very pleased to have met you, ah, Manda.' Not only did he remember to address her informally, as previously bidden, but he also went completely overboard on 'very', as if using the extra rolls of the 'r', like an impromptu drum roll, for emphasis.

'Just a word before I go,' she said, as MacDuff disappeared on his errand. 'Has Siobhan, by any chance, given you a guest list?'

'She has, that,' he replied, wondering where this was heading.

'I think you need to be forewarned because, after all, forewarned is forearmed,' she replied, taking the list he had picked up from his desk.

Inspector Glenister had listened to Lady Amanda's pronunciations of the various names with a growing look of disbelief on his face, now and again shaking his head, as he repeated each name, and an occasional shake of the head at the ridiculousness of the situation. At the end, however, light dawned, and he and Lady A shared a conspiratorial smile. 'PC MacDuff' she said pointedly.

'PC MacDuff,' he repeated, his face breaking out in a gleeful grin. 'I think I might enjoy this afternoon more than I anticipated.

As she left the study and headed for the stairs, the gong for luncheon sounded, so she betook herself off from the entrance hall and towards the dining hall instead. Inspector Glenister would have to wait for his next three interviewees until after they had eaten. As she was crossing the hall, she noticed Mary Campbell's frail figure staggering towards the dining hall under the weight of a great tureen of soup, Macdonald standing by the doorway, observing, but not anxious to come to her aid.

Taking herself off to help the girl, when she returned, she noticed that Macdonald was still standing where she had last seen him, as if waiting for a crash, or the sound of breaking china. Suddenly irked by his lack of gentlemanly response, she went over to give him a bit of a talking to.

'Couldn't you have stirred your stumps and given the poor girl a hand? She's very tiny, and not really strong enough to deal with the dish she was sent through with,' she enquired, still wearing her autocratic manner like a diadem.

'I'll nae lift a finger fer a Campbell,' he replied curtly. 'They're traitors, every last one o' them.' His accent was definitely thicker than Glenister's.

'Oh, come on, Macdonald. That was four hundred years ago,' she chided him, referring to the Massacre at Glencoe. 'That makes nae difference, lassie,' he responded.

'But, Macdonald, it wasn't your personal blood that was spilt, was it?'

'Now, I'm gonna tell ye this just the once. 'Twas Macdonald blood that was spilt there, and Macdonald bone that was smashed. I was bred from that blood and bone, and that makes it my blood.

'We took them in, and offered them our hospitality. They broke bread wi' us: they took whisky wi' us. Then they rose like the very Devil himself from Hell, in the night, and slaughtered us.

''Tis Campbell blood that ran in their veins; aye, and 'tis Campbell blood that runs in her veins, the same noo as it was then. I'll no dae it, m'lady. I'm sorry, but I just cannae bring meself' to.'

Lady Amanda walked quietly away without reply. She was not only shocked by the naked hatred in the old man's voice, but really shaken that such a strong feeling could have survived for centuries, and still walk abroad.

Over lunch, Lady Amanda related the tale of what had happened in the hall, and her host and hostess were not surprised at all. 'We went to an inn one night, having been caught out by the weather, and deciding not to continue our journey till morning,' Siobhan began, obviously relating a tale to back up what Lady Amanda had just told the table.

'We stopped at this quaint little place which looked just right to shelter from the storm. Well, there we were, standing in this sort of foyer place, shaking our umbrellas and taking off our mackintoshes, when I heard Cardew 'harumph', and when I looked up, he was staring, and pointing to a sign that said, in large red letters, 'No Campbells'.

'I thought it was some sort of joke, but Cardew told me not to say a word when we went in, for if they found out that we knew any Campbells, they'd not let us stay. The sign was deadly serious. That's how high feelings still run, even after all these years.'

There were murmurs round the table, to confirm that she was not the only one who had come upon such open hostility to the surname and, for a moment, Lady Amanda thought how strange and tribal Scotland still was, in comparison with England, and she longed to be in Belchester Towers, in front of a blazing log fire, eating muffins and butter, and sipping a soothing cup of Darjeeling.

After what passed for coffee in this household, the other three prepared for their interviews, Lady A letting them stew, hugging the secret that the policeman was a relative of PC Glenister on their own patch. She'd had to stew. Nobody could have told her; so she kept it to herself, waiting with good humour, for the wigging she would undoubtedly receive, when they came out.

While they were otherwise occupied, she began to float around, a second cup of the disgusting brew in her hand, casually getting into conversation with whomsoever she could, in an effort to find out as much about her fellow guests as she could.

She did not include Moira, Drew or Siobhan in this exercise, as she had no suspicions of them, and she also wrote Cardew off as a non-starter, as he'd hardly invite a bunch of folk to his home for Burns' Night, then murder his own piper. That way, madness lay, as far as she was concerned.

She found the effete Ralf Colcolough reading an old edition of *The Scotsman* by the fireside, and sat down next to him on the sofa, in her brashest manner. 'Hello,' she said, brazening out her unlooked-for interruption to his reading. 'How do you know dear Siobhan and Cardew?'

Ralf, too well brought-up to rebuff her, launched reluctantly into how they had met. 'It was about ten, maybe twelve, years ago, and I came here for the shooting – a little party got together by the office. When I got here, I wasn't too keen on killing things, but I found that Cardew and I got on like a house on fire. We're both very keen photographers.

'In fact, it was I who persuaded him not to stalk deer to kill them, but to photograph them. He was bowled over with the idea, and immediately invited me to come back on my own, so that we could try it out. His gamekeeper was furious, but it wasn't Macdonald's call. I've been visiting regularly ever since.'

Writing him off as a useful source of gossip, after half an hour of listening to him drone on about the technicalities of photography, she excused herself and went in search of another victim. This time she espied Wallace Menzies and Quinton Wriothesley at the other end of the room, apparently engaged in earnest and animated conversation.

Hastily pouring the contents of her cup into a pot plant, then swanning over to the coffee table to refill it, she sauntered over to them and, without waiting for them to notice her, interrupted with, 'I was just wondering what you two gentlemen thought of what happened to the poor piper. I'm sure you're both gentlemen of the world, and must have a much more sophisticated outlook on things than poor, parochial little me.'

Both regarding her crossly, Menzies lifted an eyebrow, lifted a lip in a sneer of contempt, and announced that, as they did not mix with the working classes, they had no idea how they behaved. Wriothesley – Grizzly Rizzly – nodded in ill-natured agreement, and suggested she speak to the staff, who, being those sorts of people, understood their motives much better.

'Do you have no ideas, yourselves?' she battled on bravely, in the face of intense lack of interest and hostility.

'There're plenty of pipers in Scotland. Cardew will easily replace him.'

'That's not the point, though, is it?' Give Lady A her due – once she had her teeth into something, she would not give up easily. 'His father before him was piper to this household and, if we checked, we'll no doubt find that his father before him held that post, as well.'

'And your point is?' asked Menzies, most objectionably.

That was enough for Lady Amanda. 'I offer my apologies,' she said, in her loftiest voice. 'I was of the opinion that I was conversing with gentlemen. Obviously I was mistaken.' And with that, she turned on her heel and stalked off, determined to speak to Siobhan about the people she invited into her home as guests.

While Lady Amanda was thus engaged, Hugo was resummoned for his interview with the inspector, which he approached with some misgivings. He was, after all, in a foreign country, and didn't know the ways of the natives.

A ringing voice bade him enter Cardew's study, and the gloomy-faced constable followed him into the room, taking a seat along the back wall. After the inspector had greeted Hugo, the constable turned a delicate shade of puce, and dropped his face into his notebook. That wasn't how he had pronounced the old gentleman's name at all. How could he have been so wrong, unless his list was full of spelling mistakes?

When the inspector had introduced himself, Hugo became much more amenable and, after a short discussion about the unfortunate demise of Jock Macleod, Glenister asked him if it was really true, that his nephew had actually discovered him hiding in a downstairs privy, in darkest night, in a house that was not his own.

'I tried to act casually, but I don't think he was convinced,' Hugo replied in all seriousness.

'He told me he also found your partner-in-crime hiding behind the sofa. Is that true as well? I thought he was making it up.'

'True as I'm sitting here in this tutu,' said Hugo, then smiled his ingenuous smile. 'We were caught red-handed, trespassing on someone else's property, without their permission, and your nephew had the kindness just to ignore us, and let us get on with whatever it was we were doing. The woman's case is coming up shortly. If I were the judge, I'd direct the jury to bring in a verdict of justifiable homicide.'

'Adrian thinks you two are priceless, and hopes he's got so much get-up-and-go at your age.'

'I wish I had so much get-up-and-go at my age,' replied Hugo, with unintentional humour. 'Investigating does rather keep the old noodle ticking over, though. If I'd stayed where I was, before Manda rescued me and welcomed me into her own home, I expect I'd be dead by now. Give him our regards when you speak to him, and tell him to call round for afternoon tea, or a cocktail, when he's not on duty. It must be very tedious for him, working for someone as miserable and mean-spirited as Inspector Moody.'

'He does find it rather trying at times,' replied Glenister, with a small smile, remembering the swearing that had carried along the telephone line, the last time he had spoken to his nephew.

'I say,' Hugo asked, in a small voice, 'You don't really suspect Manda, or one of us, do you?'

'I don't, so don't waste your worry on that. I've a feeling the answer to this one lies closer to home than you four.'

Beauchamp was next on the list, followed by Enid, and both these interviews were amiable and polite, Glenister having no cause to suspect that they could ever have met the piper before, living where they did, and had already confirmed this with Sir Cardew.

His nephew had described them all to perfection, and when he had finally met them, he felt he already knew them. He had absolutely nothing to worry about on the Belchester Towers front, and knew that, if he needed anyone to spy for him, or ferret out something, it was one of this crew that he would choose.

Meanwhile, Inspector Glenister's afternoon was getting better and better. He had made a copy of his guest list and given it to the gloomy and taciturn MacDuff, requesting that he bring the guests to him in the order listed if possible. The constable had already fallen foul of Cholmondley-Crichton-Crump, but restored his confidence with Beauchamp (who answered to any variation of his name, if good manners necessitated) and Tweedie. He would not make a fool of himself again.

MacDuff had sloped off, once more, to do his inspector's bidding feeling slightly more confident, and leaving, as was his habit, the door open, and his superior to mutter, 'Born in a barn, that laddie!' The door to the cavernous drawing room, in which the guests were lurking, having taken coffee, was open and, the acoustics were such that Glenister could hear every word uttered by his constable, who had one of those booming voices redolent of doom.

He heard him find his first interviewee, and the request to come to the study, followed by an audible puffing and blowing from the recipient of this request. When MacDuff reached the study door and presented his first 'catch' with the words, 'Mr Wriothesley, sir,' the bubbling of suppressed wrath finally erupted.

'You ignorant little oik! M' name's Rizzly, not that ghastly strangulated noise you made? Have you no education whatsoever, man? Rizzly! That's pronounced RI-Z-Z-L-Y, for your information, and be sure you don't forget it!'

MacDuff muttered a confused apology, blushing to the roots of his helmet, which he had retained, due to the temperature inside the castle, and he took his place ready to take notes with a very sheepish expression.

It was all Glenister could do to suppress his mirth, and the incident raised his spirits considerably. Working with MacDuff always left him feeling gloomy and depressed, and this was a considerable improvement on normal circumstances.

MacDuff's next mission was to collect Ralf Colcolough, and his first mistake was to raise his voice to ask if that young man was present. At this point, the figure of a young man suddenly swooped down on him, braying, 'Koukli! Koukli! Koukli! *Raif Koukli!*' and the constable actually ducked, thinking he was being attacked by a madman.

From his unseen desk, Glenister turned purple with glee. If MacDuff were to be habitually gloomy, then he'd give him something to be gloomy about.

A request for a Mr Smellie and a Mr Menzies variously brought forth shouts of, 'Smiley, man! That's Smiley! How dare you call me smelly!' and 'Ming-is, you moron! How can you not pronounce Ming-is when you're a Scot?'

By the time MacDuff got to Drew and Elspeth Ruthven and St John Bagehot, he was nearly on his knees with embarrassment, and adopted the policy of approaching the nearest person, indicating the name on the list of the person he wished to collect for interview, thus avoiding using a name at all.

What surprised him most of all was that the inspector had seemed to know the exact pronunciation of each and every one of these truly weird names, and he almost, but not quite, suspected that a practical joke was being played on him.

The Belchester Towers Four reassembled in Lady Amanda's room for afternoon tea, each with a tale to tell of their interview with the unexpected Inspector Glenister. Hugo was the first to speak. 'You might have said something at lunch, Manda. That way, we wouldn't have been in such jitters about the experience.'

'Why should you three get off lightly, when I hadn't had that advantage?'

'Oh, that's rather bad form, don't you think, Manda?' he asked.

'If you want to hear about bad form, I'll tell you about what happened to me while you were being interviewed. There are some uncouth louts, who are under this roof in the guise of guests, over whom I would not pour a bucket of water if they were on fire.'

'Whatever did they say?' asked Beauchamp, fluffing up his dander for possible later use. No one was going to mouth off his half-sister/employer without him having a say in matters.

'It's simply not worth repeating, Beauchamp. I merely advise you that I should be obliged if you would try to find out a bit about that bounder Menzies, and that cad Wriothesley.'

'Consider it done, m'lady.' Beauchamp was grinding his teeth as he agreed to this. The slightest step out of line, and he'd scrag them, he was compelled to announce.

'Control yourself, man. You'll scrag no one until I tell you to. Have you got that? Now, about tomorrow: I've taken a look at the three lists, and have decided that Hugo and you, Beauchamp, will go skiing, I will go deer stalking and, if you don't mind, Enid, I'd like you to stay in the castle to see what you can screw out of the staff. Do you mind staying here?'

'There's no way I want to go out in this weather. I'll be one big chilblain the day after. I can't think of anything I'd like better than to sit in the servants' hall with that roaring fire, drinking tea all day long, and gossiping to my heart's content.'

'Deal!' yipped Lady A, spitting enthusiastically on her hand and offering it to Enid to seal the deal. Enid declined the hand with a slight shudder, covering her moue of distaste discreetly with her hand.

Chapter Five

The next morning, the three groups gathered together in the hall, waiting to commence their chosen activities. Drew and Moira Ruthven and Siobhan had, as Lady Amanda had predicted, chosen the sleigh ride option, as had St John Bagehot (surprisingly) and Elspeth Smellie, whose exotic complexion would look magnificent in the snowy surroundings.

The stalking group would be led by Macdonald, and included Sir Cardew, Wriothesley and Menzies. Those headed for the nursery slope for the skiing were being led by Iain Smellie, who was an experienced skier, and had volunteered to teach kindergarten today, along with Beauchamp, the rather effeminate Colclough, and the terrified Hugo.

The stalking party would take with it, or have delivered, a picnic lunch, to be eaten in one of the many shelters scattered around the estate in which estate workers, or anyone else on the property who fell foul of the weather, and needed somewhere to seek sanctuary, could retire. Each contained a table and chairs, a camping stove and a rude cot, in case the weather was persistent in its inclemency.

The sleighing party was the first to leave, warmly wrapped in fur rugs and thick woolly hats, each with its own bright bobble nodding on the top. The stalking party stood at the large hall table surveying a map, Macdonald advising the route that he thought would be the most likely to result in good view of stags, given the latest information he had gathered from other estate workers.

When approved, he marked the route on the map with a bright pink highlighter and, checking that they all had on walking boots and sufficient layers of clothing for the exercise planned, they set off. Lady Amanda, like the other members

476

of the party, had a stout stick with her, to aid walking on the rougher ground, and had made a point of putting on two pairs of long 'janes' and two thermal vests, under her overgarments. No way did she want to become today's case of hypothermia.

Apart from Cardew and Macdonald, her only other companions were Menzies and Grizzly Rizzly, and she muttered constantly to herself to remember not to call him that to his face. The last thing she needed on a day out like this was a smack in the mouth to add to her miseries, and she was determined to gain the trust of these other two guests, to see if they could have had anything to do with the piper's death.

The skiing party headed out to the back of the castle, where there was a room that contained all they needed for their outing. Granted, the skis were not the most modern, but there were boots aplenty, in a variety of sizes, and skiing outerwear too, so that no one unexpectedly joined the Frostbite Club, and went home missing a finger or toe or two.

When each member of the party was clad to Iain Smellie's satisfaction, he warned them not to do anything they had not expressly been instructed to do, and to obey instructions to the letter. Carrying their skis, a somewhat difficult task for Hugo, as he had brought along his walking sticks, as an aid to balance in the treacherous snow, Iain led them to a promontory not far from the rear of the castle, and pointed out the slope that lazily meandered its way down towards the foot of the distant hills.

'This is what we're going to be working on today,' he announced and, in a flurry of skis, ski poles and walking sticks, all of which seemed to have a life of their own, Hugo raised a hand and asked, 'And having got down, how do you propose we get up again? I'm no spring chicken, and don't fare very well with "up".'

'Already taken care of,' answered Iain, a twinkle of satisfaction in his eyes. 'I've made arrangements with Macdonald that one of the estate workers will bring a Land Rover to the base of the slope – he should be with us within half an hour – and he'll convey us back to the top. In the meantime, we'll concentrate on the basics, if you wouldn't mind clipping your boots on to your skis.'

Beauchamp came to Hugo's aid, and ordered him to stand as still as he could, while his boots were offered up to the ski clips. Having been released from carrying the skis, Hugo ditched the walking sticks and used the ski poles, dug well into the compacted snow, to do his best impression of a flamingo, with just one foot on the ground. Finally he was ready, and Beauchamp attended to his own boot clipping.

'Right then, everybody, the first thing we're going to do is just try a gentle movement downhill. You won't need your poles for this. I just want you to turn the toes of your skis very slightly towards each other when you face the slope, before moving on to it. This should allow you to move slowly forward and downwards. If you want to stop, move the tips of the skis closer together. I shall now demonstrate.'

This, he proceeded to do, with perfect aplomb, making it look easier than walking in the snow. 'You first, Beauchamp. You look like a fairly well co-ordinated chap. If you can do it, it will inspire confidence in the others.'

Beauchamp was good at following instructions to the letter after all the years he had worked for Lady Amanda, and managed a slow glide down the shallow first section of the slope, even managing to turn himself sideways and crab-walk back up to where the others were waiting.

'Have you done this before?' Iain asked, surprised at how effortless the man had made it look.

'Never,' replied Beauchamp with a smirk, 'but I have seen it done on the television.'

'Now,' said Iain, 'I want you to have a go, Mr Colcolough, if you would be so kind. Please don't go any further than Mr Beauchamp here did, as the slope gets steeper, the further it goes. And keep to the right side, if you will, for the left side extends much further than the right, and gets a might steeper as it runs. We want to stick to the tried and tested nursery run today.'

Ralf Colcolough, a gangling mess of ski sticks and skis, his long arms and legs seemingly in the control of a malign god, managed to move himself to the top of the little slope with trepidation, frequently making little squeaking noises of fear and alarm.

'No ski poles, if you please, Mr Colcolough. You simply don't need them for this first exercise.'

Colcolough discarded his poles with rather more effort than was necessary, which immediately set him moving downwards. 'Points of skis pointing slightly inwards, please,' shouted Iain, in vain, after his retreating figure.

Gathering speed at an alarming rate, unable to do anything about changing his skis from a parallel position, Colcolough began to wave his arms in the air, and hoots of distress could be heard as he careered towards the bottom of the right-hand side of the slope.

At the foot, where the ground levelled out, he lost control in his panic, and went head over heels, shedding his skis as he went, and proceeding to produce a long drawn-out screech of a word that Hugo pretended not to understand to be 'Ffffuuuuuuucccckk!!!' just as a Land Rover approached the prone figure.

From the top of the slope, the others watched while the ghillie got out of his vehicle, calmly collected both skis and put them in the back, then went to Colcolough's aid, pitching him back upright and inserting him in the passenger seat, as if pandering to a frightened child.

Back at the top of the slope, the ghillie exited the vehicle first, informing them all that, 'It's just a wee bittie bruising. He'll be fine after a nice long soak. Nae worries.'

Colcolough eased himself out of his seat and said, in apology, to the others in the group, 'I say, I'm dreadfully sorry about what I yelled on the way down. Frightful language. No call for it. Please accept my word that it won't be repeated.'

'Your turn, Mr Cholmondley-Crichton-Crump,' announced Iain, determined that everyone should have a go at this new activity, for he had no intention of letting Hugo wriggle out of it. 'Now, let's get you in position,' he ordered, pushing the hapless Hugo across the snow like an over-sized toy.

'I don't think I want to try this,' he pleaded, but Iain was having none of it.

'I'll just give you a little push, and off you'll go. Nothing to it. Skis turned in a bit, like I told you.'

He'd already given Hugo a mighty shove before he noticed that Hugo still had his ski poles in his hands, and yelling, 'No poles for this,' made a mad grab at them, which destabilised him sufficiently for him to land face down in the snow, watching Hugo's retreating figure from ground level.

'Oh, Lord. Oh, my good gracious me!' exclaimed Hugo, wildly waving his poles, his speed increasing by the second, and his path drifting left. There was absolutely nothing he could do about it, as he approached the steeper left hand side of the slope, and he was aware of Iain shouting, 'No, no! Go right! Turn, you silly old fool. Turn right, for God's sake!'

Even through the buzzing panic in his brain, Hugo was aware of the insult, and thought, as he careered along, his poles waving wildly like antennae, that if he survived this plunge, he had a good mind to beep the blighter on the snoot. Shoving him like that was, if not exactly attempted murder – at least, it wasn't murder yet – but constituted an assault upon his person which was reckless, to say the least.

At this point, one of his ski poles made contact with the ground and catapulted him into the air, where he did a perfect somersault, then seemed to cartwheel towards the far distant end of the steep incline, making 'ooh' and 'argh' noises, with the occasional 'ouch' and, from a distance, doing a fair impression of a centipede on speed.

Before Iain could get to his feet, the Land Rover was off down the slope in pursuit of the flying figure of Hugo, who was just coming to rest in a heap of limbs, skis and poles, lying like a tangled spider at the base of the slope, shouting repeatedly, 'Bum! Bum! Bum!' then proceeding to laugh hysterically.

'Ha ha ha! Hee hee hee hee hee! Ho ho ho!' floated upwards, unimpeded in the cold clear air, to the others in his party, who could not work out whether he was hysterical with fear or had lost his mind somewhere on the way down.

Iain, in a complete fluster lest Hugo try to slap some sort of law suit on him, pushed off and skied down to join the Land Rover, from which the ghillie was just emerging at the foot of the slope. Both men reached the still recumbent form, Iain arriving in a shower of powdery snow as he made an abrupt halt as near to the figure as he could, without actually causing any further damage.

'Are ye hurt, man?' asked the ghillie, showing his concern by casually rolling a cigarette.

'Ha ha hee hee ho ho ha ha ha!' chortled Hugo, still unable to control what sounded like hysteria.

'Do you need an ambulance?' asked Iain, still concerned about litigation.

'I'm fine!' Hugo finally managed to splutter. 'All these clothes you made me wear. I might as well have been wrapped in cotton wool.'

Pulling off a glove, he wiped tears from his eyes and continued, 'I haven't had so much fun since my first ride on a rollercoaster. Just don't ask me to do it again. Has anyone got a flask about them? I could do with a "wee nip" to settle my nerves.'

At that moment, Beauchamp slid to a stop beside them and provided Lady A's second best flask, the first one now being considered as a piece of evidence in the piper's death, and Hugo took a long, grateful swig. 'I shall refrain from mentioning anything about your mishap to her ladyship, should I happen to see her before you. She'll only fret.'

'Good show, Beauchamp! Excellent idea! I say, do you think I could be dropped back at the castle? I could do with a bit of a lie down, and just ignore lunch. I'm not in the least hungry. It must be that adrenalin stuff that I've heard so much about, and now I think I've experienced it, too. I don't want to do any more skiing, though. It doesn't feel half as elegant as it looks, and I really don't think it's for me. Sorry.'

Lady Amanda's excursion started in what, to her, seemed a slightly bizarre fashion. Heading to exit the castle by a side entrance, the party came upon a pile of what looked, to her ladyship, to be a pile of old tennis racquets. 'Surely we're not playing tennis in this weather?' she quipped.

'Dunnae be so silly, girl!' growled Macdonald. 'The area immediately around the castle has been cleared of snow, but we've tae get tae the forest, and the snow's knee-deep. We'll not get there at all if we dinnae use snowshoes. Noo, get yerselves shod, and we'll be off.'

After about five minutes of puffing and blowing – some had considerable 'corporations' to bend over, to achieve this shoeing activity – the five souls braved the biting cold and went outside to start their trek to the forest, where the snow would be negligible because of the tree cover.

Lady Amanda's gait resembled that of a person auditioning for a part in a live action version of *The Wrong Trousers*, as she lifted her feet high and stepped forward, occasionally getting the back of the snowshoe stuck in the snow. After a few occasions when she nearly took a tumble, she was given an impatient instruction from the morose Macdonald.

'Lift yer feets and plant them down flat, wuman, else ye'll go arse over tit, an' at your weight, I'll nae be pullin' ye up again.'

Insulted to a degree she had only ever before suffered at school, she blushed as brightly as a robin's breast, and did 'as she had been bid', finding that – damn and blast it – the old man was perfectly correct, and it did make the going much easier. None of the others had suffered a similar problem, so she assumed they had used such ungainly contraptions before. At least now she could keep up with them.

At the edge of the forest, Macdonald called them together, so that he could explain what they were going to be doing, for the benefit of anyone who had not engaged in this sort of activity before. As he said this, he glared malevolently at Lady A, and she blushed anew.

'We'll enter the forest in silence. Any communication after that will have to be in signals, or in low whispers of the lowest kind. If we're near a deer, we'll draw attention to ourselves immediately, they have such sharp hearing. We'll be walking against the wind, so that the deer don't smell us coming. That way, we have the best chance of getting some fine photos of the grand creatures.' There was a minute pause while he sneered. He much preferred to stalk with guns. 'Is everybody ready?'

Four heads nodded in unison, each of the party heeding his instructions not to speak, and they entered the gloomy confines of the pine forest, with a final warning given in a whisper. 'Watch out for twigs. They can snap with a crack that would warn every beast of the forest of our approach, in which case we might as well return to the castle and give up. They're canny beasties who like their privacy, and to see them and be unheeded by them is a rare privilege, ye ken?'

Lady A had a feeling that she wouldn't be very good at this. Although unexpectedly light on her feet for dancing, in general she had a poor sense of balance, and tended to be just a tiny bit clumsy in everyday life, to which Beauchamp and her not-quite-complete sets of glassware would bear witness.

As the forest began to close in behind them, she looked back longingly at the pile of snowshoes they had discarded, and wondered if she should give up her plan of trying to eavesdrop on conversations at lunchtime, for that would be the only opportunity, if Macdonald didn't impose a code of silence upon them even while they were eating.

Maybe she should just let them get on with it, and wander around on her own for a while, before returning to the castle, which was, at least, a few degrees warmer than the outside. As she stood, deep in careful thought, a stag strolled across her vision, and she had to clamp a hand across her mouth to stop herself yelling out to the others.

She was downwind of it and, with no inkling of her presence, it sniffed the cold air, shook its antlers in a way that seemed to indicate its joy at being alive, then trotted off into the cover of the trees.

With a sigh of deep pleasure, Lady A smiled a smile of deep appreciation, as if she had been granted this close-up view as a blessing, then nearly jumped out of her skin as a voice at her shoulder whispered, 'What a beautiful wild creature!' Hand clamped over her mouth once again, she turned as quickly as she could, to find Beauchamp, smiling contentedly, just behind her.

'How many times have I told you not to do that, Beauchamp?' she hissed, still conscious that she should make as little noise as possible. 'Anyone else would have trodden on a twig, but, oh, no, not you. You're as silent as the wild creatures here. What do you want?'

'The skiing's finished, or at least, I've finished with it, so I just came out to make sure that you hadn't fallen or got lost. Why have you stayed behind?' He was careful not to mention Hugo's mishap, as agreed, so as not to worry her.

'For the same reason that the bear went over the mountain,' she stated bizarrely.

'I beg your pardon?' asked Beauchamp, totally uncomprehending.

'To see what he could see. That's why I'm not staying with the group. There's something out here; I'm convinced of it. I can't find anything amiss in the castle, although I haven't been down to the dungeons yet. That being the case, my nose tells me that there's something amiss on this estate, which was at the bottom of the piper's death.

'If it's not in the castle, then it's somewhere outside. I know how big the estate is, but if there's something iffy going on, it's not going to be going on too far away from the castle itself, otherwise there would be a lot of to-ing and fro-ing by Land Rover, and there hasn't been any evidence of that. It would also be inconvenient to have whatever it is secreted at a distance, when the weather's like this, and the winters in this region are long and hard.

'No, there's something within footfall of the castle, and I'm determined to hunt it out and find out what the dickens is going on here. One man's already lost his life. That needs avenging, if nothing else.'

'You could be putting yourself in grave danger, your ladyship. If whoever is behind whatever it is becomes aware of you sniffing around like a bloodhound; well, they've killed once, already. Do you think they'd hesitate to do it again?'

'It's very bad form to kill guests who are old friends of the family, Beauchamp.'

'The piper had been here all his working life, and he took over from his father before him, and they didn't hesitate to kill him. I think you're playing a very dangerous game, your ladyship. I shall do my very best to protect you, but even I have my limits.'

'That, I simply don't believe!' declared Lady A, in a slightly louder whisper.

'Hrmph!' Beauchamp cleared his throat in embarrassment at the level of confidence she had in him, then proposed something practical for the present. 'You wait here, and I'll slip off and tell the others that we're leaving the party, as you're having trouble with your arthritis, and we're just going to have a little walk before

returning to sit in front of the fire.'

'Blasted cheek! I'm as fit as a fiddle!'

'It's what's known as a little white lie, your ladyship; then we can do exactly as you please, but I shall be by your side in case ... anything happens.'

Lady Amanda unexpectedly gave in without a whimper, suddenly realising that 'anything' could happen out here in the wilds, too far away to summon help by her screams. 'Will do, old stick. I'll just hang around here in case that jolly old stag comes back for a gawp around.'

When Beauchamp returned, he found Lady Amanda on point, like a hunting dog who is pinpointing its prey. 'What's caught your attention, then, your ladyship?' he asked. She did not move an inch, merely muttering inconsequentially, 'I do wish you'd call me Amanda.'

'That is a request with which I am unable, at this present time, to comply. What has attracted your attention so strongly?'

'Look over there,' she said, pointing with her stick. Just between that tallest Douglas fir and the misshapen pine. It's quite difficult to distinguish with the sky so whiteygrey, but just keep looking.'

'For what, exactly, am I looking?' asked Beauchamp, with impeccable grammar.

'Little puffs of smoke – it may be steam, but I'm not a connoisseur of the difference between them at a distance. There goes one now!'

'I see what you mean. It's coming from quite a distance away. What do you suppose it is, your ladyship? If it were a bonfire, even at this distance, we'd smell it.'

'I have a fair idea, but I don't want to say anything until we've had a chance to explore.'

'That's a lot further away than you might think. You'd never make it on foot.'

'Then you'll have to do it, if I can come up with a reason for why you're not valeting for Hugo. Actually, I suppose that no one will really notice you're gone, if we don't say anything. If anyone asks about you, I'll say you've come down with a stomach bug that's very infectious, and you've put yourself in quarantine, as you don't want it to spread through the other staff like wildfire. How about that?'

'That will do nicely. Shall I go now, or tomorrow?'

'Go now. I'll make my way back to the castle, and if anyone asks me why I'm alone, I'll say that you've already returned because of illness, and make a huge fuss about how awful it was when your symptoms first appeared.

'If no one sees me, I'll go straight to your room, and make a loud fuss inside it, groaning on your part, and cajoling you to get to bed, on my behalf. Then, if anyone hears what's going on in your room, they'll assume that we're both in there. Give me your key, and I'll lock the door when I leave, so that no one can burst in and see that you're not there.

'When you get back, make straight for my room, and if anyone stops you, say it must have been one of those swift and ghastly bugs, but that you're feeling a lot better now, and were just going to report to me for duty, but make sure you get out of those warm clothes first, otherwise they'll know you haven't been back.'

'Neat!'

'Don't you dare go American on me! Now, off you toddle, and if you're not back by morning, I'll have to report you missing. Good luck, old bean! Happy hunting!'

'If I'm not back before morning, I'll be somewhere out here, dead of hypothermia.'

'If you get lost, there are bothies scattered all around for hunters to seek shelter. You'll never be far away from somewhere to make yourself comfortable, if you haven't got time to get back this evening.'

'Thank God for that! I had visions of you having to defrost me, so that I could make early morning tea. I don't really fancy turning into an icicle. And yes, before you ask, I do have a torch, and this little novelty,' he announced, producing a blackjack from his pocket. 'And if that's no good, I'll just have to use these,' he continued, taking some brass knuckles from another pocket.'

'Really, Beauchamp! That's disgraceful! I can't imagine why you thought you might need either of those, skiing. Well done! I'm not sure they didn't base James

Bond on you.'

Lady Amanda, by using a side entrance and a different staircase, managed to sneak up to Beauchamp's room without being seen. It was to her advantage that the servants were all involved in preparing lunch, for although the stalkers had, in the end, been sent off with a picnic lunch, the guests who had gone off for a sleigh ride and the skiers would be coming back ravenous, after all that time spent in the cold, and would, no doubt, expect to be fed extravagantly, even though there was fat chance of that happening in this establishment.

She shot into her manservant's bedroom like a guilty mistress, closing the door firmly behind her, locking it, and mentally preparing her script, in anticipation of a fine theatrical time. She'd loved acting as a child, and had actually appeared in one of the Belchester Amateur Dramatic Society's productions. (They were known as the

BADS, and for very good reasons other than their initials.)

With very mixed feelings, she got into the bed, making sure that her head made a good dent in the pillow, and wriggled around to make sure that the under-sheet was disturbed. Then she threw back the bedclothes and surveyed her handiwork. If anyone managed to get in here, they'd believe that Beauchamp was somewhere else, battling his bug.

She then pulled up an old oak chair that had been placed against the wall, and settled down to do her bit for the theatrical world. 'Groan, moan, pitiful sigh.' She produced these noises in her best contralto, sounding as male as she could, then switched pitches.

'You just lay there, Beauchamp. The bathroom's within easy reach, and there's a plastic bowl in there, should you need it. I've filled up your water container, and I'll pop up, hourly, to see how you are. Don't worry about your duties. Hugo and I can manage quite all right on our own for a short while.'

'Moooaan, slight pitiful wail of pain and despair. Groooaan.' That sounded convincing enough, and she suddenly realised she felt like Ray Alan with her hand up an invisible Lord Charles. She even had her right hand in the air, as if operating a ventriloquist's dummy and, noticing this, thanked God that she didn't have her hand up the rear end of a green duck.

'Stay exactly where you are, and I'll bring you up a cup of tea later, and maybe some bread and butter. Now, just go to sleep and don't worry about anything else, except getting better,' she said in a raised voice, as she slipped out of the room and locked the door. That should do it, she thought, bustling out of the servants' quarters and making her way back to her own room to get changed for luncheon.

Finally making her way downstairs, she ran into the sleigh-ride party arriving back from their invigorating slither through the snow. Drew and Moira Ruthven, and Siobhan their hostess, were chattering happily about the beautiful snowscapes they had seen, and St John Bagehot could be seen making a determined line for the dining hall, oblivious of his erstwhile companions.

Lady Amanda made straight for the open fire in the drawing room and found Hugo entrenched in front of it, a hot toddy in his hand and a woollen blanket over his knees. Taking the chair on one side of the blazing logs, she asked Hugo how he had enjoyed his skiing lesson, and the unlikely sportsman burst into peals of laughter.

'I never realised I was an acrobat, but I did a fair impression of one, going down that slope. I was completely out of control, but it was terribly invigorating to realise the speed at which I was travelling, and the danger that that presented. Fortunately, I was well wrapped up and must have behaved rather like a rubber ball, for when I landed in a heap of ski poles and arms and legs at the bottom, I didn't seem to be any the worse for it. I only hope there's no bruising to come out.'

'You fell,' replied Lady A, acidly. 'Have you no consideration for anyone else, Hugo. What would I do without your company, now that I've become so accustomed to it? How selfish of you.'

'I'm fine, Manda, hic,' said Hugo, with the slightest of slurs, and Lady A immediately rang for a maid and ordered a pot of very strong coffee, as Mr CholmondleyCrichton-Crump was a little tired and emotional. It was only his accident that had pried a healthy slug of alcohol out of Cook, but it seemed to have gone to his head beautifully.

'Really, Hugo. You're well on your way to being puddled. What sort of a detective are you? A lush?'

The stalking party arrived back just as the sun set and darkness descended. All were ruddy of face, their breath smoking like a huddle of dwellings, as they approached the entrance. All seemed to have had a good time, and disappeared straight upstairs to get ready for dinner at the extraordinarily early time it was served to guests of the McKinley-Mackintoshes.

Just before the dressing gong was sounded, there was a minor emergency, when Beauchamp appeared through the front door, glassy-eyed, blue with cold, and staggering. Walter Waule and Enid Tweedie had been crossing the hall carrying various accoutrements that would be needed during the meal, and rushed to his aid.

Taking an arm each, they led him to his room, halfcarrying him. Not only was he unable to walk any further unaided, but he was incoherent as well, and they feared for his health. Surprised to find his room already locked, Walter produced a master key, and went straight to Beauchamp's bathroom to run a hot bath.

Enid helped him settle into a wing-backed chair and tutted about the state of his bed. It was not like Beauchamp to be lax about things like bed-making, and she was not party to Lady A's earlier theatrical performance. After this, she made herself scarce, while Walter undressed the semi-conscious manservant and helped him into the steaming water. This was none of her business.

Instead, she headed for the kitchen quarters, and informed everyone that Beauchamp was ill, and she needed at least two hot water bottles and a hot milky drink to help revive him. After being obliged, she took these back upstairs and tapped on the door nervously. She was a coy woman, and just the thought of catching Beauchamp 'in the buff' made her blush – although not completely with embarrassment, she was ashamed to find.

Walter let her in and explained that he had already got Beauchamp into bed. 'The water went cold almost immediately,' he informed her. 'His body just sucked all the heat out of it, and I took advantage of that to get him into his pyjamas and under the covers.'

Enid pulled back the covers bravely and placed one hot water bottle at his feet and one on his stomach, and put the cup of cocoa down on the bedside table. 'Try to drink it, please. I don't know what happened to you, but I'll come back after dinner with a pot of tea, and check on your condition,' she assured the still silent figure, whose arms had clutched at the hot water bottle at his middle like a drowning man clutching at a life-belt, and was now hugging it to himself like a teddy bear.

She pulled the covers back over his now recumbent body and tucked him in tightly, like a mother putting a sick child to bed, then left him in peace to sleep, Walter following her out of the room.

'Well, what did you make of that?' he asked.

'I haven't got the faintest idea, but I'll leave him to recover a bit before I start questioning,' replied Enid with a steely glint in her eye. This was Lady Amanda's doing, she was sure, and she did not approve at all.

'And, I'd be grateful if you kept it to yourself,' she exhorted Walter, who nodded his head in agreement, wondering if there were something wrong with the manservant that compelled him to wander off into the wide blue yonder.

Lady A was going to get the rough side of her tongue, Enid thought defensively, for whatever foolish errand she had sent the poor man on, and in this weather, too.

Chapter Six

Dinner held only one surprise. As they all trooped downstairs, a pipe was making a noise like a cat in a mangle in the main entrance hall, and each of them looked at the others, to see if anyone had any explanation for this unexpected replacement for Jock Macleod, but it was a complete mystery to all of them.

Their curiosity was satisfied, however, just before the serving of the first course, when Sir Cardew banged a spoon on the table and announced that they had taken on a young piper for a month's trial, and he was sure they'd all appreciate the presence of his music, not only for dancing at the wake for the previous holder of the post, before their unexpectedly prolonged stay was over, but as a reveille in the mornings. He didn't look very happy as he announced this.

Hugo groaned, and leaned towards Lady A to whisper, 'Not again! I had forgotten that there were two seven o'clocks in one day. I haven't had to cope with that since I did my stint in the army. At that hour, I haven't finished with the night, and would appreciate being left alone, to an hour that I consider to be the start of the day, and not at a time when I'm well away, and just getting my best quality sleep. And I'd completely forgotten that we were supposed to be having a wake for Macleod.'

'I'll slip you a pair of ear plugs, Hugo. Now do stop moaning. A wake won't hurt you, unless it's far too early in the morning,' replied Lady A acidly, quite exasperated with a Hugo who saw ghosts, did cartwheels down nursery slopes, and then got squiffy.

Conversation was all about their day's outings, the cold, the beauty, and the atmosphere in the ice-encrusted forest. As the meal ended, and the guests adjourned for 'coffee', Sir Cardew left them. He always smoked his daily post-prandial cigar outside at the base of the west tower.

Leaning contentedly against the stone wall, he looked out on the winter scene of clusters of light, and the great shadows of the forest and hills, black lumps weakly illuminated but unidentifiable in the dim light of the stars. The moon was new, and hiding modestly behind a cloud on this, her debut night.

Puffing contentedly on his cigar, appreciative of the rich, pungent smoke it produced, and which Siobhan hated so much, he was a happy man, with the exception of one fly in his metaphorical ointment, but he wouldn't allow himself to dwell on this. This was his daily dream-time.

Sir Cardew looked deep into his mind and dreamt.

Sometime later, back in the drawing room, coffee was now over and a ghastly non-alcoholic liqueur was being served (these being kept separate in this household). Lady Siobhan gathered her guests close enough to listen, and asked them if they had ever seen the family broadsword. On receiving a uniformly negative answer, she offered to take them to view it in one of the south tower rooms, which was always kept locked, for it held a multitude of ancient and valuable family documents and Cardew did not consider a safe sufficient security. The locked room gave another layer of impenetrability that soothed his fears of burglary.

Everyone queued, in a very British way, at the cloakroom to get access to their outer garments, for many parts of the castle seemed colder than outside, then Siobhan led them off down corridors, round corners, and finally up a flight of narrow and very worn stone spiral steps that Hugo wouldn't even attempt to climb, waiting patiently at the foot, still glowing from the various points of the day in which he had imbibed alcoholic liquors.

Lady Amanda puffed and blew in the rear, determined to get her two-penn'orth, after all this cavorting through freezing corridors. The only thing she knew about broadswords was that they were very long and heavy, and it took a strong and fit man to wield one, and she was determined to see it.

She was thwarted, however, as soon as Siobhan opened the door to the strong room, which she referred to as the 'muniment room', she wailed in disbelief. The glass case in which the sword had been presented was smashed, and the sword had gone, taken, no doubt, by whoever had managed to get through the locked door to secure their prize, and then managing to relock the door, before departing with the filched weapon.

Disappointment was palpable in the air. They had made quite a trek to view this historical sword, and now it proved that their efforts had been all for nothing. A buzz of disappointment echoed round the chamber, joined by the faint voice of Hugo calling, 'Are you going to be much longer? It's brass-monkey weather down here.'

His plea had momentarily halted their chatter and, in the silence that followed there was a scream from outside, cut off almost as soon as it was audible.

'Whatever was that?' Lady Amanda was the first to ask. Another silence followed, in which Siobhan began to moan softly. 'Whatever's wrong, my dear? It's hardly something that can be put up for sale on the open market, and I'm sure it'll be recovered soon. If not, the insurance will take care of it.'

'It's not that,' she replied, her voice rising in panic. 'Cardew's outside. What if something dreadful has happened to him? I must go out and look for him.'

'Not on your own, you don't,' stated Lady A firmly. 'We'll all go. If he's fine, which I'm sure he is, we'll just say we're having a little starlight stroll, and then encourage him back inside, so that you can tell him about the theft.'

Collecting Hugo into their midst on the way down, they headed outside. Siobhan had explained to them Cardew's nightly ritual of smoking his only cigar of the day, so they all began to approach the west tower en masse. As they walked, slowly now, in case there really was something ghastly waiting for them, Lady A rummaged about in her handbag and produced a fair-sized torch.

Hugo glanced at her with amazement, but she merely replied, 'I just like to be prepared for all eventualities; that's all,' and quickened her step slightly, to catch up with the others, who were chattering about what might have happened. As they turned to go round the west tower, however, there was complete silence, and it was only Lady Amanda's out-of-breath question that broke this stunned silence. 'Anything afoot?' she puffed, as she arrived slightly tardily, then saw what they had already seen.

Sir Cardew was pinned to the ground, literally, the handle of the mighty broadsword sticking out of the top of his head, the point of the blade embedded in the grass between his feet, beside which his cigar slowly smouldered into extinction.

Another scream rent the air!

What to do? An out-of-hours call to Inspector Glenister threw up the fact that he would not be able to get a helicopter to the castle before daylight, having not long departed, and so it was decided, there would have to be a guard kept on Sir Cardew's cadaver overnight, so that foxes and the like wouldn't nibble at it. It would also have to be a guard comprised of two people, so that the murderer would have neither time nor opportunity to destroy any evidence left behind, due to there being a witness with him – or even her.

The sword must have been dropped: the thing was so heavy, Siobhan explained, that she couldn't even lift it. The west tower being the highest, just dropping it would prove fatal. Its own weight, aided by the process of falling, would easily slip through flesh and bone like a hot knife through butter, and the fact that it had actually pinned Cardew to the ground was put down more to luck than judgement, on the part of the murderer.

No one could have foreseen that incredible accuracy occurring. The original objective was evidently just to kill him. But why? And who? They already knew with what. There was absolutely no need to search for a weapon.

It was finally decided that the outdoor staff would be roused and rostered, in pairs, to be on guard throughout the night, and Macdonald was summoned to drag an ancient brazier out from some disreputable part of the nether regions of the castle, so that no one froze to death before morning. Moira took the weeping Siobhan back inside, and the others dispersed for the night. There was nothing more to be done until Glenister arrived on the morrow.

When Lady A and Hugo reached the comparative warmth of the entrance hall, they found Enid Tweedie standing at the bottom of the staircase wringing her hands, a look of great relief flooding her face, when she caught sight of the two friends.

'Thank God you're here,' she cried. 'I went to the drawing room after dinner and found no one there. I had no idea where you'd gone. It was like finding a landlocked Marie Celeste.'

'I thought there was someone missing at dinner. Have you been expelled from serving because you can't recognise a plate?' asked Lady A, facetiously, then softened her manner as Enid burst into sobs. This wasn't like her at all and, between gulps and sniffles, she explained that she'd been looking after 'poor Beauchamp'.

'Whatever's wrong with Beauchamp? As far as I know he's never had a day's illness in his life,' his half-sister said, speaking rather more softly.

'Robust chap, Beauchamp!' declared Hugo. 'Can't imagine the man ill.'

Edith explained how he had arrived back at the castle earlier, the parlous condition in which he'd arrived, and what Walter Waule and she had done to treat him. 'He was on the verge of hypothermia, you know. He couldn't walk or speak when we got him inside.

'Once he was sleeping, I excused myself from any other duties, as I am supposed to be your lady's maid, and I've been sitting by his bedside ever since. I only came down again because I looked out and saw a group of people heading for the front door, so I rushed down to see if you were amongst them.'

She had hardly finished speaking when Lady A went tearing up the stone stairs, two at a time, shouting, 'Beauchamp, Beauchamp, are you all right?' Enid and Hugo followed at a more sedate pace; one that suited Hugo's two still-unreplaced joints, and allowed Edith to recover her aplomb.

When they were all gathered together in the manservant's bedroom, Enid was absolutely dumbfounded to see Lady A throw one arm around Hugo and another around Beauchamp and burst into tears. This was a unique occasion, and she kept her silence in respect for this bombshell behaviour.

Lady Amanda's shoulder shook as she wailed, 'I nearly lost both of you in one day. Whatever would I have done? Life wouldn't have been worth living without the two of you. I sent you off, Hugo, on a fool's errand, to try skiing, and I sent you, Beauchamp, on what turned out almost to be a suicide mission. How can you ever forgive me?

'What a fool I am, never to consider the consequences of my little whims, but you know what I'm like when I get the scent of blood in my nostrils. I'm like a stupid bloodhound: nose down, following, and damn what the rest of the world's doing.'

Hugo disentangled himself from her embrace: he found close contact with another, whoever it was, intensely uncomfortable, but patted her on the shoulder in an avuncular manner. Beauchamp also freed himself and commented, 'No harm done, er, Manda. How's the sleuthing coming along? I do have some news.'

Enid approached the bed and asked if he'd like a nice cup of tea – the panacea of the masses – thinking that the manservant even looked formally attired in his pyjamas. The jacket, which was the visible half, appeared to have been freshly ironed while he was wearing it and, although he was still a little wan-looking, he seemed none the worse for his experience.

'I'll bring a tray so we can all perk ourselves up, shall I?' she chirped, and made her way down to the kitchen. When she arrived there, there was a black cat curled up in front of the range, and the sight cheered her. A noise from the doorway alerted the animal. It took one look towards whoever was entering, fluffed up its fur in fear, and shot out of the room as if its tail were on fire.

Looking over her shoulder, Enid espied Sarah Fraser approaching the huge old fridge, and thought that the lump of a girl looked exactly like a Rottweiler in lipstick. It would be a brave man who took that on for a wife.

The lump of a girl looked at Enid and commented,

'That cat thinks he's Russian.'

Enid fell for it. 'Why's that?'

'Because anyone who sees him tells him to bugger off – Buggerov – get it?'

Enid merely sniffed, being very fond of cats herself, and had actually had one until quite recently.

Through the back door, Angus Hamilton the chauffeur, who had just finished polishing the cars, came in rubbing his cold hands together and called out, 'Sarah, will ye make a wee cup o' tea for the two of us, and we can have a nice bitty chat?'

Sarah glanced briefly at him in/ disgust, and replied, 'Feck off, ye dirty owl man,' before stumping out of the kitchen in high dudgeon.

Enid shook her head, thinking that, with a face and figure like that, Sarah should take every chance she was offered. Hostility never produced any orange blossom, and that was a fact.

When she returned with the tea tray, Beauchamp had been apprised of the details of Sir Cardew's grisly fate, and was as flummoxed as the others as to who or why anyone would attempt something so macabre. 'We need to make some associations!' declared Lady A. 'There's something very improper,' (so typical of her to use a word like that) 'going on around here, and two people have died so far.

'We're actually in situ, and we have the best chance of sorting out the good guys from the bad. After all, this won't be the first time we've done it. I suggest we have a meeting in the morning, to pool all we can about who associates with whom, who might have been observed in a place they were unlikely to be found ... and all that jazz,' she concluded.

'And now, Enid, we have managed to suppress Beauchamp's eagerness to tell us of what he discovered on his ill-fated trip into the forest, so I suggest that, if we are all sitting comfortably, he begin.'

Beauchamp put down his cup on the bedside locker, cleared his throat, and launched into his story. 'Lady Amanda,' he began, a little embarrassed that that was the second time he had uttered her forename this evening, 'sent me off ... no, let me start at the absolute beginning.

'I had gone to the nursery slope with Mr Hugo, but the skiing didn't last long after Mr Hugo's display of acrobatics. I decided that I would catch up with her ladyship, as the stalking group had left later than the skiing party, and eventually caught up with her on the edge of the forest.

'Something had caught her eye in the distance, and I was dispatched to investigate what was causing the thin spiral of white smoke that was rising in the distance. It was a lot further away than either of us had imagined, and it took me some considerable time to reach the source. And it seemed that the stalking party had wasted no time in taking advantage of you "bunking off", your ladyship.

'They were all there, outside this wooden construction, and it was from this that the thin spire of smoke was rising. Sir Cardew, Wriothesley (we call him Rizzly Grizzly in the servant's hall), Wallace Menzies – he's known as 'Mingin'', and Macdonald were all gathered together in a huddle. When they went inside, I got as close as I could, to see exactly what was going on inside the building, if I can dignify such a ramshackle structure as that, as such, and I managed to get a peek through one of the filthy panes of glass.

'They had a huge still going in there: a huge and completely illegal still, I might add. Well, I scarpered after that, and it was just as well I didn't' hang round, for the light was going, and I'm afraid I was led astray a few times. I never realised before how much one tree looks like another. It's all so much more difficult at twilight.

'Anyway, I think that answers a lot of our questions as to why. We need to work on the fine details, however. How on earth did the piper get involved in all this? Was he part of the 'gang', for want of a better word? Who took the sword? Was it a lone action, or part of a conspiracy? And why Sir Cardew? We still have a long way to go, with respect.'

'Oh, Beauchamp, it's so good to have you back on form. When you didn't come back and there were no cocktails, I had the most enormous senior moment, for I thought you'd stayed on at the ski slope to perfect the art, knowing what you are for getting things exactly right. How can you forgive me for such laxity?'

'Precisely!' cut in Hugo. 'I had to make us a gin and tonic, and very poor it was too. I know it's only two ingredients, but it tasted foul, and had no kick whatsoever.'

'That's because I usually mix two parts gin to one part tonic,' Beauchamp informed him, with a knowing smirk. Things were back to normal. For now.

The day, with all its unfamiliar activities, was followed by an equally disturbing night. Lady A and Hugo had had a brandy in front of the former's fire before turning in, leaving Enid to pander to Beauchamp's every whim, and didn't get to bed until well after the witching hour, Lady A completely forgetting to furnish her friend with earplugs in defiance of the, now forgotten, new morning piper.

Her ladyship went out like a light, to use a rather vulgar expression, but Hugo tossed and turned, regularly discovering new parts of his body that seemed to be developing what felt like spectacular bruises. He managed to doze for a while, then dreamt that he was tied up and being terrorised by some terrible brute.

When he awoke, in a muck-sweat, he found himself so tangled in the sheets that he could barely move a muscle, and spent some time undoing the knot that he had made of himself and the bedding, huffing and puffing and muttering, 'Damn!'

'Blast!' and 'Tiddlywinks!' under his breath, as his over-exercised muscles protested at such brutal treatment.

Eventually getting himself settled again, although he had had to get out and remake the bed, he tried once more to go to sleep, but such a benison eluded him still, and it wasn't until two-thirty that he finally slipped into a light doze. What seemed like only a minute or two later, but was in fact over an hour, he became aware of something in close proximity to his head, opened his eyes, and found himself staring into the same dark-veiled countenance as he had, on one previous occasion.

When Hugo screamed, it was in a surprising falsetto pitch, and this noise pierced Lady Amanda's deep sleep of the innocent. Realising immediately that the noise was coming from Hugo's room, she leapt from her bed, ready for action, grabbed a poker from beside the fireplace, and shot through the adjoining door – or, at least, that's what she had intended to do.

She, herself, in an inattentive moment, had slipped the bolt on her side when Hugo had left her for the night, and she merely rebounded from its solid surface and landed in a heap on the floor, the poker committing an act of gross indecency upon her person. As she rose to hands and knees, she could hear shouting from the adjoining room. 'Manda! Manda! Are you being attacked? Someone's locked the door? Who's in there with you?'

Slowly she rose to her feet and slipped the bolt, and the door shot open from the other side. This was unfortunate, as it opened into her room, and she went down with the poker again with a not surprising feeling of déjà vu. 'Manda! Manda! What's happening in there?' bellowed Hugo, just making things worse by pushing the door and shoving her further across the floor.

'Oh, there you are,' he said, espying her prone figure. 'I thought the door was unconscionably heavy. Are you all right?

What's been going on in here? It sounded like you were being murdered.'

'I merely reacted to your screaming,' she declared, with as much dignity as she could muster, being helped from the floor in her nightshirt by Hugo's gallant efforts.

'But what was all that banging and bumping I heard?'

he enquired, not understanding why there had been such a rumpus from the adjoining room, and why his friend was holding a brass poker in such a threatening manner. 'Don't hit me, please.'

Lady A returned the poker to its usual position, sat down in a fireside chair, and indicated Hugo to follow her lead and take a seat. 'I heard your screams, grabbed the poker in case you were in mortal peril, then threw myself at the adjoining door to come to your rescue. Unfortunately, I must have unthinkingly slipped the bolt when you went to bed – boing-ed off the dratted thing like a ricocheting missile, and then got into a terrible tangle with my nightshirt and the poker. That's all.

'Then you barged in and pushed me along as if I were a mop with which you were washing the floor. Just look at the state of my nightshirt! Really, these flagstones are a disgrace. I shall complain to housekeeping in the morning. Someone is being lax in their duties in this establishment, and I will not stand for it; even if I do know how a mop feels, being pushed around with no will of its own.

'So, why were you making all that fuss in the first place? The noise was enough to waken the dead.'

'I think it actually did, Manda. I had a terrible time trying to get off. The first time I dozed off, I woke, practically mummified in the sheets, then, when I'd sorted that out and remade the bed, I managed, at last, to go to sleep. But it wasn't for long.

'I felt something vile hovering over me, and when I opened my eyes, there she was again – that awful woman with the black veil, and I just started to wail like a banshee. Honestly, I couldn't help myself. Then, of course, I heard noises that I thought were you being attacked, and it seemed like someone had sussed what we were up to, and was determined to wipe out both of us, before we found out any more. Shall I pour us a brandy to settle our nerves?'

'I should think so!' agreed Lady A vehemently, as she slid into a dressing gown, modesty insisting that she should not be in a bedchamber in the presence of a man – even if it was only Hugo – dressed in just her nightgown.

They had barely settled to sip their nightcap that was nearly a 'morning-cap' when there were noises from beyond the window. It sounded exactly like the jingling of bottles on a milk float, but no milk float would come out to this isolated dwelling.

As Hugo rose to investigate, Lady Amanda grabbed him by the tail of his nightshirt and insisted, 'No, Hugo! Not with the lights on! Let's turn them out, then we can peek through the curtains, and they won't know that we're watching, whatever is going on out there.'

Hugo realised the logic of this, and extinguished the lights, before they approached the draughty regions of the window. There was a low whistle as the wind entered through the ill-fitting frame, and made the room several feet away from it as icy as right next to it.

The castle being situated so far north, there was already a dim light in the sky; certainly enough for them to distinguish what was going on down below on the frontage. There might not be a milk float down there, but there was some sort of cart, filled with boxes that rattled and jingled every time one of them was lifted from its rear. Just beyond the intimidating entrance doors, a small door had been opened in the wall, and men could be seen transporting said boxes through this door, and disappearing slowly into the ground.

'It must be an entrance to the cellars-cum-dungeons,' Lady Amanda breathed in Hugo's ear, then added, 'and I don't think that's milk they're delivering, either. That's a hooch float we can see down there. They're transferring what they have manufactured in the hut that Beauchamp discovered, and they're making sure that nothing is discovered there, when the police return. They're stashing it in the cellar, and I bet there's some sort of concealed entrance down there where they think they can stash it, undetected.'

'What shall we do?' Hugo breathed into her ear, tickling her with his night-time wayward mop of white hair. Such close proximity between them had not prevailed since they had danced together in times that seemed a lifetime away, and they both slipped apart, ending up at opposite ends of the window, without a word being said.

'Meeting, tomorrow morning,' hissed Lady A, 'and not a word of this to Glenister. I don't want him plodding his size fourteens all over the place, and giving the game away that someone's on to them.'

'What about my ghost?' asked Hugo, peeved that his experience had been relegated to the bottom of the division, in the light of this new occurrence.

'Indigestion!' was the only reply he got, before Lady A stumped over to her bed, slipped off her dressing gown, and got in, pulling the covers over her. 'Draw the curtains when you leave, Hugo. I don't want to see you again until the morning. And if you get any other visits from wandering females, kindly instruct them to get a mop and bucket and do something about these filthy flagstones and at least be of some use, instead of just frightening the bejeezus out of you, and disturbing my rest.'

Chapter Seven

The auspices for the next morning were not good, with so much sleep lost, and then the unwelcome serenade by the new piper, who excelled himself, and made a noise like half a dozen cats caught in a giant bicycle, but Beauchamp came up trumps, as usual.

Although he did not know of their wee small hours disturbances, he wanted to show his appreciation for the care and concern he had been shown the day before, after his awful experience in the snowy forest, and had raided the kitchen to the tune of one frying pan, a stick of lard, four eggs, numerous rashers of bacon, two tomatoes, and a hunk of uncut bread.

These he transported into the little room beside Lady A's room, from which he produced cocktails and afternoon tea, and treated them to breakfast in bed, which went a considerable way to reining in their grumpy moods, and getting them off to a good start to the day. Above all, it was such a treat to get tea that tasted of something other than dishwater.

He had actually been heard singing, as he prepared the food, and Lady A immediately identified the song as a very old one: 'If I were the only boy in the world ...' warbled tunefully into her room, startling her beyond comprehension. She had never known Beauchamp to sing, as long as she had known him, and that seemed to have been forever.

When she ran into Enid, she found out that the police had already arrived, along with a team of photographers and evidence gatherers, and that the giant human kebab had been removed from public view. That was a relief. She still could not get out of her mind the vision of the poor man speared through like a pig ready for the fire pit. Even the adventures of the night before had not wiped it out, and it had haunted her dreams during what little sleep she had managed to get.

'... and I couldn't help but laugh afterwards. It was so incongruous,' she heard Enid conclude, and had to apologise.

'I'm sorry, Enid, but I was miles away, wondering what Siobhan will do now. Of course, this is her ancestral home, so I suppose she'll just try to keep things going the way she always remembered them. After all, the castle has come down through her family and not Cardew's.'

'I was just telling you how unlikely it was to see Beauchamp in a bobble hat, yesterday. I've only ever seen him in his chauffeur's cap or his 'going into Belchester' bowler. If he hadn't been in such a bad way when he got back here, I don't think I could have stopped myself from laughing."

'Good grief! I was so taken up with what I had just seen and wanted investigated, that I didn't even notice. We must get him to put it on again, so I can enjoy the experience thoroughly. What colour was it?' she asked, inconsequentially.

'Blue and white, with a little red in the bobble,' replied Enid, who would never forget the sight.

'That's Beauchamp – patriotic as ever.'

Their conversation was interrupted at that moment, as Evelyn Awlle came squawking down the main staircase, her hands in the air, and a look of total despair on her face. 'Whatever's the matter, Evelyn? You look in a rare old state,' asked Lady Amanda.

'It's the mistress, your ladyship. I left her a little late this morning after what happened yesterday an' all, but when I took some tea up to her room, she wasnae there, and her bed had nae been slept in. I don't have any idea what could have happened to her, but I'm afraid for her life, after what happened to the master yesterday.'

Others, having heard the cries of distress of Siobhan's lady's maid, were gathering in the hall at the foot of the stairs to see what was occurring, and Lady A immediately took charge of things. 'Can someone get Inspector Glenister? It would seem that Siobhan has disappeared, maybe as long ago as last night, and poor Evelyn here is concerned for her safety.

'Now, it could just be that she used another room, as she was so upset at what had happened to Cardew. That has to be checked out first, so if someone would kindly fetch the inspector, he can organise a search of the castle, before we cast our worries any further afield.'

By the time Glenister arrived, it seemed that the whole of the household had assembled in the great entrance hall, staff included, and it didn't take long to explain to him what the problem was. He rounded up his men, and they were allocated different floors and wings to search.

He then took Lady A to one side and, with an ironic smile, informed her that he hoped that none of her belongings would be found in connection with this most recent body. 'Otherwise it would have rather a damning implication for yourself, would it not, your ladyship?'

She gave him a very old-fashioned look, then gathered together Hugo, Enid and Beauchamp, and led them off to the library, where they could talk in privacy. She and Hugo possessed information that the police did not, and she was determined that they would form a plan to uncover all the nefarious doings, before anyone else was hurt.

It would not only be quicker that way, bureaucracy being what it was, it would also be more fun. She had read rather more Enid Blyton and Agatha Christie books than were good for her in the past, and sometimes she forgot that she was as mortal as Jock Macleod and Sir Cardew had been.

'We have to find some way into where they keep the hooch,'
declared Lady Amanda. 'We can't just approach it boldly from
the front, as they did last night. We'd be seen immediately. We
either find out where there is a key to the inside door and use
that, or wait until tonight, and try to get in from the outside,
when everyone else is asleep. Enid, it is getting imperative, in this
career of sleuthing that we seem to be adopting, that you devote
your spare time to knitting us some black or navy-blue balaclava
helmets for future use.'

'I'll ask my mother, but I don't really have the time to
produce four such pieces of headgear at the moment. I do have
a life, you know?' declared Enid more boldly than she had ever
addressed Lady Amanda before, and she didn't even blush.

'I should be most grateful if your mother would oblige. I
shall provide everything she needs, plus remuneration for her
time, when they are knitted. Thank you, Enid. We shall convene
again in my room at nine o'clock tonight, if none of us is
successful in locating a key. If, of course, we get our hands on one
sooner, I shall round you all up for a little exploration. You and
Enid start in the servants' quarters, Beauchamp, and Hugo and I
will try a little desk and bureau exploration.'

Everyone assented to this plan, and they went their separate
ways for now, Enid quietly crooning, 'The boy I love is up in
the gallery ...' Goodness! She and Beauchamp both seemed to be
steeped in old music hall songs at the moment, thought Lady A,
and wondered whether something about this visit had brought
that on.

Lady Amanda began her search with the big visitors' book
that everyone had signed on arrival, and which was lodged
overtly on the big hall table, so that anyone who cared to could
have a peek through the names, to see illustrious visitors from

the past. It was a prodigious volume going back several decades, rather like a burials register, she thought.

Heaving back the heavy pages, she certainly saw recognisable names from the political world of the past, along with a few raves from the showbiz grave, when Siobhan's parents had moved in higher circles than their daughter did today. But this wasn't getting the baby bathed, so she turned, rather reluctantly, back to the present and considered the entries made by her fellow guests, making a note of the addresses they had given. For some reason, this action seemed important, and she always followed her instincts.

Hugo had merely hung around while she did this, and when she questioned his inaction, he declared that he'd never been to the castle before, and had no idea of the layout, so he'd have to tag along with her, and let her direct his searching.

'I know there'll be no chance of getting into Cardew's study, because that's where Inspector Glenister will set up his lair, as before. I suggest we go in search of keys. We've just got to be careful whom we ask. There are a couple here whom I think are rather dodgy, but I do have a plan.

'I suggest that we ask to borrow the key to that tower room where we were shown that terrible broadsword. In the past, I've heard Mama refer to that as the muniment room, as Siobhan did when we discovered the sword was missing. If we can get in there, there should be a lot to sift through. Probably in all those chests that are around the walls. There may even be a key to that cellar door, whether it be inside or out. It's the sort of thing that might be kept there, locked away, so that there wouldn't be any unnecessary shenanigans with the staff. Old habits die hard.'

'But Manda, I couldn't get up those stairs last time I tried, and I certainly haven't got any fitter since then. In fact, I'm covered in bruises, and ache from head to toe from that blasted skiing fiasco. You really are too trying! You'll have to do it on your own, or get Beauchamp or Enid to help you.'

'I'll go and see if I can find Enid. She's supposed to be my lady's maid, so I shall say I need her to do some 'maiding', right now.'

She found Enid taking her morning coffee with the other staff, and announced that she had need of her services. Draining her cup, Enid scuttled after her, bursting with curiosity. 'What are we going to do?' she asked, excitedly. 'Are we on the hunt?'

'We most definitely are, Enid. Oh, damn, I forgot to ask.'

'Ask what?'

Sliding back into the kitchen, Lady Amanda put on her most appealing smile (fairly frightening to those who did not know her well) and asked if she could have the key to the room where they had intended to view the sword even as it was being put to such dastardly use. 'Siobhan said I could borrow it for a few hours, but I didn't like to disturb her, this morning of all morning, and then I found out she had gone missing, so I've come here instead.' she leered at them. 'Just for a little research I'm doing, you know?'

There was no question; she was a guest, and they were staff. Cook handed over the large key without a murmur, dismissing the request as just another loony passion of one of the weird guests who sometimes stayed.

Having gathered her gang together, Lady Amanda explained what she had done so far, and suggested that they go, forthwith, to said muniment room to see what they could dig up. She hadn't wanted to chance asking outright for the key to either of the cellar doors, as someone might have been alerted to their intentions, but she felt confident that they would find a copy of at least one of the keys in their target room. And who knew what documents they might come across, perhaps ones referring to nefarious doings hidden from all eyes up there, for who was likely to want to go into such a dead room, were they not being shown the sword?

Hugo had suggested that he go into the library and start shaking out books, as he was too infirm to reach the muniment room, and Beauchamp said he had a little errand to run before he joined them. That left just Enid and Lady A, puffing up the stone corkscrew, grasping for dear life at the rope that represented a handrail, and squeaking slightly as they met particularly worn steps.

It took them so long to get up there that they were still staring at all the old trunks that needed searching, when Beauchamp bounded into the room behind them, a beaming smile on his face – a most unusual occurrence, as he, by nature, wore a poker face, both on and off duty. 'That didn't take long, Beauchamp. Any luck?'

'More than you could imagine, your ladyship. I betook myself to the cellar entrance, and the key was actually in the door. It seemed the obvious place to look – handy for anyone engaged in nefarious activities, and perfectly natural for anyone innocent. Why should the key not be in the door? It's not as if there would be a fortune in fine wines down there, now is it? This is, after all, a dry house, and the most one could expect would be a few bottles of whisky for future Burns' Nights.

'There's only a short flight of stairs down, for it's lowceilinged down there. Anyway, inside the first cellar, just behind the door and not in one's sightline, were one just taking a peek inside, were three other keys. One was labelled for 'outer cellar', and another, 'exterior door'. There are, in fact, two chambers on that side of the castle. The third key was just labelled 'dungeons', and of the location of those, I am afraid I know nothing, as they certainly don't lead off from the cellars. I took the lot!'

'Beauchamp, you are worth your weight in rubies. What was in there?' declared Lady Amanda, still a little out of breath from her climb up to the muniment room. Now, she decided, they might as well go back down. The keys were the main objective, and they could spend a fortnight up here, easily, going through the trunks. She believed that, with possession of the keys, and the addresses she had copied down from the visitors' book, they had something to work on.

Beauchamp replied in a rather frivolous manner. 'I shall not disclose the contents. I think it would be more fitting if we all went there together and took a look, and I suggest we leave that until rather later, so as not to arouse anyone's suspicions. It might be injurious to our hostess, should she have had the misfortune to have been kidnapped, although I assume she must be in the dungeons themselves, as I didn't come across her on my little factfinding mission.'

Halfway back down to the ground floor, Lady Amanda bade the other two go on ahead. She was absolutely knackered, although she would never use that word aloud. She'd 'snail' her way down to Hugo to see if he'd dislodged anything interesting from the library books. As she plodded doggedly on, she wondered about Enid.

She had changed enormously since Hugo's arrival, and the events that had followed on from that. The woman was always in and out of hospital with some minor complaint like in-growing nose-hairs and septic toe (Lady A was not the most sympathetic of creatures) but now she had, it seemed, a new lease of life – and health.

She must just have been bored before, she decided, and seeking attention in the only way she knew how. She had, after all, had her demanding old mother living with her and a smelly old cat that did nothing but destroy things and leave intentional messes, although she was fond of both.

Hugo had, of course, found nothing. She had only given him the task because she didn't want him feeling left out, and eventually they all came together again in Lady A's room. Beauchamp having produced refreshments, Lady Amanda informed them of what she had gleaned from the visitors' book, and declared that they now needed a map. Those addresses were important in some way: she could feel it in her water. Hugo winced as she said this, and turned his head away at the very thought of Lady A's personal eau, wrinkling his nose in disgust. There were limits!

'No need for cumbersome old maps, your ladyship,' Beauchamp announced, 'for I have one of those electronic tablets that give one access to the internet and global maps, with zoom capabilities.'

'I have no idea at all what you're talking about, but I'm sure it's marvellous. Perhaps you would explain it to us?' Lady A wasn't very up on the latest technology, although she had a laptop, and a mobile phone, albeit a very ordinary model.

The manservant went to his half-sister's wardrobe and reached to the highest shelf. 'I left it in here for security,' he explained, bringing out a relatively small, flat, black plastic thing. 'This is the tablet,' he explained, 'and it works just like a computer, with a few other functions that are rather unique. I can log on to a global map site, type in the location of the addresses, and it should bring up a picture of that area. We can then zoom in for quite a close look, although it might get a bit fuzzy if we try to look too closely.'

'Whatever will they think of next?' exclaimed Lady A. 'I want one as soon as we get back home.'

'I can also search their names. If they're listed, we might learn a few interesting things from that service,' he continued.

'Actually, I want one NOW!' Lady Amanda had never been known for her patience.

The only addresses that were actually in Scotland were those of Wallace Menzies and Quinton Wriothesley, although both men had excruciatingly posh English accents due to being sent away to school.

Menzies lived furthest north, on the coast, and it was possible to see what looked like a fishing business on the coast that was part of his land. Although Wriothesley lived further inland, a quick look for him on the internet revealed that he had a small haulage business. These two facts were very encouraging when allied with the other information they had gleaned.

Their meeting was interrupted, at that point in the proceedings, by Evelyn Awlle, who announced that Inspector Glenister had requested the presence of Lady Amanda in Sir Cardew's study, and he awaited her even as she spoke. Muttering under her breath, 'Bum! More dashed stairs,' Lady A rose, grabbed one of Hugo's walking sticks, and followed her from the room. Much more of this castle-exploring and she'd be after his walking frame when they got home.

Inspector Glenister greeted her with a hearty handshake and a smile. After requesting that she take a seat, he said, somewhat facetiously, 'No article belonging to you was found in connection with the corpse this time, so it would seem that I can eliminate you as our prime suspect for the piper's murder, and that of Sir Cardew.

'It appears, though, that someone is planning to go into the kebab business. What an extraordinary way to go about a murder. Do you have any idea about what's going on?'

Not wishing to lie, she decided to prevaricate. 'I can't imagine what could link the death of a piper with the death of our host,' and in a way, this was completely true. She didn't have a clue what linked these murders, but she was damned sure that they had something to do with the illegal hooch business that was being carried out on the estate, but hunches were not fact, so she felt quite justified in keeping her silence.

'I understand that no one was present – save for the murderer – when Sir Cardew was done away with. Can you confirm that?'

'I think we had all been taking some filthy non-alcoholic substitute for brandy in the library, but I can't be sure. They're such big rooms, and people were coming and going, and talking in pairs and groups that constantly reformed.'

'Come on, lassie! There were hardly hundreds of guests there,' the inspector declared, with a modicum of impatience.

'No, there weren't,' she retorted in a challenging voice, 'but then, no one told us we were going to have to make a statement about who talked to whom, who went off to the lavatory or to tidy their hair or make-up, and who may have gone to their room for something. We had no idea that we were to be held to account because there was going to be a murder. None of us has a crystal ball, you know!'

'I'm sorry if I sounded a little testy. It's just that I cannae seem to get an accurate picture of who was where, when the fatality occurred. And to top it all, we have Lady Siobhan's disappearance, and we don't know whether she's run away in distress, or whether she's been kidnapped, which seems vera unlikely, but we have to consider every avenue of possibility.'

As he finished his speech, there was a sharp rap on the door, and Constable MacDuff burst into the room waving a piece of paper in a gloved hand. 'There's a note, sir. It was nailed to the outside of the front door. I went outside for a wee toke on ma pipe, and there it was. It's a ransom note!' He was very excited, not just at the turn of events, but that he had been the one to find the note. The length of his rolled 'r's had increased with the progression of his triumphant tale of discovery.

'That confirms it, then,' declared Glenister. 'It is kidnapped, she's been. I'll need to get a search party together to go through the estate with a fingertip search. Do we know how many bothies and shelters there are in the forest? No doubt there are dozens, and the trees are vera dense in some parts. Have the evidence lads left yet? No? Right, well tell them to stay on, and procure as many members of the outside staff as you can. They know the estate better than anyone else, and their knowledge could prove invaluable.'

The constable bustled off full of self-importance, and Glenister once more turned his attention to his interviewee. 'I'm sorry, lassie, but this is of prime importance, now we know that Lady Siobhan has been taken against her will.'

'No problem, Inspector. I quite understand. And don't forget to pass on my best wishes to Adrian, when you speak to him next.'

'Ma wee Sassenach nephew? Aye, of course I will. I don't know if I've mentioned it before, but ma brother's no better than all these nobs who were born in this glorious country and whose parents sent them to posh schools and universities south of the border. Ma aen brother didnae want any children of his to speak with a Scottish accent, snob that he was. I must be off, but I'll need to speak to the rest of your party before I go, so don't leave the castle grounds, now will ye?' He seemed to have suddenly become more Scottish with the excitement, and begun to repeat himself in his agitation. 'And I'd better summon a hostage negotiator too,' he concluded.

Lady Amanda knew that his request not to leave the grounds was an order and not a polite request, and left him to it, as he was obviously eager to get on with the search for their hostess. She'd hobble her way back to the others, so that they could make plans. They certainly knew a lot of things. Now all they had to do was to put them together in a coherent story, and make plans for how to uncover all the dastardly deeds that were being committed on this estate.

Hugo was in the drawing room reading an old edition of *The Scotsman* which he had found lying around, and was apparently absorbed in it. Of Beauchamp and Enid, there was no sign. 'Hey-ho, old thing,' Lady Amanda greeted him wearily. Where are the other two?'

'Well, they were with me, but then Iain Smellie joined them, and informed them that Elspeth's maid had been doing a bit of eavesdropping, and had heard talk of some illegal goods being stashed somewhere. Anyway, the maid told Elspeth, Elspeth told Iain, and he went to Sir Cardew with the information. This was just before dinner last night. Iain said 'I don't know if it means anything with regard to what happened later, but I think we'd better inform the inspector, don't you?'

'I said he ought to do what he felt was right, and left it at that, and he scuttled off. Immediately, the other two took off for the staff quarters, to see if they could get anything more detailed from that Campbell girl, and then you arrived.'

'Good!' declared Lady Amanda, her spirits lifting. 'He won't find the inspector because he's getting a search party together. That constable – what was his name? MacDuff? – found a note nailed to the outside of the front door. I didn't get a good look at it, but they said it was a ransom note, so we know more than anyone else, at the moment.

'He won't have time to interview him, but he might get him to round up the other guests to help in the search party. I certainly hope so, because that'll give us the castle more or less to ourselves. We can plead age and infirmity, Hugo. Don't look at me like that! It's true! And we can plead that we need Beauchamp and Enid to help us. That should give us enough time to get together, assemble this new information, and come up with a plan.'

'You're using one of my walking sticks. You might have asked,' Hugo exclaimed, having just noticed it.

'See, I am infirm!' she declared, trumping his ace.

Now all they had to do was wait for the return of Beauchamp and Enid, to see what they had managed to winkle out of the dazzlingly ugly Mary Campbell.

When Beauchamp and Enid returned to the drawing room, they were bursting with news, the first item being more of culinary importance, than of interest in their investigations. 'We are charged with fending for ourselves until an early supper is laid out. It will be a cold collation for those returning from the search, to be self-served, as and when they return. May I offer you some smoked salmon sandwiches for your midday sustenance?'

'Butties be damned!' burst out Lady A, while Hugo murmured,

'That would be very nice, and good of you to suggest it, Beauchamp. Thank you.'

'Come on, man! Give! What did you find out? I'm bursting to know.'

Beauchamp gave them both a sweeping glance, and bowed his head slightly at Hugo, to affirm his appreciation of his good manners. 'It transpired that when the constable went to the staff quarters to ask for volunteers for the search party, he told them what was in the ransom note.'

Lady A and Hugo both sat forward in their seats eagerly, waiting for him to continue with the details. 'It appears that the note was written in disguised capital letters, and asked for safe passage for three, from the country, before they would return their hostage. If this was not complied with, they would kill her. The note was found nailed to the front door.'

'What lousy pen-pals they'd make,' was Lady A's comment on this last. 'Well, we know who two of those three are already. One member of the little gang has been eliminated, and it's obvious that Siobhan knew nothing about any of the monkey business going on right under her nose. We need to foil those three, whoever the third member is – probably one of the woodsmen – and rescue Siobhan, before we can let any of what we know out.'

'Precisely,' agreed Hugo. 'Who'd believe us, with all these people of seemingly impeccable reputations under this roof? And if we say anything and let them know what we know, then they'll realise we know, and make a run for it before they can be taken into custody, don't you know?'

'Pardon?' asked Enid, confused with who knew what about whom, and what the result would be.

'Ignore him, Enid. He gets a bit like that sometimes. I don't know whether they're senior moments, or whether he's somehow related to Winnie the Pooh,' Lady A reassured her. 'The important thing now, is to decide what to do, and when to do it.'

'Well, whatever it is, I suggest we carry it out under cover of darkness, when everyone is safely asleep. We don't want to put poor Lady Siobhan in any more danger than she is in already,' declared Beauchamp, with impeccable logic, as usual. 'I'll get those sandwiches now, while Enid rustles up a nice pot of tea, then I suggest you two have a nap this afternoon, because it could be a very busy night for all of us.'

Chapter Eight

It was a very dark place, the only light filtering in from a tiny piercing of the wall, and Siobhan had no idea where she was, what time it was, or even if it was a different day. All she knew was that her ankles were in irons, as were her wrists. She could not stand, but could manipulate food and drinks.

These had been brought to her twice since she had been seized by someone wearing a dark ski mask, but she had no idea whether it was someone from the castle, or a complete stranger, seeing an opportunity she didn't understand.

She was lucky she had been wearing her dressing gown when she was taken, for it was cold here, wherever here was, and she'd had no idea that there had been a set of stone steps inside the walls of the castle. She thought she was in the dungeons, but she couldn't be sure, because a handkerchief soaked in something sweet and disgusting had been put over her face once the perilous staircase had been descended. In reality, she could have been transported anywhere. She had no way of knowing.

The food was delivered by the masked man, but she couldn't be sure whether it was the same one who had kidnapped her, or an accomplice. All she knew was that he didn't utter a word, so she had no way of identifying him from his voice.

Whoever it was had some sense of decency. There was an old china commode within her reach, and a roll of necessary paper, and this object had been emptied and returned on both occasions when she had been brought sustenance, so her captor couldn't be an out-and-out monster. She just wished it was either a little warmer here, or that they would bring her a blanket.

Her mind was in a turmoil about everything that had happened. It had started with the murder of their beloved family piper. Then Cardew had been brutally murdered, and here she was, kidnapped. Whatever she could have done to deserve all this, she had no idea. She hadn't thought that anyone hated her enough to deprive her of a member of staff, a husband whom she had grown rather used to over the years, and then her own liberty. She wondered how long it would be before she regained her freedom, if she were that lucky.

Then the terrible and terrifying reality struck her. What if she were never released, and spent the rest of her life in captivity – like the Man in the Iron Mask? Only without the mask! What if they killed her because they couldn't get whatever it was they wanted? If they (whoever 'they' were) would only ask, she'd give them anything she had, to get out of her current situation.

She was far too young to die, despite having reached what other people might consider a reasonable age. She simply wasn't ready. There were far too many things that she had never done, too many places that she had never seen. She wasn't ready for the castle to be handed down to the next generation. Was anyone even looking for her, or had they assumed that she had decided to go away for a few days, after the shock of the tragedy that had befallen her husband?

A thousand fears beset her racing mind, as she heard someone approaching the place where she was being held prisoner. Would this be food? Or was it Death, who came for her this time?

'If the ransom note was found nailed to the front door,'

Lady Amanda was expounding, 'then why did no one hear it being done, and investigate. And surely someone would have seen them.'

'Because the note was merely speared on an extant nail, that has probably been there for decades,' said Beauchamp's distinctive voice just by her ear, and she shrieked with shock.

'How the heck did you get there? Oh, don't tell me. You have a tread with the lightness of a cat's,' she scolded her manservant, then, as he approached the coffee table in front of them, she saw his face, and her spirits soared. His expression was one of suppressed glee, and there was news in his eyes. 'You've got information, haven't you, Beauchamp? What is it? Was it that Campbell girl?'

'All in good time, your ladyship,' he advised, maddeningly, and proceeded to pour the tea for four, Enid joining them from behind his rather larger frame.

'Come on, man! You know you've got us in suspense.' Even Enid looked excited, and a little triumphant, knowing something that Lady A and Hugo did not.

When they were all seated, it not making any difference if guests and staff sat together, with the absence of almost all the usual characters who might disapprove, he told them what he had discovered. 'I didn't get any more from the Campbell girl ...'

Here, Enid interrupted him with a comment that was extremely un-Enid-like. 'When they handed out "pretty" she must have thought they said "shitty" and said she didn't want any. I've never seen anyone who looked so

like a medieval gargoyle in my life.'

'Enid!'

'I'm perfectly entitled to have my own opinion, and state it,' she replied rebelliously, not at all like the meek little thing she had been until recently.

Beauchamp noisily cleared his throat. He was supposed to be the centre of attention, and he wasn't ceding that position to anyone, not even not-so-meek-mannered Enid. 'She couldn't actually identify the voices she heard, because she had her ear pressed to a door. She only knows that they were male voices, and the situation frightened her.'

There was a double sigh from his employer and her friend, and he quickly put them out of their misery, that he had found out something of worth. 'BUT,' he said, in capital letters, 'I was in the scullery looking for a teastrainer – I don't know where they get to in this household. I think something must eat them. Anyway, while I was in that dismal cave of a room, I tripped over something: something that the old rag rug in there must have covered previously.' He stopped at that point, and smiled like the Cheshire Cat, teasing them with his reticence to finish the story.

'Go on, you rotter. You know how you've got us on tenterhooks.' Lady Amanda was losing her patience, and was getting ready to cuff her manservant round the ears, even if, or probably because, he had turned out to be her half-brother.

'It was an inset ring that hadn't been seated properly in its groove. There was no one around. Cook had gone off for her afternoon nap, Sarah Fraser had some mending and ironing to do for Mrs Elspeth, and Mary Campbell sloped off to have a soak in the bath with scented candles. Oh, the temptation to push such an ugly woman under the water and hold her there, thus putting her out of our misery, and yes; I did mean to say that.'

'Come on, Beauchamp, before I play the big sister with you. And stop being so cruel about the poor girl. She can't help the way she was born.'

Beauchamp actually chuckled, then went on, 'I pulled it up, having pushed the scullery door shut, and found that it led to a flight of stone steps. I feel certain I have discovered the entrance to the dungeons, and it seems fitting that it should be from the servants' area of the castle, for you wouldn't want to have to drag prisoners through the living quarters on their way to be incarcerated, would you? Sounds of pain and suffering do not sit well when one is entertaining.

'I believe we have our opportunity to explore what's down there, after nightfall and, as the castle is, at this moment, almost empty, I suggest we go to the cellars and have a good look around there, while the coast is clear.'

'Is there any lighting down there?' asked Lady A, stuffing her sandwiches down her throat as if she were in an eating competition.

'I believe there are some of those flaming torches, but I'd suggest we take electric torches. We might have to get out quickly, and, if we've lighted torches, they'll be a dead giveaway,' he commented, lapsing into the vernacular in his excitement. 'I believe I can supply all of us from the emergency kit in the Rolls.' He had also changed recently, but Lady A put it down to the fact that the truth about his parenthood was now common knowledge in Belchester Towers.

'Now you know why I have such a large handbag, Hugo,' Lady A told her friend, who was always moaning that she had room in its capacious interior for a hundredweight of coal, with space left over for the kitchen sink. 'I can put four torches in my bag without anyone noticing anything odd. Think how we'd look, just in case someone did see us, trotting off to the cellars, each carrying a torch. It would be frightfully suspicious.'

Hugo had to admit defeat on this occasion. A large handbag could be a very useful accessory when one had something to keep hidden. Finishing off his sandwiches, he rubbed his hands together with glee, and asked when they were setting off on this particular adventure.

'I would suggest as soon as Enid and I have returned the tray to the kitchen. We should still have quite a bit of time before anyone returns when the light starts to go. If Lady Siobhan is discovered and brought back, everyone will be in a mood of such relief that no one will notice where we are, or what we're doing, in their mood of euphoria. Come along Enid. You can load the dishwasher while I rinse out the teapot.'

Within a quarter of an hour, they were inside the interior cellar door, Lady A surreptitiously handing out torches before they ventured any further into the dark. Beauchamp locked the door behind them, and they all four slunk inside and down the shallow flight of steps, keeping a keen eye out for anyone who might catch sight of them, but they proved to be totally alone.

The interior of the room smelt of damp and mould, and closer inspection revealed an earth floor. This part of the castle had, in all probability, not been altered since the place was built.

One by one the orbs of light descended, bringing into view a rough stone interior that was quite large, and contained, near the door, the remains of what had, at one time, been quite an extensive cellar. The few dozen bottles of wine that were still stored there were of superb quality and vintage, but they hid the secret of the room behind this more conventional screen of respectability.

Behind were rows and rows of bottles of the illegal spirit brewed in the forest, those in the front bearing labels, those to the back still awaiting this badge of apparent verity. In one corner, a table cowered in the darkness, its top covered in an assortment of labels, a small cabinet beside it containing what looked like a variety of greatly condensed flavourings.

This was the heart of the operation, with easy access, large storage space, and privacy; for who else would ever come in here, with this being a dry house, except Sir Cardew himself and his co-conspirators? It was the perfect set-up for the bottling and labelling of illegally manufactured liquor.

Entering the room that had access from the exterior of the castle, they found large plastic containers filled with a clear fluid, stacks of empty bottles, funnels, even a deep Belfast sink so that bottles could be sterilised before being filled. It was apparent that this operation was not a start-up side-line, but must have been in existence for some considerable time.

It seemed probable that Siobhan had not been aware of it, for they could not believe that, if she had suspected what was going on down here, she would keep quiet about it. She was a very honest woman who, quite obviously, lived in an otherworldly way, with her mind above such sordid things as had been going on in the castle itself, as well as out in the forest. She would have been mortified, had she been aware of such criminal goings-on.

'I think we should adjourn to our rooms for a rest now,' Beauchamp suggested. 'We don't want to chance our arms any further at this juncture.' There he went again, resorting to the vernacular. He just wasn't one to use slangy language, and now he'd done it twice in one day.

It was a sensible suggestion, though, and they obediently slunk out of the cellar rooms, leaving the manservant to lock up. Enid decided that she would have a lie down in her room as well, and the three of them left Beauchamp to his own devices, with an arrangement to dine at six-thirty from the cold collation left out, and meet again in Lady Amanda's room at midnight.

The search party trickled back in ones and twos, no sign having been found of Siobhan, or any clue to her whereabouts, and the cold collation was consumed in a gloomy silence. The only thing that could be said for dining a la buffet was that the food was rather more edible than some of the hot dishes had been. The Cullen skink and haggis had been the last really good things the party had eaten, with the exception of the Belchester Four, who had dined on smoked salmon sandwiches, with just a hint of horseradish mayonnaise, at luncheon.

After-dinner conversation also proved not to be brisk, and the only animated conversation to be seen, for it took place at a distance from which no one could hear it, was between Grizzly Rizzly and Wallace Menzies. They may have taken the decision not to stand somewhere where they could be eavesdropped upon, but they looked to Lady Amanda just like villains in a cheap Victorian melodrama plotting the overthrow of the hero, and Hugo agreed with her when she broached the subject.

Knowing what time they had planned for their meeting, Hugo and Lady Amanda took themselves off to bed very early, in the hope that they could complement their afternoon naps with a little pre-exploratory sleep. They had to take account of their age, and they didn't know how long they would be out of their beds in the wee small hours.

At five minutes to midnight, Beauchamp knocked discreetly on Lady Amanda's door and was bidden to enter, in a low voice that indicated that her ladyship was up and about, and wouldn't need wakening. The manservant was greatly relieved, because not only was waking his half-sister a thankless task – in that she slept like the dead – but if woken before she was ready, meant that she acted like a bear with a sore head, until midday.

A discreet knock on the door of Hugo's adjoining room produced no response, and Beauchamp, after two more attempts, was forced to open the door and hiss at the lump under the covers to wake up, for it was time to go. This also produced no response and, eventually, he had to shake Hugo's unconscious form, quite vigorously, to get any response.

'Whassup?' asked Hugo blearily.

'It's time to wake up. We have to leave, now, Mr Hugo,' Beauchamp replied, patiently.

'Wake up? I wasn't asleep! Couldn't get off at all. Damned cheek, thinking a fellow's asleep, when he can't get a wink.'

'You were snoring, Mr Hugo, with respect.'

'I was?'

'Very loudly, as it happens.'

''Straordinary! Was I really? Well, well, well! Amazing what one can do and not know a thing about it. Sorry about that, old chap. Give me five minutes or so, and I'll come through to Her Nibs' room.'

Lady Amanda was wearing a pair of black stretch trousers and a black jumper for, as she always said, if one goes away, it's as well to go prepared for a funeral, when one's friends are the age of hers. Beauchamp was similarly attired in black, knowing that anything pale would pick up any light that there was, and pinpoint them immediately, if someone were looking out for them.

When Hugo finally appeared, he had on the same light beige slacks, white shirt, and oatmeal jacket that he had worn during the day. 'HUGO!' hissed Lady Amanda, with real exasperation in the word. 'Just what do you think you're wearing?'

'What I had on earlier. I didn't want to soil anything fresh, and this is likely to be a messy job if we're going down to the dungeons,' he replied, with perfect logic – perfect logic for the daytime, maybe, but not for their secret explorations at this time of night.

'Think about it, man! If you go out dressed like that, you'll positively shine from any light source. We don't want to be discovered poking around where some believe we have no business to be. Go back to your room and put on the darkest clothes you've got!' she ordered him, in an imperious hiss.

'Sorry! Didn't really think it through, did I?' he intoned in a voice full of chagrin. He hated to be found wanting, and his garb was rather ridiculous, when one thought about it.

He reappeared after a considerable amount of drawer opening and shutting, and rather a lot of mild cussing, wearing a pair of slate grey trousers and an old navy pullover. His reaction to their glances at the vintage of his jumper was to say, in mitigation, 'Sometimes I wear it in bed over my pyjamas, if it's particularly cold. In fact, I've got my pyjamas on under this lot. It's probably darned chilly down in those dungeons.'

Lady Amanda picked up her black handbag containing the torches and, just as they were about to go, Enid arrived, huffing and puffing. 'Sorry I'm late,' she said. 'I set my alarm and put it under the pillow so I wouldn't wake anyone else, but the dratted thing was a quarter of an hour slow. The battery must be running out. Sorry, sorry, sorry!'

'That's all right. We'd have given you a knock on the way past. I see you've sensibly dressed in dark colours,' said Lady A.

'Of course! Light-coloured clothing would be asking for trouble, wouldn't it?' she asked, and Hugo had the grace to blush, even though neither of the other two said a word about his first attempt at dressing for underhand deeds.

Before they could get out of the room, however, there was a rumbling sound from outside, and a screech of elderly brakes outside the window, and they all stopped short. That sounded very like the arrival of an elderly lorry, and three of them approached the window with caution, Lady Amanda staying behind to switch off the light before the curtains were drawn back.

There, illuminated in the starlight, was a truck big enough to hold everything they had discovered in the cellar rooms, and more. Someone they could not identify got out and unlocked the exterior cellar door; his passenger, just as unidentifiable, followed and, between them, they started loading the moonshine into the back of the vehicle.

'Oh my God!' Lady A exclaimed quietly. 'It looks like they're clearing out. This must be a reaction to Sir Cardew's death. We've got to get away from here before they go off to fetch Lady Siobhan. If everything's gone wrong for them, she may be killed like Cardew – if she's not already dead.'

'Leave this bit to me,' said Beauchamp, with determination in his voice. 'You three wait here. I'll only be gone a short time – ten minutes at the very most.' 'Where are you going?' asked Lady Amanda.

'What are you going to do?' queried Hugo.

'You're not going to do anything dangerous, are you?' pleaded Enid.

'I'm just going to put their truck out of action,' he replied to them all.

'How?' This was Lady Amanda again.

'I'll tell you when I've done it, to save valuable time now. The longer they're stuck here, the longer we have to try to rescue the damsel in distress, and summon outside help to round the blackguards up.'

'Damsel, my big fat hairy bottom!' floated out of the door after him, as Lady A made her feelings clear about there being any resemblance whatsoever between Siobhan and a maiden.

He was gone only eight minutes, and explained that he had gone down to the kitchen for a bag of sugar, which he had then poured into the petrol tank of the old vehicle. He had also collected a potato from the vegetable store, and shoved that up the exhaust pipe for good measure, having been lucky enough to arrive during a short period of the villains' absence in the cellars. 'I did hear them mention Lady Siobhan, though,' he told them, 'so I think our window of opportunity is short.'

This quickly conjured up tale of horror galvanised even Hugo, and they decided that there should be no delay in them commencing their search of the dungeon regions.

Chapter Nine

They stepped quietly out of the room, finding only one torchiere burning at the stairs end of the corridor, but Beauchamp steered them the other way, explaining, 'Best to use the back stairs. Someone might not be able to sleep, and might have got up for a late nightcap.' As he spoke, Hugo grabbed a small hunting horn from the wall and stuffed it into the capacious pocket of his disgraceful woolly, with no thought of what he would do with it, but just a vague idea that it might prove useful.

'That's nowhere near as likely with one of the staff,' the manservant continued, 'they're usually whacked by ten o'clock, not just because they have to work so hard in this stone maze, but because they have to get up so early, with there being so few of them, to light fires, make early morning tea, and all the other chores to which owners of properties like these never give a thought.'

'Nice grammar,' hissed Enid, following closely on his heels.

'Good God, it's spooky on these old back stairs.' Hugo, no hero in the dark, was more nervous of ghosts than he had ever been in his life, because of his two experiences during the night on this trip.

'Grow a backbone,' whispered Lady A, unsympathetically.

'Please could we have a little quiet, until we get to the trapdoor? We need to listen carefully, in case there's anyone else about.' This was Beauchamp feeling rather like an infants' school teacher on a school outing, in charge of a small group of unruly charges.

Totally ignoring this order, Hugo asked, with a quiver in his voice, 'What's that tapping noise,' fearful that they might be in the company of a spirit who had been walled up on the staircase, hundreds of years ago, and was still waiting for his remains to be found.

'It's your walking stick!' – Lady Amanda, in exasperation.

'Damn! Silly me!' – Hugo, once more embarrassed.

'Is it much further?' – Enid, who wasn't very fond of confined spaces, and this staircase was very confined indeed. They were almost treading on each other's heels.

'Sssh!' – Beauchamp, in incomprehension at their inability to obey a simple order.

Somehow, they made it to the foot of the winding stone staircase without mishap, and made their way, as silently as four people who are in a state of fearful anticipation can, and Beauchamp led them to the scullery, where the mat had now been moved, to cover the trapdoor he had found earlier.

He was just about to lift it and reveal the hidden staircase, when a noise produced little yips of fear from three of the party, and they all froze as if they were playing the old-fashioned children's game of musical statues. The fear of discovery coursed through all their veins, as they wondered who it could be that had rumbled their plan.

Could it be Grizzly Rizzly? Menzies? Were they here already? Was it possible they had already cleared out their contraband? Surely there hadn't been sufficient time for them to move all that gear? If it were one of them, they were in real trouble. Maybe he, or they, if it were both of them, really did have Siobhan hidden down below, and were coming to fetch her?

They hadn't thought the chances were very high that they might actually be right about where the miscreants had stashed their hostess. It was surely more likely that they would have used one of the out-of-the-way bothies for such a purpose. This was really supposed to be a bit of an adventure, not a life-threatening experience. What would be done to them? Would they, too, be kidnapped; or hurt; or even killed?

Lady Amanda felt as if her head would burst, and Hugo was certain that his heartbeat was as loud as that of a big bass drum. And, as for Enid, she was shaking so much she could hardly stand, and feared that she might faint with fear and trepidation. Only Beauchamp remained calm, out of sheer habit.

Eight eyes swivelled round in the direction from which the noise had come, their gaze acknowledged by, 'Meow!'

'It's the bloody cat!' exclaimed Lady A, breaking her own rule of never swearing. The object of their relief wandered haughtily over to the range, and flopped down in front of it to worship the source of the heat, then swept a languid tongue over the fur of one of its front paws, having no idea what terror his night-time entrance had caused. He was just glad he had found a way in, and no one had, so far, attempted to eject him.

Sighs of relief echoed round the scullery, as Lady Amanda handed out the torches, and Beauchamp led the way down the steep stone steps, hissing, 'Mind your footing. The steps are steeper than you might think.'

At the bottom of the steps, they thought they were to be thwarted by the presence of a locked door, but Beauchamp was one step ahead of the others, and had spent his free time that evening after they had retired for a pre-adventure nap, searching for any large key that he could lay his hands on, just in case the one he had located earlier did not fit. He had quite a few, in this eventuality, but the original one he had found in the cellars did the job successfully, and granted them entrance.

Torches were turned on, while the manservant opened the door, surprised to find that, not only had the key turned easily, but that the door swung open without a creak. The hinges must have been recently oiled, to produce no resistance whatsoever.

The chances of finding Siobhan suddenly went up several rungs of the ladder of luck.

The first area that they passed through smelt similarly of damp, earth and decay for, after all, who would think of making dungeons comfortable and sweet-smelling? Piles of mouldering sacks lay around the place, as did broken chairs and tables, with rats scurrying hither and thither, surprised by this unexpected visit to the one place they called their own, by two-legged giants.

Enid made a series of 'ee, ee, ee', noises, in fear and disgust, sounding rather like a rat herself, and hopped around, trying to achieve the impossible act of keeping both her feet off the ground at the same time. To add to this distraction, Hugo was also doing his best to jump around, issuing distressing little noises of disgust.

'I say, Manda, this place is absolutely crawling with arachnids, and you know I've got a phobia about the eight-legged little horrors.'

'Can it, Enid! Be a man, Hugo! They can't hurt you,' ordered the less squeamish Lady A, and shone her torch around the dismal chamber.

'But rats can bite and scratch, and they carry disease,' whined Enid, still doing her best to levitate.

'Just look straight in front of you, and ignore them.' Lady Amanda was not putting up with this childish behaviour, when they were on an important mission. Fortunately, at that point in the proceedings, her torch hit paydirt, so to speak, bringing to light another stout wooden door in the opposite wall. 'Over there, Beauchamp,' she indicated, leaving the yellowish orb of her torch-light to dwell on the further barrier.

He responded by jingling the collection of keys he had brought with him, and shining his own torch to light his way over the uneven floor. 'We'll soon have that open,' he informed her, with confidence, and proceeded to try the keys again, one by one. While he was thus engaged, they heard a feeble sound from within this second chamber, which sounded very like someone calling for help; someone female.

'By George, I think we've got her!' exclaimed Lady A, rushing over to join him.

Beauchamp, finding the right key, opened the door gingerly, worried that there might be someone in there with Siobhan, if it was Siobhan, but the moving door caused no calls of alarm or threat, and they followed him into the darkness of a large chamber, in a corner of which was their hostess, in chains and rather grubby, due to her unexpected holiday in this unfrequented part of her domain.

'Thank God you've come at last!' she exclaimed. 'Mind the commode! You don't need light to find it; your noses can do that job adequately enough.'

'There are never any commodes in films, when someone's locked away and kept prisoner,' commented Hugo, absent-mindedly, to keep his mind off the spiders. 'I've always wondered how they coped, when someone was locked up for a long time.'

'Hugo, don't be coarse,' replied Lady Amanda, then added, 'But you do actually have a point. They're not like real life, those films. They just ignore the nitty-gritty, which is ridiculous, when you think about it. I mean, everyone's got to "go", haven't they?'

Picking their way over the uneven earth of the floor, and avoiding the large lumps of masonry that had been dumped down here for some long-forgotten reason, Beauchamp produced a small hip flask and held it to the prisoner's lips.

'We'll soon have you out of here,' promised Lady A. 'All we have to do is alert Inspector Glenister, and he'll be here in a jiffy, with something to cut through those chains. Beauchamp can sort that out, and the rest of us will stay with you. Cut along there, Beauchamp, old chap, and fetch the cavalry, please.'

Beauchamp cut along, and the other three tried to comfort poor Siobhan, who had been cold, hungry, thirsty, and, above all, terrified that she would not live to tell the tale of her abduction. They managed to get her to her feet, leaving their torches balanced on pieces of stone to light them adequately, then Enid and Lady A massaged her hands and arms, and Hugo put his arm round her waist to help her regain her balance.

As they were thus engaged, there was a noise at the door of the room, and Ralf Colcolough strolled in, not showing any surprise at the presence of the kidnapped woman and her rescuers. 'Thank God you're here, Mr Colcolough,' said Lady Amanda. Perhaps you can help Siobhan regain her balance, because Hugo here's not very strong and ...'

Looking at the expression on his face, as he crossed the chamber and entered the lit circle, she realised that he was not a member of the cavalry, but a previously unsuspected member of the gang, and her blood ran cold. The 'third man' was not a woodsman, after all. He was another of the guests, and he would lock them all in here and leave them. She had to let the others know not to tell him that Beauchamp had gone for help, or he'd hunt him down after he'd dealt with them.

'I wish my manservant had come with us tonight,' she declared, in ringing tones, with particular emphasis on the wording of her coded message. 'He'd have known what to do. Such a pity that he stayed in bed,' she said with even greater emphasis, partly to warn the others, and to make Colcolough think that she hadn't twigged yet that he was not on their side.

Hugo began to say something, but received a vicious kick on the ankle, just out of the circle of light, and fell silent in rather a huff. He didn't know why he'd been silenced and was willing to trust Lady A's judgement, but did she have to kick quite so hard? Why was she telling this nice man, who had come to their rescue, that Beauchamp was in bed, ill? She must be going mad.

'Yes, that's a really dreadful cold he's come down with,' piped up Enid, who had been quicker on the uptake than Hugo. 'He was as weak as a kitten when dear Lady Amanda let him off duty early.' Now Enid was at it as well, and Hugo set his mind to unravelling why both women were determined to deny the fact that Beauchamp had been with them, until just a few minutes ago.

Suddenly, Hugo realised what was going on, although he didn't know why the two ladies wanted to conceal the fact that Beauchamp would soon be on his way back, so he put in his two-penn'orth. 'Poor chap could hardly speak, and his nose was as bright as a beacon, sweat running off him.' He might not fully comprehend what was in their minds, but the least he could do was support them in their insistence.

'I'm so glad you've come to our rescue. Perhaps you'd be good enough to alert the inspector that we've found Siobhan, and we can get on with cutting her out of these barbaric irons,' twittered Lady A, having no intention of alerting him to the fact that he'd been outed as 'batting for the other side', in more ways than one.

'Oh, I'm not here to rescue you,' he drawled, curling his upper lip into a left-sided sneer. 'I'm here to eliminate you. Did you really have no idea? It was to be only one more death, but now you three have turned up, I don't see how that's possible. I think, on the whole, the best plan would be to lock you all down here. This place was built a very long time ago, and, even then, they didn't want the sounds of suffering from the dungeons to permeate to the living quarters of the castle.'

The trio of new captives blanched, although this was not obvious in the little light that was available to them They had never suspected this particular guest as being in on the racket, and they all knew they would have to think on their feet, to try to extricate themselves from this perilous situation. Unusually, it was Hugo who girded his loins first.

'You can't do that, you utter cad!' he spat, suddenly becoming aware of the whole game that the two women had been playing, and identifying the man as an unexpected enemy.

'Oh, I think you'll find that I can. I don't know how you got through the door at the bottom of the steps from the scullery, or through into here, but this door opens outwards. I wonder if you realise what that means. All I have to do is to get a couple of the others, and barricade it with the boulders strewn around the place, and you'll never get out.'

As he spoke, Lady Amanda's fear slipped away, to be replaced with a blind, red rage. How dare he treat his hostess like that! How dare he tell them, so languidly and callously, that they were all going to die in this hole, and that there was nothing they could do about it! Well, Beauchamp was on his way back, and that'd stir things up a bit. Little did she know quite how much they would be shaken, in the next half-hour.

'There'll be no commode services for you; or food and water, as Lady Siobhan has had,' he continued, with brazen insolence. 'It'll be black as night, and if you don't die of hypothermia, given your ages, you'll starve, but eventually die of dehydration.'

Now, he really looked as if he was enjoying himself, the perverted, treacherous oaf, and anger began to stir in Enid, too. She might be an insignificant person in the great scheme of things, but she had plans for the rest of her life, and she had no intentions of being deprived of that time, because of some small-time crook, no matter how toffee-nosed he appeared to be.

'It's a particularly unpleasant and long-drawn-out way to die, but if you play the game, you've got to be prepared to take the consequences, and this was a particularly dangerous game to get involved with. You're going to die down here, in awful pain, and your last breath will be filled with the stink of your own waste, not that there'll be much of that, after a day or two, when you're all husked out,' he concluded, casually pulling a gun from his jacket pocket, and leering at them triumphantly.

'And I expect this little fellow here,' he said, brandishing his weapon, 'will dissuade you from trying to overpower me. The first one who moves in my direction will be signing dear Siobhan's death warrant.'

'What a bounder you are, sir,' Hugo growled, now also full of fury at the way they had been trapped. Ralf Colcolough didn't know it, but he was now holding at bay three dangerously angry old-age pensioners.

'May your black soul rot in hell!' Lady Amanda cursed him.

'May you have long, dangling external haemorrhoids' spat Enid, drawing the puzzled eyes of her two companions. 'Well, it's the worst thing I could think of. If you've ever suffered from them, as I have, you'll know just what an evil curse that was,' she justified herself.

'Not a moment without pain, day or night, and a hospital waiting list to get through, before you can get anything done about them.' She paused after this explanation, remembering the suffering she had gone through, and how surgery had given her the greatest relief from pain she had ever known.

As Colcolough drew breath to reply, there was a shout from the doorway and, just discernible in the dim borrowed light from the circle of torches, stood two figures, both appearing to hold double-barrelled shotguns. Who had arrived now? Friend or foe? It was impossible to tell until they approached the light.

'Armed police!' yelled the voice of Inspector Glenister, who was accompanied by PC MacDuff. 'Drop that gun, or we'll fire!'

Thank God the cavalry had arrived, but where on earth was Beauchamp? thought Lady Amanda, now thoroughly alarmed for her manservant's safety.

Colcolough sulkily complied with the order, as two shotguns outranked one pistol. 'Now kick it away from you!' Glenister ordered, as he and the constable moved further into the chamber. Once again the miscreant complied. He'd evidently been thinking, however, for he now didn't look either crestfallen or defeated.

'I'm going to send PC MacDuff over to you to handcuff you, and if you resist, it will be my pleasure to shoot you, you murdering swine.' Glenister didn't mince his words. How dare this fop threaten three elderly people in this way? It was barbaric!

But before MacDuff could move, yet another voice sounded behind him. It was that of Menzies and, as they turned, they became aware of both him and Wriothesley standing behind them aiming pistols at them.

'I think not, Inspector. This is way off your beat. You're in our manor now, and we run things, not you.' Colcolough retrieved his gun, and it was now three firearms against two, in his favour. The stakes were getting higher, and there didn't seem to be anyone to trump the enemies' ace.

'My God!' exclaimed Lady A. 'This is the first time I've ever seen a real Mexican stand-off. I thought they only happened in films. I shall be most interested to see what happens next.' Her words were brave, and her temper still sky-high, but that still didn't stop her stomach churning with apprehension.

There was no way out of this predicament that she could see, without someone being either seriously hurt, or even killed. Yet, she still had a little something up her sleeve that might prove useful, given the circumstances to utilise it. If only Beauchamp

were unharmed and would return soon, she thought, sending up
a little prayer of forlorn hope, to whoever might be listening.

Chapter Ten

Yet another voice, from the now deserted doorway, suddenly rang out round the chamber, refined and confident. 'Anyone for cocktails? I've mixed a good selection,' and there stood Beauchamp with a large silver tray in his hands, loaded with full glasses of every hue imaginable.

This unexpected event riveted all eyes on the new arrival, astonishment evident on each of the three criminals' faces at such an extraordinary thing happening: to bring cocktails to what was going to be either a series of executions, or an incarceration until death. Was the man completely out of his mind? Had he risen from his sickbed and decided that cocktails were just the thing, if only he could locate his mistress?

Beauchamp looked Lady Amanda straight in the eyes, and widened his just enough to let her know that it was time for action. They might not have made any verbal plans, but the shared genes must have linked them mentally, somehow, for she behaved exactly how he'd needed her to.

He had been sidling across the room to the more recent entrants with his tray, as he offered his drinks. 'Roman Candle? Brandy Alexander? Grasshopper? Manhattan? Blue Lagoon? Can I not tempt any of you with this fine selection of cocktails? They're on the tray just waiting to be drunk,' he called out, like a refined fairground barker.

Lady Amanda suddenly kicked Hugo again, and as he began to yell, turning all eyes in his direction, Beauchamp yelled too ('Geronimo!' in fact) and threw the contents of his tray into the faces of Menzies and Wriothesley, and they flicked back in his direction, as his cry had been a fraction of a second after Hugo's cry of pain and incomprehension, at being assaulted yet again, with no apparent cause, and no warning whatsoever.

547

Hugo's loud acknowledgement of pain was followed immediately by a piercing scream from Lady Amanda, and all the confusion caused Enid to start shrieking too. As the echoes of the sounds of the assault on the silent cavern, of four different voices died away, a completely different configuration held sway.

Hugo suddenly remembered the hunting horn, and gave a blast on it that would be enough to raise the dead, then descended into a fit of coughing at the amount of breath he had had to use to produce the sound.

In the confusion, Enid kneed Colcolough in the unmentionables. No way was she going to give up what she had planned for her future, and no one would take that away from her. Beauchamp, his belly aflame with determination, bashed Menzies over the head with his heavy tray, denting it in his enthusiasm, then both he and Lady Amanda drew guns. Lady A held a small mother-of-pearl-handled pistol, and Beauchamp had retrieved a slightly larger version from a special pocket in his tailcoat.

Both had independently decided to bring along a weapon and, although Beauchamp knew all about Lady Amanda's dangerous little trinket, she had no idea that he carried such a weapon in his everyday uniform of tailcoat and pin-striped trousers. Neither knew why they had brought their guns with them, but instinct had suggested that something might occur when they would be advantageous. Some hunches should be taken seriously, and this had been one of those, born of shared blood.

Both Glenister and MacDuff had turned their shotguns towards the two men who were now doubled over, groaning with pain, and Lady A had one well covered. She was feeling very ticked off that none of them had identified Colcolough as being part of the gang, and she took this personally. How dare he fool her for this long!

'In our pockets,' said Glenister with urgency, 'we have a pair of handcuffs each. Take them, Beauchamp, and use them to link the three together. That'll hold them till we get back upstairs where we can tie them up individually, while we get an explanation of what all this has been about.'

The inspector did his best to sound butch and masculine, but he had had to get Cook to open the gun room for him to get the shotguns, and he was uneasy with any firearms, especially ones he held himself, but only the slightest of tremors gave away his state of mind, given the fact that the shotguns were not loaded, and had only ever been intended to act as a bluff.

'But we know ...' Lady Amanda started to utter, but was immediately silenced by Glenister.

'I know you probably know every little detail, but I need it from the horses' mouths, so just keep shtum for now. Remember, I know your reputation from talking to my nephew, and I'll give you the opportunity to let me know just how clever you've been, later, when I've got the goods from this little lot.'

'Before we all leave this delightful area of the castle,' she cut in, 'I suggest that you have a word with Macdonald. I'm sure there's someone else involved, and someone from the outside staff would fit the bill admirably. Don't ask questions, just do it!' I'll explain when you've got him; or rather they'll do that for you.

'They could never have run this little scam without someone who really knew the castle and the woods like the back of his hand, and Cardew didn't know the woods sufficiently. They also needed someone who would not be out of place anywhere on the estate, or in the less used parts of the castle.

'Who would suspect a head game-keeper? He'd need to be inside to consult his employer, check the guns and ammunition, and for meals and refreshments. He's rather like a postman – not even noticed as a person in his own right; just someone that one would expect to see about, just getting on with his job.

'Mind the broken glasses as you go out, and I suggest you let these three go first, Inspector. If Macdonald has got wind of this, he'll be waiting at the top of the stairs. Just tell them to be as silent as the grave or you'll plug one of them. And if you don't, I will. They can't get far, all handcuffed together like that.'

With a smile of superiority on her face, she muttered, 'Well done, Beauchamp! That really was thinking outside the tantalus, let alone the box.'

Macdonald hadn't proved difficult to locate. He knew that the racket was clearing out of the castle and, therefore, his domain, and he was making the most of his last opportunity to be a taster for the product they had manufactured.

He'd made himself scarce during the loading of the lorry, and had been drinking in solitude in the servant's hall, when Lady A et al had gone down the dungeon steps. It was he who had alerted Colcolough, and then been sent off to find the other two. While he waited for them to emerge, he had sipped his way rapidly into an alcoholic stupor at the great kitchen table, and it was there they found him now, the bottle knocked over by his arm, his head on the wood, snoring the snore of the absolutely blotto.

'Cook's OK,' Beauchamp announced, apropos of nothing, but was understood perfectly by Glenister, who also believed Cook to be on the side of the angels, since it was she who had given him access to the arms he and MacDuff had used to bluff their way through the potential disaster that never materialised, down in the dungeons.

'When we've got this little lot's hash settled,' he pronounced, 'I'll send MacDuff to fetch her, and she can watch over him until reinforcements arrive. I've already put out a call, but we're not being treated to any more fancy and expensive choppers. The minor roads are all clear now, so they'll be arriving by road.

We spent quite a bit of time down in the dungeons playing 'who's going to shoot first', so I don't think she'll have long to stand guard before they get here, then she can get back to bed.'

'I doubt she'll do that, Inspector. Knowing Cook, she'll want the ins and outs of a duck's arse, before she'll rest.'

'ENID!' bellowed Lady A, and the head gamekeeper twitched in his sleep. 'Where did you learn language like that?'

'From my mother,' Mrs Tweedie replied, with a smile of sweet innocence on her face.

'Well, I'll be jiggered!' exclaimed Lady A, in flabbergasted tones, and followed the others to the library, where there was sufficient seating for them all, including an extra-long and extremely uncomfortable sofa, to accommodate the three who were joined together with a bond that was, without a key, unbreakable, and probably a darned sight stronger than the loose business arrangement they had been enjoying, from what was now, and always had been, Lady Siobhan's estate.

As it turned out, the three aristocratic co-conspirators couldn't wait to rat on each other, and the tale of the manufacture and distribution of the moonshine was soon unravelling with a plethora of cross-accusations about who had done what.

It was as Lady Amanda and the gang had suspected. The illegal liquor was made in the still in the forest, then transported to the castle cellar. There, it was bottled and labelled, and flavour was added, so that the product had some variety.

After that, it was collected by lorry, courtesy of Menzies' haulage business, and taken to the coast, where it was ferried over to an agreed spot in the wilds of the Irish coast, boats courtesy

of Wriothesley's so-called fishing business. The only mystery was
how the slimy Colcolough fitted into the deal, and he gave this
information to them of his own free will.

He was the money man. Both the haulage business and the
fishing business of two of the partners had been in a parlous
state, and he had been persuaded to invest in what they were
doing, in order to get them each out of a financial hole. Cardew
was similarly financially embarrassed, having enjoyed a fondness
for horseracing and poker, about which Siobhan had known
nothing, as he indulged in both of these gambling activities via
the internet. He had been more than happy to offer the castle
and its estate for the manufacture of the product.

The money was split four ways, with a small remuneration to
Macdonald, for his part in their nefarious activities, which had
been going on for a few years now.

'But why the murders?' asked Glenister, genuinely interested
in how the piper had got involved, and what had caused the
fall-out that resulted in Sir Cardew's bizarre murder.

'Jock Macleod overheard us planning to move the latest
batch. My God, what an innocent the man was.' This was Grizzly
Rizzly speaking, and he appeared eager to share the simple
honesty of the ex-piper with them as an act of unbelievable folly.
'He ought to have asked for a "wee cut", as he'd no doubt have
referred to it, and he'd probably have got away with that. The
poor lad, though, threatened to turn us over to the police. He
had no idea what danger he was putting himself in.'

They were all quick to point the finger at Macdonald for
the murder of the piper, but they fought like dogs over who had
dropped the broadsword so accurately on Cardew, thus turning
him into a giant, human, late Saturday-night-snack of meat on a
skewer. It was still stomach-churning even to think about what
he had looked like, and it appeared as if the three were on the

verge of blaming that on Macdonald as well, when the small sinewy man himself joined them, hanging by the scruff of his neck from the ham-like hand of Cook.

He looked to be in a bad way, still blurry with sleep, and still suffering more than a little from the effects of his ingestion of the illegal alcohol. She dumped him unceremoniously on the sofa, saying, 'Yer wee man woke up, so I thought he ought to join the party, as he was one of the party-planners in the first place,' before stumping out of the room to take a look at Siobhan, who had been sent straight to bed, with the doctor summoned to check her over.

Cook had no intention whatsoever of waking Evelyn Waule, and retiring to her bed, where she'd miss any of the excitement still to come, if she didn't have to. That way, she'd have a real tale to tell at breakfast, and she'd be the centre of attention for some time to come, as well as making Evelyn as jealous as hell, that it had been her who had looked after the lady of the house, and not her, her own lady's maid.

Picking up the threads of where he had been in his questioning, Glenister next asked, 'Why did you kill Cardew? Was there a falling out between you?'

'You bet there was,' replied Colcolough. 'I put up the money to get this thing started, and provided the contacts across the water, but when I sneaked a look at the books, when Cardew was otherwise engaged, I could see he was skimming off money for his own personal use.

'A quick break-in of his computer, with a well-guessed password – he never was cunning enough for this sort of life – clearly showed that he had a bank account in the Cayman Islands, and there was a ticket in his desk, one way. He was going to have it on his toes with the majority of the money, leaving us to take the rap should word ever get out. What a bastard! He got no more than he deserved!'

'And so shall you, Mr Colcolough. So shall you, along with your partners in crime.' This statement hadn't quite the drama that Glenister expected, as it was accompanied by loud snores and snorts from Macdonald, who had fallen asleep the moment he settled on the sofa Cook had dropped him on. 'And he's in for a shock when he wakes up,' the inspector concluded, glaring at the old man who had just rained on his parade.

'But who was the woman in all this?' asked Hugo, eager to solve his own personal mystery.

'What woman?' asked Menzies, as all three of the handcuffed men looked puzzled.

'When you were about your night-time activities, moving the stuff about. Manda and I sleep on that side of the castle, and have rooms that overlook the exterior to the door to where you stored your hooch.

'Twice, I woke up to find a woman in a black veil leaning over me, while I'd been sleeping, so I assumed she was just checking that neither of us was awake. She wouldn't have woken Manda, because she sleeps like the dead, but she woke me and scared the living daylights out of me.'

'There was no woman!' exclaimed Colcolough indignantly.

'We'd never trust a woman with that sort of secret!' declared Menzies with fervour.

'Nothing to do with us,' confirmed Wriothesley. 'You must have been dreaming. Nobody checked on any of the guests to see if they were sleeping.'

Hugo went as white as a sheet, and clammed up like an oyster – or a clam, come to think of it. He'd have to pretend he hadn't heard those emphatic denials, if he were to spend any more time in this ancient building, and there was no way he was going to sleep in that room again. No way!

At that juncture, the police summoned to help take the three reported, but now four, men into custody arrived with a van. The danger had passed, but they had with them a police marksman, in case a state of siege had been in existence when they arrived. Thanks to Beauchamp and Lady Amanda, this had been prevented, but the armed policeman might have proved very useful if half-brother and sister hadn't thought to come armed on this visit, with nothing but a hunch to cause them so to do.

With the wrong-doers in custody and out of the castle, the stragglers decided that it was necessary for them to get at least a few hours' sleep, so that they would be fresh to speak to Siobhan in the morning, to get her side of the story.

Cook reappeared after the van had left, and informed them that she had stripped the rooms of the three no-longer-present guests, for use by the police, should they wish to take advantage of the accommodation. They would be much more comfortable there than in the cots that had been put out for them in an empty staff bedroom, and both the inspector and the constable agreed with alacrity, being dead on their feet, without actually being deceased, which had been a distinct possibility earlier on in the night.

Hugo, who was still as silent as the grave, asked if he might use one of the rooms, as he had taken a sudden dislike to his quarters, and could do with a change, and was given the thumbs-up. And that was everything that could be done, dealt with for the night.

As they left, to go upstairs, Lady Amanda turned to her old friend and said, 'Hugo, that blast on that horn was completely off-the-wall. Where did you get it?'

'Yes!' replied Hugo, enigmatically, and disappeared into the room he was about to vacate.

There, he collected his necessary possessions for spending the night in a different room, and retired to bed tired, but unworried about surprise night-time visitors. He had only been asleep for an hour, however, when the strident skirl of the pipes woke him, and he was so incensed, that he waited for the piper to round the castle and, when he was just below his window, hurled his alarm clock at him with great accuracy, and a roar to 'Bloody well shut up!'

There was a cry of pain, followed by the dismal sound of a set of pipes deflating, and Hugo was, at last, able to get some well-earned rest.

Chapter Eleven

None of those involved in the previous night's caper woke before noon, and didn't arrive downstairs until nearly one o'clock. The doctor had called, hours earlier, to examine Siobhan, to check that she had suffered no long-lasting harm from her incarceration, and she had ventured downstairs just before noon.

By the time the other guests involved in the previous night's activities appeared, she had ordered lunch for onethirty, and instructed Cook that dinner was now never to be served before eight. She was already taking over the reins of the running of the castle, and was raring to go, as far as the rest of the estate was concerned.

She had already summoned the outside staff and ordered them to remove all trace of the still, once the police had all the evidence they needed, and was already planning residential shooting parties in season, and a host of other activities that would support the running needs of the castle without resorting to crime. She was a woman reborn.

Once it had dawned on her that she and her husband lived totally separate lives, and that the love between them had been lost some time ago, she also woke up to the fact that the castle was, in fact, hers, and had never been his, to run. Not only did she intend to really live now, but she might even look for a like-minded partner who would share this brave new world with her, although she would never again contemplate marriage.

Without her heavy make-up and elaborate out-of-date hair-do, she looked ten years younger, and after the shock of all that had happened, felt it as well, flooded with relief and gratitude to still be alive, and with the opportunity to rearrange her life to her own satisfaction.

'I've organised a celebratory dinner for tonight:' she informed her remaining guests at luncheon, 'one that will help to erase the terrible events that have taken place here during your stay, and perhaps encourage you to believe that Castle Rumdrummond isn't such a bad place after all. It will represent a wake for Cardew and Macleod, and celebrate the fact that I've got my common sense back, after years of living in a fugue state. I've also arranged for the piper to play for us, for some dancing.

'Funny, but he had a lump on his forehead when I spoke to him earlier, but he didn't seem to want to talk about how he got it.'

Hugo sat and blushed quietly to himself. He didn't feel in the least guilty; just justified. Just before luncheon was served, he toddled round to the side of the castle from which his room looked out, and retrieved his alarm clock, unharmed, from the bare twigs of a shrub, into which it had ricocheted from the piper's head. He slipped it to Beauchamp, whom he ran across on re-entry, to be returned to his new quarters, leaving no one any the wiser about how the piper had been injured.

Lunch proved to be a much jollier affair than usual, with a couple of bottles of the excellent wines that the amateur sleuths had discovered in the cellar sitting on the table for their enjoyment. Once again, Siobhan was in her element.

'I never really approved of this being a dry house,' she informed them. 'I have always been of the opinion that a man who doesn't drink has something to hide; that he would be afraid of what he might reveal under the influence of alcohol, and I seem to have been proved right.

'From now on, this is a normal household, which will have wines upon its table and sherry before dinner, for all who wish to indulge. And as for that terrible bilge that Cardew insisted was served after dinner, I've had Cook pour it down the sink. From now on there will be port and brandy for all who want them.'

As they left the table, Lady A whispered to Hugo, 'I think we'll still indulge in our private cocktail session this evening, don't you? After all, we'll be going home tomorrow. Beauchamp and Enid will leave as soon as cocktails are partaken of, and we have flights booked for tomorrow afternoon. I took the liberty of using the telephone just before you came down, having apprised Beauchamp of my decision.'

'Oh, goody-goody-gumdrops!' exclaimed Hugo, with an unexpected return to nursery language. 'I do so miss our normal everyday life, and I shall be very grateful to get back to just pootling through life with no alarums and scares.' Hugo's memory could be very fickle at times. 'And now I think I'll go for another little snooze. Long night, what ho?'

At six-thirty sharp, Beauchamp and Enid entered Lady Amanda's room to find Hugo there, waiting for them, Lady Amanda sprawling in a chair before the blazing grate, half-asleep. The arrival of the drinks tray, however, soon had her back to full consciousness.

'I have taken the liberty of providing two turbo-charged Snowballs for the ladies, one a double for your ladyship, and a much smaller one for Enid. I have also brought a double Scotch Mist for Mr Hugo, and a rather more innocuous cocktail for myself – an Apple of my Eye – as I shall be driving after this last of our evening meetings.'

'Golly, you can sound pompous at times, Beechie, old stick,' Lady Amanda ragged him, then realised what she'd called him. 'Oh, I'm terribly sorry about that, Beauchamp. I didn't mean to offend you. I don't know what came over me!'

'No offence taken. And I did address you rather informally, twice, in the aftermath of my misadventure in the snow, so perhaps we ought to call it quits.' Although neither of them would admit it, they both felt a half fraternal affection for each other, not only because they had known each other for so long, but also because of the blood-tie, of which both of them were now aware.

Draining his glass, Beauchamp announced, 'And now Enid and I must be off. I've already got our luggage packed in the Rolls, along with all the other miscellaneous items I brought up with me, plus the bulk of your and Mr Hugo's luggage, so we shall get a good start, and find somewhere to stay for the night, as late as possible, so that we can make good speed to welcome you home.'

'Here's mud in your eye,' Lady Amanda toasted them both, and blew a kiss to Enid, who was so surprised that she actually ducked, as if a missile had been launched at her.

As the Rolls rolled through the imposing castle gateposts and on to the winding country lanes that would eventually lead to what Beauchamp thought of as 'a proper road', the inside of the car was alive with the sound of singing.

'Daisy, Daisy, give me your answer do. I'm half-crazy, oh, for the love of you,' rang out Beauchamp's pleasant baritone.

'It won't be a stylish marriage, for we can't afford a carriage,' Enid continued, an octave higher, and thoroughly enjoying this shared interest they had discovered.

'But you look sweet ...'

At the end of the song, they both burst into peals of delighted laughter, and argued amongst themselves as to which number they should carol next.

By the time they were approaching an old inn to take their overnight break, their approach was accompanied by: 'O, o, Antonio, he's gone away,

Left me alonio, all on my ownio,

I'd like to see him now, with his new sweetheart,

And up would go Antonio, and his ice-cream cart,' a pleasant lullaby for them both after all the excitement of their little trip to Bonnie Scotland.

Back at the castle, Lady A and Hugo had managed to make it downstairs just in time for a refill of sherry before the first course, their appetite really whetted for the vintage wine that was on the dining table, the white, in an ice bucket, the red on a wine coaster, having a good old breathe.

From the quality of the food served, it was quite obvious that Cook had been let loose on the telephone to the local suppliers, and been allowed to order exactly what she liked, instead of having to keep inside Cardew's miserly budget. At last she could let her talents have free range, instead of having to work miracles with second-rate ingredients, and the results were superb.

Siobhan almost purred as she ate, sometimes breaking out into a contented humming. This is what life had been like before Cardew had cultivated his mean streak, which was probably when he had started squirrelling money away in the Cayman Islands for his escape.

The wines were not only wonderful, but did their job admirably, of loosening up all the diners, ready for some rather uninhibited dancing, after a suitable period for decent coffee, brandy and a little digestion.

As both coffee and cognac were sipped and conversation buzzed with the events of the last few days, the piper could be heard just inside the front door, inflating his pipes and warming up. While this was going on, some of the staff joined them, for Siobhan wanted an eight-some reel, and an eight-some reel she was going to have, come hell or high water.

Those from the staff perched on the spindly chairs that everyone else had avoided, and Siobhan, who was sitting with

Lady Amanda, pointed out the variety of tartans they wore. Evelyn Awlle, Walter Waule, and Cook, Janet MacTavish were all dressed in the MacIntosh tartan, which was the house tartan, and had red as its predominant colour.

It must have taken a mort of tartan to kit her out, thought Lady A, but she looked good dressed in her national material, her face almost girlish, as she did a few cumbersome skips in preparation for the dancing. She'd make a man a damned good wife, she considered, especially if she could hook up with someone like Angus Hamilton. He might be a mite older than her, but they both had the same employer, and wouldn't have to make too many changes in their way of life, but could enhance each other's. Golly, she must be turning into a sentimental old matchmaker in her old age!

Mary Campbell was in her family tartan of dark blue, green, and yellow and with the application of a touch of make-up and a smile on her face, looked as if she'd just had her application to join the human race accepted. Sarah Fraser also wore her own tartan of red and black with white lines, as did Angus Hamilton, the chauffeur, about whom she had just been speculating, and whose tartan was very similar to the Fraser, but with a slightly less complicated plaid.

Sandy Gunn, the new piper, when he appeared, already playing, proved to be wearing the MacIan tartan, which was a dark one with a little red in its pattern. These last two were allowed to wear their own tartans, as they were not inside staff, as were the two visiting inside staff. Altogether they made a very colourful bunch.

Lady A and Hugo had not taken much notice of the other guests' tartans, as they had arrived just before dinner, in time to guzzle down a sherry and, as the first dance started to gather speed on the floor to the blood-stirring skirl of the pipes, Lady

A and Hugo sat out with Siobhan, who wanted to share her knowledge of tartans with her Sassenach guests.

But just before she started on her explanation, she whispered to Lady Amanda, 'I don't know what I ever saw in that rat Menzies, and I've a good mind, now the entail's been broken, to put this whole bang-shoot on the market and make my home permanently on a good-quality cruise ship. Although I won't, of course, but it's a bit of a pipe dream, if I can't do something with the old family estate.

'By the way, the inspector found Cardew's fingerprints on your hip flask, as well as Macdonald's, so he must have stolen it from your room. Sorry. I'll return it to you before you leave,' then began to point out the different patterns of plaid.

St John Bagehot was in full Cameron fig, a complicated pattern with its red standing out against the darkness of the background. Drew and Moira Ruthven were cousins on their mothers' side, and wore the Buchanan, the yellow and oranges of which glowed like jewels against some of the blander tartans.

Ian Smellie's mother had been a Barclay, and they were both attired in the screaming yellow of the Barclay plaid.

Siobhan, herself, wore the house colours of the MacIntoshes and, after all her identification of the clan colours, bade the two of them join them in a dance.

'But I can't dance,' protested Hugo.

'And I haven't done any Scottish dancing since I was at school, when we had this Scottish geography mistress who was mad about it,' pleaded Lady A, similarly dismayed at having to cut a Scottish rug. They had managed to do a little hoofing round the floor to look as if they were taking part, when there had been more people there for Burns' Night, but there were four less people now, their host being dead, and three of his guests arrested. Even Duncan Macdonald was in police custody, and he had been an enthusiastic – not very accurate, but enthusiastic – dancer on that occasion.

'Come on!' Siobhan exhorted them. 'Angus and I will show you the steps at half-speed, away from the melee, then you can join in when you feel ready to.'

There was no way to refuse her, after all that she had been through, and come through more positive than she had been in years. Lady Amanda rose and held out a hand to Hugo, who was slowly creaking to his feet. 'Come along, old chap, you can't refuse the chance to say that you took part in Scottish dancing in a Scottish castle, on a Burns' Night visit, now can you? People will be so surprised when you tell them, back home,' she encouraged him.

Lady A soon picked up the steps she had not danced since childhood, but Hugo was the hit of the evening. Not really knowing what he was doing, even after some tuition, he allowed himself to be hurled and swung around the floor willy-nilly, whooping with a mixture of excitement and terror, as he swung at great speed from one partner to another.

In the middle of the Gay Gordons, which can be a very boring dance, he enlivened it considerably by getting himself in a tangle, when arm movements had to swivel the dancers to dance in the opposite direction, and it took two other participants, and a short break in the proceedings, to set him and his partner back on the right track, and facing in the right direction. He still managed, however, to make such a mess of the steps that, at one point, he seemed to be positively skipping.

After three energetic numbers, he retired to a sofa to become the elderly and retiring gentleman that he usually was, puffing hard to get back his breath. He was content just to watch the others 'cutting a rug', and noticed, as Lady Amanda had done earlier, that the usually surly Mary Campbell, with the sheer joy of the dancing, looked less like a gargoyle and more like a woman, which he, personally, thought would have been impossible.

And that new piper was pretty much up to the minute. He'd noticed that, instead of a sgian dubh in his sock, he wore a mobile phone: rent-a-reel, 24/7. How modern was that?

They departed the following afternoon, leaving for the airport directly after lunch, with only hand baggage to take on the plane, as Beauchamp had taken all but their travelling clothes and their tartan with him and Enid, in the Rolls.

As they were on the point of leaving, Angus waiting for them by the car door, Siobhan thanked them for coming, and especially for their help in ridding her nest of so many undetected vipers. 'Don't leave it so long before you come back again. We've not had a Golightly at a Burns' Night since your mother died, and that must be twenty years ago.'

Lady Amanda forbore to correct her and, secretly never wishing to cross the castle's threshold again, bade her a fond farewell, adding an invitation to Belchester Towers whenever she felt like it. She then reassured Hugo, as they entered the back seat of the car, that she had no intention of ever coming north again. That was her finished with Burns' Nights north of the border.

When they arrived home, by taxi, from the airport, Lady A was delighted to see the Rolls parked ostentatiously outside the front doors, elegantly announcing that Beauchamp had, indeed, got home first.

Inside, there was a fire burning in the drawing room, the beds were freshly made up, and the smell of cooking wafted all the way from the kitchens, to tantalise their nostrils. Beauchamp had sorted the mail that had arrived in their absence, and put it on their respective desks, for Hugo had been assigned his own 'work station' in the library, now that he was a permanent resident.

They were both, in different rooms, opening their mail happily, glad to see that Enid was there too, as she served them with a very welcome cup of tea. Say what you will about the facilities available on aeroplanes and in airports, but no tea tastes as good as that made in one's own kitchen in one's own home.

Epilogue

Lady A was just reading a missive from an acquaintance, about the approaching murder trial of her old friend Porky, when Hugo flung himself through the door, wailing like a banshee, and making little whooping noises.

'Whatever is the matter, Hugo? Have you won a chance to take part in a Readers' Digest prize draw?' she asked, with a little titter.

'No, Manda. It's Tabitha! My younger sister! She's coming on a visit. She's coming here! Do you remember her?'

Lady Amanda's face clouded over like a stormy summer's day, and her brows drew together in distaste. 'Do I remember her? Do I remember Tabitha Cholmondley-Crichton-Crump, Hugo? Well, I bally well ought to. She bullied me mercilessly all through school. That girl made my schooldays an absolute misery, and I was so relieved when she finally left, that I actually cried with joy. So, yes, I should say I jolly well do remember her, with no fondness whatsoever, and you've actually invited her here?

'Can't you put her off? Say I've got bubonic plague, or something similarly ghastly – smallpox, say?'

'Not really, Manda. She's arriving in the morning. It's just that we're a bit later back than we intended to be, what with all the palaver in Scotland, so she thought she was giving me adequate warning – I mean, notice. I'm sorry. But she is my sister. Do you think you could just grit your teeth and bear it for a little while? You can always come down with suspected plague if you can't stick it. I'm sure Dr Andrew would play along, for the sake of a quiet life and a bit of a laugh.'

While she was digesting this bit of ghastly news, Hugo went back to his post and, it being later than it felt, what with the flight and everything, she was still on her own when Beauchamp came in carrying a tray with three glasses on it. 'Is it that time, already?' she asked, in surprise. 'I had no idea. Do you want to give Hugo a bit of a yell?'

'Not just at the moment, your ladyship. I have something of a private nature to discuss with you before Mr Hugo joins us, if that's acceptable to you,' he replied, mystifyingly.

'You're being very cagey tonight, Beauchamp,' she replied, feeling slightly queasy, having already had one unpleasant surprise, from Hugo, since their return.

Beauchamp put down his tray carefully on a small table, and Lady Amanda was horrified to notice that there was a slight tremor in his hand. Whatever was he going to say? He wasn't ill, was he; maybe with something incurable? He must be all right. He was her Beauchamp, and she simply wouldn't be able to manage without him, especially since she had learnt (and accepted) that they were kin.

'I wish to request your blessing, for I am planning to get married,' he stated bluntly, then just stood there with a poker face, staring at the wall above her head, and waiting for a reply.

Oh, my good Lord! He was going to leave her, after all this time! She'd lay money on it being one of the women from the castle. And she'd be left here, hundreds of miles away from him, with no possible replacement.

He'd be off back to Scotland, and she'd be left here all on her own – she had forgotten Hugo in her moment of great distress – with no one to do for her in the impeccable manner that Beauchamp had evolved over the great number of years that he had worked here. He wasn't ill at all. He wasn't dying. This was even worse, for he was leaving her, and he'd work for someone else, and not her, any more.

Her scream brought Hugo at what, for him, passed as a run. 'Whatever's the matter, Manda? You sound like the end of the world is nigh!'

With a face distorted with horror, she announced, 'Beauchamp's getting married!'

The words went straight over Hugo's head, or rather, their import did, and he casually asked, 'What have you made for us tonight, old chap? I'm dying for a change of cocktail.'

'May I offer you both a 'Goodness Gracious',' he replied, proffering the tray politely. 'I shall be having a 'Slippery Surprise.'

THE END ... ALMOST ...

COCKTAIL RECIPES

SNOWBALL

2 measures advocaat
    ¼ measure lime cordial
    5 measures lemonade
    Add all ingredients to an ice-filled glass and garnish with a cherry.
    To turbo-charge, add a generous slug of vodka.

SCOTCH MIST

2 measures scotch whisky
    Shake with a glassful of crushed ice, pour and add a twist of lemon peel.

GOODNESS GRACIOUS

1 measure cherry brandy

1. measure white crème de cacao
2. measures cognac

1 teaspoon egg white
Shake and strain into a glass ¾ filled with broken ice.

SLIPPERY SURPRISE

½ measure scotch
    ½ measure crème de banane
    2 measures peach juice
    2 measures grapefruit juice
    ½ measure passion-fruit juice

Shake with broken ice. Garnish with seasonal fruit and a straw.

HIGHLANDER

½ measure Drambuie
½ measure scotch
½ measure dry vermouth
1 teaspoon lemon juice
4½ measures dandelion and burdock or cola
Mix and add to ice-filled glasses and garnish with mint and a straw.

FROZEN MELON BALL

½ measure Midori
½ measure vodka
2 measures pineapple juice
1 teaspoon lime juice
Shake and strain over crushed ice and garnish with a melon ball and a slice of lime.

FROZEN SPIRITS

1. measure of vodka or other spirit, chilled until gelatinous

Serve in a frosted glass
APPLE OF MY EYE – Beware, non-alcoholic!

1. measures apple juice

½ measure blackcurrant syrup
1 measure pineapple juice

1 measure coconut cream

Blend with half a glass of crushed ice and garnish with a cherry and slice of banana.

ABSOLUTELY THE END! CHEERS!

Milton Keynes UK
Ingram Content Group UK Ltd.
UKHW040712201123
432908UK00001B/318